THE LAST LIVING DIVA

A NOVEL

MATTHEW STEVENS

ISBN Ebook: 979-8-9925352-2-8
ISBN Paperback: 979-8-9925352-1-1
ISBN Hardcover: 979-8-9925352-0-4
ISBN Audiobook: 979-8-9925352-3-5

To myself…
for making this happen when everyone told me I couldn't.

PROLOGUE

Alexis had been screaming all day. Up and down the grand staircase of her home she paced, stopping occasionally to let out bone-chilling howls at the top of her lungs, over and over again, as if she were in some sort of trance.

In the kitchen, I hid behind the island, holding back tears of frustration and fear, hoping she wouldn't find me. I felt bad but I couldn't speak to her anymore. I was too exhausted.

Was she having a nervous breakdown? This had been going on for three days and she still hadn't slept—which meant that I hadn't slept either. I was starting to wonder who was crazier—her for behaving this way, or me for staying?

It had been days of paranoid rambling as she rattled off lists of her enemies and rivals, both real and imagined. The younger singer, to whom Alexis was often compared, she had nicknamed "Donut Licker." The rapper who was publicly dragging her was "Troll Doll." And the woman who'd tried to steal her career, actually *wasn't* from the block—instead, Alexis said she just "blew a lot of cock." She talked so fast it didn't warrant a response. The only thing I could compare it to was the cocaine-addled party girls I'd seen traversing West Hollywood on the occasional Saturday night out. But Alexis was in a full-blown psychosis.

"I'm the star, Hayden," she'd say, her body here but her eyes staring at some distant horizon only she could see. "*I am the star.*"

Once an hour she disappeared for a few minutes to change her outfit, but other times she insisted I come with her to the closet. On our way there, she always gave me the same tour—as if I'd never seen it before—of this Beverly Hills compound, which she was renting to the tune of

$150,000 a month. When I was a kid, I'd watched Alexis give a tour of her house to Robin Leach on *Lifestyles of the Rich and Famous*. She was in her prime then, and I never would have imagined I'd end up working for her. Now, the tour ended with her shutting me in her bedroom as she undressed, insisting I get underneath the sheets with her.

"I'm gay, Alexis!" I said.

"I don't care!"

Sometimes I got lucky and she'd tire of me. Walking out the front door, clutching her car keys in hand, she'd turn the car alarm on and off before telling her head of security she was taking the car to outer space. He'd eventually wrestle the keys from her, as she was forty and had never learned to drive. She got famous too young.

The house was quiet now. Too quiet. I pressed my back up against the island and closed my eyes, praying to wake up from this nightmare. After only three months, I knew I couldn't take much more of this. *What was wrong with her?*

A floorboard creaked, and I glanced up. Alexis was standing over me. We locked eyes.

"Hayden," she whispered, then let out another horrific scream. I whimpered, tears flowing down my cheeks. "Don't be scared, Hayden," she said. "You do believe in God, don't you?"

I rose to my feet and started for the door. I heard her running behind, trying to catch me. Just as my hand touched the cold brass handle, she screamed again.

"Don't leave me, Hayden! Please! Everybody leaves me!"

The woman behind me wasn't just anybody. Alexis Shane was the most famous woman in the world, the best-selling female artist of all time, the recipient of countless accolades and an idol to millions of fans.

And now, she was ruining my life.

Turning the handle, I sprinted out into the street, looking out at Beverly Drive, picturesque and tree lined. It all appeared so perfect. It was hard to imagine something so awful could be happening here.

As I ran toward Sunset Boulevard, not knowing where I was headed, one thought kept ringing through my head.

How the fuck did I get here?

CHAPTER ONE

Three Months Earlier

"Help me, Daddy!" the self-proclaimed world's first supermodel, now sixty, flirtatiously whined for me to dress her after her spray tan. She was underfed and the bronzer was streaky between her botched breast implants.

One room over, a Real Housewife needed me to pull her leggings up over her surgically enhanced ass and began shouting my name.

I didn't know what was with these crazy rich ladies, but they always seemed to be clamoring for my attention. Maybe it was a generational thing and they felt they'd missed out on the opportunity to grow up with a gay best friend.

I turned to abandon the half-dressed supermodel for the Housewife. As I exited, she smacked my ass for the third time that day. *I can't fucking do this anymore*, I thought, gritting my teeth and exhaling slowly. "Hayden! There you are. Where have you been?"

Jesse Toleman's voice cut like glass as I returned to the front desk. No matter what she was trying to communicate, she always did it coldly and with an air of superiority. Jesse was my boss, and the owner of the salon. Beverly Hills legend has it that she used to be a sweet, normal girl from the Midwest, but the years of success and constant stream of celebrity clientele had undoubtedly morphed her into an egomaniac who thought she was more famous than the A-listers whose bodies she perfected.

"Hi, Jesse. I was help—"

"It doesn't matter," she interrupted, holding her open palm to my face while peering down at her iPhone. "Schedule says you're off the next two days, but that's just not going to work. The SAG Awards are coming up and our appointment books are full. I'll need you open to close both days." She turned sharply on her heels, madly tapping away on her phone, and started walking away.

"Jesse, I can't do that," I said. I hadn't had a day off in almost two weeks. "Tomorrow Grayson and I—"

"Also, I'm going to need you to redo the display in the lobby. Let's stock it with my new candle line. All the scents are named after my dogs, and I have a very specific strategy in mind for the layout." As she continued down the hallway, something inside of me snapped.

"*NO!*" My voice reverberated through the most famous salon in Beverly Hills. Jesse stopped cold, turning slowly to look at me, dumbfounded. "No, Jesse," I repeated, mustering up whatever confidence I could manage. "I'm done! I can't do this anymore! Find someone else to hawk your bitch candles." Somewhere between blind rage and utter exhaustion, I looked around and realized I had an audience, as the semi-famous, middle-aged women with mannequin-like faces stared at me, jaws agape.

"*Bitch* candles?" the supermodel repeated.

"It's a double entendre," I shrugged, and walked out the door for the last time.

Once I was sitting in my car, the reality of what I had just done set in. To be clear: I'm not an asshole. I was just a guy who'd had enough. I was approaching thirty years old, barely able to make ends meet, and nowhere near where I'd hoped to be in life. And it didn't help that I lived in Los Angeles, where everyone I met seemed to be succeeding in ways I couldn't fathom.

The population grows every month in Los Angeles as the most beautiful and charming young people from small towns in flyover states hop on a bus to chase their dreams. What kind of dreams? Famous actress. Pop star. Blockbuster film director. Or maybe they just want to get TikTok-famous by interviewing strangers on Rodeo Drive. Everyone in LA is striving for the same thing—to be the best, most glamorous version of themselves.

Some of these people eventually realize they'll never be the next Sabrina Carpenter or Jacob Elordi, and end up moving home. But the ones who stay become a special breed of LA hellion—one with which I've become all too familiar. The actress-turned-Beverly Hills housewife. The ladies who, although perhaps still beautiful for their age, were once young sexpots that never quite reached A-list status. And so, they married lawyers, studio heads, and celebrities—anyone who could save them from having to move home to Oklahoma. Now they spend their days shopping, attending charity parties, and being colossal pains in my ass.

Since my fiancé Grayson was still climbing the rungs at a talent agency and couldn't bankroll an extravagant lifestyle, I actually had to work for a living. And suddenly I was unemployed.

A feeling of panic rose over me. I hadn't thought this through. Whenever I felt stuck, I always immediately reverted to calling the one person who could manage to calm me down. My grandmother, or as we called her, Oma. She was, without a doubt, my best friend. I even moved in with her during my senior year of high school, when my father kicked me out after walking in on me with an older man. She was the only person who loved me unconditionally, and I always knew I could turn to her when I was in a bind.

"Hello?" her warm voice greeted me on the second ring.

"Hey, Oma, do you have a min—"

"Hi, honey! Oh, it's so good to hear from you!" she said. "How are things going over there? You know, I saw on *TMZ* yesterday that Taylor Swift—God bless her—said that she—"

"*Oma!*" I interrupted. "Oma, please just listen." I inhaled deeply. "I quit my job."

There was silence. And then—

"*What?* But... what are you going to do? You don't have any money saved! Do you have another job lined up? What about your rent? And don't forget about your car payment! I really can't handle another financial burden right now, Hayden. What were you thinking?"

The truth was, I had no fucking idea. All I knew was that I couldn't take it anymore. But had I made a mistake? Working at a major salon in Beverly Hills definitely had its perks. Every woman I dealt with was either a music executive, a television producer, or an A-list celebrity like Jennifer Lopez, Kate Beckinsale, Christina Aguilera, and Paris Hilton.

Had I just wasted five years for nothing?

My well-connected clients had all asked me over the years, "What do you want to do?" But I had no idea, and now I had no access to them. No more baby showers with Kate, no more drunken birthdays with Christina, and definitely no more Halloween parties at Paris's house.

"Oh, honey," Oma said after a long pause. "It's all going to work out. You'll see."

THE NEXT MORNING, MY ANXIETY was at an all-time high. I ate a pomegranate weed gummy from my nightstand and tried to take some deep breaths, but my mind was racing.

"It's gonna be okay, babe," Grayson said, before rolling over and kissing me on the cheek. "This is long overdue. You've been miserable there for years, and now you can focus on finding a job that you love."

He was right. But what did I *love*? Grayson had always known he wanted to be a talent agent and had a very clear path on what he needed to do to get there. He was putting in the time as an executive assistant before his inevitable promotion. I envied his self-assuredness and laid-back demeanor. I wanted the right decisions to be more obvious for me, like they were for him. I grabbed another gummy.

An hour later, my phone began vibrating. It was a number I didn't recognize, but I took the call.

"HAYDEN," a familiar voice shouted, "I heard from one of the girls that you quit the salon and are looking for a new job."

Shit. I was too high for this.

The voice on the other end of the line was that of Samantha Fox, a successful documentary producer turned music manager. A regular client of ours at work, Samantha was unforgettable—we nicknamed her "the Tornado." Her red hair was as loud as her foul mouth, and she always had her equally obnoxious, also redheaded preteen daughter, Blair, a few steps behind. Samantha was under the impression that I took good care of her because I never charged her for being late or missing appointments. But the truth was, I just wanted to avoid her wrath at all costs.

"Alexis is looking for a new assistant," she said.

"*Alexis Shane?*"

Samantha had been managing Alexis for the last several years, which was surprising considering how frequently Alexis switched out the players on her team.

Alexis Shane was the biggest star in the world, as famous for her vocal range and record-breaking sales as she was for her diva antics. I grew up listening to her. She's a legend—one of a small handful of people mentioned in the same breath as Michael Jackson or Whitney Houston. However, just two weeks prior, her reputation had taken a massive hit. She was facing tremendous backlash and public ridicule after a disastrous performance at the Super Bowl halftime show, where she was clearly lip-syncing—something she'd promised fans she would *never* do.

"I think you would be *perfect* for this," Samantha said. "I have never met a crazy rich lady who doesn't just love you. Maybe because they can tell how badly you want to be one of them." She was teasing, but it was true. "I just love you. I'm so proud of you—fuck that place! So, what do you think?"

"I think..." I said, unsure how to respond. *How many gummies had I eaten?*

"*HELLO?*" she shouted in her thick New Jersey accent. "Are you there?"

"Yeah, uh—yeah. Sounds great," I stammered.

"Perfect! Come to Alexis's in Calabasas tomorrow at eight p.m. I'll text you the address. She'll fucking love you. I just know it."

THE INTERVIEW WOULD BE POSTPONED four times that week before it finally happened—something I should have expected given Alexis's reputation. I sat on the 101 in an hour of brutal traffic before finally getting off onto exit 30—Parkway Calabasas. Over the past decade, the Kardashian family had made this pocket of Los Angeles famous. It felt like a world away from the city, and the gated communities within promised exclusivity and privacy from cameras—ironic being that they hosted reality TV stars who don't exactly shun the glare of media attention.

I drove down a long, quiet road that felt like a breath of fresh air compared to the bright lights and loud noise of my own neighborhood in West Hollywood. Almost out of nowhere, a small guardhouse appeared to my left. As I approached, a security guard in uniform leaned out the window, I assumed because he could hear the squeaky brakes of my ten-year-old Toyota Corolla.

"Hi!" I said, aiming to sound confident, "I'm trying to get to Alexis Shane's home."

He stared at me intently before asking for photo identification. I handed it over, watching as he picked up a phone and began mumbling into the receiver. After several minutes, he handed back my ID along with a barcoded pass. "This is for you to go through the second gate."

I made my way toward the second gate, nearly half a mile into the development. I'd lived in Los Angeles and worked in Beverly Hills for nearly a decade—it wasn't new for me to be around people with money, but I'd never been to a house where I had to pass through security *twice*.

After driving through the second gate, I finally caught my first glimpse of her compound. It was spot-lit, so big it could only exist in a Disney fairytale. The "home" was surrounded by a cobblestone path with giant steps leading up to the grand, castle-like mansion. It was framed by rich green, perfectly manicured landscaping, and behind a third gate to my left was a fleet of sports cars: Rolls-Royce, Ferrari, Bugatti. I parked my car as far away from the entrance as I could, embarrassed of what Alexis Shane would think of a Corolla on her property. After a few minutes marveling at how beautiful the grounds were, I nervously approached the entrance. More security greeted me, double checking my name was on a master list before one said, "Right this way, I'll show you to the office." As I followed behind him, I heard someone shrieking, "*SARAH!*"

The marble foyer enhanced the castle-like theme, with floor-to-ceiling pillars, a grand staircase, and a scintillating chandelier. A man in a baseball cap shouted directions at what appeared to be a lighting crew. A flurry of determined faces blurred by, a cross between helpless and haughty. A sense of preciousness pervaded the room—clearly everyone understood the magnitude of the personality who employed them. Was I beginning to sweat already?

Then suddenly, I heard it, rising above the din of the chaos—the unmistakable sound of Alexis Shane's voice pumping out from dozens of speakers. It was a pop song I'd never heard before. That's when I realized I wasn't there for just anything—I was there for the shoot of her comeback music video.

Just months after her disastrous Super Bowl performance, I wondered if the rest of the world would be as taken aback by this unheard melody as I was. For a super-fan of my stature, disappointment was rather quickly and inevitably replaced by being in awe of her sassy, unapologetic attitude, though I assumed not everyone felt the same. Nowhere close to a football fan, the only reason I'd tuned in this year was to witness what I imagined would be one of the most legendary performances to ever grace the field. Instead, Alexis awkwardly paced the stage back and forth in silence, interjecting every few seconds to complain about the backup vocals or to state, "I want to have a Super Bowl party, too. Can I not have one?" Her lack of enthusiasm and indecipherable-yet-clearly-sarcastic remarks filled me with joy, as she was simply living up to her legacy. Though I'd hoped for her to belt out those high notes instead of the back-track filling in for her while she insisted, "I'm trying to be a good sport here," I couldn't help but chuckle into my chardonnay. The rest of her fans, I wasn't sure about. I knew no one wanted to work with her after that, thanks to the incomparable journalism of *TMZ*. But in that moment, standing in the marble glory of her foyer as her caramel voice drifted into my ears, I couldn't imagine the world could stay mad at her for much longer.

"*SARAH!*" I heard a deeper voice calling out the same name in a desperate howl.

As I entered the office, which was larger than my apartment, I couldn't help but notice the extravagant furnishings. The shelving, the desk, the chaise, and the statues. Everything looked expensive, but gaudy. I knew if I asked, I'd be told how each piece had been flown in from some obscure part of the world.

"Wait here," the guard said, leaving me standing awkwardly on my own.

A few minutes passed. Finally, a mousy blonde, heavy-set girl in glasses and a frumpy gray sweater walked into the room, breathing heavily. She sat down at the antique desk and oversized snakeskin print throne, looking overwhelmed and out of her element.

"*SARAH!*" yet another voice screeched, this time echoing through the foyer.

The girl in front of me looked exasperated, and I didn't need to ask her name. This was obviously Sarah. She stood up and rushed out the door.

A second woman entered the office. She too was heavy-set, dressed in an

Adidas tracksuit and Fenty fur slides, with red hair similar to Samantha's, but in a messy bun on top of her head.

"Are you Hayden? I'm Amber, Alexis's executive assistant. I'm her *number one*." She spoke about being number one with such pride that you would've thought she herself was the star. "Usually prospective employees only have to wait about two hours to meet Alexis. But tonight, it's looking like you'll have to wait at least three!" She laughed.

She was right. One hour went by, then two. All the while, I heard Samantha's loud voice echoing through the mansion, making perpetual demands. Eventually she passed by the office and seemed surprised. "Oh, you're here?"

"*Only* for three hours or so," I said. "But I'll wait all night if I have to."

Samantha was used to people waiting on her. But instead of being irritated by my biting tone, she laughed. I knew she liked it.

"Let's walk and talk," she said.

As we began walking through the mansion, her loud, echoing voice suddenly turned into white noise. My eyes darted around as if they belonged in a pinball machine, moving from corner to corner of each room, observing a way of life I'd never witnessed before. A uniformed chef in the kitchen, a nanny chasing twins, an enormous portrait of Alexis over the fireplace, and an incredible view of the grounds. Mountains rose past the open French doors. Calabasas felt like a vacation away from Los Angeles. I suddenly understood the appeal.

"Um, *hello*?" Samantha said, pulling me back to the present. "So, what do you want to do?"

"What do I want to do? I mean… you called me. Be an assistant?"

"But do you think you can handle it?" She looked at me quizzically. "This is not a forty-hour-a-week job. This is a *full-time job*. I'm talking twenty-four hours a day."

"I can handle it," I said. After this small taste of Alexis's world, I now desperately wanted the job. I wanted a piece of this extravagant lifestyle, to bask in the glamor and luxury of stardom without the cruel spotlight of fame.

"Alexis needs help. Real help. Good hard-working people. Not just bodies. Come. Meet her."

I followed Samantha's thigh-high Christian Louboutin leather boots and perfectly tailored dark denim jeans up the grand marble staircase.

Suddenly, I was nervous. The first album I'd ever purchased was Alexis's. At that moment, it suddenly clicked that I was meeting an actual living legend. No longer would my childhood idol be confined to the flat static of MTV music videos and Grammy awards—soon she would be right before me in flesh form. My palms began to sweat as I realized I'd actually be close enough to smell her perfume.

As I turned the corner, there she stood—the woman I had seen my entire life on television, just staring at herself in the mirror as if she were a normal person. But she wasn't a normal person. In that moment, she looked like a goddess.

"My beautiful girl," Samantha said. "I want to introduce you to a *potential* new assistant."

Alexis turned in what felt like slow motion. Her hair was chocolate brown, wavy, and full of volume. She was wearing a black lace bodysuit with a built-in bustier. It had to be custom-made. She was taller than I expected her to be. The all-male glam squad, who I initially hadn't even noticed, paused their primping to allow me to introduce myself.

"Hi, I'm Hayden!" I sputtered, thrusting my hand out, not realizing hers were full—an iPhone in one, and a glass of champagne in the other. She proceeded to hold out what little of her hand she had available to shake, presenting it to me as royalty might do. *Was I supposed to kiss it?*

"Thank God," Alexis said to Samantha. "That new girl you have downstairs—she won't even look at me." I wondered if that had something to do with the article on *TMZ* years ago about how Alexis fired anyone who looked her in the eye.

I stood frozen in time as she began examining me from head to toe. Her eyes were so dark, they were almost black—but at the same time, they were mesmerizing.

"Girl... I'm not afraid of you," I said. I was trying the funny, beguiling, gay-best-friend routine that had always worked for me in the salon, but it didn't land—and more importantly, I was lying. I was already terrified of her. I could tell that she wasn't amused by how cavalier I'd been. She forced a smile anyway.

She and Samantha discussed the logistics of the video shoot while I tried to keep my cool. I tried to absorb as much of Alexis as possible without creeping her out, stealing glances at her every few seconds in lieu of leering.

"It was nice to meet you!" I said as Samantha pulled my arm, guiding me out of the room. It had only been a few minutes, and the brevity of the meeting made me nervous I'd lost my opportunity. They say you should never meet your idols, which initially made me unsure if I even wanted the job. But after breathing the same oxygen, I'd never wanted anything more.

While waiting for the shoot to start, I noticed her backup dancer boyfriend, Brody, pacing the hallway upstairs, puffing his chest to make it clear he was the man of the house. He was tall, dark, and handsome in a generic way, but his fit body had made a lasting impression on Alexis's wandering eye. He'd been heavily featured in her documentary, and now he too was famous—for getting Alexis to leave her billionaire fiancé, Mark Kauffman. From an outsider's perspective, something about Brody felt inauthentic, reminiscent of Kevin Federline. I wondered what kind of man could get me to leave a billionaire. His dick had to be *huge*.

Sarah made her way over to formally introduce herself.

"So, what do you think they'll have you do?" she asked.

"Honestly, I have no idea," I said. "I mean, I would *love* to go on tour."

"Listen, I don't care what you want to do—as long as I still have a job." She laughed awkwardly, and then told me stories about how she'd formerly toured with the Backstreet Boys, the Jonas Brothers, and One Direction.

"So, you've been doing this awhile?" I was in awe that Samantha would have me, someone with no experience, come interview.

"I have. My first tour was actually with Backstreet, and let me tell you, those boys—"

I stopped listening as Alexis exited her dressing room. I stared at her silhouette from behind as she posed at the top of the stairs. She immediately began giving direction on the lighting, guiding the cameramen around and pointing to where she wanted them to station. Clearly, she'd been doing this for a lifetime. Her easy commands only increased my awe of her, to see her live and in action choreographing a roomful of people. She fixed her dress, nodded to the director to begin, and suddenly the music kicked on. Goosebumps covered my body as I heard what I knew was destined to be a hit song.

Watching her perform was mesmerizing. She moved in a way that I felt emulated Marilyn Monroe: sultry, sexy, confident. She knew her angles, what poses to hit, and exactly how to make love to the camera. She wasn't afraid to cut the music abruptly to pick one of the crewmen apart when the lighting was bad or she thought an angle was off. Even in her impatient incisiveness, there was such an elegance to her, an underlying allure that felt magnetic.

The sun was nearly up by the time they wrapped. By this point, I could barely keep my eyes open, and Alexis seemed to have vanished as the crew started to tear down. I sought out Samantha to say goodbye, and as we hugged, she promised she would call me.

I got into my car, pulled out my phone and wrote a text to my grandmother.

"*It's in the bag,*" I typed.

CHAPTER TWO

B ut it wasn't. Team Alexis went dark on me. Samantha didn't call as she promised, so I tried calling her. No answer. What happened? Did Alexis not like me?

Weeks went by. I spent my time either moping or applying to salons—even though I knew I didn't want to work in another salon. I only wanted to work for Alexis Shane.

Regardless of time passing, I convinced myself I still had a chance. I mean, they hadn't said 'no'. So, four weeks after the interview, I called Samantha over and over until she finally answered.

"Hayden, listen, I'm sorry," she said. "I'm not ignoring you; I just don't think the job is for you. It's a lot of work. I mean it when I say that you won't have a life."

I could feel my face turning red from frustration. "Please," I begged. "Just give me a chance! If it doesn't work out, it doesn't work out. But at least let me try. Unless Alexis said she doesn't like me or something?" I had nothing to lose at this point.

"But we're friends," Samantha continued to push back. "What if it doesn't work out and I have to fire you?"

Friends? We weren't friends. She was a client at my last job, and if she didn't hire me, I would probably never hear from her again.

"Plus this isn't exactly the *ideal* time to be joining the team. I'm sure you've read what the media's saying."

"That only makes me want to help *more*," I pleaded. "I promise to worship the ground she walks on every day until the press remembers what a legend she is." I cringed, unsure if my devotion was too fanatical for Samantha's intolerant New Jersey disposition.

She sighed heavily. "Fine. Maybe I'll just fire Sarah. Alexis isn't thrilled with her anyway. Meet me this afternoon at the house. We're hosting an after-party for the Grammys tonight. But here's the deal—I am *not* guaranteeing you a job. This is just a test."

Fire Sarah? I flashed back to Sarah panting while we watched the music video shoot. *"I don't care what you do—as long as I still have a job."* I felt bad, but my excitement overshadowed it.

An hour later, as I pulled up to the gate, Samantha called.

"Where the hell are you?" she hissed.

"Just getting to Calabasas now. I'm in line at the gate."

"Are you serious? Did you fucking forget to read *TMZ* today? Alexis moved to *Beverly Hills.*"

Suddenly I felt sick. How could she expect me to know that? Why wouldn't she just tell me? I did my best to remain calm, as I was now not only going to be late, but will have wasted two hours in traffic. *This is a test*, I reminded myself.

ALEXIS'S NEW PLACE WAS NOT in a gated community, but still hidden behind a gate so high it made the home invisible. Parking on the side of the street, I walked down the cobblestone driveway until a silver call box appeared on my left-hand side. I pressed the button, and a woman answered.

"Hi! This is Hayden. I'm here to see Samantha." The nervousness in my voice made it crack. The person didn't respond—they simply buzzed me through.

The gates opened in slow motion, the glistening sun highlighting the mansion. The yard was lush with green landscaping, florals, and fruit trees. I took my time stumbling up the cobblestone driveway in my knock-off Saint Laurent boots from Zara. Heading for the front door, I anticipated security to jump out at any moment, but they didn't. To the left of the house was another driveway that wrapped around the perimeter. I noticed the same luxury cars I'd seen at Alexis's home the night of the music video shoot. To my right was a pool, a guest house bigger than most "normal" homes, a tennis court, and even further down what appeared to be a second guest house. Squinting, I peered through the French doors. It wasn't a second guest house. It was a *bowling alley*.

Anxiety gripped me as I tiptoed up the steps to the front door. Should I knock? Call Samantha? I decided to knock.

The door cracked open slightly, just enough to see through—and it was *Alexis Shane*. She opened her own doors? Isn't that what assistants, security guards, nannies, and house managers are for? She frowned at me, confused.

"Hi!" I said, and smiled. "I'm Hayden. We met in Calabasas. Samantha told me to meet her here."

"Oh! Yes. I remember," she said, holding a phone to her ear. The expression on her face told me she was lying. "Excuse the mess, sweetie. We just moved in and it's *impossible* to find good help." She rolled her eyes and forced a smile. But her teeth were so big and perfect, even a fake smile looked real. "Samantha left but is on her way back." She held out her phone to show me it was Samantha on the other end.

Alexis was barefoot in a silk leopard print Dolce & Gabanna tank, matching shorts, and what looked like yesterday's makeup. Most noteworthy was her blinding jewelry. She was still wearing the 30-carat engagement ring from Mark Kauffman. However, it now resided on her middle finger. Around her neck was a choker made of rubies and yellow diamonds resembling a phoenix. The necklace had become a part of who she was, an iconic piece of pop-culture paraphernalia. I knew from researching her life in the weeks I'd spent waiting for a call back that it'd been present in every photo taken of her over the last two decades.

While Alexis released many successful albums, *Phoenix* was her most famous, and the highest-selling of the 2000s. Prior to that, she'd been represented by powerful music manager, Tracey Bass. At eighteen years old, Alexis had snuck into an exclusive Hollywood party to meet her. With Alexis's vocal range, Tracey was quickly impressed, and single-handedly turned Alexis into the biggest pop sensation in the world—seemingly overnight. There were rumors in the press about the nature of their relationship, which only intensified after Tracey's abrupt firing. *Phoenix* was the first album Alexis had produced without her, and in the title track she revealed the truth about their romance. Alexis's authenticity touched fans and catapulted her into the highest levels of superstardom.

Alexis welcomed me into the mansion when Brody appeared, FaceTiming a friend to gloat about *his* new home. I sensed that everyone close to her took ownership of her success. Looking past Brody, I saw the scene inside Alexis's house was alarmingly normal as her twins chased one another in the foyer. Rhythm and Blue, nicknamed R&B, were from Alexis's marriage to Rich Revolver. Rich was a celebrity in his own right and had attempted to conquer all aspects of the entertainment industry, but he'd never quite reached Alexis's level of fame. After four years of marriage, the relationship crumbled as the tabloids fueled rumors of Rich's infidelity.

Even having just moved in, accomplishments adorned the walls of her new home: gold albums, platinum albums, ten million, twenty million. In the hallway alone, I quickly tallied over three hundred million albums sold. Brody directed me to the office, and as I walked in, the oversized door was quickly closed behind me. Inside awaited a familiar face—Sarah.

"Hi! How are you?" I said, knowing the poor girl could potentially be fired.

A back door to the office opened and Amber walked in. She was dressed almost the same as the last time I'd seen her: an oversized Adidas sweatshirt, fur Fenty slides, with a messy bun on top of her head. However, this time, she wore see-through leggings which exposed her neon green thong.

"Hi Hayden," she said. "How are you?" Her pleasantries felt forced— and before I could respond, she rapid-fire interrogated Sarah as if she herself were the one writing the paychecks. "I need the updated schedule. Where did you put the boxes? Did you ship everything out through FedEx? What time is glam coming? What time will Samantha be here? Has Noah started making lunch for the twins? Speaking of, where is the twins' activity schedule? Have the nannies turned in their time sheets for payroll?"

Jesus. If these were all Sarah's responsibilities, then what did Amber do? The girl couldn't get in a word edgewise and just sat there staring at Amber like a deer in headlights. "Do I have to do *everything* around here?" Amber mumbled to herself as she exited the office's front door. Before she could close it, I heard Samantha's unmistakable voice ring out like a siren as she praised Alexis on how beautiful she looked.

Samantha entered the room. "Great, you're here!" In the same breath, she turned to Sarah. "Listen, Sarah, *honey*. I'm sorry. It's not gonna work out. There's no hard feelings. I just think this is all a little too fast-paced for you. I'll cut you a check for two weeks." Her delivery was cold and direct. And to my surprise, Sarah didn't put up a fight.

Uncomfortably, I said goodbye to Sarah, knowing it was my persistence that cost her job. After she shuffled out, Samantha continued talking to me as if nothing had happened.

"Here's the deal. Like I said, this is a *test*. Okay? We're hosting a Grammys after-party tonight so the radio executives can hear Alexis's new song that we teased in the documentary. This party is *everything* to Alexis, especially after the Super Bowl performance. We need to remind everyone who she is. Do you know what people think of her now, Hayden?"

"Me?" I flinched, not knowing if I was supposed to answer. "Well, I—"

"They think she's a *joke*, a has-been, one Louboutin heel into retirement. So, it needs to be perfect. If you want to be on the team, your foremost concern is her image, at all times and at all costs. And if you do well, you can stay."

A FEW HOURS LATER, I stood nervously against an ivory dresser as Samantha sucked in her cheeks while her twelve-year-old daughter Blair, doppelgänger and giver of sage life advice, applied an unflattering shit-colored blush to her cheeks.

"You should keep Hayden on, Mom," Blair said encouragingly. "He's just like the gays in all the movies. Alexis *has* to love him!"

I tried to like Blair, as she was the unofficial photographer of Alexis's social media and therefore a supposed crucial link to the expansive entourage, but the solemnity with which Samantha listened to her opinions disturbed me.

Suddenly Samantha straightened up, nodding toward me with a frown. "This is the *most* important advice I will give you about this job," she said gravely, flicking her lacquered lash extensions toward me. "Do not trust *anyone*."

I laughed nervously, twisting my fingers. "What do you mean?"

She sighed and then smiled as if I was a naïve child. "Listen, I'm serious. You can't trust anyone. Not security, not the chef, not a nanny. Everyone will use the first opportunity they have to throw you under the bus and get rid of you. Be kind, be short, and be professional. Nothing more."

I nodded silently as I thought of the previous hour I'd spent running around the guest house fetching Amber's accessories and setting her dirty dishes in the sink, which she allowed to pile up outside her bedroom door like a hungover kingpin. The most important thing I'd done all night was show the DJ where to set up outside—between the tennis court and the bowling alley, of course. Everyone seemed nice enough, and why shouldn't they be? We were all here for Alexis. We all shared a common goal, so I didn't understand why anyone would want to sabotage anyone else. Certainly nobody *seemed* cutthroat so far.

Samantha jerked her phone violently from her pocket. Her alertness inspired and frightened me. "Alexis wants to go directly from the party to The Parker in Palm Springs," she announced, then looked back to me. "Book the spa room for her."

I didn't know if this was how she always operated, or if this was part of the test. Soon I'd discover Samantha liked to tell me to do things, but would never tell me how. The spa room? Did she mean spa services? Was there literally a spa-themed suite? Also, I was going to need a credit card. But I couldn't ask her any questions because she was already back on the phone. I exited the office and began wandering the mansion, hoping to find Amber.

I tiptoed up the stairs, looking for signs of life. As I arrived at the top, I paused, unsure if I should go left or right—until I heard the cackles of gay men coming from my left. I turned the corner and saw white velvet sofas draped in fur throws.

"Amber?" I said, "Amber?"

"Yes, babe?"

"I need some help."

I continued around the corner where I heard the voices coming from and was greeted by a cavernous room of maybe forty or so rolling racks full of designer clothing. Furs, leather, denim, coats, blouses, skirts. At the far end of the makeshift closet was another well-lit room. In the door frame, I saw part of Alexis's figure. She was seated, and barely visible from where I stood.

It was the glam room. Alexis would never be seen in public without a full face of makeup. She basically invented the trend. You would never catch a sallow-faced snapshot of her in *People* dredging down the remains of a Starbucks frappuccino or bending down to pick up dog shit in sweatpants. She only ever emerged in goddess form.

I started walking toward the glam room toward Alexis and Amber's voice—when Samantha appeared out of nowhere and jumped in front of me. "Excuse me, *what are you doing*?" she hissed.

"I'm sorry, I—I was confused," I said. Amber saw the commotion and made her way over.

"Amber, what the *hell* are you doing to him?" Samantha said. "Why didn't you tell him to go back downstairs? You know he can't be up here!"

Samantha began guiding me back downstairs, this time via a hidden staircase. "Hayden, no one is allowed to see her without hair and makeup," she said. "Not even her children. The only people allowed in that room are me, Amber, and the glam boys."

"*Not even her children?*" I asked. That sounded a little dramatic. I mused about the Super Bowl show and figured the crux of diva-hood must have rested more in glamorous appearance than performative capabilities. After all, who cared if her voice cracked as long as her bodysuit shimmered so violently everyone sprouted a pair of cataracts?

The staircase led to the kitchen where we opened the door to R&B causing chaos. They each had personalities as big as their curly brown hair, and as the offspring of a superstar, I couldn't help but intuitively know that one day they would be stars in their own right. I wondered if they would be singers or actors, or just simply tabloid-fodder.

On some level it was even more bizarre meeting the twins than it was their legendary mother. I had seen these two grow up on TV—not in a reality television sort of way, but in an untouchable way, frozen in photographs. They were both incredibly smart, speaking like grown-ups, yet still wild like children.

"Who are you?" Blue asked me. "Do you work here now?"

"I'm Hayden," I said. "And we'll see. But I hope so!"

Through the kitchen windows, I looked into the bowling alley where the party was being held. It was lined with French doors that were all open, facing the outdoor tennis court. It was starting to get busy, and Alexis was still nowhere in sight.

Confidently, Rhythm walked up and grabbed me by the hand. "Will you take me to the bowling alley?" he said with an adorable lisp. He knew because there were strangers in the house that he couldn't go alone.

The uniformed bartender greeted us with a knowing smile.

Rhythm looked up at me with puppy-dog eyes. "Will you get me a Coke?"

The second he uttered those words, another nanny I hadn't yet met was sprinting across the tennis court from the kitchen to stop me. "Rhythm!" she said. "You know what Mommy told you."

He began to pout and stomp his feet. "She said I can have this much!" he said, spreading his thumb and index finger as far apart as they could go to give a demonstration.

"No, Rhythm," she corrected him. "She said you can have *this* much." She pushed his index finger closer to his thumb, leaving them about three inches apart.

As she handed him the acceptable-sized Coca-Cola serving, she turned to me and smiled. "You've got to be careful with this one. He knows exactly what he's doing. I'm Porsha, by the way."

Porsha was a beautiful, fit African American girl with impeccable braids. She wore what appeared to be an Alexis Shane employee polo adorned with her iconic phoenix logo.

I laughed. Rhythm was much smarter than I'd given him credit for. He knew I was the naïve new guy who would give him exactly what he wanted. Porsha and I turned our heads to look at the crowd for a moment, and Rhythm had already run loose—through the legs of the partygoers and back to the tennis court, where he stopped in front of the DJ to show off his moves.

After following Rhythm back to the kitchen, a visibly irritated man entered. "Excuse me!" he groaned. "How much longer is she going to be? This is ridiculous. I have the heads of SiriusXM, Spotify, and Apple Music here. They're going to leave."

I glanced at the clock; it was just after ten p.m. The party started at eight, but the hostess had yet to make an appearance.

"I'm so sorry, sir," I said. "Let me find out what's going on."

But the moment I turned to find Samantha, Alexis descended from the hidden staircase. She was again moving in slow motion. The compliments from the staff flooded my ears like a choir as they oohed and aahed over her.

"Alexis, you look amazing!"

"You look *beautiful*, Alexis!"

"I am speechless!"

"You look *so* skinny!"

I had no idea who was saying what. It all kind of rolled out of everyone's mouth at the same time. It sounded excessive, but the truth was she did look amazing. She wore a white velvet Saint Laurent motorcycle jacket, metallic gold Tom Ford stilettos, and her hair and makeup were flawless, as if she'd just come from a magazine cover shoot.

I openly stared as Samantha gave Alexis a rundown of the evening, while Alexis picked at the hors d'oeuvres that were about to be passed around. "You'll walk over, say hello, they'll play your song, take a couple photos, and we're done. Forty-five minutes and then I'll kick everyone out."

Alexis sighed dramatically. If this was as important to her as Samantha had stressed, she had a funny way of showing it.

I fell in line with the entourage, watching iPhones from the crowd in the bowling alley rise above eye line as everyone photographed and recorded Alexis's every move. I wondered what percentage of the attention was genuine admiration, and what percentage was just waiting to see how she could humiliate herself next. I scrutinized Alexis's face, but it was impossible to tell how she truly felt beneath her veneer of glamour.

"Hello, sweeties!" Alexis said. "I apologize for my tardiness. I promise it had nothing to do with my getting ready. You know, I wake up just looking like this." The crowd laughed.

Standing in the corner, I watched her work the room. She was effervescent, moving seamlessly through the crowd of wealthy industry folk, lighting up the faces of everyone she passed. I made sure to keep checking in with Samantha and Amber to see if there was anything I should be doing, but they both just encouraged me to enjoy the party, so I snuck a glass of champagne. Was this what *work* would be like?

As everyone made their rounds, I tried to familiarize myself with the bodyguards, of whom there were three: one for the property, one for Alexis, one for the twins. Then there were the three nannies who rotated every twelve hours. And lastly, my favorite—the handsome twenty-something chef named Noah. I made sure everyone knew I was willing to help with any task, hoping my officiousness would secure me a spot on the team for good. Everyone's face wore the same expression: exasperated composure, like they were one thread away from unraveling, but were too well-compensated to allow it to happen. I wondered what that meant for me.

As Alexis continued taking photos with the partygoers, I made my way back to the kitchen to meet the glam boys who were sitting at the table enjoying Noah's multi-course meal.

I introduced myself and quickly forgot the names of the stylist, hair-stylist, and their assistants, because I was too enamored by the tall, strong black man whose arms were covered in tattoos.

"I'm Dylan," he said.

Dylan. I watched his full lips intently, replaying his name over again in my head. He sounded as sexy as he looked. My pulse began racing as he made intense eye contact.

"So, what is your role here, handsome?" he said.

I did my best not to blush, but I was notorious for turning the shade of a tomato.

"I'm the new assistant, *hopefully*," I said.

"Well I hope to be seeing you around here more often then." He winked.

Eventually I checked my phone to see it was almost midnight. The champagne was still flowing, and Alexis didn't seem to mind having exceeded her forty-five-minute requirement. I was exhausted after being there all day, but snapped myself out of it, remembering Samantha's words from my interview. "*Full-time job*." I stood up to find her to see what I could help with.

"You did good today!" Samantha said. "You can go home. Be back here at ten a.m. on Monday."

"Oh, thank God!" I exhaled, injected with a new flush of joy and excitement. Whatever vague rites of passage were required of me, I had miraculously succeeded in all of them. I couldn't wait to tell Oma that my childhood superstar was now officially my *boss*. No more catering to the plastic wives of B-movie directors.

When I made my way back to the kitchen island to say goodbye to everyone, I found Amber berating Noah. "This steak is so fucking *dry*," she said. "I can't eat this, Noah."

"Don't talk to me like that, Amber," he said. His tone indicated this was a normal interaction for them.

I cut in. "I'm sorry—is your name Alexis?" I teased Amber. The group laughed, and Amber blushed.

"Hayden," she said. I prepared to be scolded. But instead, she smiled faintly. "Welcome to the family."

I SPED HOME THAT NIGHT to find Grayson half asleep in bed with his book of the month in hand.

"Guess who's an official member of Team Alexis?" I cried, bursting into the room and flipping my nonexistent locks.

"No," he said, a smile cracking over his face as he let his book fall flat on the mattress.

"Yes!"

"Babe!" he shouted, springing up from bed and pulling me in for a bear hug. "That's incredible! I knew they'd love you!"

"Well, *love* isn't the word I'd use. I told like five different people today I'd happily clean any of the eight bathrooms with a toothbrush if that's what it took, so I think that really gave me an edge."

Grayson laughed and kissed me on the cheek, his bright blue eyes gleaming. He was genuinely proud of me. He was the hardest-working person I'd ever met, working up to sixty hours a week at the agency. Any day now, we figured he'd be promoted from assistant to agent. I was only slightly worried that my job news would be a sour reminder to him of his own situation, as he'd deserved the promotion *years* ago, but he was genuinely happy for me.

"I'm so proud of you," he said, holding my face in his hands. "Do you think this means she'll officiate our wedding?"

"I'll have to get on her good side first."

What's that—her left side?" he teased, having learned from me that Alexis considered the right side of her face to be her *bad* side.

"Oh my God!" I cried, suddenly remembering. "I gotta call Oma!"

"It's like four a.m. in Maryland! Call her tomorrow."

CHAPTER THREE

While I thought my test had gone well, my interactions with Alexis herself were still limited.

I arrived early for my first official day, full of anxiety and nerves, when the cleaning lady opened the door wearily and told me Alexis and Amber were still asleep.

"Oh," I said, surprised, then waited in the office, unsure what to do. I imagined by nine in the morning the whole house would be bustling with the chaos of stardom. Instead, anonymous snoring wafted down the halls.

Two hours later, Samantha arrived, steeped in her typical urban neuroses. I fiddled with my pen as she walked into the room to make it look like I was doing something.

"So Hayden," she huffed, plopping her oversized leather Prada bag onto the swivel chair across from me. "Here's the rundown of your new gig. Brace yourself. You're not just an assistant. You're the liaison between myself and Alexis. It is *your* responsibility to make sure deadlines are met, and she always gets out of bed. Meetings can never be canceled, no matter how much she whines." Samantha's voice was serious, and her eye contact was intense. "My number one priority is to prove people wrong, to show them that her reputation is a myth, or at least a thing of the past. We have to make people see the Super Bowl performance as an endearing quirk of her prima-donna-ness instead of writing her off. This is a crucial time for her, do you understand? You are now in part responsible with helping me transform her image as the media currently sees it, and that's no easy feat. I've done my best to show people that under my management she is not who they think she is, and you are vital in maintaining this."

I wondered how I could successfully do this, as no amount of scheduling or wine runs could undo the damage Alexis had done to herself during that performance. What good was keeping up an illusion that most people were beginning to see through? But I nodded emphatically anyway, blindly loyal to whatever alchemy would be asked of me.

Samantha explained that the schedule was our bible, and never to be messed up or shared with anyone outside of herself, Amber, and Alexis.

"So, things we need to add—we're going to Australia. I need you to get in contact with the travel agent and add our itinerary to the schedule. Alexis is headlining a festival there, so make sure Anna has glam scheduled. She's due on stage at eight p.m., and always needs two hours for glam, so schedule that at six. I also saw on Instagram a place where you can meet baby koala bears. Alexis would *love* that, so figure out how we can fit it in. I'm forwarding you the invite to Kendrick Lamar's birthday party, which is the day we return. Make sure our flight lands with enough time for Alexis to come home, change, and glam. She normally needs a day off for vocal rest before a performance, but the day after that, she's performing on *Jimmy Kimmel Live!*"

Writing feverishly, I wondered when the instructions would stop, and what exactly I'd be lucky enough to attend.

"And no—in case you're wondering," Samantha said intuitively.

"In case I'm wondering what?"

"You're not coming with. You need to prove yourself first. You'll start out just working here in the office."

My dreams of jet-setting crumbled, until I heard a familiar raspy voice over my shoulder.

"Hello Miss Samantha," Alexis cooed.

"Hello my beautiful girl! You remember Hayden, don't you?"

"Hello Hayden," Alexis said. "Yes, I remember." This time she actually did. "Nice to see you again."

"Hayden is officially your new assistant," Samantha said.

Alexis smiled at me, then beckoned Samantha with a freshly manicured nail to come closer. Samantha walked around the desk so she and Alexis could speak privately. While I was now on her radar, that wasn't enough for her to feel comfortable speaking freely in front of me.

Alexis pointed in the direction of the bowling alley and began to whisper, "Rich is here to visit with the twins, but I want to go to the studio. I don't want it to look like I'm *abandoning* them."

"Why aren't you using the studio that's in your house?" Samantha laughed.

"We just moved in! It's not set up the way I like yet."

"Alright, princess. Don't stress," Samantha said, "I'll take care of Rich."

Samantha always had a solution, and it was clear her job far exceeded that of a normal manager. I watched as Alexis and Samantha quietly joked with one another. I admired their relationship, which was playful like best friends, or even sisters.

As they discreetly whispered, I again found myself staring at Alexis. Looking at her wasn't just like seeing someone famous—Alexis was a *star*. Today she was decked out in a $10,000 gold and turquoise sequin Gucci bomber jacket, red Christian Louboutin platforms, and a diamond necklace easily larger than what Old Rose had dropped into the ocean at the end of *Titanic*. Showing off her look to Samantha, Alexis playfully unzipped her jacket to give a peek at her new red lace Agent Provocateur bra.

"Your tits look incredible," Samantha said.

"*Hello?*" Alexis cried, pointing to me.

"Who the fuck cares?" Samantha smiled. "He's gay!"

"Oh, I'm sure he forgot, Samantha. He really needed you reminding him!"

"Um, who said I was *gay?*" I said, trying to insert myself into their friendly banter. And this time, it worked. They both laughed, and Alexis grazed my arm approvingly before exiting the room.

Alexis Shane just touched my arm. Every inch of the twelve-year-old in me dancing alone to *Phoenix* in my room exploded in prophetic joy.

Samantha walked back and took a seat on the white snakeskin-print throne.

"All right! She's going to the studio, and it's even harder to be permitted access there than it is to the glam room. So, just come back to the house at the same time tomorrow."

I glanced out the glass door over her shoulder and noticed it had started drizzling. Security ran from the bowling alley to the kitchen, umbrella in hand. He then opened up the umbrella, grabbed Alexis daintily by the hand, and led her down the steps.

"I'm sorry," I said. "Did I just see that right? Did he just run across the property with an umbrella so she wouldn't get wet?"

"Honey, buckle up," Samantha said, "we're just barely scratching the surface."

Samantha left the office to get rid of the ex-husband, and I looked down at my desk to see a pile of Sarah's new hire paperwork. She had only lasted a few short months. I slowly pushed them off the edge of the desk and into the waste basket.

"Sorry Sarah," I said with a grin. "But it's my turn now."

WORKING FROM ALEXIS'S MEGA-MANSION WAS nothing like I expected it to be. Each morning I arrived promptly at ten a.m. and one of the cleaning ladies quietly opened the front door for me, careful to not wake Alexis, as the master suite was just above the entrance. I then tiptoed into the office, petrified that my mere footsteps would rouse the queen from her slumber.

Amber was never any help either, always leaving the second I got there to go work out with a personal trainer. "Oh no, babe, you're good," she'd say. "She won't be up for hours." She was right—Alexis never left her bedroom. I'd then call Samantha for instruction, but often received her voicemail. So, to kill time, I made up things to do. I reorganized the office, set up a new filing system, and created a birthday calendar for the other employees.

I'd been working all week from ten to six, and had yet to see Alexis. At least on Friday, Samantha finally graced me with her presence. This time she came with a woman who I hadn't yet met, who wore an outdated plum sweater wrap and had a brand-new Apple laptop in hand. She resembled a mean-looking Melissa McCarthy, but with red hair that matched Samantha, Blair, and Amber's. I wondered if it wasn't a coincidence that the women looked so similar. She walked confidently behind Samantha into the office as if it were her own, rearranging my desk to make room for herself.

"Hi, I'm Hayden!" I said, greeting her with a smile and a handshake, still eager for everyone to like me.

"I know," she said. "I'm Vanessa, part of the management team. More specifically, the tour manager. But I do a little bit of everything here."

It felt like she wanted to make clear to me she was in a position of power.

Her expression was one of those that looked perpetually unimpressed.

"It's nice to meet you," I said.

"This is yours." She placed the new laptop on my desk and began setting up my new Mac with the apps I'd need.

"Thank you," I said. "I'm so excited to be on the team." Wanting her to warm to me, I changed the subject. "Has anyone ever said that you, Samantha, and Amber look—"

"Related?" she interrupted. "Yes, of course. We're *sisters*—Samantha didn't tell you?"

"She didn't. But the shade of red you girls have is so specific. It's this gorgeous ruby meets auburn color," I said, knowing exactly what I was doing.

I like him, Vanessa mouthed to Samantha, who was on a call.

A little compliment always went a long way. That was the benefit of being a gay man working with a group of women. I learned from my years in the salon that women could be catty and competitive with one another, but never with me. They loved me because I was non-threatening and I loved them for naturally embracing me. It was much easier than the toxic masculinity work environments my hetero brothers had to endure.

"Did you see *TMZ* this morning?" I asked Samantha, wanting to impress her after showing up at the wrong home. "They reported Alexis leased this house for one-hundred-fifty grand a month! How do they even find that out?"

She laughed a little too loudly. "Who knows? I'm just glad they didn't mention it was a downgrade, being that Kauffman isn't footing the bill anymore."

Vanessa shushed her and pointed up to remind her Alexis's room was right above us.

"Have you talked to the boyfriend at all?" Samantha whispered to me.

Her inquiry confused me, as in the documentary it appeared Alexis and Brody had a great relationship.

"I mean, I ran into him in the entry the other day. We said hello, but that's really it."

"Listen," Samantha said, "you're going to be privy to a lot of confidential information, both business and personal. Which reminds me, Amber needs to have you sign an NDA. But regardless, you can never tell him *anything*. Even if you know the answer, say you don't."

I didn't understand but didn't question her. I was just happy to be on the *inside* of any kind of information.

"I'm gonna need you to connect some calls. And then I'll need you to run out and get this new bubbly rosé Alexis wants to try."

"Sure!" I said, excited to finally feel useful. I eagerly connected Samantha to each conference call, genuinely excited to listen in on the potential new projects. Most fascinating was a scripted series she had sold about Alexis's life. Alexis had made it known throughout her career that she'd had a difficult childhood. She often spoke about how challenging it was for her to grow up as a little black girl adopted into an all-white family. In an interview with Drew Barrymore, she explained the white kids at school weren't allowed to play with her, and the black kids would bully her for "acting white."

"I have Samantha on the line!" I said to the callers after connecting her.

"Hi, guys!" she said. "Quentin is on my other line. Let me conference him in. He's *so* looking forward to directing this."

Quentin Tarantino was how Samantha and Alexis met. Knowing he and Alexis were close, Samantha had reached out, wanting to do a documentary after her separation from Rich. Alexis had turned into tabloid-fodder, and Samantha wanted to help her spin the narrative.

Samantha covered the speaker to her phone with her overly spray-tanned hand and whispered to me, "Alexis just woke up. I need you to connect her to the call as well."

"But—" I stammered, "I don't have her number."

Within seconds my phone buzzed with a contact share from Samantha that read, *Alexis Shane New Number.*

Holy shit. I have Alexis Shane's phone number. I started fantasizing about the friendship we were about to embark on. The late-night phone calls, pajama parties, vacations. I was so nervous to call her for the first time, I began to sweat as I dialed. On the fourth ring, she answered, sounding as if she were still beneath the covers.

"Hi Alexis, it's Hayden!" My voice was shaking. "I have Samantha and the team from Netflix on the line for you."

I was grateful just to know she was alive. There was something unsettling about witnessing this other side of my childhood superhero, a grimness there I did not expect. After not seeing her all week, I began to wonder if she was an alien, a vampire, or even better, a member of the Illuminati. I couldn't help but imagine this reclusiveness was due to the torrent of cruelty the media had been unleashing upon her for the past few months. I probably wouldn't want to get out of bed much either if the entire globe was looking for every opportunity to slander me into ruin, just to make a few bucks.

"But it's *so early*," she groaned. "This is abusive, Hayden."

I pulled my phone away from my face to see it was two p.m. Unsure what to do, I connected the call anyway, wincing.

"I have Alexis on the line!" I cheerfully informed the team. The excitement from the other callers was palpable, streamer executives' voices imbued with a sudden liveliness after she spoke.

Once the Netflix team disconnected from the call, Samantha reminded Alexis they had a meeting later that afternoon with N.J. Sax, the head of the record label.

"Nooooo, Samantha," she whined. "Can't we reschedule?"

"I let you reschedule it twice last week, Alexis. This is serious. I'm sorry, but we have to go. Nap for a little while longer, and Amber will wake you when glam is here. I'm going to have Hayden come with us so he can start getting acquainted with everyone."

"Ugh, fine." She hung up.

OVER THE PAST WEEK OF my employment, I had gotten into the habit of leaving the back office door open, as the office could sometimes feel like a cage. I also knew the twins passed by on their way to and from "school" in the guest house, and they had come to accept it as an open invitation to interrupt my normally slow-moving day. They'd barge in like little tornados, asking me questions, hiding my car keys, stapling my papers together, and taking selfies with my iPhone. Today was no different.

"Miss Samantha!" Blue shouted, running into the office. "Miss Samantha, do you know Hayden?"

"Of course I know Hayden, silly," she said. "I hired him."

"Hayden is my best friend," Rhythm interrupted. He then jumped into Samantha's lap. "My best, best, best, best friend!"

While I had never been very fond of children, hearing him say that made my heart skip a beat. He then jumped off her lap and toward me, pleading to show me the newest games he'd downloaded to his iPad—but the nanny on rotation interrupted to guide him back toward school. I couldn't help but laugh at his pouting face as he walked off. Was I beginning to actually *like children?* Then again, not all kids had the personality of R&B. They were special.

"Nice of you to show up for work today," Samantha said sarcastically to Amber, who suddenly appeared from the back door. "Take Hayden with you so he can see the private entrance to the glam room. But send him back down before you let Alexis know they're here. Oh, and don't forget to have him sign an NDA!"

At some point, my phone began to vibrate. *QUEEN*—Alexis was calling me.

"Hayden, is it just us on the line?" she asked.

"Of course!" I said, confused by her question. Why wouldn't it be?

"I need you to head to the bank and pick me up fifty grand in cash."

"Of course," I said again, pretending picking up 50 racks was as casual as going to Starbucks for a cold brew. "I'll go right now."

I ran back to the office in a panic, hoping Samantha could help. But Alexis asked if anyone else was on the line—was I not supposed to ask for help? It was the first task Alexis herself was giving me, and I couldn't fuck it up. Still, I had no idea what I was doing, and needed Samantha's guidance.

"Which bank does Alexis go to? Do I need to talk to someone specific? Are they actually just going to hand me fifty grand of Alexis Shane's money?" I rambled. "And why did she ask me if someone else was on the line? Should—"

"Calm down, psycho!" Samantha interrupted. "I'll call Karen at the business management office. Just drive down to Bank of America. It's off Little Santa Monica. Go in and say you're picking up for Alexis Shane. All you need is your ID."

As I climbed into my car and glanced at the clock, I noticed it was only an hour until Alexis's meeting at Capitol Records. In Los Angeles traffic, that meant they'd need to leave right now. I sped down the hill for Little Santa Monica, and when I spotted the bank there was no time to find a parking spot, so I pulled up directly in front and put on my flashers. I ran in, anxiously approaching the front desk.

"I'm here to pick up for Alexis Shane," I whispered.

"Sir, you'll just go around the corner right there," the teller pointed. "There's a telephone. Pick it up, tell them what you're here for, and they'll buzz you in."

In my ten years of living in Los Angeles, I had never seen anything like this. I headed down the white oak-paneled hall, where I was met by two large double doors and a telephone mounted on the wall to the left. I picked up the phone and repeated myself, "I'm here to pick up for my boss, *Alexis Shane*."

The door made a loud buzzing noise. I hung up the phone and opened the door to the private back room of this Beverly Hills bank. There were rows and rows of cubicles full of employees, and the walls were adorned with iconic photos of Hollywood royalty like Elizabeth Taylor and James Dean. I walked down the hallway between the cubicles until I reached a glass window at the end, where I repeated myself for a third time.

"Hi, I'm here to pick up for my boss, Alexis Shane." Was this as weird for people to hear as it was for me to say? The teller asked for my driver's license, photocopied it, and had me sign a release form. She then handed me a large plastic envelope which I'd previously only seen in bank robbery movies.

As I headed for the door, I felt like I was doing something wrong, like someone was going to try to stop me, but no one did. I climbed into the driver's seat of my car and looked down at the shiny envelope that had "ALEXIS SHANE $50,000" in black Sharpie across the front. It hadn't been sealed, so I opened it to make sure it was all there. But also, because I had never held $50,000 cash in my hands before. It kind of turned me on.

When I returned to the mansion, security opened the gate for me just as Alexis and Samantha were climbing into Samantha's four-door Porsche 911. She rolled down the window as I reached across her to hand Alexis the envelope of cash.

"Hop in the back," Samantha instructed.

I climbed into the very tiny leather backseat, and immediately had butterflies. This was my first time seeing Alexis all week. I sat quietly, listening to the two women talk business and admiring Alexis's chocolate locks that whipped through the wind of the open window.

"I guess Live Nation has decided to push the tour to July," Samantha said. "The ticket sales just aren't cutting it. So, I'm going to have to get you out there to do some press, you know, because you still personally haven't addressed the Super Bowl halftime show."

Alexis was quiet, and I couldn't see her expression from where I was sitting. I felt uncomfortable, wondering if Samantha should be having this conversation in front of me. While Alexis's Super Bowl performance was a nightmare—with a myriad of memes referring to it as the end of her career—it still hadn't crossed my mind that someone with her legacy would ever have a problem selling tickets. After all, what was *one* bad show compared to twenty years of unequaled talent?

We pulled up to the guard house at Capitol Records. "We're here to meet with N.J. Sax," Samantha said. N.J. was the most powerful record executive in the music industry—famous for working with Drake, Rihanna, Justin Bieber, and even her rival Jessica Rodriguez.

"I just need some identif—" The guard trailed off after spotting Alexis in the passenger seat. "Oh, I'm so sorry, Ms. Shane. No need for that. Welcome back."

I sat in the corner of N.J.'s office admiring the accomplishments adorning his walls, when he entered. He was a well-groomed black man with a bald head, gray beard, of average height and build, and wearing reading glasses that looked too costume to be prescription. He hadn't even managed to say hello to Alexis before Samantha went for the jugular.

"Listen N.J., I'm not here to waste time and give fake pleasantries. I know what you're trying to pull here. Alexis isn't twenty anymore, I get it. However, she is still the bestselling female artist of all time, and you need to start treating her accordingly. Ever since the Super Bowl performance, you've been taunting us via the media with anonymous sources claiming she could be let go from the label."

"Samantha, you're paranoid," he said.

"N.J., *shut it*. You think I don't know how this works? I've been in the business for twenty fucking years. You're trying to pressure her into recording the final album from her contract since there's buzz around this disastrous performance. Well, you're not going to push her into a comeback album that she isn't ready for. She needs to be able to be creative, not just record for the sake of it."

"I mean, it's been five years since her last album, Samantha. If she doesn't soon, she may as well just—"

"Just what? She's gone through a divorce *and* a failed engagement! She's a single mother. I mean, come on! Are you fucking kidding me? She's going to record another album when she's ready, okay? But since we're here, we do need to discuss said contract. I've seen the terms, and it's absolutely ludicrous. Two-hundred-fifty thousand dollars for three albums? That won't even cover the cost of her *assistants* for a *year*!"

"Samantha, we're not adjusting her contract. That's completely out of the question. So, you can just forget about that right now."

Samantha stood and walked around to N.J.'s side of the desk and whispered so that only he could hear. I watched as his fingers closed into fists and his jaw clenched. What was she saying to him?

"You're renewing her contract *today*—and a press release will be going out tomorrow." Samantha now spoke loudly, so the whole room could hear. "Whatever manager made her last deal is a fucking amateur, and you're going to put just as much effort into her next album as you do with Fifth Whore-many. Three million dollars for two albums, and one greatest hits. Oh, and we're going to need an advance."

I imagined if Samantha were a man, N.J. would have punched her square in the jaw. I sat quietly in shock at Samantha's ability to not be afraid of someone with his reputation and expertise. Of course, a man with that amount of power wasn't going to take an ultimatum like this lying down. But Alexis *was* a legend, and Samantha refused to let up. We weren't leaving until there were signatures on a dotted line.

And we did leave, with exactly what Samantha demanded.

I followed the ladies in silence to the car, and once the doors closed, Alexis let out a high-pitched noise I'd only ever heard in her songs.

"You did it again!" she whistled, grinning from ear to ear.

"No, beautiful, *we* did it again." Samantha's off-key screech was as ecstatic as Alexis's.

Goosebumps covered my body, thrilled to be a fly on the wall in this genuine moment of excitement with Alexis. Seeing her this happy made me excited for our future together.

IT WAS RARE IN HOLLYWOOD for a couple to get divorced and still spend time together with their children. But this evening, Alexis would be attending the Teen Choice Awards with the twins and their father, Rich. It was rare for anywhere, really. When my parents divorced when I was twelve, they avoided each other entirely, so the idea of co-parenting was foreign to me.

Alexis slept well into the afternoon the day of the awards show, while I sat in the office preparing the schedule. But my train of thought was interrupted when I noticed Brody on the phone, pacing in front of the office door. I pretended not to listen in as I heard him complain about the family outing and how he wasn't invited.

"Why does she think she can just parade around in public with her ex-husband and *without me*?" he said.

Why would he not want his girlfriend and the father of her children to get along? His comments reeked of insecurity. But I guess, how could he *not* be insecure? Her ex was a wealthy celebrity adored by millions, and he was the backup dancer on her payroll.-

My phone began to buzz.

"Listen," Samantha said, "we had a pair of custom Christian Louboutins made for Alexis. They're saying they were shipped to the house in Calabasas. Maybe they were delivered after she moved out, but *someone* signed for them, and Alexis is freaking out because she wanted to wear them tonight. You guys need to find them. They're covered in Swarovski crystals, and have her signature phoenix logo on the back of the heel. They're ten thousand fucking dollars, so look *everywhere*. I swear to God, if that new homeowner is trying to steal them, I will drive there myself and cut off his fucking balls!"

I was able to find the tracking information through Sarah's old emails, but when I looked it up online, I saw a photo of Amber's signature. I was sure of it, as I'd seen it multiple times over the past few weeks. But if she signed for them, why didn't she say anything? Knowing how reactive Samantha could be, I walked to the guest house to ask Amber myself.

"I found the tracking in Sarah's email, but it's showing that you signed for them?" I turned my new MacBook screen to show her.

"That's so weird, babe. I did *not* sign for those! It must have been Sarah. *Stupid bitch*," she said. "I'll call myself and take care of it. Don't worry."

Don't worry? I glanced up from my screen to see the racks and racks of designer clothing in her room and wondered if she was lying.

"Alright, *babe*," I said. "Sounds good."-

The gate phone started ringing. It was the glam squad. I buzzed them in, but then it immediately rang again.

"Boysssss!" I answered flamboyantly, "I already said you can come in!"

But before I held down the number permitting access, a deep-voiced man on the other end laughed. "It's Rich Revolver."

My stomach dropped, humiliated that I had just addressed Rich Revolver thus. I buzzed him in quickly without apologizing, too embarrassed to hope for redemption. Maybe he was a bigger fan of the beguiling gay act than Alexis—I prayed he was, anyway.

I opened the front door to greet him, but he instead waved me over to his matte black Range Rover, which had his initials "RR" emblazoned all over in a pattern resembling the signature Gucci print. Slightly out of breath, I forced a smile to cover my embarrassment and introduced myself.

"I'm Hayden," I said. "Alexis's new assistant."

Rich was more famous for his comedy chops than his good looks, but in person he was jaw-droppingly handsome and extremely fit. His shoulders were broad, and he wore a white tank top exposing his large, defined biceps. His skin was a rich chocolate brown that showed no sign of imperfection, and accentuated his Crest commercial smile. He was charming before even speaking a word.

"Good luck, buddy," he joked. "This is Rhythm's outfit for tonight." He handed me a red Gucci tracksuit in a clear dry-cleaning bag, as well as a Neiman Marcus shopping bag full of hat and shoe options. "Let the queen know I said hello, and tell her I'll be back in time for the cars to take us. I'm gonna head home and get ready. Nice to meet you, man."

I turned around, star-struck, failing to remember that Dylan and the hairstylist, Lion, were right behind me, patiently waiting for direction. Flustered, I led them to the private entrance for the glam room, then texted Alexis to let her know they were here.

Back in the kitchen, the twins were still in their pajamas eating lunch with Porsha. I handed her Rhythm's outfit, which did not escape his line of vision.

"*Let me see!*" he said.

"Where's mine?" Blue pouted.

"Mommy already has yours upstairs," I said. "Rhythm is matching your dad, and you're matching your mom."

Porsha peeled the dry-cleaning bag away from the tracksuit and then pulled the hat options from the shopping bag. There was a red baseball cap, a red beanie, and a red turban. While not attached to a specific religion, Rich was very public about his spiritual journey and had been wearing different spiritual garb, to the confusion of many. Alexis was not shy about criticizing him for it. Regardless, for Rhythm there was no choice—he wanted to look like Daddy, immediately putting the turban on his head.

"I'm gonna show Mommy!" he said.

Rhythm stood up on the bench, grabbed me by the hand, and began leading me upstairs. As he made his way toward the glam room, I begrudgingly pulled his hand from mine, staying a safe distance away.

"Mommy! I look just like Daddy!"

Porsha hesitantly approached, knowing the importance of avoiding the glam room, but also not wanting Alexis to think he'd been left unattended. I held back as I saw half of Alexis's face appear through the doorway, jaw clenched and eyes glaring. Suddenly Samantha's voice saved me, echoing through the house. Pulse racing, I hurried back downstairs to the office and sat at my desk. I sat silently as she wrapped up her call—but as soon as she hung up, it began to ring again. Her ringtone was Alexis's new song from the music video shoot where my interview had taken place. Samantha answered on speakerphone.

"Hi my beautiful girl!" she said. "I just got here, I'm in the office."

"Get rid of her, Samantha. Get rid of her *now*," Alexis hissed.

"Get rid of *who*?"

"THE NANNY!" Alexis shouted. "Whatever her name is! Rich dropped off outfit options for Rhythm, and she didn't deem it necessary to show them to me first? She just lets Rhythm put on whatever he wants? Rich gave him a fucking *turban* to wear, Samantha. Rich can wear turbans all he wants, but he's not going to push them onto our children!"

While I personally would have tried to defuse the situation, Samantha's response showed me that wasn't how things worked in Alexis's world. Was this my fault?

"I'll take care of it," Samantha said, before hanging up the phone to tell me, "Get Porsha."

As I made my way to the kitchen, I felt as if I were going to throw up.

"Porsha, Samantha needs you," I mumbled, before walking side by side with her down the long hallway, as if I were walking an inmate to the electric chair.

I felt nauseous sensing what was coming.

"*Hi*, Porsha. Sit down. I've been meaning to talk to you."

I started to exit the room, but Samantha shook her finger at me indicating not to leave. She wanted me to watch.

"As you know, the tour was postponed. So, for right now, we're a little overstaffed. But once it gets busier, I'll give you a call, okay?"

Porsha's jaw dropped and I watched her eyes fill with tears. Why couldn't they just have a conversation with her? Security appeared at the office door. Porsha didn't say a word as Samantha continued, "Don't say anything to the twins. Just go ahead and gather your things. Security will walk you out."

Samantha's reasoning had *nothing* to do with why Porsha was being asked to leave. I could only assume it was an attempt to squash a potential lawsuit or splashy headline on *TMZ* that would read, ALEXIS SHANE FIRES NANNY OVER TURBAN. I watched security escort Porsha out the front gate from the office window, covering my mouth in disbelief.

I'm not going to make it.

I heard Alexis's heels descend the grand staircase, followed closely by the glam gays. Before she was even in eyesight, Samantha shouted across the office, "Alexis, you look *stunning*!"

Alexis's chocolate brown hair appeared before she did, and her face wasn't visible from behind her large sunglasses. She wore a black Valentino mini dress with long sleeves, the front altered to expose a significant amount of cleavage.

"Thank you, Miss Samantha," she said in her smoky voice. She turned for the kitchen, informing everyone, "I need a *drop* before we go."

This was Alexis's preferred euphemism for an alcoholic beverage, which of course was necessary before a children's awards show. When Alexis returned to the foyer, *drop* in hand, she sat on a leather bench as Amber and Dylan attempted to change the shoes on her feet.

"It would have been nice if someone actually found the shoes I wanted to wear," she said. "You know, Michelle Obama told me never to let anyone think I can't put on my own shoes." She laughed. "But some shoes really are too abusive to put on yourself."

I stood there uncomfortably, as Alexis had yet to acknowledge my presence. But I then reminded myself, *Just be yourself.*

"Alexis, you look *so cute!*" I said.

"*Cute?*" she responded without eye contact. "Thanks—if that was a compliment."

I felt the heads turn from Samantha, Amber, and the glam gays, as if I'd just committed the most humiliating faux pas in recorded history. Today was *not* my day. It's much easier to feel like a total idiot when you're surrounded by highly important people. But luckily the gate phone rang, providing me with an exit. I opened the front door and watched as Rich's Range Rover and two black Escalades pulled into the driveway. Alexis, Samantha, Rich, and R&B climbed into one, while Amber, the glam squad, security, and I climbed into the other.

"Are you crazy?" Amber nudged me. "Don't ever call her *cute.* Sexy, beautiful, gorgeous, stunning, amazing... yes. But never *cute.*"

The glam squad laughed behind us. We hadn't even pulled out of the driveway and Samantha was calling me.

"Hello?" I answered, to no response. It was a pocket dial.

I listened as Samantha explained how she'd gotten rid of Porsha. But Alexis had another target.

"What about that boy? Why would he give the bag to the nanny instead of me?"

It felt like a punch in the stomach as I listened to her complain about me for the first time. I was damned if I did and damned if I didn't. How would I ever figure out when I could and could not approach her? How would I figure out what words were and were not acceptable? Luckily, Samantha had taken a liking to me.

"He's great. I swear, Alexis. Just give him a chance."

The fantasies in my head of being Alexis's new best friend quickly dissipated. Her non-diva side rarely came out around me. She was still the idol beyond my reach. I guess my collection of her albums on vinyl wasn't going to automatically make her like me the way I hoped it would.

We pulled up to the red carpet and the famous family stepped out. Rich still treated his ex-wife like they were married, standing in front of her to guard from any unflattering photographs. While the glam squad primped Alexis, she handed me her iPhone and black leather Chanel boy bag. Security flanked the family as they made their way down the carpet, fans and paparazzi screaming, *"Alexis! Alexis! Rich! Alexis! R&B! Alexis! Alexis…"*

I was at once overwhelmed and invigorated by the electricity around me. Ecstasy rippled through the faces and reaching hands of the surrounding fans as they clamored and cried. As frustrated as I was at myself for not winning her over automatically, looking around at the adoration of thousands reminded me of the magnitude of my position. Though it was hard for me to imagine, some people were even *bigger* superfans than me—a truth made undeniable with one cursory glance at any screaming face. Suddenly Alexis's phone began buzzing incessantly in my hand. I looked down to see they were all texts from Brody, the most recent saying, *"You need to come home NOW. This is so disrespectful to me and our relationship."* I locked the screen and followed in the footsteps of Samantha and Amber behind the photographers in the press line.

I thought I would be excited attending my first awards show, but by the end I felt depleted. For my entire life, I'd wanted to feel like I was a part of this world. Now here I was, finally on the inside, in a position that would be considered enviable by anyone's standards, yet still somehow peripheral. Sure, I was now an official part of Alexis' entourage, but what did that really mean? To her, I was just another replaceable stranger.

CHAPTER FOUR

A nother month went by, and it was still normal for me to spend entire days at Alexis's mansion without her ever leaving her bedroom. I was always on my way home by six p.m., sometimes a few minutes earlier, since I knew no one would say anything. But today as I climbed into my car, Samantha called.

"I need you to come by my house," she said. "We have to plan St. Patrick's Day for Alexis."

Plan St. Patrick's Day? I'd been at Alexis's since ten that morning, and the last thing I wanted to do was drive to Calabasas. Without traffic it took an hour, and during rush hour it would be closer to two. Samantha's home was in the same gated community that Alexis had just moved out of.

I pulled up to see one of Alexis's black Escalades parked out front, meaning Amber had to be here. Not only did Amber live with Alexis, but she also drove her cars. No rent and no car payments made it a little easier for me to understand how she was able to afford her designer duds.

I heard Samantha, Amber, and Blair shouting from outside, so after knocking and knocking to no response, I let myself in. I was overwhelmed to find an obscene number of moving boxes.

"How the hell are you living like this?" I looked around, mouth agape.

"We just moved in!" Samantha was sitting at the bottom of her white marble staircase. She always looked so polished when with Alexis, so it was surprising to find her in sweats. "Alexis hasn't let me leave her side for almost three years now—well, until this boyfriend came along. She's wanted me there for everything! Why do you think my kid is homeschooled? Why do you think I was living in her house? I've had no time to take care of my own life!"

The doorbell interrupted Samantha's speech. I turned to open it.

"Hi, sir. I'm here from Diamond Auto. We're here to deliver a car to Samantha Fox."

I peeked my head out the door to find my dream car—the brand-new 2025 Mercedes G-Wagon. Matte silver exterior, black leather interior, and oversized black rims.

Before Samantha could even stand up, Amber charged for the door, grabbed the keys from the delivery man's hand, and hopped into the driver's seat. As she turned on the car, the engine revved, and my mouth began salivating. Amber ignored Samantha's attempts to stop her and backed the new car out of the driveway. She sped away, circled the quiet Calabasas gated community twice, and returned to tell us, "I think I'm gonna get one too."

I'd been hired at $60,000 a year, so the fact that buying a $250,000 car was even an option for someone on an assistant's salary boggled my mind. Did the Fox family come from money? But if they did, why would Amber want to spend her time kissing Alexis Shane's ass?

Samantha aggressively pulled Amber from the driver's seat.

"Let me drive my car, *you bitch*!" she said. "Alexis just texted me anyway, asking where the hell you were. She keeps saying you're never there. I know you're obsessed with me, but you really need to remember who your *actual* boss is!"

The two bickered over the validity of Alexis's statement before Amber left in a huff, climbing behind the wheel of another car that wasn't hers.

Samantha signed for her new car and led me back inside, then pointed to her office and instructed me to sit down.

"You've got some work to do," she said.

I stared at her, bewildered.

"The holidays are very important to Alexis. *All* holidays. We always need to go above and beyond to make them special for her. Here, write this down," she said. She handed me a notepad and pen. "First things first, the house must be over the top. You'll need to find a party store, or maybe a company to come decorate. Get one of those large rainbow balloon arches made to flank the driveway and place a pot of gold at each end. Coordinate with Noah to make some festive St. Patrick's Day-themed foods for dinner. We're also going to need to rent out an Irish pub, and she wants to show up there in a glittery green Ferrari. Oh—and four leprechauns."

I finished writing and looked up at her, thinking I'd misheard.

"St. Patrick's Day is *tomorrow*, Samantha—and what do you mean, *four leprechauns?*"

"You know," she shrugged, "four little people. But dressed as leprechauns. Is that the politically correct way to say it these days?" She laughed.

I looked over her shoulder through the office's double doors, which overlooked the hills of Calabasas. I felt anxious as I watched the sun begin to set. I thought I might burst into tears as she left me to my own devices, unsure where to start. Well, the rainbow couldn't be that hard, so I called a local decorating company to explain what I needed.

"*Two thousand dollars?*" I yelped, placing them on hold to find Samantha.

When I found her in the kitchen, she looked at me as if I were a moron.

"Okay, *so?* Just pay for it."

I placed the order for the balloon arch, justifying it by knowing I could never make it myself. I'd save money in other ways, I thought, like decorating the rest of the house with things I could find from *Party City*. Hopefully Amber would help, too. I looked down at the next item on my list, the Irish pub—and remembered last year, when Grayson and I had gone with our friends to one named Jameson's on Hollywood Boulevard.

I called and immediately asked for the manager to avoid having to make this odd request more than once.

"I'm sorry, sir," she said, "but St. Patrick's Day is our busiest night of the year. Renting out the pub just won't be possible."

I wasn't sure if I was supposed to be name-dropping, but I didn't see any other way. Immediately her tone changed.

"*Alexis Shane?* Well, I'm sure we could manage to rope off a section for her. But I have to ask—is it true?"

"Is what true?"

"That she only eats the brown M&Ms, and makes her assistants separate them for her?"

I was getting somewhere. But how would I ever manage to find four little people, and how could I ask them to dress up as leprechauns without offending them? But then again, I suppose this *was* Los Angeles, so maybe there was a casting company I could hire them from. I spent hours googling and making calls, but had reached a dead end. I started feeling anxious again at the now pitch-black darkness outside, when Grayson texted me.

"You're working late today! I miss you. Circus tonight with the boys when you're off?"

CIRCUS! That was it! Circus was the club in West Hollywood that was famous for, well, *little people.* Little people were the servers, the bartenders, the go-go dancers, and they even did performances as little versions of Britney Spears, Beyoncé, and, of course, Alexis Shane. Not to mention, I knew the owner was also Samantha's friend.

I heard Samantha upstairs in her bedroom and ran up to ask for his contact info. It was much more comfortable working from Samantha's home. I didn't feel like I had to walk on eggshells.

She interrupted me before I could finish my sentence, "You're a fucking *genius*," she said, dialing him. It wasn't rocket science, but I did appreciate her telling me I was doing a good job—and the owner was more than willing to provide us with four leprechauns, and for free, under one condition—"I'm coming with!"

"Okay, so we've got the rainbow arch, the Irish pub, and the leprechauns," I said. "I'm gonna go pick up the pots of gold and decorations from *Party City*, and then I'll have to wake up early to figure out the car. I mean, this is *LA*, so somewhere will have one."

"You know what," Samantha said, "when I was driving home, I noticed a house just a couple blocks over that's decorated completely over the top for St. Patrick's Day."

I looked at her, waiting for the next instruction, but there was none.

"So, you want me to go over and ask where they bought their decorations?"

"We don't have time for that," she said. "They have these giant pots of gold outside that would be *perfect* for each end of the rainbow."

Fishing through her bag, Samantha pulled out a large wad of hundred-dollar bills. "Take this and go buy their pots of gold. Actually, why don't you just ask if you can buy *all* of their decorations?"

I took the cash and counted out three thousand. I stood speechless for a second.

"You can't be serious," I finally said.

"As a heart attack."

"You want me to walk over to a stranger's house, and ask to buy decorations off their lawn?"

"No, *silly*. I don't want you to walk. Drive my car," she said, throwing me the keys to her brand-new G-Wagon.

Blair appeared in the master bedroom's entry.

"Relax, gay boy. I'll go with you," she said, before tossing a Louis Vuitton miniature backpack over one shoulder.

"This isn't normal," I said to Blair as we pulled up to the house, before remembering she hadn't lived a normal life, maybe *ever*.

"Go get 'em, tiger!" she laughed.

"*What?*" I asked. "You're not coming with me?"

Blair laughed maniacally now.

"Yeah, right! I just came to watch this train wreck!"

It was too bad I couldn't call a twelve-year-old a "bitch." But Samantha was right. The home was decorated incredibly. If this was what she wanted, *Party City* was not going to suffice. Most people didn't do this much for Christmas, let alone St. Patrick's Day. But then again, this was Calabasas. The lawn wasn't visible to the eye, and had instead been replaced by a field of four-leaf clovers. The front porch had giant pots of gold, filled with candy for the neighborhood children as if it were Halloween. There was also the same rainbow balloon arch I'd just ordered, and inflatable leprechauns in the yard, on the roof, and peeking over the hedges.

I climbed out of the driver's seat and tiptoed toward the front door. Hesitantly, I pressed the doorbell, and a security camera turned toward me. All of the lights in the home were on, but there was no answer.

"They aren't answering!" I whisper-shouted to Blair.

"Try again!" she said, twirling her long red ponytail between her fingers and rolling her eyes.

Why was I letting this little girl bully me? I pressed the doorbell a second time, but there was still no answer.

"Okay, *we're leaving*!" I shouted again, before hurrying back to the car and climbing into the driver's seat.

Suddenly, a white Mercedes pulled into the driveway. With a flushed face and heightened heart rate, I meekly walked over, trying not to startle the older couple as they opened their car doors, though there was no way to shake the feeling that whatever the hell I was trying to do was, at the very least, creepy.

"Hi!" I said. "I have a strange request for you guys." They looked at one another, bewildered. "You see, I work for Alexis Shane..."

"*Okay...*" I could sense the older woman was wondering where I was going with this.

"I have to decorate her home for St. Patrick's Day like, *tonight*. Her manager lives just around the corner and loves what you've done to your home. I have three thousand dollars in cash, and I wanted to see if there was any way I could buy your decorations off you?"

The couple laughed at me.

"I'm sorry, young man. But we do this for every holiday, and everyone in the neighborhood really enjoys it. They aren't for sale."

I guess not everyone was impressed by name-dropping. Besides, I was only important by proxy of Alexis, a humble position in comparison to whatever seat these hotshots approaching seventy were sitting in. If they didn't find me worthy in connection to a superstar, I definitely had no other angle to take. I sighed.

"I understand. Thanks anyway," I pouted, walking back to the car.

But, given that she was Samantha's daughter, Blair thought I was letting them off too easily. She hopped out and tried to convince them herself. Her persistence toward the couple made me uncomfortable, and the end result was the same.

Back at the house, I explained to Samantha I was getting nervous about finding the car *tonight*. It was nearing ten p.m., and nowhere was open.

"Can I just find it in the morning?" I begged.

"No, Hayden. First, call the decorations company you used for the balloons. See if they can add on what you saw at the neighbor's house, and then I'll help you with the car."

I called them back, and again my mouth dropped at the prices.

"The cost doesn't matter!" Samantha snapped before I could even ask for confirmation.

I completed the order just as her email notification went off. Her eyes widened and she let out a loud, dramatic gasp.

"What is this?" she said before reading aloud, "*Happy to see that*

Brody didn't give up clout-chasing after being fired by both Rihanna and Beyoncé. Looks like he finally found a pop star desperate enough to take him in. Good luck with him."

Samantha flashed me the email, and then went into panic mode. Who would send this? When I googled the email address, it came up with a website where people could send emails anonymously. She spent the next hour gossiping about it on the phone with Alexis's publicist, Kelly, as I continued trying to track down the Ferrari.

"Samantha, *please*. I need your help with the car," I said.

"Ugh, I'll call you back," Samantha said, before finally hanging up on Kelly. "Did you ask Amber yet?"

"I talked to her, but all she said was Alexis had seen it in the window of a dealership for exotic cars on Sunset. I know exactly which one she's talking about, because I pass it on my way to her house every day. But it's almost midnight and they aren't open—and everywhere that *is* open just laughs at me."

Samantha picked up her phone and dialed her friend, the owner of the company who had just delivered her G-Wagon.

Luckily, he knew what we were talking about, as the glittery-green Ferrari was rarer than I expected—even in Los Angeles. The guys in the exotic car industry were well-connected and he was able to get the dealership's owner on the phone.

"This could have been helpful hours ago," I said.

But there was one problem—a billionaire visiting from Singapore had rented the car and driven it to San Diego. I listened to Samantha play phone tag, until the billionaire finally agreed to let Alexis have the car for the day, *if* she would foot his bill for the week—$35,000. Samantha agreed effortlessly in a way that sounded as if he'd asked if she was okay with paying extra for guacamole.

"Thank God we've gotten that squared away," she said to me. "Now, are you going to need coffee?"

"*Coffee?* No way. I won't be able to sleep."

"That's the point," she said. "You're going to San Diego."

"*What?*" I asked.

"Well, someone needs to pick up the car!" she said, and then laughed. "You didn't think I was doing it, did you?"

"Samantha, I've been at Alexis's since ten this morning. It's past midnight and—"

"Did you forget already?" she interrupted. "I told you this was a twenty-four-hour-a-day job."

Fifteen minutes later, a black Escalade arrived at Samantha's home to take me to San Diego. As I walked out the front door, she shouted after me, "Get ready! Tomorrow is going to be a paparazzi *frenzy*!"

"I'M ON MY WAY HOME from Circus. Are you already in bed?" Grayson said. He answered on the first ring. It was so nice to hear his voice—gentle and deep, a welcome contrast to the constant squawking of the Jersey sisters. "I thought you were gonna meet us for a drink?"

"I wish," I said, rubbing my forehead. I knew he wouldn't like what I was about to say. "I'm actually on my way to San Diego."

"*What?* What do you mean?"

"Gray, I'm still working."

"You're *still* working? But it's after midnight."

I recounted the events from my day, careful not to say any names as my driver was listening. Grayson was laughing so hard I could hear him crying. Despite my exhaustion and irritation, I couldn't help but laugh too.

"If it weren't *you* telling me this, I wouldn't believe it," he said.

"I'm glad you find this amusing," I said. "I guess I've had it pretty easy up until now. I was kind of waiting for something like this to happen. I mean, they don't call her the biggest diva in the world for nothing."

"Jesus, so you won't be home 'til when, four a.m.?"

"I think I'm just gonna get a hotel room down there, if that's okay? I've been at work since ten."

"I get it," he said. "Just text me before you go to bed, so I know you made it safe. Okay? I love you."

"I love you, too," I said, frowning as I hung up. It felt strange not seeing Grayson every day anymore. He was always my source of solace in the tempest of the city, the one grounding force beyond all the plastic tits and bloated lips.

I told myself we'd have time soon to sit down and discuss what we wanted for our wedding. Just a few months ago, I had been all over

Pinterest for hours at a time, gathering ideas and looking up possible locations. It all felt so imminent, so exciting. But now it was a bit harder to imagine having enough free time to myself to even decide what flowers we wanted.

"Soon," I told myself, suddenly missing him terribly, and leaned my head against the window, resisting the urge to fall asleep.

After arriving in San Diego, I waited for almost an hour in the lobby of the Four Seasons for the billionaire's assistant to hand deliver me the glittery-green Ferrari. Like most people, he had been sleeping. I breathed a sigh of relief as I sped away, astounded at the miracle I just pulled off.

I kept my eyes peeled in search of a hotel I could afford, and then checked into the first motel I spotted. It felt bizarre walking up the steps to my $49 room while glancing down at the $200,000 Ferrari. I was halfway into a new world. Well, a *quarter* way into a new world. I just needed to quadruple my $60k salary, and then maybe Calabasas residents would be willing to sell me their blow-up leprechauns.

I JOLTED OUT OF BED in a panic. I was so exhausted last night, I'd completely forgotten to set my alarm. Reaching for my phone, I saw my fear was a reality. I had *twelve* missed calls from Samantha. I dialed her quickly, before gathering my thoughts.

"Where in the *hell* are you?" she said.

"I am *so* sorry," I said. "I was exhausted, and by the time I finally got the car, it was three a.m. I had to pull over at a motel to sleep for a few hours. But I'm on my way back right now."

The phone was silent.

"Let me get this straight. You go pick up a rare Ferrari, and you leave it parked all night outside of a *motel*? In the middle of *nowhere*?"

Another rush of anxiety came over my body and I ran for the door, swinging it open, only to quickly breathe a sigh of relief as I found the Ferrari shimmering back at me. A man at the corner of the parking lot smoked a cigarette and nodded his head toward it approvingly.

"Samantha, it's *fine*," I said, now catching my breath. "I'm in the car right now, and on my way back. I'll be at Alexis's as soon as I can."

A neighboring motel room catcalled me, reminding me that I was only in white Calvin Klein briefs. I hurried back inside.

"Just *hurry*," Samantha said. "All of the deliveries will be happening soon, and the last thing you want is for anyone to ring that gate while Alexis is still asleep. Call security and tell them to be on the lookout."

I quickly dressed in my clothes from the day before, ran down to the car, and came to an immediate halt as I realized I had no idea how to open the door. I fumbled with the keys until the door opened, then realized I had no clue how to start it. The billionaire's assistant had left it running as he handed it over to me. Thank God for YouTube.

I drove cautiously back to Beverly Hills, terrified of damaging the car, but also praying, *Please, don't let today be the day Alexis is up and looking for me. Please don't let me crash this car. Please, God, make sure there are enough little people to make this day festive enough for her.*

I was able to breathe a sigh of relief two hours later, once I finally pulled into the driveway.

Brody stood at the front door, doubtlessly attracted to the sound of a $200,000 engine pulling up. I started to park the car, and he ran down the steps of the mansion to greet me.

"I'm gonna take it for a spin," he said. He began patting the door, looking for a handle.

I started to panic. I didn't know what to do, especially after how Porsha had just been fired.

"Shouldn't Alexis see it first, though?" I said.

Amber appeared faintly over his shoulder, shaking her head 'no' aggressively.

"Don't worry, dude. I'm just gonna take it around the block," he said, wriggling his way into the driver's seat as soon as I stood up.

Just like me, he had no idea how to start the car, so I showed him with the begrudging willingness of a hostage. I bit my thumbnail as I watched the front gate close behind the Ferrari's taillights. Amber ran over and nudged me so hard that I almost fell over.

"What the *fuck* is wrong with you?" she said, her sloppy bun bristling around her skull like a shitty halo.

"What was I supposed to do, Amber?"

"You can't let him take the fucking car before Alexis even sees it!"

Amber dialed Samantha and recounted what had just happened, giving me no opportunity to respond. Samantha was so loud on the other end, I could hear her shouting from ten feet away, "Put him on!"

I placed the phone up to my ear and said nothing, wincing.

"What were you thinking?" she asked. "Have you lost your mind? Did you not just see what happened with Porsha? It was a liability having *you* drive that car up here, Hayden. Brody won't be insured to drive it for a few more hours, and he definitely isn't going to be as careful as you were."

"I'm sorry, I didn't realize," I said. "I just don't feel comfortable saying 'no' to him."

"Well, *get comfortable*. The only people you aren't allowed to say 'no' to are me and Alexis. You need to remember, *Alexis* is the star, not him. Always keep that in the back of your mind when making decisions. No one is to see or touch anything that is for her, until she sees or touches it herself. Do you understand? Text me as soon as he gets back so I know the car is safe."

Soon the decoration crew arrived. I watched as the team framed the driveway with a rainbow balloon arch the size of a goal on a football field. Pots of gold were placed at each end, so large that both R&B could be hidden inside of. I helped the crew unload large brown boxes filled to the brim with fake lawn made entirely of four-leafed clovers. A second team of men wrapped the driveway and the entrance stairs in metallic gold. Green spotlights framed the mansion, and finally two large bounce houses were unloaded—one shaped like a giant shamrock, and the other like a leprechaun's hat.

Just as security opened the gate to escort the decoration team out, Noah pulled in. Luckily for me, it wasn't his first holiday in Alexis's world, as I'd completely forgotten to ask him to prepare a festive dinner. He picked up Irish beer and was making corned beef and cabbage—my Oma's favorite. For dessert, there'd be a layered rainbow cake.

"Here, I thought this couldn't hurt either," he said, handing me grocery bags full of shamrock confetti, gold coins, and leprechaun hats.

"You're the *best*," I said, as he began to unpack the groceries in the kitchen.

I leaned across the island to scatter the confetti, when I felt small pinches from each side of my abdomen.

R&B had snuck up behind me in matching olive-green Balmain ensembles. They both giggled excitedly.

"You aren't wearing green!" Rhythm teased in his raspy voice. "And you know what happens when you don't wear green on St. Patrick's Day!" Blue said, continuing to pinch.

I'd forgotten I was still in my clothes from yesterday. Brody walked into the kitchen, dropping the Ferrari keys on the confetti-covered island, and immediately reached for one of the beers Noah had just dropped green food coloring into. I pulled out my phone to text Samantha that he was back, and she quickly responded, "*It needs to look brand new before Alexis sees it. Wash it.*"

Every time I thought the most difficult part of my day was over, I was wrong. Running through every possible expletive in my head, I gritted my teeth and looked for a bucket and sponge. Thirty minutes later, I returned inside, now sopping wet. I caught my disheveled reflection in the entryway mirror, then turned the corner to hide in the office, hoping they would leave for the pub before anyone saw me. I just wanted to go home, shower, and get a good "night's" sleep.

I sat down in the white snakeskin throne behind Samantha's desk when the gate phone rang.

"It's the leprechauns, reporting for duty!" a small voice said.

I buzzed them in.

Oh my fucking God. I couldn't help but laugh at how ridiculous this looked, watching four little people walking down the now gold driveway underneath the rainbow arch. I put on a big fake smile and escorted them to the kitchen, where Brody and the twins had started making shamrock cookies. Instead of looking at the leprechauns, their heads all turned toward me. I'd forgotten what I looked like after washing the car. Not skipping a beat, Alexis appeared from the hidden staircase dressed in a glittery jade, body-hugging Charbel Zoe dress to match the Ferrari. Amber trailed behind her with a shamrock-patterned t-shirt in hand. She walked over to Brody and insisted he put it on.

"Well it sure is festive in here, Hayden!" Alexis said. I couldn't tell if she was being sincere or sarcastic, until she turned to Amber and continued, "But remember *last year*? All of the furniture was removed from the house and replaced with green furniture for the day."

Amber snickered, taking pleasure from the implied criticism.

I thought of Samantha's comment about not trusting anyone. Maybe she was right. I had been working my ass off for the past twenty-four hours to make today come together, and what had Amber done?

"Just wait until you see outside!" I said.

Samantha and Blair announced their arrival as soon as they entered from across the mansion. "*Happy St. Patrick's Day!*"

"What are you still doing here?" Samantha scolded me as she reached the kitchen. "Shouldn't you be at Jameson's making sure everything is ready?"

I had no clue I was to go ahead of them. I had no clue I was going at all. Flustered and now more frustrated than ever, I turned to head for the door. "And Hayden," Samantha said, giving me a head-to-toe examination, "you may want to try and look a little more presentable at work."

I turned red. Samantha took pleasure in correcting me in front of Alexis. I knew it made her feel like a boss. I fumed silently as I shut the door behind me, wondering if she was trying to toy with me purposefully. She knew perfectly well I had barely slept, and it wasn't my fault that I'd showed up looking like shit.

"Trust no one," I whispered as I fell into my car, beaten and angry, but unwilling to quit.

Remembering tonight was due to be a *paparazzi frenzy*, as Samantha had described, I sped home quickly to shower and change. I had hoped to catch Grayson after not coming home the night before, but instead found a note.

"*Work dinner with potential client, won't be out too late. Love you.*"

I threw on an olive-green bomber jacket from Urban Outfitters and ordered an UberX which dropped me off right in front. The line of patrons waiting to get in was so long, I couldn't see where it ended from the entrance. I tried to explain to the bouncer checking IDs who I was, but he didn't care. I stepped aside to call the manager from my phone, who then proudly marched to the front of the pub, pushing aside security to escort me through the crowd of drunk early-twenty-somethings to our roped-off area.

"It's almost nine!" she yelled over the noisy bar. "She will be here *soon*, right?"

"They should be here any minute," I said, taking a seat in our booth behind the out-of-place velvet ropes.

"Well, you're already an hour late. I don't know if you've noticed, but there's a line down the block. That's money we could be making filling up this section of the bar. You need to tell her she has to hurry if she's coming."

The woman who was so friendly the night before at the mere mention of my boss's name was suddenly rude and pushy. Had she lost her mind? Did she really think I could call *Alexis Shane* and say, *Hi, sweetie! You really need to hurry it along or you'll lose your seat!*

So, instead I tried Samantha—but it went straight to voicemail.

The pub was getting more crowded as the hours passed, and everyone was now staring at me as I sat alone in the large roped-off booth adorned with "reserved" signs. I held my head down to ignore the drunk partygoers, scrolling on Instagram to find Alexis posting shots of herself sitting in the Ferrari surrounded by the leprechauns and the twins.

A middle-aged gentleman sat next to me and introduced himself. "I'm the owner," he said. He waved the bartender over to bring me a drink. I wasn't sure at first if I should have one. I mean, I was technically *working*. But at this point I had been waiting for close to two hours.

"I'll have a vodka, sugar-free Red Bull," I said. I told myself it was okay, because I was tired. Plus it was a bonafide get-shitfaced-drunk holiday, so a little tipsiness wouldn't hurt anyone.

He was a nice man, but like everyone else, he was wasted and wanted something.

"Do you think I could get a picture with her?" he asked.

I appeased him, telling him I'd ask when she arrived, and thanked him profusely for accommodating us on such short notice. The manager came to interrupt us, now not being so subtle about her impatience.

"She's not coming, is she?" She rolled her eyes. "Is this some sort of prank?"

Suddenly, through the large open windows at the front of the pub, bright lights flashed like fireworks. It was the paparazzi. I watched excitedly at the series of incessant camera flashes, listening to the people in line begin to scream Alexis's name. I ran for the door to greet her and was met by pandemonium.

"*Alexis!*"

"*I love you, Alexis!*"

"*You are so hot, Alexis!*"

I tried to make my way toward her, but she and the glittery-green

Ferrari were swarmed by dozens of paparazzi. Samantha was right. It was a frenzy seeing Alexis Shane pulling up in front of an Irish pub on Hollywood Boulevard on St. Patrick's Day—in a sparkly green Ferrari, in a green dress, flanked by leprechauns. Only she could do something this over the top and get away with it.

Brody opened the passenger door to let Alexis out, and the crowd went crazy, some fans breaking out into tears. The crowd screamed and laughed with excitement at the sight of Alexis exiting the Ferrari with four leprechauns trailing close behind.

I led Alexis, Brody, the leprechauns, Amber, Samantha, and Blair inside the pub to our roped-off area and became nervous. Not because we had a twelve-year-old with us in the bar, but because every single person in the place was looking in our direction. I wondered how it made her feel. Did she love it? But Alexis was unbothered, acting as if she didn't even notice. She sat down in the middle of our roped-off booth, but then quickly stood up.

"I don't like this one," she said, squinting. "I don't like the lighting." Alexis pointed at the largest table in the center of the bar, where she knew everyone would be able to see her. The manager suddenly reappeared and had adopted a completely different tone, eager to kiss Alexis's ass. She ran to the table in the middle of the pub and insisted they swap.

As Alexis and Brody took their seats, Samantha shook her head at the rest of us, and told us not to sit yet. I didn't understand. Samantha then instructed the leprechauns to sit at the table next to the one Alexis chose. Apparently, they were only acceptable for the entrance. The rest of us just stood around the table, unsure what to do in the crowded pub, waiting for further instruction from Samantha.

"What's going on?" I asked.

"If you want to sit, then *sit*," she blurted out, pointing to the table of leprechauns.

"Are you being serious?"

Samantha looked nervous, but I didn't understand why. She just stood there, observing Alexis for fifteen minutes who acted oblivious and giggled with Brody, before finally giving us permission to sit. I sat across from Alexis and Brody as they ordered drinks. This was my first time going out in public with her, and I wanted her to like me.

"I haven't been to an Irish pub in so long. Have you?" I asked, trying to make small talk.

"Of course I have, Hayden." She rolled her eyes. "My adoptive family is Irish."

Her sarcastic response pushed me back into my shell. The way she said it, it was like I was supposed to know her entire biography. I thought, with time, that Alexis would warm up to me, but even speaking to her made me feel like a nuisance.

Alexis's music began to blare through the pub speakers, and the owner who had introduced himself to me came back to introduce himself to Alexis. He'd started undoing the velvet rope, when one of our security guards grabbed him by the wrist.

"Excuse me," the bar owner said, "this is *my* bar."

I tried to interrupt and explain to our security, but the bar owner was wasted and began to push one of our six-foot-five, two-hundred-and-seventy-five-pound guards.

"I don't care who you are!" he yelled, physically picking up the owner, before removing him from his own place.

I was nervous about Alexis's response, but as I turned around, she was oblivious to anything but her boyfriend. An arm then rested on my shoulder, and I turned to see who it was. It was the evil manager, leaning across me to take photos of Alexis. I was taken aback by her audacity, and as she turned to walk away, Alexis reached across the table and violently grabbed me by the arm.

"*Hayden*," she spat, "if you ever see someone taking a photo of me, you better grab their phone out of their hand, *immediately*. That is, if you want to keep your job. I don't care if you have to fucking throw it."

I sat paralyzed, unsure how to respond. No one had ever spoken to me like that before, let alone my idol. I turned around to see hundreds of iPhones taking photos and videos. *Am I supposed to grab all their phones?*

"I'm sorry, I didn't know," I said.

Uninterested, she turned away. How could I know? Not only was the request impossible, but we came with three security guards. Wasn't that *their* job?

"Alright, this is bleak," Alexis announced to the table after finishing her martini. "Let's go to Catch."

Samantha handed me a credit card and I could barely pay the check before Alexis exited the booth. Leaving the pub was even more chaotic. The cameras, the shouting, hands reaching for her, her song blaring, our entourage trying to squeeze out the door with security and the leprechauns. Once we finally pushed through, I looked around at the chaos in disbelief, watching Alexis hop into the passenger side of the Ferrari, waving at fans as if this were completely normal.

"What is happening, Samantha?" I said, grabbing her elbow as she attempted to climb into the waiting black Escalade.

She wouldn't give me an answer, but the look on her face told me something was wrong.

"What is going on?" I asked again. "Something is *off*. Why were we all standing around and waiting to sit? And did you see how hard she grabbed me by the arm?"

Amber looked at me with compassion, like she knew what was going on, then she and Samantha looked at one other. Samantha hesitated before saying, "Amber did have you sign a non-disclosure, *didn't she?*"

"Of course I did!" Amber interjected, her eyes now glaring at me.

"*Hayden?*" Samantha pushed for confirmation.

"She did," I lied. "I signed one."

CHAPTER FIVE

"I don't think I can do this anymore," I said to Grayson as I closed our apartment door behind me.

"What do you mean?" he asked. "What happened?"

"She was such a fucking bitch, Gray. It's like I can't do anything right. I just spent the past twenty-four hours preparing for this ridiculously over-the-top St. Patrick's Day party for a forty-year-old woman who couldn't have been less grateful. I mean, I went to fucking San Diego at one a.m. for a sparkly-green Ferrari!"

"Babe, I definitely wouldn't do this job ever expecting a 'thank you' from *Alexis Shane*."

"She's not what everyone says she is. She's *worse*," I said, and then sighed. "What am I even doing? We haven't even had time to plan the wedding, and just a few months ago it's all we were talking about."

"Babe, calm down," he said, grabbing my face like he always did when I was upset. "What's there to worry about? A small ceremony in Palm Springs isn't hard to pull off. How much more planning do we *really* need to do?"

"We only have seven more months to figure it all out! It just feels like we haven't even had time to *think* about getting married. I feel like I'm getting married to Alexis Shane, and I can't believe I'm saying this, but I really don't want to."

Grayson laughed and wrapped his arms around me. "Whenever you want to divorce her and marry me, just let me know."

I slept soundly for the first time in weeks, happy to finally be in Grayson's arms again.

BACK AT WORK, I SAT at my desk anticipating the worst when Samantha texted me.

"*Great job yesterday. We're giving you a 15K raise. Xx.*"

What? I was blindsided and didn't know what to think. Despite Alexis's openly bitchy demeanor toward me, I guess they did see how hard I'd worked. I didn't know whether to smile or cry, as the anxiety still hadn't worn off yet. At least I had good news to bring home to Grayson. My shock was interrupted when the twins ran in.

"Are you two staying out of trouble?" I teased. The sight of them instantly changed my mood.

I stood up from my desk, and Rhythm ran to hug me. But Blue suddenly beat me as if I were a dummy from her karate class. Any time she did this, which was fairly often, Rhythm felt the need to protect me.

"No, Blue! No! Get off him!" he shouted.

"Hayden! Hayden!" Blue yelled over her brother, to grab my attention. "We're going to the Getty today!"

"You guys are going to have so much fun!" I said.

Rhythm scowled up at me.

"No, we're not. It's just some dumb garden," he said.

He was so honest, I couldn't help but laugh. Sometimes it seemed they were the only two I could count on for a straight answer. Their playfulness and childish honesty always provided a much-needed respite from the ambiguous intentions of my coworkers. I wondered who they would grow up to be in such an environment, and something in me soured at the thought—knowing that their playful ignorance would eventually be replaced with the hyper-awareness of their family's stardom.

The new nanny who followed them in first glared at my response and then laughed herself. "You shouldn't encourage him," she said. "I'm Teddi, by the way." She held out her hand to shake mine. Teddi was young with blonde hair, blue eyes, and already wore the signature nanny polo shirt.

The front office doorknob turned. I felt a pit in my stomach when I turned to see Alexis. She was *never* awake this early.

She approached me with a warm smile and a *hug*. I froze in fear and awe.

"Good morning, Hayden," she cooed, then directed her attention to the twins. "Are you two ready for school? Or are you just going to stay in here and give Hayden a hard time?"

"Mommy! Blue hit Hayden!" Rhythm said.

"I did *not*!" Blue shouted back.

Alexis rolled her eyes and smiled at me.

"I'm not sure why she does that to everyone. I actually did the same thing as a child, now that I think about it," she said, giggling.

The nanny led the twins back toward school, without her or Alexis acknowledging one another.

"*Haydennnnn*," Alexis whined, "I desperately need a massage. It was a late night."

I was taken aback by how warm she was being after how rude she'd been the night before. I'd prepared in my head over and over again what I was going to say. But how could I, now that she was being so nice, and had presumably approved my raise?

"I actually know the best masseuse from the salon," I said with a smile. "Her name is Mai Lee. She treated *all* of our celebrity clients."

Before Alexis could respond, I had Mai Lee on the line, eager again to demonstrate my worth. At the mention of Alexis's name, she was on her way.

"Wait, Hayden," Alexis interrupted me, but hesitated over her words. "What does she... *look like*?"

It had been widely reported in the press for the past two decades that Alexis did not like any women around who could be considered younger, thinner, or prettier than her. I'd forgotten what a sensitive matter this was, as to me, she was the most beautiful woman I had ever seen. It didn't even compute that she could be insecure.

"*What does she look like?*" I asked, and then laughed. "Her name is *Mai Lee*."

Shocked by how cavalier I'd been, I covered my mouth and blushed. But Alexis let out a kind laugh. Still, I backpedaled, trying to correct myself.

"I mean, she's short, thin, Asian."

Alexis continued laughing, now loudly.

"What's so funny?" Amber said as she marched into the office, interrupting our moment.

"Amber, there's a stack of scarves on the island in my closet that I need you to return to Hermès. They were a gift from Kauffman, and aren't exactly my style. Just have them put it under my name as store credit." Alexis exited the office doors, heading for the grand staircase. "Hayden, I'll be upstairs. You can just bring the masseuse up whenever she gets here."

Amber was red-faced at not being included in our banter. She sat down next to me with a stack of credit card statements and receipts.

"I'm going to need your help with this," she said. "I need you to look up every credit card transaction from Saks Fifth Avenue, Gucci, Versace, Louis Vuitton, Saint Laurent, and Hermès. Then match it with the receipt. If there isn't one, contact the store and request a receipt. Just make sure Alexis was not charged for anything she wasn't supposed to be."

"But how am I supposed to do that? I can get copies of the receipts, but I don't know what she's actually purchased and what she hasn't. This is from before I was here."

"Well if there's a *receipt*, obviously it's for her. All you need to worry about is having one on file, *okay*? If they don't have one, we shouldn't have been charged." She then waddled out of the office.

This made no sense. But still, being the new kid, Amber knew I wouldn't push back. I made sure to at least have a receipt for every charge, but there was no way for me to actually determine those charges were only made for items in Alexis's closet. Again, I wondered about the endless rolling racks in Amber's room.

GIVEN THAT I'D STAYED LATE to finish organizing all the credit card statements and receipts going back *six months*, I was startled to see Mai Lee leaving the mansion the same time as me. She had taken turns massaging Alexis and Brody over the course of six hours. As we said our goodbyes, Samantha called.

"I don't know if you're aware, but it's Alexis's birthday this weekend. Or as she likes to call it, her *holiday*." She laughed.

I had barely survived St. Patrick's Day, so the mention of this made me wonder if I could mentally handle another celebration. But then again, maybe last night was a fluke? Maybe she was just drunk? She had been so kind to me today.

"Birthdays are a sign of getting older, and holidays are simply a celebration of life," Samantha said. "Anyway, we're going to Puerto Vallarta. Well, *we are*. Not you."

Thank God.

"I WANT THE SALESPEOPLE ON Rodeo to be familiar with Hayden, too. Just in case I ever need him to run down for anything," Alexis said. "I don't want them to give him a hard time using my accounts."

She'd already asked Amber to return the scarves to Hermès three times that week. So, to make sure the job would actually get done, she now included me.

Amber crossed her arms, annoyed at the request, but forced a smile anyway.

"Just take a seat right there," Amber said as we walked into Hermès, pointing to two open chairs in the center of the store.

"Doesn't that defeat the purpose of having me come? Alexis said she wanted you to introduce—"

"Hayden, it'll only take a minute! Can you *relax*? I'll take you down to Gucci after this. That's where we shop most of the time anyway."

Reluctantly I took a seat as she scurried across the shop to greet an employee with a hug, making it clear the two were familiar. After this, we made our way to Gucci.

I met so many employees, it was impossible to remember all their names. However, Joshua made it clear he was a massive Alexis Shane fan, and insisted I always come to him if I needed anything.

Amber turned to me. "Do you want to pick up anything while we're here?"

"Oh, I'm fine," I stammered. "I've never actually bought anything from... here. I'm not sure I could afford—"

"*Come on*," Amber said, rolling her eyes. "Alexis gets a thirty-percent press discount, and we can use it."

"*Really?*" My eyes lit up. "Well, I'm not gonna lie, there's a pair of silver glittery sneakers in the window that caught my eye."

"I have those too!" She waved Joshua back over. "Can you bring out a pair of those sneakers for Hayden in a size..."

"Ten and a half," I said.

"Oh, sweetie," he laughed. "You're so cute. Gucci is in European sizing. You're a forty-three and a half."

When he returned with the shoes and placed them on my feet, I *had* to have them. I felt like Cinderella. But glancing at the box, I saw the price: $795. Amber and Joshua gossiped as I calculated the discount on my phone. They would now be $556. I justified the purchase, as they were $239 off. But the reality was, they were still more than double what I'd ever spent on a pair of shoes. Still, I talked myself into doing it. That is—until we reached the register.

"Oh, the discount can only be used on things for Alexis," Joshua said. "I'm sorry."

"Maybe another time then," I said. I was mildly disappointed, but also semi-relieved. I could justify the five hundred dollars, but not eight.

"Yeah, when using the press discount, we have to use the card on file."

"Don't even worry about it," I said.

Amber's face had gone white.

"Hayden, why don't you go take a seat over there?" she said again, just as she had in Hermès. "I'm gonna talk to Joshua."

I went and took a seat at the opposite side of the store and watched Amber intently. Was she trying to talk him into giving me the discount anyway? She too had picked some things out. Not only for Alexis, but for herself. Was she going to put them back?

She didn't. She completed the transaction, then waved me towards the door with one bag for herself, another for Alexis, and nothing for me.

I tried to hide my puzzlement as she blabbed on like there was no reason for me to be suspicious. She wouldn't use Alexis's account to buy her own things. *Would she?*

IT WAS A BALANCING ACT being the second assistant, constantly trying to figure out how to do my job without upsetting Amber or making her feel like I was stepping on her toes. Something important to her was that she dressed Alexis, so I made sure to never interfere with that, or ever give my opinion. Even if she was dressing her like a porn star. So, when I told her Samantha had instructed me to pack for that weekend's trip to Puerto Vallarta, she glared at me with such intensity, I could feel myself melting into the floor.

"I know you dress her, of course. So, if you want to pull the outfits for me, I'll just physically pack the bags," I clarified.

"Oh," she breathed a sigh of relief. "Okay, well, let me show you where the bags are."

Amber led me to the garage on the other side of the property. It was lined with industrial shelving, and the only thing they held were large black rolling bags so large I could comfortably fit inside of them.

"Alright, I'll pull clothes for Alexis and the twins for the five days we're in Mexico and put them on a spare rolling rack in Alexis's closet. Then what you'll need to do is pack them according to the numbers on the bag tags." She pointed to show me, "Each bag is numbered #1 for Alexis, #2 for Rhythm, and #3 for Blue. That's how the bellmen know which room they're to be delivered to when we travel."

"I figured she'd only use designer luggage," I said.

"That's what poor people do," she scoffed. "Packing in these makes it less likely for someone to riffle through them."

My phone vibrated in my pocket.

"Hey Samantha!" I answered over speakerphone. "I'm just starting to pack right now with Amber."

"I'm forwarding you the deal memo from Airbnb for Alexis's holiday this weekend. I need you to sign it immediately with a copy of Alexis's credit card and get it back to them. Tell her it's just for incidentals." Airbnb had become famous for gifting their luxury rentals to celebrities in exchange for a social media post. "Also, Blair is texting you a picture of a handbag. I don't know who makes it, but I need you to find it before we leave on the jet tonight. It's my holiday gift to Alexis. I'll text you my credit card info too. So, once you've got the bag, just bring it to my house in Calabasas."

"Okay. I will as soon as we're done pack—"

"Do it now!" Samantha yelled out of nowhere. "If Amber is insisting on pulling the clothes, then she can pack them herself!"

Amber's skin flushed and her jaw clenched.

Getting to leave the house during these long days was somewhat of a reward, and these tasks that were normally asked of Amber were now being delegated to me. Samantha had clearly taken a liking to me, making Amber resentful.

"Trust me, it's not like I want to go," I told her. "I would much rather stay here."

And it was the truth. I would much rather spend time trying to build a relationship with Alexis than running errands for Samantha. I didn't really even understand why, if I was on Alexis's payroll, I was being asked to do things for Samantha. But being that she *did* get me the job, I didn't want to push back.

Back in the office, I printed the deal memo and researched the house where they would be staying. It was a thirty-million-dollar estate which normally cost $30,000 a night, but for Alexis it was free. All for a simple post sent out to her fifty million Instagram followers about how much she enjoyed her time at *Casa Vallarta*. A fleet of black SUVs would scoop the team from the tarmac and drive them to the compound—the most private home at the top of the tallest hill overlooking all of Puerto Vallarta. A uniformed staff including a house manager, chef, butlers, and maids would be awaiting their arrival to festively welcome them to Mexico with shots of tequila and a tour of the fourteen bedrooms, ten bathrooms, movie theatre, and infinity pool.

It looked so amazing that, even after St. Patrick's Day, I wished I was being included. But I stopped drooling over the photos and the fact Chris Hemsworth had been there the week before to scour the internet, typing in any kind of description that might match the bag in the photo Blair had texted me. After a half hour of searching, I was able to find the designer, a rare French brand I hadn't heard of, and it was only carried in three locations in California—two in Beverly Hills, and one in Newport Beach. The only store with the bag was, of course, in Newport Beach—a two-hour drive in afternoon traffic.

Driving from Beverly Hills to Newport Beach to Calabasas to deliver a handbag took up almost five hours of my day, so I didn't arrive at Samantha's home until just shy of nine p.m. Walking in, I was again greeted by chaos as Samantha and Blair frantically packed their Louis Vuitton rolling bags in the primary suite. I handed Samantha the wrapped gift, which Blair snatched out of her hands and unwrapped as if it was for her. She examined the bag approvingly.

"Alright ladies," I announced, "have the best time in Mexico!"

"Wait, wait, wait. Not so fast," Samantha shouted after me. "I need you to call Noah and get a grocery list from him for the house manager in Puerto Vallarta. The kitchen needs to be stocked with all of Alexis's favorite things when we arrive. Also, don't think because we're not here that you have days off. You need to stay on top of the schedule and all of our travel. Departure time is midnight tonight, but you know Alexis. We probably won't take off until two a.m."

I called Noah on my drive home, expecting I'd be able to remember the list, but he insisted on emailing it to me. Probably because the grocery list I received reminded me of when my Oma had feared Y2K would be a reality and stacked her garage from floor to ceiling with bottles of water, canned food, and toilet paper. When I parked, I forwarded the email to the house manager and hurried inside, excited to have a few less demanding days to spend with Grayson.

"She's going to P.V. for five days? So, you're leaving?" Grayson said. "But I had something special planned for us this weekend."

"I'm sorry, babe." I enjoyed letting him ramble for a minute before confessing the truth.

"A few days ago, you were saying you couldn't handle it, and now you're flying to Mexico," he said. "Well, I guess this is just gonna be our new normal. Maybe we *won't* have enough time to plan the rest of the wedding."

"Grayson, come on. It can't be easy being that famous and trusting someone new. She was just having a bad night. Anyway—I'm not going."

He lit up. "You're *not* going?"

"No, I guess I'm not included on trips initially. I just have to be available by phone."

Grayson bearhugged me and started kissing my neck. He worked his way to my ear, and then my mouth. I was undoing the button on his pants when my phone rang.

"I'm sorry," I said, and then laughed. "But it's Samantha."

"*Seriously?*" He continued to take off his pants.

"Ugh, Hayden," Samantha groaned. "She hasn't even started glam yet, so there's no way she's going to make it by midnight. If we don't get to the jet by two a.m., the crew will go into rest time and we'll have to leave tomorrow."

"Rest time?"

"What are you, *new*? Have you never flown private before? Yes, *rest time*. Anyway, if we don't fly out tonight, you'll need to get to Alexis's in the morning and help them out the door."

I hung up.

"My weekend may have just gotten one day shorter," I said.

Grayson took my phone and tossed it onto the couch.

"Well, at least we have tonight."

FLIGHT CREWS GO INTO REST time for eight hours, which is why the next time the team could fly out would be ten a.m. However, Alexis doesn't wake up that early, and once she does wake up, she goes into glam for two hours—*no exceptions*. All she'd need to do was get to the jet before the next rest time at six p.m. This couldn't be too hard, I thought, but then remembered how many days I had finished my work day at six without having seen her once. I didn't understand how it didn't bother her to have all these people waiting, or worse, how much money she was blowing. But according to celebritynetworth.com, she was worth just shy of seven hundred million dollars, so I guess money wasn't really a concern.

I called Amber before heading to the house.

"Morning! I just wanted to see what time you guys were headed to the jet?"

"Why, babe?"

"Well, Samantha called last night and said you guys might not leave until the morning, and I should head over to help you guys get out the door."

"Oh, babe," she said, "we're totally fine. I've got it under control."

I hated how many times she used the word *babe* in a sentence. The insincerity of it made my skin crawl.

"Okay, *babe*," I said. "But, are you sure? I don't want Samantha to be upset if I don't come help."

"Yeah, we're totally good, babe. Security will load the luggage into the Sprinter. Glam is at three, we'll leave the house by five, and take off by six."

It was nice to spend my day doing almost nothing, before meeting Grayson that afternoon for happy-hour drinks at Cecconi's on Melrose. We hadn't ever spent this much time apart since we first started dating over four years ago, but I was too distracted by all the chaos for this estrangement to truly register. The sense of importance I derived from being near Alexis overshadowed any negative impacts it had on my personal life.

Plus, I assumed whatever sacrifices I'd have to make would be temporary.

As I waited on the patio for him to arrive, I scrolled through Instagram to find Samantha had just posted a photo with Blair, Vanessa, and her two best friends, whom I was acquainted with from the salon. Samantha's own entourage posed in the photo with their *designer luggage* outside of the jet as if it were their own. *Poor people*, I remembered Amber saying. I had noticed the glamorous photos and tag-a-long friends were a regular occurrence for Samantha since being employed by Alexis. Something about it felt icky to me.

"Hey handsome." Grayson kissed my cheek and took a seat across from me. "How was your day? Relaxing?"

"I can't lie, it was pretty nice to be left alone. How was yours?"

"I don't know," he said. "It was alright."

There were dark circles under his eyes, and his hair was disheveled.

"Alright?"

"An assistant from the literary department was promoted to an agent position today. He started a year after me. I just don't understand. I do everything right. I go above and beyond. I don't know how much longer I can wait."

Grayson was rarely ever down, so when he was, I worked extra hard to be the optimistic partner that he always was to me.

"I'm sorry, babe," I said. "But remember, he's in the *literary* department. You're in television. Your department is so much more competitive. You've said it to me hundreds of times. So, don't get too down. It'll happen soon. I just know—"

My words of encouragement were interrupted by a call.

"Sorry, it's Samantha," I said. "Hey, Samantha! What's going on?"

"*Wowwwww!* World's worst assistant!" Samantha said, to which I could hear the rest of the passengers on the jet laughing.

"What?"

"No, Hayden. Not you. We're still waiting for Alexis to get to the jet, but Amber just texted me that she left Alexis's Bible behind, and Alexis never flies without it."

I looked down at my phone: 5:58 p.m. She had to arrive within two minutes, or the flight would be canceled.

"Where are you anyway? I told you to help them get out of the house!

This would have never happened if you were there. Amber told me she never heard from you today."

What a fucking liar.

"No, I mean, of course, I was going to. But Amber told me—"

"Miss Fox?" the pilot interrupted. "I'm sorry, but it's not looking like it's going to happen today."

"No, no, no! Wait, wait! She's here!" Samantha shouted. I heard her nails tapping up against the window to show the pilot.

He, like everyone else always did, changed his tone as soon as Alexis Shane's six-inch Versace platforms hit the red carpet in front of the jet. I heard the private plane quickly fill with voices from Alexis's entourage. From the passenger list I provided to the jet carrier, I knew almost every seat on the plane was taken. It wasn't a public misconception—Alexis really did travel with a large entourage. But as I heard everyone's voices, it made me sad to realize her entire *holiday* celebration was only with people on her payroll. I wondered how she felt about that, or if she was even aware.

"Listen, I don't know she knows that Amber forgot it," Samantha whispered. "As long as we take off, you should be good. But I just want you to be prepared that you may have to get on a plane and bring the Bible to Puerto Vallarta. I'll talk to you later. Bye."

I sighed, setting down my phone.

"What happened?" Grayson asked.

"Oh, nothing. I just may need to fly a Bible to Mexico this weekend."

Grayson rolled his eyes.

These people are fucking nuts. For real, how are we supposed to plan a wedding if you can't even get through two days without having to fly to another country to deliver a *Bible*?"

I sighed, pulling my hands through my hair. "Well," I shrugged, "maybe we can delay the wedding by a few months? What if we had a bigger wedding?"

"But I thought you wanted something intimate. You always said you weren't into those big, flamboyant weddings."

"Yeah, but... it wouldn't hurt to make it a *little* more extravagant. I mean, we're only going to get married once, right?"

"Hopefully," he joked, though something in his smile seemed heavy.

SHOCKINGLY, I WAS LEFT ALONE for long enough to enjoy my surprise weekend staycation with Grayson in Malibu, and all I ever heard or saw from Alexis and the team was what I could see via social media. It did make me a little jealous when I saw a mariachi band appear, marching through the house with guitars and maracas, loudly singing and dancing, then leading the team outside where they presented Alexis with her own private fireworks show. This was the kind of thing that only existed in movies, and it made me smile to see the twins' excitement.

I was more excited to celebrate my recent raise by going with Grayson to the Mercedes-Benz dealership to pick out a new car. I chose a 2025 black A-Class sedan, which may sound basic, but looked sporty, and its sunroof, surround sound stereo, and backup cameras were a major upgrade. I told myself I deserved it now that I was making almost double what I had at the salon, even if it was going to take me six years to pay off. But it was also because I'd been embarrassed pulling my rusted Toyota Corolla through Alexis's gates. Everyone on staff, including the nannies, drove luxury cars.

On her actual *holiday*, Alexis didn't respond to my text message or phone call. *I'm sure she's busy*, I thought, remembering the homeowner had chartered a yacht for her for the day. What was odd though, was neither she nor Brody were seen in any of the social media posts on the boat. But everyone else from the entourage was posting photos and videos of themselves, snorkeling and swimming with the twins. I wondered if it made her feel taken advantage of.

Hours later, I checked Instagram again to see Brody had now been uploading stories of himself with Alexis. It looked like they'd opted out of the yacht day, and instead were in the hot tub taking tequila shots and smoking what looked like a blunt resting on a ledge in the background. Alexis was normally so poised and aware of the image she was portraying, not wanting to be seen from the wrong angle. But now she seemed carefree, so much so that her bikini top looked like it was about to come undone.

Seeing they had chosen to spend the day alone, I was beginning to understand the friction between Samantha and Brody. When Samantha and Alexis had met, it was two single mothers taking on the world. But now with Brody in the picture, Alexis was consumed with entertaining her boy toy's desire for luxury and partying—which of course didn't include her children.

Grayson peered over my shoulder as we laid in bed. "Bummed you didn't get to go?"

"Absolutely not. This is where I want to be." I set my phone on the hotel nightstand and cuddled up next to him under the crisp white sheets. Eventually, of course, Samantha called.

"Did you think I was gonna let you off the hook that easy?" she said. "Listen, I've been getting lots of emails and calls because everyone wants the address to the new house so they can send flowers. You need to swing by and bring them all inside."

"What kind of flowers are her favorite?" I asked. "I should probably get some for her, too."

"Stick with white roses."

I remembered Alexis had a song titled "Tulips", a dedication to her deceased birth mother. I knew mine would stand out, and hopefully she'd appreciate my familiarity with her catalog.

"Is Alexis not with you guys on the boat? I've tried calling and texting to wish her a happy holiday, but I've heard nothing."

"No, it's a long story. She's at the house with her *boyfriend*. Anyway, the handbag was great, thanks again for finding it. Alexis loves it. But Vanessa is here and has the best idea for something she wants to gift Alexis. You'll need to have it ready by the time we get back. Here she is."

Grayson looked at me confused, before reaching across to press mute on my phone.

"Who the hell is *Vanessa*, and why are you doing things for *her*?"

"As you know, the phoenix is Alexis's thing," Vanessa said. "Obviously, I'm aware it's a mythical creature, but there's an exotic pet store I was walking by in Beverly Hills, and they have the most beautiful birds in the most obscure shades of red, orange, and yellow. I want you to purchase half a dozen and install a large cage outside her home, you know, like at the Playboy Mansion. Rainforest-like, with lots of greenery and flowers. Make it festive. Gay men are great at that!"

Grayson rolled his eyes at the stereotype. And he was right—why was I setting up some crazy gift for some random woman from her management team? I was Alexis's assistant, not Samantha's, and *definitely* not Vanessa's.

I zoned out, agreeing with everything she said, until I heard Samantha scream in the background. No matter how she screamed, which was often, it always sounded the same. I never knew if what was going to follow was something exciting, or something terrifying. This time it was exciting, as Blue's first tooth had just fallen out—a big milestone for any mommy.

"Hold on, Hayden," she said, then frantically shouted for Amber to get Alexis on FaceTime.

"Try again! Try again!" Samantha said over and over.

There was no answer, so she tried Brody.

Samantha clearly sounded upset but was trying to keep calm in front of the twins. Instead, she instructed Amber to begin recording a video on her phone.

"Blue, tell Mommy what just happened!"

"My tooth fell out! I want to show Mommy," she said. "Why isn't she answering?"

Blue's words felt heavy in my gut as I wondered how many milestones Alexis would miss. It felt especially sad she missed this rite of passage, not because she was working or on tour, but because she was too busy getting high with her boyfriend.

The entourage of temporary people that surrounded them could not replace their mother.

CHAPTER SIX

I found the exotic pet store on the corner of Beverly Drive and Wilshire Boulevard. It was hard to miss from across the street as the fluorescent flurry of birds looked like a bag of Skittles had just exploded. I took two of the orange golden pheasants, two of the yellow canaries, and two of the red lorys. When the manager, Tyler, explained to me he'd been the one to set up the store's display cage—which appeared "rainforest-like" as Vanessa had described—I offered him a few hundred dollars to follow me back to the house and replicate it.

As I typed in the code, the gate opened to the mansion, and I saw Tyler's jaw drop. We searched for an opening in the staircase that led up to the front door. It was invisible due to the excessive amount of flower deliveries, almost all white roses as Samantha had predicted. But two arrangements stood out, both yellow tulips. What I thought would be a nice hundred-dollar tulip arrangement from myself paled in comparison to the other—a decadent display that stretched to my height, five-ten. Suddenly aware I'd just brought a stranger back to Alexis's abode, I asked Tyler to wait out front while I searched the office for an NDA. And given that Amber had forgotten to have *me* sign one, I contemplated signing one myself.

But as I approached the office door, I heard Brody's Rottweiler uncontrollably whining inside. Why was she here? Alexis had given Amber specific instructions to drop all the dogs off at a pet hotel. Slowly, I opened the office door, and Bella charged for me, making loud howls I'd never heard from a dog before. To my left were her bowls, bone dry and empty. The floor was covered in urine and feces. Amber had taken it upon herself to drop all of them off, except for Bella. How could she leave *any* dog locked up in the office when no one was home for five days? I spent a few minutes consoling Bella, before printing an NDA off of Samantha's computer.

Outside, Tyler had already unloaded his car, so I directed him to a shaded area on the right side of the house, which I felt was the most visually appealing spot for the cage. Unfortunately, it was also in earshot of Bella's deafening whines. I hurried Tyler to sign the NDA so I could get back inside.

"She's okay," I lied. "It's just because she knows a stranger's here."

But the noises were getting worse. I felt horrible leaving her there for even a second longer, but I couldn't let her out into the yard for Tyler to see, as she was covered in her own mess.

"I'm good with animals," Tyler said. "Can I see her?"

"No, no, no. She's really mean," I lied again. I was dripping sweat but couldn't tell if it was because of my nerves or the 100-degree weather. "Go ahead and just start putting this together. I'm gonna go keep her company for a few."

I was anxious at the thought of him finding her in the office covered in piss and shit and calling animal control. The *TMZ* headline would read, ALEXIS SHANE: ANIMAL ABUSER. Everything became precious around Alexis, which meant that ruin and disaster were just a bad photograph or Freudian slip away.

Inside, I filled Bella's water and food bowls, cleaned the filthy office, then led her to the kitchen, where I washed her in the oversized chef's sink. She had a sadness in her big brown eyes that told me not to leave her alone, so when I finished, I sat with her on the floor to pet her for a while. I didn't understand. Did Amber intentionally leave her behind? Would she really use an innocent animal to torment Brody?

Thirty minutes later, I reluctantly closed her back into the office to give myself time to carry what felt like a hundred flower arrangements inside. I tried spacing them out nicely throughout the first floor, but I wound up covering the entire kitchen island, kitchen table, fireplace mantle, and any other open surface. I saved the table in the entrance for mine, hoping they would catch Alexis's eye.

When I finally made my way back to Tyler, he'd finished assembling the cage and was filling water bottles with a hose.

"These hang on the inside of the cage," he said. "You should only have to fill them a couple times a week."

"Thank you so much. This looks amazing," I said, pulling two hundred-dollar bills from my wallet.

"Listen, the cage is in the shade now. But does it stay like that? Because if it doesn't, it really should be moved. It's too hot out here for them right now."

"I'll keep an eye out," I promised, before thanking him again.

After he left, I made a video of the birds flocking around the cage while playing Alexis's song "Phoenix" in the background. I proudly sent it to Samantha, along with a text that the job had been completed. The pool water glistened in the corner of my eye, catching my attention. Sweaty and inspired, I made my way over. Security was gone, and the team wouldn't be home for a few more days, so there was nothing wrong with putting my feet in. *Oh, what the hell.* I stripped down to my briefs, and dived in.

As I came up for air, the front gate began opening. *What the fuck.* I panicked, climbing out as fast as I could and hurrying for the guest house just behind me, where I knew a basket of fresh towels would be waiting. I threw on my clothes and picked up my phone, which had a text from Samantha.

"*OMG looks amazing! Had to leave Mexico early. On our way back to the house now. Leave before we get there, Alexis needs rest.*"

Two black Mercedes Sprinter vans were parked in the driveway. Samantha was the first to exit, scowling at the sight of me. "What are you still doing here?" she hissed. "I don't want her to see you. Get back there!" She pointed toward the guest house as I walked toward her.

"Why are you being so weird? I'll just say hello, ask how her trip was, and then leave. What's the big deal?"

"No!" she said, then waved Blair over who hurried toward us.

"Guard him!" Samantha said, as if Blair were my own security. "He can't see her!"

Blair stood in front of me, trying to force conversation while attempting to block my view as the entourage started unloading. Two security guards came out, each holding Alexis under her arms. I'd have assumed she was dead, if I didn't notice the tight grip she had on a very large glass of Pinot Grigio. Once off the van, she pulled away from them. It looked like she didn't have time to change before catching the flight, as she was still in a bathing suit.

"Hello Hayden!" she shouted enthusiastically. She hobbled up the cobblestone steps toward the home's entrance. "I love your *ensemmmmmble*, sweetie."

"Thank you!" I shouted back.

Unfortunately for Samantha, she'd seen me. But what was there to hide? Alexis seemed happy. Even if she *was* drunk, it couldn't be worse than St. Patrick's Day. Security escorted the glam boys out, and Alexis, Brody, Teddi, and the twins made their way inside. Thinking I could leave now as well, I attempted to walk around Blair, but she continued guarding me. We silently watched as security, Samantha, and Amber huddled. Unable to keep quiet for long, Samantha finally snapped.

"Listen, I've got to get out of here for a minute, okay? I need to clear my head! I've been dealing with this bullshit for three days. I'm exhausted, I'm fucking starving, and my kid is starving! We're gonna go get something to eat. Blair! Let's go!"

"But what am I supposed to do, Samantha?" Amber whined. "Don't leave me alone with her when she's like this!"

"You have security! And well—" Samantha looked to me. "*Fuck it.* Hayden, you're gonna need to stay with Amber for a bit," she said, climbing into her G-Wagon. "I'll be back in a few hours."

I stood in confusion, watching Samantha's taillights pull out of the driveway.

"Well, today is the day the curtain gets pulled back, Hayden," Amber said. She laughed as we headed for the front door. "You're about to see it *all*."

"I don't understand. What's going on? She's just drunk, *right*?"

But Amber didn't respond. I followed her to the kitchen, where Noah was preparing dinner.

"Will someone please tell me what's going on?" I said.

"I don't really know how to explain it, man," Noah said. He looked concerned. "You just kind of have to be around it to understand."

Suddenly, Alexis appeared in the entryway to the kitchen, now in a completely mismatched outfit. Her gold bathing suit and Versace caftan had been replaced by a cowboy hat, the sexy Santa costume from her Christmas show, and neon pink knee-high Balenciaga boots. She was not only dressed bizarrely, but her eyes were glossed over in a way that made her appear vacant, as if she were possessed, not in control of her own body.

"Hayden," she paused, "what's your favorite book of the Bible? It's Matthew, isn't it?"

Amber laughed. The question caught me off guard, and before I could respond, she had an unrelated follow-up.

"Did you vote for Donald Trump?"

"I didn't." I smiled uncomfortably. Whatever was happening was *not* because of alcohol.

"Everyone's talking about Caitlyn Jenner. Caitlyn, Caitlyn, Caitlyn," Alexis said. She stared at me blankly.

The more ridiculous Alexis's statements became, the more Amber laughed at her. I didn't understand what was happening, or how to converse with her. Yes, she was looking at me, and she was talking to me, but she spoke so rapidly that she didn't leave any pauses for me to respond.

Alexis walked toward me without breaking eye contact, and my palms began to sweat. She grabbed me aggressively by the wrist, and I gasped.

"I'm sorry!" I said. "You scared me."

But it didn't register to her. She pulled me toward the front of the house. Amber's cackling became louder.

"Have fun, you two!" she shouted after us.

Alexis led me to each room to admire all the flowers. She dragged me to the dining room, then to the formal sitting room, each time pulling the cards out, reading for a second, and then tossing them aside. She finally spotted the yellow tulip arrangement that was much larger than mine in the hallway. She pulled out the card.

"Who sent these tulips?" Alexis said to no one. She read it aloud, and then rolled her eyes. "Ugh, *Rich*."

She grabbed me by the inside of my elbow and led me to my much smaller tulip arrangement on the large mahogany entry table. She pulled out the card. After reading it, she scowled, picked the flowers up, and forced them into my arms.

"Did my mother make you do this?" Alexis growled. "Did she make you send these, Hayden?"

Goosebumps swept over my body and I froze, struggling to find the right words. Her mother had passed away years ago. But she didn't wait for a response, and led me back to the kitchen. I struggled, still carrying the flowers while trying to avoid spilling water. She reached the first kitchen cabinet and opened it, pulling out Blue's Barbie lunchbox. She pushed that into my arms as well.

"Come on, fabulous Hayden," she said. "Carry your purse. And I'll go change my ensemble!"

She walked away, as if the previous interaction hadn't happened. Amber was now laughing so hard she was crying. But I actually burst into tears.

"Amber, what is going on? I'm *scared*," I said, tears streaming down my face.

Before she could answer, Alexis appeared in the kitchen.

"You guys, I'm black!" she shouted. "And the KKK is after me! You all know they hate black people. So, why did you invite them here? Why do you think all of our security guards are white men with shaved heads? Because they're skinheads! You guys don't want to acknowledge I'm black, but I'm black! I'm black! I'm BLACK!"

I backed away from her in genuine fear. And again, the subject changed.

"Are you *Keeping Up with the Kardashians*? Those fucking whores."

She never left room for a response and bounced between the Bible, Donald Trump, Caitlyn Jenner, and the KKK. I searched her eyes for a glimmer of life, but she wasn't there. She just continued rambling, and eventually left the room again.

"What the *fuck* is going on?" I pleaded through tears with Amber and Noah. "Someone tell me! Is she fucking okay?"

Alexis whirled into the room. "Where's my phone?" she demanded. "Where's my phone?"

Alexis repeated herself at least a dozen times as Amber ignored her. Each time her voice got louder.

"It's getting fixed, kitten," Amber lied, finally caving after becoming annoyed. She often used 'kitten' as a term of endearment, although Alexis never seemed amused by it.

Alexis repeated herself incessantly, before growing bored and leaving the room. She reached the top of the grand staircase and let out a bone-chilling howl that echoed throughout the house.

"Where are the kids?" I asked. "They shouldn't be around this."

"Where's my phone, Hayden?" Alexis shouted. "*WHERE'S MY FUCKING PHONE?*"

Unfazed, Amber continued laughing. Noah just shook his head while continuing to prepare dinner.

"Why is she asking for her phone, Amber?"

"We have to take it from her when she's like this. She tries to call people she shouldn't."

I didn't trust her. Whatever was going on with Alexis, the way Amber was treating her felt inhumane.

Alexis reappeared.

"Where's my phone?" she hissed. "Someone give me a phone! Where's my phone?"

I watched as Noah subtly slid his phone from the marble island into the closest drawer. Amber continued to use hers in plain sight of Alexis, ignoring her pleas.

"Don't be fooled by the rocks she's got. She still blows a lotta cock," Alexis mumbled about one of her rivals, before she again walked away.

Amber pulled Alexis's phone from her own back pocket and typed in random passcodes to intentionally deactivate it. When Alexis reappeared again, Amber handed it over. Alexis was oblivious to the fact that it wasn't working and started shouting into it.

"Siri, call Drake! Call Drake, Siri."

My mouth dropped open in disbelief. Years earlier, Drake had publicly spilled the juicy details of their secret relationship, which she denied and then released a song about how he was a stalker. He retaliated by humiliating her, releasing her desperate voicemails in a song of his own. I now understood why her phone had been taken away. God forbid she actually reach him in this state of mind.

Feeling threatened after hearing Drake's name, Brody emerged from wherever he'd been hiding to check out the commotion.

"Alright, Alexis, it's time to get to bed," he said, guiding her toward the staircase.

"Show him! Show Hayden your vagina, Brody!" she spat. "Do you know how much bigger A-Rod's dick is than yours?" She had famously dated the baseball player in the early 2000s.

One of the cleaning ladies was now sweeping the foyer, unaware of what had been happening.

"Can I get you anything, Miss Alexis?" she interrupted in broken English, then smiled.

"Are you trying to sleep with my boyfriend?" Alexis shouted and charged for her. She high-kicked her to the ground, startling us all. The woman fell down with a thump, peering up at her in shock.

"Baby, stop!" Brody shouted.

Security ran in from the front door after hearing the shouting and pulled Alexis from the scene. He and Brody guided her upstairs.

"Are you okay?" I asked the petrified woman, helping her up. "Maybe you should just go home for the day."

Brody pulled a joint from his pocket as he descended the stairs, this time alone. He lit it as he made his way to the kitchen. I didn't understand what was happening, but she had to be on drugs. Brody returned from the kitchen, now passing me with a joint in one hand and a bottle of Patrón Silver in the other.

"Brody," I said, following him up the stairs, "I don't think she should drink anything. She's clearly not okay right now."

Brody opened the door to the primary suite, and Alexis had changed again—she was now wearing a baby pink see-through nightgown, multiple plastic grocery bags around each wrist, and one over her head styled to resemble a hat. It was like I was in *Grey Gardens*. Alexis began untying her nightgown, exposing her naked body, when I felt my phone vibrating in my pocket. It was Samantha.

I headed back downstairs to take the call in the restroom at the front of the house so Alexis couldn't hear me. When she figured out her phone wasn't working, I didn't want her to ask for mine. She was my boss, and I didn't feel comfortable telling her 'no'—but I also wanted to protect her.

"What's going on over there?" Samantha said over the bustle of a busy restaurant. "Amber isn't answering her phone."

"Samantha, why will no one tell me what's going on?"

"What do you mean? Does she not remember who you are?" Samantha had trepidation in her voice.

"What do you mean, *does she not remember who I am*? Of course she does. But she keeps changing into these really bizarre outfits, saying all these things that don't make sense. One second she's talking about the Bible, the next about Donald Trump, the next about Caitlyn Jenner. But it's not, like… conversational. She just keeps talking and talking and one statement rolls into something completely unrelated. It's like she's in a trance or possessed or something. Oh, and Amber just deactivated her phone because she was shouting at Siri to call Drake… and *then* she kicked the cleaning lady after accusing her of hitting on Brody. Did she take something in Mexico? Is that why you guys left early? I feel like we might need a doctor here or something."

"*Fuck!*" Samantha shouted, audibly silencing the patrons in the restaurant around her. "Okay, I'm coming back. Get Amber on the phone, *now*."

"Hold on, let me find her." I turned to open the door. I opened it slowly, peeking through the crack to make sure I was still in the clear. "*OH MY GOD!*" I yelped. Alexis was standing in the doorway, staring at me. "*ALEXIS!*" I said, my body trembling. "You scared me!"

Alexis didn't respond and instead mumbled to herself with clouded eyes, "She blows a lotta cock, and the KKK is after me. I'm telling you the truth."

It was chilling to watch a woman who millions idolized completely out of her mind like this. Never could I have imagined that this seemingly perfect icon had such a frightening side to her—much less that it apparently emerged regularly. I stood paralyzed, unsure how to respond or get around her, until Amber appeared again, laughing at the fact that I was now trapped.

"Hayden, you need to *relax*. Seriously, you can say whatever you want, do whatever you want. She doesn't remember *anything* when she's like this."

Amber approached Alexis and physically pushed her back by the shoulders and out of my way. It startled both Alexis and me. Amber looked her in the eye in an attempt to intimidate her.

"Fuck you, Alexis!" Amber said, then laughed mirthlessly. "See? She has no clue what's fucking going on."

Jarred by the interaction, I didn't respond. I simply handed her my phone, to which she walked away and began whispering to Samantha.

"Are you okay, Alexis?" I asked.

"Why didn't anyone pull me off stage at the Super Bowl?" she demanded. "Is my mother here? Where's my mother? Did the KKK get her? It's all the Donut Licker's fault. I know you voted for Donald Trump. Caitlyn Jenner did too."

Well, the second part was true.

Amber returned to pull me away. "Why do you keep trying to talk to her? She's not going to understand you. Look, Samantha is on her way back. She said we need to get rid of all the alcohol in the house because the doctor is on his way."

"So she's just *drunk*? That's not possible. It has to be drugs."

"Hayden, we don't have time for this right now! If you have questions, you need to ask Samantha. Now let's just load all the booze up into Noah's car before she starts looking for a *drop*."

I followed Amber and Noah around the house, looking for any trace of alcohol. There was a bar in the formal sitting room, another in the office, one in the movie theatre, and a cabinet full of liquor in the kitchen.

As we snuck the now boxed-up alcohol outside and into the trunk of Noah's car, Samantha pulled through the gate.

"Hayden!" Samantha shouted through her open window while parking. "Take Blair to the office. She needs to get started on her homework!"

AN HOUR LATER, I WAS with Blair in the office when I heard Samantha's high-heeled boots click around the home's entrance. She was with an unfamiliar voice, an older man with a thick New York accent. *It must be the doctor.* I stood by the door to eavesdrop.

"What happened this time?" he sighed. "It seems like these calls have been happening more frequently."

"Doctor, it's the exact same thing that happened in November and January," Samantha said. "When she's working, she's busy and vibrant and great! But with this boyfriend around, she doesn't want to leave bed. All *he* wants to do is drink and smoke weed, so that's what they do."

"You've got to be kidding me. Brody didn't take anything I said to him seriously? I mean, one time, okay. But three times? It's almost as if he's *trying* to kill her."

"Of course he doesn't take you seriously! He's a fucking kid! He doesn't care about anyone or anything but himself!"

"Alright, where's Amber? *AMBER!*" the doctor shouted, to which she came running in from the kitchen, nearly tripping over her Fenty slides. "Bring Brody to me, *now*," he said.

Amber ran up the steps of the grand staircase. Things had been so chaotic that I didn't even wonder where Brody had gone. The last I saw him, he had closed Alexis into her bedroom with a bottle of tequila. I stood by the office door, peeking through the crack to see Alexis descend the stairs first. She didn't acknowledge Samantha or the doctor, just looked at the ground and mumbled about the same topics as she had before. The doctor followed as she paced the foyer. He observed her every move and speech pattern.

"Yes, Samantha. She's manic. She's absolutely *manic*," he said. "This is the third time in six months. This is *not* good. We're in dangerous territory here."

Amber delivered Brody to the foyer and quickly caught a glimpse of me spying. She stepped away to join me. We watched as Samantha and the doctor stood across from Brody. The doctor shook his head and held his chin.

"Brody," the doctor said, as a parent would before scolding a child, "I told you when this happened in both November and January that someone with her condition can *not* under *any* circumstances handle hard liquor, and absolutely *no* marijuana. Her brain doesn't process substances the same way yours or mine does. Do you recall this?"

Brody stood quietly, looking down at the hardwood floor.

"Of course you do. But somehow, she's been drinking tequila for days, and you were stupid enough to post videos of the two of you smoking weed in Puerto Vallarta. What's it gonna take? Do I need to get the police involved? Do you understand when she goes into these manic episodes as she gets older, that some people just don't come out of them? She could be stuck like this *for the rest of her life*."

Brody still refused to make eye contact.

"*LOOK AT HER!*" the doctor shouted. He grabbed Brody's face to make him watch Alexis. "Do you want her children to see her like this? She can *die*, Brody. Mania leads to the inability to sleep for weeks on end, which leads to seizures. You just don't get it, do you?"

Brody was still quiet.

"I am telling you this for the *last time*, Mr. Smart. If something happens to her, if she tries to harm herself while in this state, or if—God forbid—she dies, I will personally hold you responsible. I will have her estate sue you for her death, and you will wake up one morning to every paper in the world reading, BRODY SMART TO BLAME FOR THE WRONGFUL DEATH OF ALEXIS SHANE."

"IT'LL JUST BE FOR TONIGHT," Samantha said, insisting I spend the night with Alexis. "She can't be alone right now, you know, in case of an emergency. But don't worry, security will be right outside."

"What about Brody? And the kids?"

"The twins are staying at my house tonight, and Brody left. He's gonna stay with some friends in San Francisco until she's better. I would have Amber stay, but she's been dealing with this for days on end in Mexico and really needs a night off. We'll have a nurse here tomorrow morning. The nurse who normally comes isn't available tonight, and for confidentiality reasons, I don't feel comfortable having just anyone come."

But she still wouldn't tell me what was going on. All I knew was what I overheard from the doctor and his consistent use of the word *manic*. I had heard a lot of people using the term on social media, but I fear they may have been misusing it.

Eager to help Alexis, I stayed. Especially after seeing how horribly Amber treated her, I felt like it was the best thing I could do. But I didn't realize what I was agreeing to. Alexis didn't sleep all night, nor did she attempt to—which meant I didn't sleep either. She had inexplainable energy with no end in sight. She now added other topics to her one-sided conversations, rambling about a female rapper she publicly feuded with, and another young artist the media was calling "the next Alexis." Communicating with her in this state of mind, I felt it was best for me to agree with whatever she was saying. But doing this for hours on end made me wonder if I was the one who was crazy.

I followed her all night through the mansion, up and down the stairs. Every hour or so she'd change into something new, but equally outrageous, and insisted I help. As the night went on, she became delusional, ignoring that I was gay, coming on to me, and moments later, attempting to jump off the second-story balcony, convinced she could fly.

"If R. Kelly can do it, so can I!" she shouted.

"No, I promise that you *can't*!" I cried, pulling her back into the house and attempting to distract her with the dress she wore to the 2010 Grammys, which luckily worked for a minute.

Grayson kept calling and texting, but there was no way for me to adequately explain what was going on. All I managed was to send one quick text saying I wouldn't be home tonight, and that I'd explain in the morning. Alexis required more vigilance than a newborn, and I wasn't willing to risk running to the bathroom for longer than a minute in case she decided to jump off the roof next. It was the most exhausting night of my life. But I could only assume not hers.

THE FOLLOWING AFTERNOON, SAMANTHA FINALLY returned with the doctor and nurse to find the two of us sitting in the formal sitting room. I'd been watching Alexis reapply the same shade of lipstick while staring into space for hours. I nearly cried at the sight of them. The nurse carried an IV stand inside, then led Alexis upstairs to her bedroom. Samantha and the doctor came over to console me—until we heard a scream.

"She's having a seizure!" the nurse cried out.

Samantha chased the doctor up the staircase. I sunk into the sofa and started sobbing uncontrollably. I was so exhausted myself, I felt I was experiencing some sort of dissociation. I listened in horror at all the commotion, more confused than I'd ever been. The glorious façade had melted away so quickly. All the accolades and magazine covers and worldwide tours precariously propped up the woman now shaking and seizing on the hallway floor, because the man who was supposed to love her was willing to destroy her to get what he wanted.

Twenty minutes later, Samantha returned.

"Samantha," I said, wiping tears from my eyes. "That was the scariest night of my life. Please tell me what's going on. I was *not* prepared for that. The doctor kept using the word *manic*, but what does that mean?"

"Hayden, she's going to be fine. She's just... I don't know. She's *eccentric*." She didn't seem convinced of her own words. "Don't worry!"

"She just had a fucking seizure! I know you want to protect her privacy, but you should at least tell *me*!"

"I've got it under control. Now go ahead and take a break. Go for a drive, grab yourself some food, take a nap, whatever you want. Oh, and here." She pulled a prescription from her pocket. "I need you to get this filled for her on your way back."

I hadn't eaten in almost twenty-four hours, but I wasn't hungry. After experiencing the severity of the situation, I also didn't want to leave Alexis knowing Amber was coming back soon. The way Amber had treated her, laughing in her face and antagonizing her while in this state, made me sick.

But I took the drive, only to pick up Alexis's prescription—and to call Grayson.

"What the fuck is going on? Do you know how worried I've been?" Grayson answered his cell at his desk—something he *never* did. "You were just supposed to run an errand and then come home."

I tried to respond, but I didn't even know where to start. Instead, I cried.

"Babe, are you okay? What happened?"

"No. I'm not fucking okay, Grayson. They came home early yesterday, just as I was about to leave."

"Well, I figured that much. So, what? Did she make you go out drinking with her? Did she grab you again?"

I recounted the events from the night prior, and when I finished, Grayson stayed silent.

"Gray?"

"We need to have a deeper conversation about this when you get home. I'm genuinely concerned about you working for her. Something is clearly wrong, and you aren't a professional when it comes to mental health or drug addiction. And I mean, Samantha won't tell you anything. Imagine if Alexis had—"

"Don't say her name out loud," I said. "You're at fucking work."

"Okay, I know. *I'm sorry.* But imagine had she really hurt herself last night, and you were the only person there. What do you think the headlines would read?"

"Don't even say that," I said. "Let's just talk about this later. I just wanted to tell you I was sorry I didn't come home and explain what happened. I've gotta run into Rite Aid, then back up to the house."

"Alright," Grayson sighed. "Just please be safe and try your best to keep me in the loop. I love you."

"I love you, too."

On the way back, I paused at the stop light, wondering what exactly it was that I had just picked up. I opened the bag, turning the orange translucent bottle around. It was Lithium, something I'd heard of but wasn't sure what it was for.

I googled and began to read. "*Lithium treats and prevents manic episodes of bipolar disorder.*" Bipolar disorder? I thought bipolar disorder meant one minute you were in a great mood, and the next you were sad, or angry. I continued reading. "*Bipolar disorder is also known as manic depression. When untreated, one goes through times of mania and times of depression.*"

Mania was certainly what I witnessed last night, and it could last for weeks at a time. Symptoms included restlessness, like her walking up and down the stairs obsessively and changing her outfits. Rapid speech, to the point of not allowing anyone to respond. Increased energy, demonstrated by her inability to sleep. Unusually high sex drive, proven by her coming on to me. And of course, drug and alcohol abuse. Depression would then follow the manic episode, because those who are bipolar live for the manic high. It makes them feel like they're invincible and can do anything. Depression would include sadness, lack of energy, and sleeping all day. *Everything finally makes sense*, I thought, remembering the days upon days when I started and she never left her bedroom.

Suddenly the infamous divahood of Alexis seemed only relative. I wondered how much of her initial guardedness was due to her star status and how much was due to self-protection, or even fear of being "found out." Surely maintaining a high-profile identity would be exhausting with such a volatile disorder. I thought of the spinning roster of assistants that came before me, and finally understood. It wasn't that Alexis was evil, or that she refused to look into the eyes of those she employed. She was *ill*. She couldn't control her behavior in these states. These episodes were more than just the rambling tantrums of a demanding woman—they were the manifestation of a broken person who had been manipulated and taken advantage of her entire life.

I thought of the doctor's voice, the desperation in his plea toward Brody. That she could *die* because of this seemed incomprehensible. I always imagined with Alexis's infamously extensive entourage that she had more than enough people looking after her best interests. But now, considering Brody's behavior and Amber's malicious amusement, it was apparent she was basically fending for herself. I wondered what Rich Revolver thought, leaving the mother of his children to make sense of such a circus. Who was looking after her? Was Samantha? Now that I understood how exhausting it was to be around that behavior for days on end, I understood her frustration, but why would she leave her alone with Amber, knowing how poorly she treated her? Why was she including her own friends on these luxurious vacations? Though I still didn't understand the scope of the dynamic, I could tell she was being failed. If anything, weren't they at least *paid* to care?

I sighed, trying to recollect myself before driving back to the property. This job was nowhere near what I imagined it to be, but somehow after witnessing Alexis in that state, I felt more committed than ever. If I were going to be a witness to all of this, I at least needed to be an ally to Alexis.

As I pulled back through the gates to Alexis's, I remembered the birds, and how Alexis hadn't even seen them. *I should check on them.* I headed for the far side of the house. But as I approached, something felt off. There was no chirping. As I got closer, I panicked: not one bird was flying. *Who let them out?* But the cage was closed. When I finally reached it, I covered my eyes and turned away in horror. Every single bird was on the bottom of the cage, dead. It had been too hot for them. I started hyperventilating, panicking about what to do, overwhelmed by the past twenty-four hours—until the sound of a car alarm erupted at the front of the house.

I ran back to the front of the mansion, not knowing what to expect, when suddenly there was Alexis. She was on the steps, turning the car alarm on and off, over and over again. She walked over to the car, opened the door, climbed in, and then climbed back out. Turning on the alarm and turning it off again. The noise was so loud I hardly noticed the new gown she was wearing, until she returned to pose on the front steps as if she were on a red carpet. Bored with posing, she perched herself against the brick wall, and pretended to smoke as she stared into space.

I hesitated. "Hi Alexis." I thought maybe if I spoke normally, she would too.

But she didn't make eye contact. What did the doctor and nurse even do? She was just as neurotic as before, the circles under her eyes deepening. Her lips twitched as she spoke, as if even she didn't know what was going to spring forth next.

"Hayden," she said, "get Rhythm and Blue ready for dinner. Elvis, Whitney, and Marilyn will be joining us. They need to look their best."

Chills covered my body as she spoke to me about her deceased guests. I smiled awkwardly and slowly slid past her for the kitchen, where Amber was eating as if it were any other day.

"She just told me Elvis, Whitney, and Marilyn are coming to dinner," I said.

Amber laughed, shaking her head as she bit into a sandwich prepared by Noah. It felt odd to see her so unbothered while Alexis was clearly suffering. I'd never seen anyone act like this around a genuinely ill person. It made me sad to think that even the people she paid couldn't conjure any modicum of empathy toward her.

"So, where did Brody disappear to anyway? Samantha said something about San Francisco?"

"The doctor made him piss his little panties," she said. "He may think he's coming back, but we won't allow it. I had the gate code changed and informed security not to let him back on the property. When I finish eating, I'm going to pack up his things. Not that he paid for any of them."

I wondered how long Alexis would stay like this. From what I'd read, manic episodes could last anywhere from three days to three weeks. But also, as the doctor said, when you get older, the episodes get worse and last longer—she might never come out of it. I couldn't imagine the horror of a perpetually detached reality, or worse, leaving R&B without a mother for the rest of their lives.

Given such terrifying prospects, Amber seemed awfully unmoved. The world in general didn't care about Alexis the human. They only loved her for the entertainment fodder she provided them—the hit songs, the glamour, the meltdowns, the mishaps, the memes, and now the potential permanent dive into madness. Who would really care if she were to lose herself forever, as long as it made for a juicy headline? It was best for Brody to be gone, but at the same time I imagined when she was "better" she would want him back. Conditional love was better than no love at all.

"Let me know if you need any help," I said. "I'm gonna lie down in the office for a minute. I didn't sleep a wink last night."

"Oh, trust me, I've been there," she said.

I closed the office door behind me and laid on the chaise lounge to close my eyes. I couldn't believe how drastically things had changed since my first day, when I was sitting at that desk with nothing to do. I drifted off for seconds, but heard a knock at the door.

"Come in!" I said, expecting Samantha.

I turned to find Alexis, peeking her head through the door in yet another new ensemble.

"Hayden, a *gentleman* would have opened the door." She rolled her eyes and quickly closed the door behind her. Her two Pomeranians—normally locked up in her bedroom—came trampling in by her side. She sat next to me, pulled her deactivated phone out of her robe pocket, and handed it to me.

"Can you get this to work? I will give you ten grand in cash. I just need to get out of here. They're trying to poison me."

Is that why she had me pick up cash? For emergency bribes? While this normally would have sounded appealing, I refused.

"What's wrong with it?" I asked, playing dumb. "What's the code?"

She stared at the phone blankly. I knew she didn't know.

"We'll just have to go to the Apple store later," I said without thinking.

"Then let's go." She stood up and pulled car keys out of her other robe pocket.

I imagined the chaos that would ensue if she were to leave the house. It would resemble something that hadn't been seen since Britney Spears in 2007. I knew she couldn't drive and was prepared to scream for security, but instead she began to "rapid cycle" again—interrogating me about the books of the Bible. When I stopped engaging, she left the room and walked up the staircase, then immediately back down. And then up, and then back down again. She stopped, I assumed disappearing to change her outfit again—when I heard Teddi and the twins coming through the front door.

"Mommy!" Rhythm and Blue shouted, running into the foyer.

"Shhh! Shhh!" Teddi shushed the twins. "Mommy's sleeping! She's not feeling very well, *okay*? We're just gonna get some clothes, toys, and your iPads to take back to Miss Samantha's house."

But before they could make it anywhere, Alexis appeared again, descending the staircase.

"Security!" Teddi yelled, hoping for help to distract the children. But it was too late.

"Mommy!" Rhythm shouted again, running for his mother. "Are you feeling better?"

"I'm not your Mommy, *little boy*," she said bitingly, walking right past him.

I started choking up. Now I knew why Samantha had asked if Alexis recognized me. She didn't recognize her own son.

"YOU ARE MY MOM!" Rhythm screamed, his face breaking into scared confusion.

The six-year-old stormed away screaming, and I held back my own tears to scoop him up and hold him like a baby as he cried. Blue chased after us and tugged on my shirt, tears forming in her own eyes.

"What's wrong with Mommy?" she said. "Why is she acting—" She rotated her pointer finger in a circular motion at the side of her head to symbolize crazy.

They didn't have the words for it, but they knew something was wrong. What could I tell them? What comfort could I possibly provide, knowing there was a chance she could stay this way forever? This was the flipside to the red carpet pomp of their childhoods—raised by a roster of nannies and a mother who didn't recognize them depending on the day. Rhythm's tears soaked my shoulder as I took them to another room.

What I couldn't see was, at the same time, Samantha had walked in the front door and witnessed the entire interaction. She finally cracked, bursting into uncontrollable sobs, and hyperventilated. Security grabbed her by the shoulders and encouraged her to breathe—but she couldn't.

"*I SWEAR TO GOD,*" she shouted through gasps for air, "*I WILL FUCKING KILL THAT MOTHERFUCKER! I WILL PUT HIM IN JAIL! HOW COULD HE DO THIS TO HER? WE'VE ALREADY TOLD HIM!*" She continued to sob. "*SHE'S A MOTHER!*"

Samantha's real and raw emotion emerging for the first time made everything clear. She was desperately, truly trying to help Alexis, and Brody was so callous and self-serving he didn't care if taking advantage of Alexis led her to death. Alexis was merely a stepping stone in his quest to achieve fame. And he was now damaging her relationship with her children. Samantha, a single mother, couldn't just stand by and watch that happen.

That evening, the Beverly Hills sheriff showed up at the door, and Samantha successfully issued a restraining order against Brody—ensuring he would *never* see Alexis Shane again.

CHAPTER SEVEN

The following weeks didn't get any easier. Alexis's mental illness was now putting a strain on my relationship. Even when I did get the chance to leave her, I couldn't. Grayson understood the severity of her bipolar diagnosis, but he didn't understand why I refused to leave her with Amber. I had even been lying to the team, saying things weren't going well with my fiancé to instead take up residence in the guest house. I couldn't just relax at home anymore knowing Alexis was left to the whims of whoever happened to be with her.

The primary doctor promised us Alexis would come out of it soon. But I couldn't see an end in sight, as most of my days were spent listening to deafening screams or rejecting Alexis's sexual advances. Nurses came each night to hook her up to an IV to put her to sleep. They explained she needed complete silence to "catch the wave." And when it worked, I'd breathe a sigh of relief. Still, it was upsetting to see my childhood superstar stripped of all illusion, tucked into bed like a child and hooked up like a hospital patient. To witness her so deeply vulnerable, so helpless, made me feel completely bewildered as to how to genuinely support her. Part of me felt presumptuous for wanting to "help" without truly knowing her, but I also realized I was now privy to a side of her that most of the world didn't know existed, so there was an inherent sense of responsibility toward her.

But if something distracted her from this induced tranquility, I'd often wake up screaming at the sight of Alexis hovering over me, clad in feather boas and pajama shorts, hysterically giggling or solemn, tranquilized or neurotic. I never knew which combination it would be.

"I want to die, Hayden," she'd tell me. "I want to die just like Marilyn."

There were huddles outside the home with Samantha each afternoon about what the next steps should be. Different doctors came to observe, lawyers came to give advice, and even Brody eventually came back to the house with flowers—only to be handed a copy of the restraining order and told by Amber to never return.

Each night when the team dispersed, I'd convince Amber I was alright staying up with Alexis, that she could go to bed. And as the weeks went on, Alexis was slowly coming out of her episode. There were times when her gaze would teeter on the edge, and I could sense some awareness reaching out. But just as quickly as I felt her lucidity, she'd slip back into mania. It was almost as if she wasn't ready to step back into reality—with all its implications and responsibilities—to bear the gravity of her infamy, the dizzying shuttling from event to event—every moment curated, all eyes staring, international performances and expectations. In some ways, it seemed this was how she protected herself—by retreating into a world of her own where no one could touch her or demand anything of her.

Despite my empathy, it was exhausting. The more time I spent around her, the more I lost my own sense of reality. After weeks of being locked behind the gates and trying to shield her from Amber, I snapped. My anxiety reached an all-time high, and I made a run for it. I just needed a moment outside of the gates, to remember there was life outside of there.

I could leave Amber alone with her for a day. I just had to.

"PLEASE DON'T ASK ME ANYTHING about her today," I said. Grayson had opened the door to our apartment to find me sprawled out on our couch in sweats, eating chocolate chip cookie dough ice cream from Salt & Straw. "I'm actually starting to lose it. I want to protect her, but I need a break from the madness. So, *please* can we not talk about her?"

"Of course." Grayson made his way over to give me a hug. He was just happy to come home and find me for once.

I pressed play to resume the latest episode of *The Real Housewives of Salt Lake City*, and cozied up beneath the fleece blanket Oma had gifted me a few Christmases earlier. Grayson's well-defined biceps drew my attention away from the television, until my phone pinged with a text message from Samantha.

"I'm just so glad you're home," he said. "Especially *today*."

"Oh, yeah?" I was half-listening as I texted Samantha back, fearing some new disastrous development.

"Yeah, I was um…" he paused, waiting for me to put my phone down. But I didn't. "I was promoted, Hayden. I'm an agent."

"Oh, really?" I said, feverishly texting Samantha. For some reason, Alexis was up looking for me.

"Did you hear me?"

"Yeah, babe. One second."

"*HAYDEN!*" Grayson yelled, prompting me to quickly drop my phone. Grayson never yelled. I'd only ever heard him raise his voice maybe once in four years. "Are you serious?"

"What? What's wrong?"

"You're not listening! You're never home, and now you are, and I'm trying to tell you something important. But you're just sitting there, fucking ignoring me."

"I'm sorry," I said. "I'm listening."

"I just said I was *promoted*."

"*NO!*" I jumped up from the couch, throwing my blanket aside. "You're an agent?"

"I am," he said, and grinned.

"Oh my God, Gray," I said, kissing him. "I'm so proud of you."

"Thank you. I'm just glad you're here. So, can you *be here*?"

"I'm here! I'm here! Now what the hell are you doing putting on those sweatpants? Go get changed." I waved him away, toward the closet. "We need to celebrate!"

"Honestly, babe, we haven't spent any time together in weeks," he said. "The only thing I really want to do is be at home with you." He smiled wearily and pulled me down beside him, resting his head on my shoulder.

"Alright, well, I'm at least ordering us some champagne on DoorDash," I said. "And there's nothing you can do to stop me."

Grayson wrapped his arm around me tighter. "I won't argue with that."

I sunk deeper into the couch, deeper into Grayson's arms, and inhaled his familiar scent—a combination of Le Labo's Rose 31 and Santal 33.

I really did miss him. I had just been too busy to miss him. Now that he was beside me, I could feel *human* once again—loved and in love, not just some hyperactive robot flittering from task to task or trying to yank superstars off balconies.

"My boss wants to take us to dinner. But his schedule is jam-packed. So, it won't be for a few weeks. Will you just *please* make sure that you have that night off?"

"Of course," I promised. "I wouldn't miss it for the world."

WHEN I RETURNED TO ALEXIS'S the next day, Samantha was waiting in the office.

"Thank you," she said before I could even sit down. "I know how hard you've been working, and I know your number one priority has been the same as mine—to get Alexis *better*."

I appreciated that she was initially relentless in trying to keep Alexis's medical condition a secret from me. But once it had become impossible, she started opening up and even wanted my help in creating a plan. Step one was to get her vibrant and healthy, and step two was to pack the schedule—so when she *was* feeling good again, she wouldn't have the time to worry about Brody.

But unfortunately, because of the Super Bowl performance, no one was interested in booking Alexis for *anything*. The requests had completely stopped coming in, which meant all of Samantha's calls would be outgoing. But she didn't let that stop her.

"In life you have to remember, you always need to be crazier than the next person to get what you want."

"I have to ask..." I said.

"Ask what?"

"Well, after the Super Bowl, I remember you releasing that aggressive statement to the media. You told them her inner earpiece wasn't working, and you blamed it on the NFL's production company."

"What's your point?"

The statement had created a media firestorm, and what actually happened became a major topic of debate in the press for the weeks following. Some understood she couldn't hear herself over a crowd of

80,000 people—but many thought she was a flat-out liar.

"They *were* working, weren't they?"

Samantha scoffed.

"She was manic, wasn't she? You were just covering for her."

She knew she couldn't lie at this point, and instead threatened me. She slammed her hands down onto the table and squared her eyes at me like a fiery little bulldog.

"If you tell anyone, I swear to God, I will fucking kill you."

"I won't," I promised. I couldn't help but feel a bit taken aback, as the idea of allowing Alexis to perform in that state of mind seemed cruel. How could someone clearly disassociated from reality be expected to perform for millions of people?

"You have no idea how many professional relationships I have ruined trying to cover her mental illness. After that performance, I felt like it was the perfect time for her to come forward and talk about it publicly. She doesn't need to be ashamed, you know? I told her she could inspire so many people. But she didn't want to listen. She doesn't *have* to live like this, Hayden. She chooses to."

I didn't understand what she meant. It was barely as if she had a choice. To disclose something as personal as a mental disorder to the vulture of the mocking media hardly seemed like a plausible option. Nobody *chooses* to be mentally ill in the first place. At least she should have the power over whether or not she wanted the entire world to know.

Samantha changed the subject.

"I need you to put together a press binder, because apparently her publicist thinks it's fucking vacation time or something. Check your Google Alerts and read all the articles about Alexis from the past few weeks. Maybe if she sees some positive news, it'll help snap her out of it."

"Kelly normally does this?"

"No, Kelly normally does *nothing*. I'm not sure how she's still on the payroll. Alexis doesn't even like her, and prefers it when I handle the press."

I printed off *People* magazine talking about her multi-million-dollar Puerto Vallarta vacation, *Page Six* reporting on her new record deal, and the *Daily Mail* informing fans that new music was finally on the way. I separated the articles with color-coded dividers, made a cover with her signature phoenix logo, and handed it to Samantha. Samantha was always quick to appreciate what I considered simple organizational skills—maybe because Amber didn't have any.

I joined Samantha on her side of the desk as she flipped through the articles. She immediately began to rip out pages.

"Nothing with a mention of Brody, and nothing with photos from the right side of her face. That's her bad side. When she was nineteen, shooting her first magazine cover, Tracey told her that, and it's always stuck with her."

At forty years old, with all her fame, beauty, and money, she was still affected by something someone had said to her twenty years earlier. She was much more self-conscious than people knew. It was clear that not only did everyone else expect her to live within the well-defined confines of what they expected of a glamorous superstar, but she expected it of herself as well. The amount of pressure involved in that kind of role-playing was evident—no wonder she boiled over every few months.

Samantha's phone vibrated against the glass desk. It was Karen from business management. She answered the call just as someone began knocking at the door.

I walked over, anticipating Alexis, but when I peeked out, it was Noah.

"Hi boyfriend!" I said, greeting him with a smile. "What's going on?"

"Man, *shut up*," he said.

Noah was not the straight guy who was super comfortable with his sexuality, which only made me love flirting with him more. He waved me out of the office to speak privately.

"Listen, man." He shook his head. "I hate to bother you with this, but I just don't know who to talk to."

"What's the matter?"

"Well, I haven't received a paycheck in a while..."

"What do you mean? What's *a while*?"

"Eight weeks."

"*Eight weeks?*" I repeated in disbelief.

"I've called Samantha, emailed her. Tried calling Karen too, but she just sends me straight to voicemail."

"There must be some kind of mistake," I said confidently. "Don't worry, I got you."

This didn't make any sense. Was it because Alexis had been incoherent and unable to approve payroll? But *I* had still been getting paid. What made me take precedence? I assumed keeping her alive.

I closed the office door behind me. Samantha now looked flustered, covering her mouth as she whispered to Karen. I'd never normally interrupt, but with the conversation I just had, and who she was speaking with, I felt it was necessary.

"I'm sorry to interrupt," I said, "but I just spoke with Noah and he said he hasn't received a paycheck in *eight weeks.*"

"BECAUSE SHE HAS NO FUCKING MONEY!" Samantha shouted.

I stared back at her, bewildered by both her reaction and the statement.

"Samantha, stop!" a muffled Karen shouted back through Samantha's earpiece.

"Karen, I'll call you back," Samantha said, quickly hanging up.

"That's not true. It can't be," I said. "It says on celebritynetworth.com that Alexis is worth seven hundred million dollars. She's been in the industry for twenty years! She has to be making millions off of residuals alone. I don't believe you. It's just not possible!"

"Are you kidding me? Celebritynetworth.com? You really believe everything you read online? She has *no* money. For years she surrounded herself with users who took advantage of her, charging ten grand a day for glam, a quarter-mil a month for security. She was living off *loans* when I met her. I came in, fired everyone, provided affordable options, and have since brought in a hundred and fifty million. But she still has absolutely nothing to show for it! She just doesn't fucking get it!"

While I couldn't wrap my head around the details, I suspected she wasn't lying.

"Don't say anything to Noah. Just give me a minute to figure out how to bring more fucking money in the door that I'm sure she will just piss away."

Samantha's phone vibrated against the desk with call after call from Karen.

"I'm doing everything I can, *okay*?" Samantha said before Karen could say a word. "She needs to get better first, that's our number one priority. And when she's lucid again, you need to start having these conversations with *her*, not *me*!"

I stepped out in disbelief and ignored Samantha's instruction. It was my job to protect Alexis, but Noah was my friend. I relayed the info to him in the most delicate terms possible.

"Please just keep this between us," I said.

"Dude, this isn't the first time this has happened," he said. "I figured as much. But I still need to pay my fucking rent."

"I don't even know when to tell you to expect it. But I'll help as much as I can, and I'll stay on them to make sure you're paid."

Back at the office, I closed the door behind me. Samantha had broken down.

"People just don't understand." She was sobbing, mascara running down her cheeks. "No one understands how hard I work! These are not normal circumstances! Her financial situation is *dire*. Do you understand the pressure I'm under? The criticism I get? When I started, the IRS was beating down her door, telling business management if she didn't pay her taxes, they'd come and arrest her on stage to make an example out of her."

I couldn't help but feel sorry for Samantha, a single mother who had her own child to take care of, let alone the forty-year-old diva and her entourage. Her tears were interrupted by her phone vibrating yet again. I picked it up and handed it to her, noticing the caller ID read *Jill TMZ*. So, that's how they knew the house cost $150,000 a month. I squinted at her, trying to understand that she had her feet in both camps—protecting Alexis the human, while creating enough of an edge around Alexis the idol to pump her name back into the headlines.

After everything I'd witnessed—the mental illness, the con-man boyfriend, the financial ruin—I'd finally gained Samantha's trust. She didn't ask me to leave the room for what once would have been considered a private conversation. I was in too deep; there was no room for secrets anymore. She answered on speaker.

"*Jill?* Here's what I want it to say: *ALEXIS AND BRODY BROKE UP*. Say she grew tired of being used for fame and footing the bill for this backup dancing boy-toy. And make sure you go into how jealous he is of her relationship with the twins' father."

I listened to the phone conversation, my mouth open in disbelief at seeing how the gossip blogs operated. Stories were planted by a credible inside source to fuel their own agenda. She was the primary alchemist of Alexis's image, leaking specks of information that would bolster her public extravagance. *She* was the one who drew on the mask so tactfully day by day. It didn't matter whether Alexis still loved Brody, so long as

Samantha deemed it unacceptable. And once it was in the media, it was cemented in the public consciousness.

"Is Alexis on board with this?" I asked when Samantha hung up. "You spoke to her in a clear frame of mind?"

"Don't worry about it," she said.

"But they didn't break up, Samantha. He was kicked out of the house. Why did you need to say anything at all?"

"It's the only way. The restraining order will only get us so far. I need to change the public perception of him. When she comes out of this and reads all the negative comments, she won't *want* to be with him. He is the one keeping her in this place. He is the one feeding her drugs and alcohol, which lead her into mania. He is the one keeping her away from her children. He is the one encouraging her to buy him diamonds and Gucci. We have to get rid of him. *For good.*"

Based on her argument and what the doctor said, I understood. However, Alexis was not her daughter. This was not Samantha's decision to make. People have to learn life lessons on their own. She couldn't just play the puppet master of Alexis's life.

But it was too late. Google Alerts went off on each of our phones. The headline read, ALEXIS SHANE DUMPS FAME-HUNGRY BOY-TOY!

"SECURITY JUST TEXTED ME THAT the paparazzi are already outside waiting to get their first shots of *single* Alexis," Samantha said. "But we can't let her go out there until I speak to her. She needs to hear it from me, not from one of them shouting at her."

Samantha and I spent the day in the office brainstorming how to bring money in the door, and when Noah began cooking lunch, the smell was enough to get Alexis out of bed. I caught her slowly descending the staircase and waved to get Samantha's attention.

"Hi, my beautiful girl!" Samantha said.

Alexis approached the office doorway looking disheveled with her hair up, and in a wrinkled silk robe. But she was clearer than I'd seen her in weeks. She was aware of what was going on, and what she was saying. *She must be close to coming out of it.*

"Where is he, Samantha?" she asked.

She *was* coming out of it, and wanted Brody home.

"Where's who?"

"I want to speak to Brody. Call him from your phone," Alexis said. "And when can I have mine back?"

"We'll talk about everything tonight over dinner, *okay*? I'll have Noah make your favorite, and Hayden will go get you a new phone tomorrow."

My heart hurt. She had no idea the whole world was talking about her "breakup." It wasn't right that she should be the last one to receive the news about her own love life.

"He's *my* assistant. Why can't he go get me one right now?"

"Because there's more pressing things going on *right now*. You haven't been working, and employees are starting to go unpaid."

As Alexis continued to push, Samantha finally snapped.

"He's a bad person, Alexis! *Okay*? He's fucking evil! He's been using you for your money and fame. How do you still not see this? And worst of all, he's been separating you from your kids! Do you even remember what happened with Blue in Mexico?"

Alexis didn't respond because she *didn't* know what happened with Blue. She barely remembered going to Puerto Vallarta. And now she was worried.

Samantha picked up her phone to show Alexis the video of Blue losing her tooth. Alexis took the phone, sat down, and watched the video over and over again, wiping tears from her eyes. Suddenly I felt guilty for judging her before. Clearly she *wanted* to fulfill all the roles of a mother, but her spontaneous episodes precluded her from being totally present. When she was manic, she could barely take care of herself. Here was a woman witnessing a rite of passage she'd missed because of her illness, reacting to what she had lost. I wondered how terribly she'd feel if she remembered telling Rhythm she was not his mother, and how horrifying those gaps of memory must be. Even in her waking life she was only privy to parts of herself.

All the while, Google Alerts continued to pop up in the corner of my screen. A story came in from St. Patrick's Day, and a waitress was now claiming Brody had been flirting with her all night.

It blew my mind that one phone call *minutes* ago had already created a media firestorm.

Alexis handed Samantha's phone back to her without question.

"Can we at least go out somewhere for dinner?" she said. "I need to get out of the house."

"Of course, beautiful."

THAT EVENING, SWARMED BY PAPARAZZI, Alexis, Samantha, Blair, Amber, and I headed to Craig's in Beverly Hills. I'd gotten accustomed to Alexis's routine and allowed her to walk in first so she could choose the best seat at the table—based on the lighting. I sat at the far end, wanting to give Alexis and Samantha privacy.

"Why are they all shouting about Brody?" Alexis whispered to her.

Amber sat her phone down next to me before heading to the restroom. It grabbed my attention as it continuously lit up. Text message after text message came through with contacts that ended with *TMZ*, *Page Six*, and *Entertainment Tonight*. She was in on it too. Was I the only one who saw both sides? How could they justify cultivating the perceived reality of a grown woman? Didn't everyone have the right to tell their own story?

"What are you doing down there?" Alexis said. I looked up to find her glaring at me.

"Oh, I just wanted to give you girls some privacy."

"I don't even know why I speak to you at all, Hayden," she said, rolling her eyes.

"I'm sorry. I thought you had personal things to talk about."

Why was Alexis suddenly being so mean to me? I had just given up weeks of my life to spend by her side during her episode. My memory flashed back to St. Patrick's Day. I guess that was the last time she was actually *mean* to me. Maybe this was what it was like when mania wore off? Maybe the feeling of it made her agitated. I was still trying to delineate where her illness ended and her personality began, though I wasn't sure this was achievable.

"Well, another holiday is almost here!" Samantha said, trying to change the subject. "Can you believe it? What should we do for Easter?"

Alexis ignored the question, asking the waiter for a glass of Pinot Grigio. Even after all we'd just been through, no one tried to stop her. I wondered idly what made any of them better than Brody. Maybe they weren't.

"Hayden should dress up as a bunny," Alexis said.

"I was able to find leprechauns, so I'm sure I'll have no problem finding someone to dress up like a bunny." I laughed.

"*NO!*" she spat. "I pay you, so *you* will dress up as a bunny. Samantha, is this how an assistant should be speaking to me? Are we just going to let assistants decide what they will and will not do?"

I sat quietly for the rest of dinner as the topic of conversation between Samantha and Alexis returned to Brody. Maybe not the best idea, given that Alexis was clearly still not herself. I reminded myself not to take it personally and that I had to be patient. I did my best to read their lips. Samantha was trying to play it off as if she had no control over the situation.

"It's out of my hands," she said. "This is between you and your doctor."

But Alexis knew better. Samantha was only loyal to her own agenda, and she was willing to dominate every aspect of Alexis's life to ensure it.

WITH BRODY GONE AND ALEXIS so close to coming out of mania, I continued spending my days with Samantha, devoting our attention to the cash flow.

"I don't know what to do," she said. "The chef is one thing, but as soon as the security, hair, makeup, and stylist invoices start going unpaid, they sue. The documents become public record, and *everyone* will know she's broke."

"I don't understand," I said. "How is it that some of us are getting paid and some not?"

"There's a priority list. First me, of course. Then Amber, you, and so on. But if you're worried about other people getting paid first, I can always move you down on the list," she said with a scoff.

"I know how much you want to help her, but her financial ruin isn't your fault. It's not your responsibility to tell her how to spend her money. That's why she has business managers. Your job is to *make* her money, that's it. If she needs to learn the hard way, then she needs to learn. But she won't learn if you keep cleaning up her messes."

"I know, I know," she said.

"Have her business managers even tried telling her she can't afford to get hair and makeup done every day? Has anyone actually sat down with her to go over finances?"

"Come on! Of course! I tried getting her to pull back for years before I found out her diagnosis. But the doctors all say excessive spending is a symptom of bipolar disorder. So, I *have* to care. I mean, do you want to keep getting paid? Because *she's* not worried about paying you."

Samantha returned to flipping through her calendar of the past year, brainstorming money-making ideas aloud. I listened as she made calls to agents and networks, trying to fill up the schedule. Within hours, Samantha had secured our first deal. She walked from her desk to mine, shaking my shoulders, then holding her hand up to give me a high-five.

"I did it!" she squealed. "We're going to Austria, baby!"

"What?" I said, jumping from my seat.

"One-million-dollar performance! And they're advancing fifty percent of it, *today*."

"How did you—"

"They just love her in Europe, and I was thinking about how many deals I was able to pull together during the tour last year. I remembered Alexis had performed in Vienna at a private event for Mrs. Blade. This woman owns the largest knife company in the world, and every year she hosts an extravagant birthday party and flies out her favorite celebrities to celebrate."

"Okay, *and*—" I said.

"I just thought I'd tell her that Alexis and I were chatting about how we had such a great time last year. She was so excited, she immediately asked if we'd be willing to come again. One million dollars, plus jet, and accommodations for the whole entourage! See what happens just by putting yourself out there?"

"Do I get to go?" I asked excitedly, remembering I was not to be included when it came to travel.

"I can't *not* let you come, after everything you've been through."

I jumped up to give Samantha a hug, but she immediately pushed me away. She wasn't a touchy-feely person.

"Alright, *calm down*. Now, I need you to print off the new record contract. That's three million, and I just talked them into a quarter-mil advance. It's not much, but it's something. Then print off the Austria contract. I'm gonna go upstairs and have her sign them."

Almost two hours later, Samantha returned bleary-eyed and disheveled.

"I don't get paid enough for this shit," she groaned. "I had to crawl into her bed under a blanket fort to have her sign by flashlight. I'm not a manager, I'm a *babysitter*."

EVEN AFTER NEGOTIATING TWO MAJOR deals in such a short period of time, Samantha wasn't slowing down. When she got wind through our agent that Alexis's biggest rival was on the brink of closing a million-dollar deal with a high-end haircare line, she called the owners personally to throw Alexis's name in the ring.

"Have you guys seen Alexis's hair? I mean, *come on*. No one has better hair than her!"

The product line incorporated salt from the Dead Sea in Israel, and the job included a trip there for a photo shoot and a press conference—which coincidentally was due to commence right after our trip to Austria. With Samantha's persistence, the deal was done in days.

"Deals are always null and void if they don't include *plus jet*," Samantha told me. "Don't forget that."

With all the money starting to pour in, things felt a little lighter around the house. I made sure Noah was paid, and Alexis had officially come out of mania—although she now resumed her depression, spending entire days in bed. I wondered if she knew how much time we spent together during her episode, and was embarrassed now that she was clearheaded.

"Hi babe," Amber said as I walked into the office that morning. "I'm working on the menu for Samantha's birthday dinner tonight. We need to make it special, you know? I told her to take the day off too, and that we could handle Alexis. She deserves to relax for once."

While I didn't trust Amber, she and Samantha were sisters and clearly had a special bond. I understood better at this point it wasn't an easy work environment, and they always had each other's back.

"Here's what I've picked so far," she said. "What do you think?"

Nails began tapping against the office door.

"*Hayden?*" a voice cooed. It was Alexis.

"Good morning, beautiful!" I said.

"Do you mind taking me down to Rodeo? I want to pick out a gift for Samantha."

"Of course! I'll call the glam boys and have them come to the house now."

Dylan and Lion were always prepared for a last-minute call. They would hurry over, wait for two hours, and another two hours later, Alexis would descend the grand staircase looking effortlessly beautiful, as only someone with her star power could.

Seeing her back in her signature hair and makeup, even after all we'd been through, took my breath away.

"Let's take one of my cars," she said.

I watched as Amber's jaw clenched in irritation that Alexis had asked me to go instead of her. But what could I do? I followed Alexis to the large mahogany table in the foyer that was adorned with photos of the twins and white roses. I'd removed the yellow tulips from the house after realizing they triggered her. I followed her to the garage, where she asked me to remove the fabric cover from the closest car.

"This was my mom's," she said proudly, resting her hands in the back of her Prada jeans pockets. "I had it refurbished."

Hearing her say that, and seeing the way she looked at the car, I could see clearly—and for the first time—that she was just a normal girl. A girl who missed her mother. I imagined her childhood must have felt like a lifetime away. It was sweet to witness her nostalgia. The Jaguar was vintage, black, and the back read XK-E. Alexis handed me the key, and I anticipated her telling me to be careful, but she didn't.

We pulled out of the gate, security following closely behind in a black Escalade. The wind blew through our hair on our quiet drive down the canyon onto the world-famous Rodeo Drive. Being with her when she was clear felt electric, even in silence.

Pulling in front of a meter at Goyard, the paparazzi immediately spied us. I watched as Alexis slowly and deliberately stepped out of the car, giving them a chance to catch up and photograph her.

"*Alexis, you look beautiful!*" one shouted.

"*Gorgeous, Alexis!*"

"*Who's the guy?*"

She ignored the questions and comments, simply smiling as we glided toward Goyard where security in a pristine suit opened the door for us.

"So, what do you want to get her?" I asked.

Everyone in the store was staring at us.

"When we were in Aspen this past Christmas, there was a large trunk she wanted but wouldn't buy for herself."

Alexis's thoughtfulness surprised me, especially considering she knew Samantha was the reason Brody had gone missing.

As the employees spotted her, they abandoned their customers in a race to get the chance to assist her. The first saleswoman to make it greeted us with triumphant eagerness.

"It's a monogrammed trunk, very large. Not something you would actually travel with. It's more of a display piece for the home," Alexis said, swooping her long lashes around the room. I wondered how on earth anyone could possibly get used to the amount of attention and scrutiny she dealt with every time she left the house. All the customers and salespeople were gawking at her like they discovered a new species. It must have felt strange to be an object of awe all the time, but she seemed content with it.

The saleswoman guided us to the selection of trunks, and Alexis pointed to the largest one without hesitation. It was gorgeous, and big enough for the both of us to comfortably fit inside. Rich people sure liked to decorate their lives with useless objects.

"Hayden, will you pull out my card?" she said, holding out her Hermès Birkin.

I removed the black metal American Express card from her Louis Vuitton wallet and handed it to the salesgirl. Moments later, she returned.

"I'm sorry," she whispered, "but this card was declined."

"Ugh. *These people*, I tell you," Alexis said, "What am I paying everyone for? Can't they remember to pay a bill?"

Alexis rolled her eyes and laughed with the saleswoman, putting on a show. She intuitively knew what role to assume in any given social situation, transforming herself effortlessly into whatever anyone needed her to be. She could shoot the breeze with a stranger as easily as she could kiss Anna Wintour on the cheek.

"Hayden, call business management," she said.

My skin flushed and I apologized, quickly dialing Karen.

Karen might have been stern with Samantha about Alexis's spending habits, but she quickly catered to Alexis's instruction without question. I wondered, what was the point of having a business manager if they just let you do whatever you want? Karen made a payment with the haircare advance, the salesgirl re-ran the card, and the receipt was brought back for signature. I watched Alexis sign her famous autograph, right below $50,000. *Jesus*. I guess even if she *was* blowing her money, you couldn't call her selfish.

BACK AT THE MANSION, I turned to head for the office, but Alexis stopped me.

"Do you think you could arrange a spa night here at the house, for after dinner? You know, massages, nails, whatever."

"Of course! That sounds fun. I'm sure the twins will love it too."

"Also…" she paused, "I just want to say, you've been doing a really great job." She looked at me and smiled. For the first time in weeks, there she was. Not the sick woman or the effete diva—just Alexis.

It was the first time I'd received praise from her, and the unexpected compliment made me blush as if my crush had just handed me a love letter. It felt good to feel appreciated by a living legend. I hoped she was beginning to see that she could trust me, but I always knew how capricious she could be.

Out of the corner of my eye, I saw Amber lurking in the office doorway, hanging on every word. Her brow furrowed and she pulled anxiously at her lips. But I ignored her, flourishing in my moment with Alexis.

"Thank you," I said, trying not to smile too wide. My gratitude was genuine.

But she, of course, could not stay in the moment, and quickly changed her voice back to the sarcastic diva tone she often used in interviews. Sooner or later, she always retreated back into her armor.

"Alright sweetieeeee, it's time for vocal rest!"

I LEFT SAMANTHA'S BIRTHDAY DINNER early to set up spa night at Alexis's house. Due to my years at the salon, it was a task that came easy. The estheticians, manicurists, and massage therapists were already waiting when I returned. I led them in, helping to carry their tables and equipment down to the theatre. Rhythm and Blue were there with Teddi, playing video games on the big screen.

"Um... *hello*! I'm trying to play a game here!" Rhythm shouted at the unfamiliar women who were blocking the screen.

But when he saw I was leading the pack, he changed his tune.

"What's a spa night, Hayden?"

"Rhythm," Blue said, and then laughed, "it's when someone tickles you!"

I helped them each into an oversized white robe, then lifted them onto their own massage tables. They laid face down, and as the masseuses began to rub their backs, they both broke out into laughter.

"That does tickle!" Rhythm giggled.

I laughed, imagining how my own future would feel with children—a sentiment I'd been considering more and more lately the closer I became with the twins. They taught me to appreciate the simplicity of the world, and their sense of wonder was infectious.

While they were distracted, I changed the theatre screen to *Some Like It Hot*. I wanted to impress Alexis with my knowledge of her idol. I then began to take photos of the twins to share with her, who were now turned over and wearing face masks.

"Who put on Marilyn?" Alexis whispered over my shoulder.

"I did!" I said. "I mean, this *is* Alexis Shane's home."

Alexis smiled at the sight of the twins. She put a robe on and made her way to the only open massage table. The technicians quickly swarmed her—one doing a manicure, one doing a pedicure, and one massaging her, all at the same time. The only time Alexis flinched was when one of the girls attempted to do a facial. Her rejection was jarring. "I don't do facials."

It brought me back to my first day, when Samantha told me no one was allowed to see her without makeup.

I took a seat in one of the oversized recliners, and Rhythm climbed off his table to join me.

"Mommy, can I get my nails painted?" he asked, hanging over my shoulder.

"Yes, Rhythm. But *only* your toes, and *only* black."

Twenty minutes later, a masculine voice called, "Hello?" from the theater entrance.

It was Rich, and the unexpected visit prompted the kids to sprint toward him.

"*Daddy!*" they shouted in unison.

His presence was surprising—in my four months of employment, this was only the second time I'd seen him, and the first time I'd seen him *inside* the house. Maybe with Brody out of the picture, he felt more comfortable.

"I just came to tuck you guys in for bed." He kissed each twin on the forehead.

"Hello Rich," Alexis mumbled through the face hole of the massage table. "I'll come with you to take them up."

Rich picked up Blue, and then Rhythm ran toward me.

"Will you carry me upstairs?" he asked.

I waited for Rich or Alexis to say they would, but neither did. So I followed the famous family up the stairs, with Rhythm on my waist, in awe that I was alone with them. I remembered seeing paparazzi photographs of the family at Disneyland each year for the twins' birthday. It was hard to believe I had reached this level of intimacy with them, and I couldn't help but smile as Rhythm dozed on my neck.

At the top of the stairs, Alexis removed her spa robe, exposing a sexy pink nightie. I wondered if she knew he was coming. Rich sat Blue down on a large window seat in the twins' bedroom overlooking the property. There was plenty of room in the mansion for R&B to have their own rooms, but Alexis insisted on them sharing. She was worried about stalkers and slept easier knowing they were together—with a nanny on the sofa at the foot of their beds.

"Will you read us a bedtime story? Like when we were babies?" Blue asked, pushing out her lower lip.

"Of course we will," Alexis said. "And you're still our babies! You'll always be our babies."

She sat on one side of Blue, and Rich on the other. I sat Rhythm down, and he climbed up between Blue and his dad. I smiled at them and turned to walk out of the room.

"Hayden?" Alexis called after me.

"Yes?"

"Will you take a picture of us? I still don't have my phone."

"Of course!"

I spent so much time thinking about Alexis the superstar, Alexis the diva, Alexis the record-breaker, or even the Alexis with mental illness, I forgot that Alexis was also just Alexis—the mom to Rhythm and Blue.

Alexis grabbed the book and began reading. Rhythm and Blue struggled to keep their eyes open, and Rich began to drift off, too. To any other family, this was normal. But for her to share this moment with me felt special. She was being vulnerable, something I knew she hated. Before leaving the room, I took a dozen pictures, from her good side only. She asked me to text them to Samantha for her to post to Instagram.

I had no idea that the headlines the next morning would read, RICH AND ALEXIS—BACK TOGETHER. Nothing could be just for her. The moment that otherwise would have provided a sense of sweetness to living just *had* to be transformed into fodder. Samantha just didn't know when to quit.

THE "RECONCILIATION" WENT VIRAL, AND the public couldn't get enough. Alexis and Rich's Instagram comments were flooded, and their photos returned to the covers of the tabloids. I guess America loved seeing a family reunite. The unexpected attention also thrilled Samantha, and she began blatantly pushing for it, inviting Rich to every outing we had over the following week. And somehow the paparazzi knew exactly where we would be *every* night.

All the attention was distracting Alexis from her desire to reunite with Brody. But just in case it wasn't, Samantha filled the schedule with other dates—with billionaires, athletes, musicians, actors. She would get on the phone with their agent, and no one ever said no. It was that easy. Alexis played along, but somewhere deep down, Samantha knew Alexis was just appeasing her. So, when Alexis asked to go to dinner with Rich and the kids alone, Samantha organized a dinner with me, Amber, Vanessa, and Blair at Nobu to strategize.

"She's relaxed on asking me about Brody. But I still think we need to be a few steps ahead," Samantha announced to the table.

"Well, we are. We know every person she's been speaking with," Vanessa said.

"What do you mean?" I asked.

"When I replaced her phone, I bought two. Everything she does on hers comes to a back-up phone as well," Vanessa said.

"No, no, no." Samantha shook her head. "That's *grimy*. I told you to get rid of that phone, Vanessa. He's been ignoring her attempts anyway.

That restraining order really scared him. But I know what she's doing right now. She's acting like everything is okay, but she's not done with this guy. And if he comes back, we're *all* out of jobs."

I thought the job I had signed up for was one of fun, glamour, and travel—but it was really one of manipulation, betrayal, and mental illness. I felt like I was in the middle of some convoluted game of chess whose rules were bewildering to me.

Amber slammed her fists down on the table. "We need to stay ahead in the game!"

The game?

"She talked to me about firing you today," Samantha told Amber. "I've been trying to convince her otherwise. But for now, you really need to hustle and work your ass off. I thought she was completely out of it during mania, but she made a comment about how you're never at the house."

Amber's face turned red.

"I DARE HER, SAMANTHA! I fucking dare that bitch to fire me!" she spat. "I will take every penny she'll make for the rest of her goddamn miserable, crazy-person life!"

I sat uncomfortably, unable to believe the words coming out of her mouth. Amber's indifference to Alexis's needs had always been evident, but to speak so vitriolically about the woman who employed and trusted her when she was at her most vulnerable, shocked me. While I understood our working conditions were far from normal, I also knew we had an opportunity to turn things around.

"Samantha, I'm sorry. I know I'm still the new guy, but there's a right way to handle this. You did what you thought was right." I turned to address the entire table. "However, it's clear she's out of her manic episode now. I understand what the doctor said, and you know what? *He's right.* But Alexis is a grown woman. It's up to her how she wants to live her life."

The entire table scoffed at me.

"You don't know what you're talking about!" Vanessa said.

"You really don't," Blair agreed.

"I don't know what I'm talking about? I lived in the house with her for the past three weeks."

This group of people was not interested in trying to right any wrongs. They wanted revenge, and they wanted control.

"I am telling you right now, if Alexis even mentions firing me again, she is going to regret it!" Amber dug through her Louis Vuitton bag and grabbed her phone. She spent a minute scrolling. "I will sell this." She turned her phone toward the table. "Got it? Then I will buy myself a mansion in Beverly Hills, and Hayden, you can move into *my* guest house." She laughed.

Amber pressed play.

It was a video of Alexis. I immediately remembered the day she was wearing this bathrobe and trucker hat. The restaurant was loud and I couldn't hear what Alexis was saying, but it was clear Amber was filming without her knowledge—and during a manic episode. Amber followed her through the house. Upstairs, downstairs, upstairs, downstairs, and into her bedroom, where Amber stopped at the door. Suddenly, I came into frame. I had been picking up Alexis's clothing that had been strewn across the floor. When Alexis noticed me, she started undoing her robe. Out of her mind, Alexis pulled down her panties, exposing herself to me, and requested I get into her bed. Amber zoomed in on Alexis's naked body.

I knew how aggressively Alexis came on to me, and had to look away. I didn't just have to worry about leaving Amber alone with her, now I had to worry even when I was there. I had no idea Amber had been present. Samantha covered her face in disbelief, and Vanessa's laughter became deafening. She reached across the table and pressed pause.

"You need to hide this immediately, Amber," she said. "Do you realize what this could do for both you and Hayden? You could make a lot of money off this! I'll help you place it into a Dropbox so no one can find it."

I looked to Samantha, who shook her head disapprovingly. But instead of saying anything, she buried her face in her phone. Why wasn't she speaking up? Was she amused at having the potential leverage? Or was she merely allowing her sisters to speak of the vengeful fantasy, refusing to believe they would ever go through with it?

I was nauseous. I thought I might actually throw up. This wasn't a game. This wasn't just dark. This was *evil*. This was the twins' mom. How could Amber do this to her? Would she really do anything with it? Could I tell Alexis? And what would happen to *me* if I did?

CHAPTER EIGHT

"**D**o you know how embarrassed I felt telling my boss that the four dates he suggested for dinner wouldn't work for you?"

Grayson had enough. While he understood both the mania and depression sides of bipolar disorder, it was really hard to comprehend unless you witnessed it yourself. It also wasn't helping matters that, when I did get the opportunity to come home, I didn't want to talk about work. It was my break from the chaos. Initially he'd been understanding and concerned, but now that it was affecting something important to him, he'd completely lost his patience.

"But the fifth date he suggested worked. So, what's the problem? I'm doing the best I can, Gray. I understand this is nothing like what we thought it was going to be. But things are starting to turn around. Brody is out of the picture, she's back on her meds, and we'll be on the road before you know it."

"How is you being on the road going to help *us*? Don't you get it? You're not an assistant, you're a slave! You slept there for weeks during her mania, or whatever the fuck it's called—and now you're going to Vienna and Tel Aviv before tour? I get she has needs, but what about *me*? I barely see you when we live together, and now you're going to be gone for three months! We're supposed to get married this year. How will that work, Hayden? You're supposed to be my *husband* soon, and you're never here. You want me to marry a ghost?"

"What do you want me to do?" I said. "Tell me! What do you fucking want me to do?"

"I want you to quit," Grayson said, as if it was an obvious solution.

"You want me to *quit*? I have been waiting for an opportunity like this my entire life. I'm getting ready to travel the world—and you want me to *quit*?"

Grayson headed for the door.

"You're right," he said, turning around in the doorway. "You've been waiting for something like this your entire life. But now that you have it, are you even happy?"

I didn't know the answer to that. Despite my immediate defensiveness, I now realized how deeply my work was impacting him. All along I'd assumed he understood my absence as a necessary time of sacrifice to secure my dream job into a realized future, completely ignoring the havoc it was wreaking on my relationship in the meantime.

I hadn't even told him about what happened at dinner the night before. That wouldn't have made matters better. I didn't know what to do. Even after four months, I wasn't close with Alexis. We had special moments, sure. But these people had been around her for years. If I told her about the video, would she believe me? Or would she just confront everyone and turn them against me? I couldn't lose this job. I had never made this much money. But in order to keep it, was I going to have to compromise everything else in my life? My fiancé? My sanity? My morals?

I ARRIVED AT THE MANSION, disheveled and anxious, just after ten to find Amber in the kitchen with Noah.

"She's awake," Amber said, eyes wide.

"She's *awake*?" I sighed, bolstering myself. I double-checked the time on my iPhone. I had gotten so used to Alexis being asleep all day that I knew her being up this early meant something was awry.

"And on the phone with Regina."

I hadn't met Regina, but I knew she was Alexis's backup singer and self-proclaimed best friend of twenty years.

"I heard them talking about Brody, and when she saw me she looked nervous and asked me to go downstairs. Regina just landed at LAX. But why wouldn't Alexis tell any of us that she's coming? Why is it a secret? I mean, it's the twins' birthday tomorrow. But I swear something's up."

The gate phone rang. Noah answered, and he looked panicked. He buzzed her in. The two refused to greet her, so I headed for the door.

"Good luck, my dude!" he shouted after me.

What was there to be afraid of?

As I opened the door, there stood Regina—a heavyset black woman with magenta hair and a light mustache, who I recognized from the documentary. Before I could greet her, she said, "Who are you?" and examined me head to toe.

"Hi Regina, I'm Hayden!" I said. "Alexis's assistant."

I gave her a welcoming hug, knowing I couldn't trust what Amber said about anyone.

"Alexis said there was a room for me in the guest house. Will you show me the way?"

"Of course," I said, stepping around to take the lead.

"Well, aren't you going to carry my bags?"

There were two large black rolling suitcases and four duffle bags. She had no plans of leaving any time soon. With a forced smile, I threw two duffle bags over each shoulder, wheeled the two suitcases behind me, and led her to the bedroom where I often slept—wall to wall with Amber.

"Could you have one of the cleaning ladies unpack my bags? And have the chef make me some lunch?" Regina barely phrased it as a question, watching me struggle to carry her six large bags up the stairs.

"Absolutely," I breathed.

I led her back to the main house, passing Amber in the foyer. The two reluctantly smiled and nodded at one another, making it clear that neither was happy to see the other.

"Where's Alexis's room?" Regina asked.

I pointed toward the grand staircase. "It's the first door to the right."

Soon after she headed upstairs, Alexis shouted my name.

"Morning, beautiful!" I said, arriving breathless at her doorway.

"Hayden, we're celebrating the twins' holiday tomorrow at Disneyland. I need you to head there now to start setting up." She wanted privacy, which meant me out of the house. "Actually, why don't you just stay the night down there? There's a lot to do."

Great. This was exactly what I needed after my fight with Grayson.

"WHAT ARE YOU STILL DOING up here?" Samantha said, reprimanding Amber outside of Alexis's Disneyland hotel suite. "You need to be at Goofy's Kitchen, making sure everything is ready to go."

"Relax!" Amber said. "Everything is taken care of. I talked through every single detail with the party planner yesterday."

"I don't care what you told her *yesterday*. You should be down there double-checking and greeting the celebrity guests. I mean, you work for Alexis Shane for Christ's sake! There is no room for error, Amber! How are you so fucking lazy?"

Samantha wasn't wrong. It was like Amber just wanted to be an observer in the world of celebrity and money, but never really wanted to work. Simply put, she was replaceable.

Twenty minutes later, I walked into Goofy's Kitchen and spotted Vanessa in the back with her brows furrowed and her arms crossed.

"Where the hell is Amber?" she hissed. "Nothing is set up for the party! She should have been down here hours ago, and now her phone is off!"

Our designated area had no privacy, the tables were not set up, the cakes had not yet arrived, and there were no decorations. There was no evidence that we were having a birthday party.

I scoured the restaurant looking for a manager.

"I am so, so sorry," I told him, "but I need your help. My boss will be down here any minute, and nothing we requested is set up. We're supposed to have like tons of balloons, two cakes, the Disney characters greeting the kids as they arrive…"

"Sir, I'm sorry. But we were only told to hold the space. We were never given any instruction from your team besides that. We'll do our best to help, but it might be too short notice to accommodate everything."

While I didn't want to drive a further wedge between Amber and me, I needed Samantha to stall Alexis, so I called her.

"What's wrong now?" Samantha said upon answering.

"Please, *stay calm*. Listen to everything I say before you freak out. Okay?"

"Hayden, come on, what is it?"

Although I felt awkward telling her right after Amber claimed everything was set up, there was no other option. The notion of facing Alexis's wrath or losing any of her trust lit a perpetual fire under my ass. "Nothing has been set up down here. I need you to stall Alexis for twenty minutes while I pull this together."

But before I could even finish, Samantha was screaming at Amber.

"THIS WAS YOUR FUCKING RESPONSIBILITY! THIS IS SO EMBARRASSING! CAN'T YOU EVER JUST DO YOUR FUCKING JOB?"

SAMANTHA NOW SHOWED UP TO the office every morning—I assumed because she wanted to keep a watchful eye on Regina to make sure she wouldn't turn Alexis against her. As she took calls about promoting the upcoming summer tour, I flipped through the latest *US Weekly*.

Oh my God. I held out the magazine in disbelief. The paparazzi had gotten a shot of Alexis and me interlocking arms, walking out of E.P. & L.P. It was my first tabloid appearance. The headline read, ALEXIS SHANE THROWS DIVA'TUDE LEAVING HOLLYWOOD HOT SPOT.

The story was a complete lie, but who cares? I was in a tabloid, walking lockstep with my childhood idol. I couldn't wait to tell Oma. In fact, I was so excited I almost considered texting it to my dad.

"Hayden? *Hayden?* HAYDEN!" Samantha said, interrupting my daydream. "I need you to connect Vanessa and Kelly to the call."

I connected them and listened in on the conversation about how low the ticket sales for the tour still were. The shows had already been pushed, and now cancellation was a real possibility. I didn't get it. Alexis Shane's fans were *diehard*. If one bad performance turned them off forever, especially considering her frame of mind at the time, then they weren't true fans—or at the very least were incapable of seeing Alexis as anything other than some superhuman glambot.

"I hate to interrupt," I said, "but we're talking about canceling a tour, when no real press has been done. Like, what about *Call Her Daddy*? It's also a great way for her to talk about what happened at the Super Bowl. I mean, *everybody* loves a comeback story."

The line went silent, until Samantha spoke.

"You know what? Hayden's right. Vanessa, when we hang up, call Kelly directly and get a press schedule together before we have another one of these calls."

Amber rushed into the office, quietly closing the door behind her while waving an iPhone at us.

"Guys! I'm sorry. I've got another call coming in," Samantha said, and hung up. "What the fuck is this?"

"She just called the glam boys to come over *herself*," Amber whispered. "She never does that. Then she asked me to plug in her phone, but she didn't lock it. Look—Brody finally responded! They're talking again!"

"I don't want any part of this," I said, raising my hands and stepping away to sit at my desk.

Brody had sent Alexis a clip from *E! News* that covered her record deal party at E.P. & L.P. The clip focused on Blair and went on and on about how she was an integral part of Alexis's entourage. How they were best friends, selfie pals, and shopping buddies—followed by a montage of photos of the two together. "*Isn't this weird?*" he'd typed.

It *was* weird, and I knew it was because of Samantha.

While Samantha's whole message was about female empowerment, it wasn't Alexis's responsibility to make her daughter famous. Especially given that she wasn't in on it. Plus, what could this twelve-year-old be famous for? It's not like she was Shirley fucking Temple. Simultaneously, our Google Alerts went off.

"*FUCK!*" Samantha screamed.

The headline read, DID ALEXIS SHANE'S TEAM CONFISCATE HER PHONE?

"Brody fucking planted this! Alexis knows damn well why her phone was taken away, and now he's trying to force my hand."

Samantha had developed a reputation in the press for being cutthroat. As immediately after Alexis hired her, she fired her entire entourage. The former employees came forward and bashed Samantha for her inexperience when it came to managing a star of Alexis's magnitude. Samantha didn't help matters by playing up the role of bitchy manager for the documentary, and went on the attack against the NFL, blaming them for Alexis's lip-syncing snafu. She already looked crazy, and out of context, taking her phone away would make her look like a bonafide psychopath. But maybe the headline was so ridiculous no one would believe it? A forty-year-old superstar's phone taken away? *Yeah, right.* But it was true.

The gate phone rang, startling us.

"It's just glam," Amber said.

"Why did she call glam anyway? Where is she going?" Samantha asked. She hated not being in control.

"She's taking the twins to karate."

"Doesn't that sound at all suspicious to you? She's *never* been with the kids to karate."

An hour later, Alexis began whistling her way down the staircase; Amber vanished out the back office door.

"I'll see you guys in a few hours!" Alexis shouted, hurrying for the door.

Amber returned moments later with a grin on her face. She pressed mute on her phone, placed it on the glass desk, and then pressed speaker.

"Where the hell did you go?" Samantha asked.

"I called my second phone, then duct taped it underneath the passenger seat in the Escalade."

"Amber, what the fuck are you talking about?" Was I the only person without a second phone?

"Now we'll know what they're *really* up to," she said.

TWENTY MINUTES LATER, WE HEARD Alexis instructing security to take the kids into karate while she and Regina caught up in the car.

"I didn't want you to call from the house," Regina explained. "Because I honestly think it might be bugged. Who knows, the car could be too. Let's call Brody from outside."

While the house wasn't bugged, and neither was the car *normally*, Amber had become paranoid and was taking drastic measures due to the fear of losing her job.

"Jesus, this isn't all gonna go away, is it?" Samantha rubbed her temples with her fingers. "She told me last night she never had a manic episode, and accused me of making the whole thing up."

"What?" I interrupted. "Are you serious? Samantha, you can prove it. The doctors, the canceled meetings. Listen, I understand what you did and why you did it. But you took this too far. You should have let him come back when she asked. You need to make this right. You need to apologize."

Samantha looked down at the desk calendar.

"This shows every meeting for the past month, and it's all crossed out and moved around. She can't deny it, it's literally right here." She slapped her hands on the desk. "I'm also going to need to draw up a spreadsheet showing every deal I've set up for the year. She needs a visual of how much I bring in."

Samantha knew Brody was coming back with a vengeance, and the only thing Alexis cared about more than Brody was money.

TWO HOURS LATER, ALEXIS AND Regina returned.

"Hi, my beautiful girl!" Samantha greeted Alexis with her usual excitement. "Do the rest of you hooligans mind giving Alexis and me a little privacy? We have a few business things to discuss."

Regina returned to the guest house, and I joined Amber, huddling outside the office doors.

"You really upset me last night," Samantha said. "I know when you're not manic you don't like talking about it. But we can't just pretend like it didn't happen. Look at the schedule. We lost a whole month. It doesn't have to be like this. All you need to do is take your medication—and *no weed*."

"You just want to dull my shine," Alexis said.

"Why would I want that?"

"Samantha, you're right. I don't remember all of those days. I don't remember moving this whole schedule around. But I've been dealing with this my whole life. So, if I've made it this far, I think I'll be okay. But enough about work. I'm tired of talking about work."

"Okay."

"I'm not asking you to see Brody anymore. I'm telling you that I am. But he's refusing to meet me because you got the police involved."

"It wasn't me, Alexis."

"Either way, he's uncomfortable coming to the house being that the security team you hired locked him out. The only way he'll meet me is if *you* bring me to him. That way, he knows he won't be in any trouble. So, you're taking me to the Beverly Hills Hotel, *tonight*—and without security."

THE FOLLOWING AFTERNOON, SAMANTHA PICKED up Alexis and Amber. They were attending a creative meeting at Capitol Records about her next album.

A few hours later, I heard a commotion coming from the front yard.

I opened the door to see Mitch, the head of security, with a gun pointed at him by a six-foot-five black man with a perfect fade.

"Mitch! What the hell is going on?" I shouted, hiding behind the door. "Should I call the police?"

"Who are you?" the unfamiliar man shouted back.

"Alexis's assistant."

"I'm taking over security duties. Per Alexis's request. These guys have to go, *now*!"

"Put your fucking gun down, you lunatic!" Mitch shouted.

"Both of you, STOP! Just let me get her on the phone!"

After Alexis didn't answer, I dialed Samantha, my hands shaking with confusion at this mini coup d'état.

"Hayden, I see you keep calling Alexis! We're just recapping the meeting in my car. Can it wait?"

The clarity in Alexis and Amber's voices in the background told me I was again on speaker.

"No! No! NO! Some guy just showed up and pulled a gun on Mitch. He's saying he's the new security. Does Alexis know this guy? Do I call the police?"

The line went silent, until I heard a loud sigh from Alexis.

"Do you know anything about this?" Samantha asked her.

"Hayden, he's right," Alexis said. "I'm having the security replaced."

"Why would you do that?" Samantha asked. "Is it Big Wayne? If you wanted your old security back, why didn't you just tell me?"

I hung up. It was because of Brody. I walked outside to let the guys know that it was true, and watched Mitch and his guards leave.

"Sorry we have to meet this way. I'm Wayne," the new head of security said. He nudged past me to enter the mansion. "First things first, I need to check the house."

I started following him, but he held up his hand to stop me.

"Excuse me, I don't need your help."

"I know, I'm just—I'm not supposed to leave anyone alone."

"I've known the woman for twenty years, man."

I walked back to the front door to close it—and there stood Brody.

"What's up buddy?" he said, dropping his Gucci duffle inside the door. The king consort was back at last, ready to devour the fruits of Alexis's labor once again as if he had never gone. Immediately he lit up a joint and started looking through the contents of the refrigerator. I shook my head, ready for the meltdown to continue.

CHAPTER NINE

"I need you to do something for me," Alexis said. She stood with her hands on her hips, resuming her position as the boss. She and Samantha were having an impromptu meeting in the office after returning to the mansion. Upon the sight of Samantha, Brody stomped upstairs to lock himself in the bedroom like a child throwing a tantrum. "Brody is obviously very upset about all of the negative press. So, we need to start clearing his name."

Samantha was desperate to appease her. "Of course, Alexis. Whatever you want!"

"Well to start, everyone needs to know we're 'back together,'" she said, using air quotes. "Why don't you have the paparazzi stumble upon us at Runyon tomorrow?"

"I know you want to do this right away, but you're a *legend*. This moment should be utilized to create something viral," Samantha said. She took a minute to brainstorm. "How 'bout this? We're kicking off the tour in Las Vegas, right after Europe. What if Brody carried you out on his shoulder at the beginning of the show? Now *that's* something that would have people talking!"

"I guess," Alexis contemplated, "but that's still weeks away, and we both want this over and done with as soon as possible. Just arrange for them to photograph us leaving Mastro's tonight. *Please*, Samantha."

"Okay, *okay*. But let's keep the paparazzi out of it. We can just have Hayden go. He can discretely photograph you guys from inside the restaurant. That way, it looks like a fan spotted you, instead of going the Kardashian route."

While it was the bleakest of the options to me, Alexis loved it. And I can't lie, it was exciting to be included in this scripted moment.

When I arrived at Mastro's, I headed for the restroom and spotted Alexis and Brody. Of course, it was impossible to miss her. I stopped halfway there, requesting a table where I could inconspicuously photograph them. I then waited for her cue.

"Kiss me," she mouthed to Brody.

I began snapping away.

Brody wrapped his arm around her as she leaned to whisper in his ear. He picked up his fork, twirled pasta, and fed it to her. It looked so contrived that I myself was suffering from secondhand embarrassment.

Alexis pulled out her phone and began texting. My phone pinged.

"*Can you take one more of us kissing, but with flash?*"

Flash? The queen of lighting wanted flash. This was something I would never normally do. But for her, I'd do anything. I cringed, anticipating every head to turn, as my flash went off.

"What the hell are you doing?" a deep-voiced man shouted.

The flash hadn't turned heads, but his voice did. Big Wayne chased me to the restroom. It would have been nice if someone could have filled him in.

The headlines that evening read, ALEXIS SHANE GETS COZY WITH EX-BOY TOY.

THE COMMENTS ON THE BLOGS were brutal—my favorite was, "*Feed me the dinner that I paid for.*" I knew it made Samantha feel vindicated in a sense. But more importantly, with Brody back, she knew she had to prove her worth. The income spreadsheet was a start, but she needed more. And what does every artist want besides money? Awards.

While Alexis had thirty-two Grammy awards, more than any other artist in history, it had always been a dream of hers to win an Academy Award for Best Original Song.

Samantha now had a goal and sat tirelessly on calls with agents to book meetings with every studio head from Universal, Sony, Warner Brothers, and Fox. However, our agent wanted to slow Samantha down, unconvinced that with Alexis's history of tardiness and cancellations she'd make it to all the meetings in the same week. He was sure Alexis would bail and wasn't willing to put his neck on the line—because when you burn a bridge with a studio head, the damage is irreparable.

"I will get her there. That's my job," Samantha said. "Now I'm not going to ask you again. Book the fucking meetings, or I'll replace you with an agent who will."

True to her word, Samantha and Alexis met with every studio that week, and Samantha's idea was working as my email was flooded with options of movies to be scored, and theme songs to be written. Each enthusiastically thanked Alexis for taking the time to meet. Alexis even thanked Samantha herself, something I had never heard her do.

"I've never had someone take me into all the studios like that, in all my career," she said as we were leaving Fox. "Thank you."

"Alexis Shane!" a familiar British voice shouted. I turned to find Simon Cowell. "You look *gorgeous*!" He walked toward her from the parking lot, his white veneers glistening in the LA sun. His chest hair was even more aggressive in person, peeking out from his V-neck shirt collar.

"Simon!" Alexis cooed, before air-kissing each cheek.

"I haven't seen you in *forever*. How have you been doing, Miss Diva?"

"Oh, you know. I'm just out here, living the glamorous showbiz life," Alexis said in her signature tone. "How are you doing, handsome?"

It was bizarre seeing two celebrities interact, like watching animals in a zoo.

"I'm doing great! I just got back from the Bahamas, and we're getting ready to film my new singing competition show here on Fox." After the success of *American Idol*, he'd tried to replicate it with *The X Factor* and failed. I wondered why they were giving him yet another shot. "I know people ask you to do favors all the time, and I know you've said you'll never be a judge on one of these shows. But—would you consider being a *guest* judge? We're planning a diva-themed episode, and everybody knows there is no bigger diva than Alexis Shane!"

"Of course she will!" Samantha interrupted. "As long as we can promote her tour!"

I WAS SURPRISED TO FIND Alexis in the formal sitting room by the piano when I arrived at the mansion on filming day for her guest judge spot. She was finished with hair and makeup, but not yet dressed, wearing an ivory La Perla silk robe.

"Hi Hayden!" she said as I closed the front door behind me. "Could you come upstairs and help me with something before the stylist gets here?"

I followed her upstairs into her dressing room, excited that she requested *me*. Alexis slid open a drawer and pulled out a corset. "Will you help me get this on?" she asked. "It needs to be *tight*. Any time I have Amber do it, it just isn't tight enough."

Alexis untied her robe, and I watched it fall to her ankles. She stood only in a black lace Agent Provocateur bra with matching panties. Seeing her almost nude body reminded me of her advances during mania. I wondered if she had any recollection of that at all, but the casual way she looked at me made it seem like she had no idea. She was gaining weight, but not enough to be able to tell when dressed. I took the corset from her hands, wrapped it around her body, and fastened the metal clasps a dozen times down the front. She then turned, her back facing me.

"Just let me know if it gets too tight," I said, pulling the laces as she gripped the vanity. I pulled tighter and tighter, waiting for instruction to stop, but it never came.

"This is *perfect*." She admired her now tiny waistline in a floor-length mirror. There was no way she could actually breathe in that thing.

Once the stylist arrived, I headed down the hidden staircase for the kitchen. Grabbing the door handle, I heard Amber on the phone.

"He is such a fucking bitch! I *always* tie her corset! Every single day, and then he comes along. Like, who does he think he is? And why would she let him? Do you think she was going to ask me, and then he just insisted on doing it himself?"

I pushed open the door to see Amber's face turn white. She fumbled with her phone in an attempt to hang up.

"What's going on?" I said. "Is everything okay?"

She was unwilling to make eye contact. "The vibe is just *off* today."

"What are you talking about?"

"Well, I mean. Like, is everything okay with Samantha?"

"What do you mean?"

"I've been calling her all morning, and she hasn't responded once. We *always* talk every morning. Then I walk upstairs, and *you* are tying

Alexis's corset?"

"Yeah, I heard you on the phone. I don't know what to tell you. When I walked in, Alexis just asked me to do it. I was the closest person to her. I didn't realize it was *your* thing. And Samantha's been in meetings all morning about launching an Academy Award campaign, so I really don't think it's anything personal. You're overthinking things."

"Academy Award campaign? How come I haven't heard anything about this? Samantha told you, and not me?"

She was so paranoid. She thought that not only was I taking her place with Alexis, but with Samantha too. What she didn't realize was the only thing she needed to do to get attention and approval was her job. If all this was news to her, clearly she wasn't involving herself enough. Before I could respond, Alexis walked in with the glam gays chasing closely behind.

I was speechless for a second, as I'd never seen her—or, indeed, anyone—look so beautiful. Her hair was beachy, long, and wavy. Her makeup was flawless, and she wore a beige Tom Ford leather mini dress that looked stunning against her chocolate skin, with her décolletage covered in diamonds.

"Alexis, you look *gorgeous*! Like a movie star!" I said, examining her from head to toe.

"Are you sure? The sleeves on this are okay?" she said and frowned, fidgeting.

Her perception of herself was distorted. She thought when she dressed like a whore on Hollywood Boulevard, she looked her best, and was insecure any time she was even a little bit covered. But still, she knew there was a difference between when I told her she looked beautiful and other people did. I said it when I meant it; others used it as a greeting.

While she looked incredible, the corset and leather combination made it difficult to move, or even breathe. She wanted to sit down, but couldn't on her own. The scene began to look like *Weekend at Bernie's* as the gay-tourage and I tilted her backward in a trust fall to lay her at a thirty-degree angle in the closest chair. Lion ran behind us, delicately moving her hair out of the way to cascade down the back of the chair. I tried not to laugh.

"Alexis, are you sure you don't want me to loosen it a little?" I said.

"No, no," she groaned. "My waist looks *amazing*."

An hour after we were supposed to leave, we circled Alexis to lift her. I wrapped an arm of hers around my neck, and the other went around Big Wayne. Again, we repeated this after pulling into the studio lot—this time with an entire production staff staring.

We laid Alexis out like a corpse on one of the sofas in her dressing room, and now knowing better, I lifted her hair over the armrest. She groaned as I tucked pillows around her.

"I hate coming to these things!" she whined. "They tell you to be here, then they make you wait around for *hours*. Like, just give me an actual call time! This is *abusive*!"

The irony of her complaining about other people's tardiness was too precious to draw attention to. I simply clucked along and agreed, knowing she would have felt less *abused* if her waist hadn't been squeezed into half its size. Just as Samantha arrived, my phone started ringing with a call from the new home security team.

It's not an emergency," he said. "I just wanted to let Alexis know *a lot* of flowers were delivered. Like, fifty arrangements or so. All white roses. Are we hosting a wedding here I don't know about?"

"Does it say who they're from?" I asked. Samantha was now staring.

"I'm not sure exactly. Each arrangement is just signed, 'MKHB'."

"Does MKHB mean anything to you?" I asked Alexis as I hung up.

"*Fifty* arrangements? And who is 'MKHB'?" Samantha interrogated.

"It's personal!" Alexis blushed, still lying out like a corpse. "I don't want to talk about it in a room full of people, Samantha."

When it was finally time for Alexis to appear in front of the audience as the guest judge, we walked toward the stage in a herd. We were guided into a black curtained box with television monitors inside. I held Alexis's Birkin and watched as the glam squad did last-minute touchups.

"We're ready for you, Alexis," the producer said, peeking in.

Big Wayne held Alexis by the hand and guided her up the steps to the stage. We stayed in place to watch Alexis from the monitors.

Simon appeared on the screen and shouted, "THIS WEEK'S THEME IS... DIVAS!"

The large screens behind him displayed images of a variety of divas. But one at a time, they would fade away, replaced with one of Alexis. Then her longest-running number one single blared out through the studio.

Goosebumps covered my body as the entire audience sang along. Simon laughed and then teased them, "Ladies and gentlemen, *ALEXIS SHANE!*"

The contestants in the front row laughed, sure Alexis Shane was not there. But she was, and she knew exactly what she was doing. She paused to play up the joke, then walked out unexpectedly. The contestants and audience screamed, hugging one another in disbelief. Whenever she stood before a crowd, they reacted so strongly to her—a beautiful symbiosis that proved how pivotal she had been in so many lives. Cameras panned in on audience members' eyes filling up with tears. Participants even got on their knees to bow, as if Alexis were a queen—because to them, she was.

The audience chanted, "*ALEXIS! ALEXIS! ALEXIS!*"

Simon turned to her. "Alexis, your music has been the soundtrack to all our lives. There is no greater diva than you, and we're just so grateful for your gift. Thank you so much for being here."

I knew she needed to hear that.

In that moment, I completely forgot everything that had happened in the past few months. I forgot about her being mean. I forgot about the boyfriend drama, the manager drama, the bipolar disorder. I remembered Alexis was a star, a legend, a woman whose music had touched the lives of millions of people—and I felt honored to be working for her.

"SO, WHAT DOES MKHB MEAN?" I asked Samantha on my drive to Alexis's the next morning.

"I can't tell you!" she said, and quickly tried to change the subject.

"Oh, God. You do know! Come on. You've trusted me with a lot more than MKHB."

"Mwah, kisses, hugs, baby. I guess it's the sign-off that Rich's mom uses with her husband, and Alexis thought it was hilarious. So, Rich and Alexis have used it ever since."

"The flowers are from *Rich*? Jesus, guys are so fucking moronic. Of course Brody comes back and he pulls that. He had a window, and he should have tried harder if he really wanted to be with her."

"Oh, *please*! If Rich wanted to be with her, he would. We just did it to intimidate Brody," she said, laughing.

I paused. "What do you mean, *we*?"

"What are you, *slow*? Rich and I came up with the idea together."

With how much work we had to do, Samantha somehow always managed to schedule time for scheming. I guess Rich had enough time to mess around too, despite hosting several television shows.

"Anyway, I'll be at the house soon," she said. "Don't forget to remind me to update the schedule," Samantha said. "Universal has officially hired her to record the theme song for their big holiday picture, *Hope*."

"Wait, *seriously*?"

"This is what happens when you get out of bed, Hayden. Oh, and we're gonna jet up to San Francisco this weekend too. Because, on top of the theme song, they're considering using mine and Alexis's production company. They're hosting a fundraiser there, so I think it's important for us to show face. Make it known we're serious, you know? We'll need you to advance."

"Advance?"

"Yeah, fly ahead of us. Alexis has a rider, and the hotel will take care of most of it before you get there. But when you do, you'll do a walk-through of her suite and the twins' room to make sure everything's in place. Whatever they forget, or don't take care of, is your responsibility."

"Is Brody coming?"

"Who cares? Alexis hasn't mentioned it."

"Well, why don't you take advantage of this opportunity to extend an olive branch? You should invite him. I'm sure that would make Alexis happy."

"Hold on, that's Vanessa beeping in." The line went silent for a second, before Samantha merged our calls. "Vanessa, I have Hayden on the line. I need you to book his flight and hotel room for San Francisco."

"Hayden is traveling with us now?" she asked, not caring that I could hear.

"Is there a problem with that?" Samantha said. "He's going to advance, and you'll double-check his work since it's his first time on the road. Also, I want you to be prepared for Brody to join us. I might try and mend fences."

"Samantha, no! I don't agree with this. We should not *befriend* Brody; we should be working harder than ever to get rid of him! Don't you see we're going to be outnumbered soon? Regina's back, Big Wayne, and now Brody? If we don't make a big move first, they're coming for us."

Make a big move first? Coming for us? Vanessa and Amber really believed they were living in *Game of Thrones*. Even listening to them was exhausting. How could they exist in a world where every person was potentially an enemy?

"Vanessa, I don't have time for this right now!" Samantha said. "I'm actually *working*, okay? Just book Hayden's travel."

Vanessa abruptly hung up.

"God, she can be such a bitch. Hayden, are you still there?"

"Samantha, you've been playing offense at the suggestion of your sisters, and it hasn't been working. Don't you see? Regina and Big Wayne are Alexis's best friends. What have you been thinking trying to push them away? You need to start embracing them. You need to be the one making everyone feel like a team!"

"I got it, Hayden. I hear you," she said in a desultory tone.

"I'm not sure you do, Samantha. Because we still haven't even talked about what happened at that dinner," I paused. "You know, *about the video*."

Samantha went silent.

"You need to make sure Amber gets rid of it," I continued. "I'm serious. Because if anyone finds out, it's not just her who is going to be fired. Or sued."

"Hayden, *please*! They aren't going to do anything with it. And if they try, I'll stop them! You think I'm just going to let my sisters ruin my career? My reputation?" Samantha scoffed. "I've got it under control. Now when you see Brody today, just let him know I asked if he would like to come with us. Okay?"

I LANDED IN SAN FRANCISCO feeling like Alexis myself, carrying my Louis Vuitton duffle to meet the driver holding a sign adorned with my last name. I checked into the Four Seasons using her alias, Bette Davis, and pulled up my email from Vanessa, which had the rider attached.

I reviewed it as the concierge led me to the fourteenth floor, and *honestly*, it wasn't bad considering all the rumors I'd read. One report mentioned she liked kittens delivered to her room to cuddle with. Apparently, that was a lie. I was only mildly disappointed.

My jaw dropped as the concierge opened the double doors to Alexis's suite. It wasn't just bigger than my apartment—it was bigger than my entire apartment *building*. There were three floors, each with its own bedroom, and a breathtaking view overlooking all of San Francisco.

"Is that—" I said, pointing to the floor-to-ceiling windows.

"The Giants' ballpark? Yes, it is," the concierge confirmed.

"Where Kanye proposed to Kim?"

"Yes, that was there," he chuckled. "Alright, so here are the keys. Everything on the rider was taken care of, except we couldn't find the flavors of La Croix she prefers, and we can't light candles in here. Unfortunately, they're a fire hazard. Oh, and I'll have the vegan cheese platter delivered just before her arrival—to keep it fresh."

As if I was going to let a fire hazard stop me.

When I finished double-checking the rooms, Vanessa arrived, Apple TV in hand. Five months in, and I was still trying to figure out exactly what she did. She called herself a tour manager, but to me, she just seemed like another entitled assistant who made appearances only when it was convenient for her. I wondered how much she was getting paid.

"Thank you so much!" I said, assuming it was to hand off. "Will you show me how to set it up?"

"This is *my thing*." She nudged past me. "I created this traveling Apple TV box to set up in hotel rooms. It overrides the password-protected wi-fi."

Wanting credit for something so silly made me laugh, but I was happy to give it to her. She needed this minute task to feel needed by a worldwide superstar. "My flight was *so* delayed!" I said, trying to lighten the mood. "Was yours?"

"Yes, because I guess there was a gay member of ISIS flying here to San Francisco," she teased.

"Oh, you're so funny," I laughed. "Do you wanna triple-check the room, see if I missed anything?"

"I already see you have." She walked toward the windows. "Now this is *important*. Alexis does not like to see any daylight when she walks in. So, you always need to close *all* of the curtains."

When Alexis's jet landed, I returned to her suite with the LimonCello La Croix and three-hundred-dollar Diptyque candles. I accepted the vegan cheese platter from room service, turned on the humidifiers, and poured a glass of her favorite Pinot Grigio. I beamed out at the room, feeling exhausted and proud. There was something meaningful about familiarizing myself with Alexis's quiddities and slowly getting to know her.

"Hayden, you're going to advance to the dinner tonight too," Samantha said without a 'hello'. "Greet all of the executives as they arrive, and please memorize their names so Alexis and I don't waste our time talking to nobodies."

"Hey, where are you?" Grayson spoke rapidly into the phone, out of breath. "You left before I was up this morning and now I'm home and you're still not here. Are we gonna Uber together, or are you meeting me at Tower Bar, or...?"

I continued buttoning my shirt in the hotel room, unsure what he was rambling about. And then it dawned on me.

FUCK!

It was the night of Grayson's dinner with his boss, where we were to celebrate his promotion. I had completely forgotten.

"Babe..." I began, shaking, "I'm... I'm so sorry." I felt sick.

"You've gotta be fucking kidding me," Grayson said. "Where are you?"

"I'm..." I hesitated. "In San Francisco."

Grayson was silent.

"I'm so sorry," I said. "I just—"

"You just forgot," Grayson interrupted. "You just forgot about what I have been working so hard for, for the past five years. You forgot."

I did forget. And I had no excuse. His boss had scheduled the dinner to accommodate my own after four failed attempts, and I was now a no-show. I'd humiliated him, and there was nothing I could say to fix it. He was silent on the other end of the line as I struggled to find something to stay.

"You know what, Hayden? We really should rethink this wedding. I'm not sure I know you anymore."

A high-end Italian restaurant was holding the charity event in a private, sexy, second-story room with dim red lights and our own personal bartender. I stood by the hostess stand holding back tears, listening for anyone who was attending. I'd then interrupt and introduce myself, explaining who I worked for as I guided the way, feigning an easy spirit as my chest rolled in on itself, ready to burst at any moment.

This is what I wanted, isn't it?

After an hour of painful introductions, a Mercedes Sprinter van pulled out front. The door slid open, and Brody emerged with Alexis in hand. I ran into the brisk San Francisco night to greet them.

"Hi, you two!" I said with forced enthusiasm.

But Brody tugged Alexis right past me.

"What was that about?" I asked as Samantha exited the Sprinter. Her thigh-high Christian Louboutin boots meant she needed assistance in stepping out.

"I have a weird feeling, Hayden," she said.

I felt the same, but didn't want to fan the flames.

"Just do your best to be kind, and have fun," I said, leading Samantha into the restaurant.

But when we walked into the private room, Brody was leading Alexis around and introducing her to everyone as if *he* were her manager.

Samantha didn't let it bother her, instead asking me to point out the CFO so she could plant herself next to him. While she, of course, wanted Alexis to make the appearance—she was really there to get face time with him, to sell him on using their production company. People thought she was crazy, but she was just hardworking and unwilling to miss an opportunity. With Alexis's name and Samantha's determination, it wasn't a hard sell. To seal the deal, she pulled Alexis from Brody.

"Let's go downstairs so we can talk in private for a moment," Samantha suggested to the two, knowing it would enrage Brody.

As the ladies walked downstairs, he confronted me.

"Where are they going?" he said.

"Just downstairs. He's the CFO of Universal. It's something about *Hope*."

"You're a *liar*," Brody said. He began to pace, furiously texting for Alexis to return, pouting like a petulant child.

I'd been trying to make a nice guy out of this sociopath. He only wanted to be in this room full of deep pockets for his own advantage. But with Alexis downstairs, he didn't matter to anyone—and he knew it.

"911
EMERGENCY!
COME TO MY ROOM!"

The next morning, frantic text after frantic text came through from Samantha in a group chat with Amber, Vanessa, and me. We hurried to her suite.

"What's going on?" I asked Blair, as Samantha wrapped up a call. I had never seen her face so pale.

But before elaborating, Samantha instructed Vanessa to check outside the door to make sure no one was listening.

"I just got a call from *TMZ*," she said. "A credible source called to inform them I was getting fired, and they wanted my comment."

"I told you Brody never should have come!" Vanessa said.

The room erupted into chaos, everyone trying to speak over one another.

"*EVERYBODY SHUT UP!*" Amber shouted. "I already know! When she went into glam this morning, I went through her phone. There's a group message between her, Brody, and a lawyer."

Amber had taken photos of the messages and passed her phone around the room. The dates confirmed that the night Samantha had dropped Alexis off at the Beverly Hills Hotel to reunite with Brody, he had taken her to meet a lawyer. He was convinced Samantha had power of attorney over Alexis.

"Power of attorney? Is he fucking stupid?" Samantha said.

TMZ's source was reliable, but with Samantha's negotiation skills, they were willing to trade out the story for an exclusive about Alexis's new song and major motion picture deal. The article would be a dick punch to Brody, showing Alexis and Samantha's strength as a duo. It was incredible what she was capable of when backed into a corner—a true alchemist.

The headline read, ALEXIS SHANE AND MANAGER'S PRODUCTION COMPANY PREPARES FOR FIRST MAJOR MOTION PICTURE.

"Let's see how the boy toy likes this one," Samantha said, smiling triumphantly. She glowed whenever she knew she had won a round in this "game".

"I KNOW YOU MET WITH a lawyer," Samantha said, confronting Alexis once they were finally alone, back in the home office that evening. "*TMZ* called for my comment on you firing me. Why are you handling things like this? If you don't want to work together anymore, just tell me."

Alexis was silent.

"Listen, you have this all wrong. I don't have *power of attorney* over you. Do you realize how ridiculous that sounds? Yes, I've definitely had to make decisions for you when you've been unable to. I mean, you have children to look after, and I know you don't want me going to Rich…"

Samantha started to cry, feeling betrayed by the woman she had been so desperately trying to protect. Dark rills of mascara trickled down her face. Alexis looked away guiltily, nervously pulling at her fingers.

"You think I did what I did because I hate Brody? I don't give a *fuck* about Brody. I did what I did to *protect you*."

"I'm sorry," Alexis finally whimpered, forcing out tears. "Brody told me you must have that to be making decisions for me."

"I've been making decisions to *help* you! Based on your doctor's orders! Don't you think you would *know* if someone had power of attorney over you? He has no clue what he's talking about. He's like a child playing grown-up. He has no clue how the world works."

Alexis became confused, and was now genuinely crying, unsure who to believe.

"I'm sorry," she stammered, biting her lip. "I just don't know. He told me…"

Suddenly Samantha's text message alert went off.

"And what the fuck is *this*?" she said, holding out her phone for Alexis to read.

It was a screenshot from Brody's Instagram—a photo of him holding a gun at a shooting range. The caption read, "*It's true, redheads are crazy.*"

"Do you want to try and tell me this has nothing to do with me?" Samantha said, grabbing a lock of her red hair.

"I don't know, Samantha," Alexis sighed, looking away. Sometimes, she had the shy mannerisms of a teenager.

"Okay. Well, I'm suing him, Alexis. How 'bout that? I'm fucking suing him for torturous interference, so that he doesn't pull this shit again. You know, I invited him to San Francisco with every intention of starting fresh. But now he's interfering with my livelihood. Do you think I couldn't tell what was happening when we were there? Do you really want a backup dancer *managing* you?"

Alexis confessed that Brody was, in fact, trying to manage her. So, first thing the next morning, he was served a cease-and-desist letter from the most feared litigator in all of Beverly Hills. To avoid a lawsuit, he was required to put in writing that the accusations he made were unsubstantiated. He shouldn't have been so arrogant, as I learned, to ever count Samantha out.

"LISTEN," SAMANTHA TOLD ME, "AFTER this call about the Netflix show, I need you to decorate the recording studio downstairs with Christmas decorations. It'll get Alexis in the spirit to lay this track."

The days leading up to leaving for Europe were packed, and Alexis had still yet to record the theme song to the film, *Hope*. It had to be done before we left, as we'd be on the road for the next three months.

"Of course," I said. "Are there decorations in the garage?"

"No. You'll have to go shopping."

No problem, it was only *June*.

I zoned out, wondering where I was going to get Christmas decorations. Wandering out to the guest house, I found Amber in her room with Blair, both trying on clothes that were clearly meant for Alexis.

"There's a guy I use now for decorating," Amber said. "His nickname is actually Mr. Christmas. He decorates movie sets."

"Is he expensive though?"

"Who cares? Are you paying? Do you really want to run around to ten stores and have them dig through the back to save *her* a dollar?"

Amber led the way outside to make the call. But we spotted Regina hiding in the corner of the property, whispering into her phone. Thinking we hadn't seen her, she hid further behind two metallic gold cars I'd never seen—a Lamborghini and a Bentley.

"What in the hell is going on now?" I said. "Why is she hiding? And where did those cars come from?"

"Regina told me the house might be bugged after Samantha found out about the lawyer," Amber chuckled. "She's such a stupid idiot. She doesn't realize *I'm* the bug."

"And the cars?"

"Rich dropped them off for the kids to play with. It's his version of a dick-measuring contest, I guess. He's still trying to fuck with Brody."

"To play with? They're *seven years old*." So he could drop off a few luxury cars for his tots but was incapable of spending more than a few hours at a time with them every few months.

MR. CHRISTMAS DELIVERED MUCH MORE than I'd anticipated: three large trees, lighting, garlands, ornaments, stockings, and even holiday-scented candles. The ambiance was set up for whatever inspiration was needed, and being the queen of all things festive, I knew she'd love it. Alexis gasped as she walked in, spinning slowly around.

"Hayden, this looks *incredible*," she said.

"I'll let you get to it." I smiled, excited for her to use the recording studio for the first time since moving in.

"I actually have the chorus written. Can I sing it for you?" She avoided eye contact. I noticed her skin seemed flushed, and she was fidgeting with her hands. Was she *nervous*?

Five months in, and I hadn't even realized that I'd yet to hear my boss—so famous for singing—actually sing. And *I* was about to be the first person to hear a song she'd written. I stood in awe, unable to fathom what was about to happen; that the superhero of my youth was about to share this singular moment with *me*. I clenched my teeth with nervous excitement as she took a deep breath and began to sing, the honey-rich smoke of her voice blooming softly into the room.

"Hope is a thread, that won't ever break
Even in the dark, it learns how to wait
The sky doesn't open for those who let go
But if you hold on, the stars start to glow
Every shadow fades when the morning arrives
Hope is the fire that keeps you alive."

I stood in silence, my hands covering my mouth, until she looked up with amused suspicion. Knowing I was the *first* to hear those words, they rang deeply through me, alighting my body with goosebumps. I couldn't speak, continuing to stand there and glisten with adoration. Here was the voice I'd cherished since my boyhood, who I'd listen to in low volumes beneath the covers so my dad wouldn't hear. The angel on the radio was now a living, breathing, beautiful woman who'd just opened up a tiny piece of her heart to me. She let out an uncomfortable laugh. "So... what do you think?"

What do I think? Why does she even care *what I think?* Alexis Shane wasn't like most pop stars. She'd written almost her entire catalog. She had thirty-two Grammy awards. She was *worshipped* by millions of people. But it made me so happy to see her vulnerability. Even if only for a second. "I don't know what to say. I mean, when I hear your music... I see who you really are," I said.

Alexis grinned from ear to ear, her eyes widening. She looked truly happy.

"And I mean, *hello*! I'm the first gay to hear it! I'm having a full-blown homosexual heart attack over here!"

For the first time ever, I made Alexis laugh.

Like, *really* laugh.

CHAPTER TEN

"**D**ude!" Karen said. She was on a conference call with Samantha and me. "I just got the background check on this new assistant, the one Regina referred. She's *sixty years old* and was a security guard at Nordstrom! Should I just tell Alexis we can get rid of security now that she has an assistant who can do both?"

The two were cracking up when my iPhone lit up with a text from Alexis.

"Can you print off the new merchandise deck and bring it to the glam room?"

Seeing her name emblazoned across my screen still intoxicated me. I smiled at the message, remembering it hadn't been that long ago when I'd been forbidden from the glam room. Each time I was granted a little further access into her world, I was overcome with childish joy, and it reminded me that all my time and anxiety were worth it. That is until the message had been cleared and I saw my phone's wallpaper—a photo of Grayson the day he proposed. He had been ice cold since my return from San Francisco and I was wracking my brain on how I could possibly make up my absence to him.

Upstairs, I watched as Alexis flipped through the deck. I'd been designing the products with her merchandise team in the mornings, before she woke up. She wrote her initials on what was approved.

"These hoodies are *amazing*, Hayden. And I love the phone cases too. You did such a great job. But the photos still need to be sent to Skeleton before everything goes into production."

"Skeleton?"

"Boys, will you step out for a minute?" Alexis asked Dylan and Lion. Lion closed the door behind them.

"Skeleton is the Photoshop *master*. Let me show you. See here? They will fix the toes right there, bring my waist in here, make my arm thinner there, bring in my chin here."

Alexis circled all the areas that made her self-conscious. She was comfortable with me now. This was a huge deal considering the picture-perfect obsession that drove her to endure two hours of makeup every day, which looked more like an assault, with three men gathered around her, poking at her eyes and cheeks and pulling at her hair.

"Also, I'm sure you heard we have a new assistant coming with us to Europe. I just want to make sure you know it's nothing to worry about."

"Thanks, I appreciate you saying that," I said, knowing she meant it, though of course a new assistant would mean yet another reason for the Fox sisters to freak the fuck out.

"How is everything else going? Is there anything you need to talk to me about?"

The memory of Amber's video recording flashed before my eyes. Here was a window of opportunity, but I couldn't take it. The boys were outside the door, and she seemed *happy* now. I didn't want to ruin that. Not to mention we were hours away from leaving the country. *I just need to find a way to delete the video myself.*

"The only thing that could really help is a company card. Especially being that we're going on the road. I need to buy things to set up and I just don't have the money to keep buying things and then waiting to be—"

"So, what's the problem? Just call Karen and she'll have a card overnighted. Oh, and also," she now whispered, "Dylan and Lion are coming with us, but the day of the photoshoot in Tel Aviv, I'm having Sebastian fly out. I love Dylan, but it's an international campaign. Will you give him the heads-up? I don't want him to be blindsided."

I nodded solemnly. Great, I was going to have to tell my work crush he was taking a backseat to *Sebastian McGrath*. Sebastian was a world-renowned makeup artist who owned a successful cosmetics line and had a twenty-year history with Alexis. Gays in the beauty industry aspired to be him. While Alexis was with Mark Kauffman, she had Sebastian on payroll. But given that his day rate was ten thousand dollars, she returned to only using him when jobs would foot the bill.

A few hours later, when the boys finished glam, they descended the staircase. I stopped Dylan on his way to the door.

"Are you excited for Europe?" I said.

"I am! But no drinking for me on this trip," he said. "I'm trying to get back in shape."

There was nothing more annoying than when a muscle gay made that statement.

"I just wanted to give you a heads-up that while you're doing Alexis's glam for almost all of Europe, for the photo shoot in Tel Aviv she's having Sebastian fly out."

Dylan's very pronounced jawline clenched.

"I mean, I'm still going to need to be paid for that day. It's not like I'll be booking jobs while we're on the other side of the world," he said.

"Of course. I'm sure she realizes that."

He was trying to keep his cool but couldn't.

"It's just *so annoying*. I'm good enough for Kim Kardashian and Beyoncé to use on major shoots, but not Alexis?"

"I'm sorry," I sighed, at a loss for what to say. "But it's what she wants."

I'd pushed through months of drama just waiting for the opportunity to travel. I couldn't let Dylan's bruised ego over one day of work get me down. Plus, I had bigger things to worry about. Like if Grayson and I could survive my three months on the road. The notion of Grayson *not* being my husband fluttered through my mind, and I shivered. Somehow I had to make both of these worlds work, to nourish both my professional and personal life. It had to be possible, I told myself. The alternative was too frightening to think about.

"I DIDN'T HEAR YOU COME in," Grayson said. He stood in the doorway of our walk-in closet.

I was kneeling in front of two large black suitcases I had borrowed from Alexis. I didn't know if I was even going to see him before I left. We had become strangers, as I had with everyone else in my life. The only people I ever talked to anymore were the people I worked with. He'd given up trying after I missed his dinner, and it felt impossible to look at him now without being overcome by guilt and remorse. I would never be able to forgive myself for missing that. Some moments are irredeemable, and that was one of them.

I thought things would eventually slow down, and Grayson and I would get back to normal. We'd been together for four years, and every couple goes through things. But when I turned to look at him, a single tear fell from his eye.

"I can't let you go on the road without having this conversation," Grayson said. He bit his lip and looked away from me. Immediately my heart began racing. I knew what he was going to say. "I just don't know who this person is that you've become, Hayden. I mean, I don't know the last time we've had a legitimate conversation. We're not lovers, we're not even roommates. We're strangers now, and I don't want to share a space with a ghost anymore."

I couldn't look at him; I stayed kneeling in front of my suitcase, holding back tears of my own.

"I'm not gonna be here when you get home. I'm moving out."

I couldn't hold them back any longer. My vision blurred as tears began to stream down my cheeks.

"Grayson, you don't mean this. Don't you still want to get married? I know things have been difficult, but I just started, and we knew this would take some adjusting but—"

Grayson held his hand up to stop me from talking.

"You didn't just start. You've been with Alexis for *six months*. In that entire time we've barely had one conversation about the wedding, let alone anything else. How could we possibly get married now, Hayden? I mean, Jesus, when was the last time we even *kissed*?" He shook his head and rubbed the back of his neck, looking away from me. I could see how hard this was for him, the awful hurt in his eyes. Panic started rising up in me. "I just don't see it anymore."

"Grayson, *please*!" I said, standing up. "Just give me a little longer, just so she knows she can trust me. And when she does, I'm sure she'll give me more time off, and I want to spend that time with you!"

I stood up to hug him, hoping it would change his mind.

I thought of the first day I met him at Zinqué. I was having lunch with a friend, and he was alone, reviewing a contract for his boss. His eyes mesmerized me, I had never seen such a crystal clear shade of blue. I remembered watching his lips as he talked to himself, wondering what they would feel like. When the waitress told him I covered his bill, he blushed. He walked over to introduce himself, and I wondered if he looked at everyone that way, or if I was special. It took me months to win him over. How had I let him slip away?

"I can't, Hayden. I'm sorry. It's not fair to me, to *us*. You know we can't get married like this, right?" He now started to sob, gripping me tightly, knowing it was the last time we would be connected in this way. He wiped his tears away, and then mine. He kissed me on the lips, and then again on the forehead. "I really hope you find what you're looking for out of this."

When Grayson left, I collapsed to the floor, wondering what I had just done. I'd never wanted anything or anyone as much as I wanted Grayson.

And now he was gone.

SIX MONTHS EARLIER, I WAS in bed watching Alexis Shane travel the world in her documentary. And now, I was traveling it with her.

My first flight was to Vienna. Thirteen hours, not including the layover in Germany. Being that I kept breaking into tears, I was grateful to be flying ahead. I needed the time alone, telling myself this was my time to grieve. When I got to Austria, I was going to have to get it together. I couldn't let myself travel to Europe for the first time and be miserable. Most people would never travel like this in their lifetime—and I was getting paid for it.

I deplaned, exhausted after the long flight, and started looking for the driver who would be holding a sign with my name. I looked inside the baggage claim and outside the terminal, lugging my heavy bags with me every step of the way. When I saw no one, I dialed Vanessa—there was no answer. I searched for a concierge who could speak English. He said, "I'm sorry, sir, but I believe you have flown into the wrong airport. The hotel you are staying at is a two-hour drive from here."

I burst into tears once again. I didn't know if Vanessa had done this on purpose, or if she was actually stupid enough to fly me into the wrong airport. It felt like my entire life was toppling sideways onto me at once.

"Murphy's Law," I told myself, blubbering as the concierge helped organize a car to drive me to the hotel. I still had to pay hundreds of dollars for the car myself, as Samantha was flying behind with my new company card. I tried to stay calm, reminding myself of how lucky I was to be there, but only felt condemned. Everything reminded me of Grayson and what an asshole I was.

Two and a half hours later, I pulled up to the Schloss Fuschl, a castle-like hotel at the top of a winding hill overlooking a big body of emerald green water. Approaching its vast beauty, I felt slightly better for the first time all day. As the bellman unloaded my bags, I was greeted by the concierge. She smiled, knowing who I was, and handed off my room key attached to a large gold keychain.

The walls of my room were pastel yellow, the bedspread a vibrant baby blue with imagery of lemons and yellow roses. I stepped out onto the balcony, overlooking the property, quickly forgetting about all of the trouble it took to get here. When I collapsed into bed, my phone pinged, reminding me I was there to work.

"Make sure Alexis and the twins' suites are set up phenomenally, and then some! Also, get some flowers for the new assistant to welcome her to the team. Xx Samantha"

With three assistants now, I had to prove to Alexis why I was worth flying across the world.

I returned to the front desk to have someone give me a walk-through of Alexis's suite, when I saw Big Wayne had also advanced. His nostrils flared, he was waving his arms and berating the woman. She appeared startled, and her coworkers gathered around to show support.

"What's going on?" I interrupted.

"They won't let me do a walk-through. Apparently, they were instructed not to. And my room is at the other end of the hotel, when I always stay in the room adjacent to her."

I didn't have to ask—I already knew. Vanessa and Amber had relentlessly been in Samantha's ear after San Francisco, again insisting she push out "Alexis's people." They wanted to make Wayne's life miserable, hoping it would prompt him to quit. They didn't miss a single opportunity, and it was truly incredible to witness in the most awful way.

"Hayden, I just need to do my job. It shouldn't be this hard. I've done it in every city we traveled to for the last twenty years. Now listen, I have to get over to the venue to check out the space she's performing in tomorrow—will you please help me get this sorted out before I get back?"

"Of course," I said. "Let me find out what's going on."

As Big Wayne walked out the front doors, I apologized to the flustered staff, and dialed Samantha—but Vanessa answered.

"What's going on? Is Big Wayne losing it yet?" she said.

I was right. What a predictable bitch.

"The hotel won't let him do a walk-through of Alexis's suite, and he said his room is always supposed to be next to hers."

"Duh! We told the staff not to let him in her room, and to place him at the opposite end of the hotel," she admitted. "I can't *wait* to see his face when he sees that I advanced in two security guards from Tel Aviv too. Now don't tell him anything. And if he has a problem, he can talk to management, not *you*."

"But do you really think Alexis would be happy with all of this?"

"It's not really your position to be asking a superior that question anyway, is it? Now don't let him intimidate you into making any room changes. *No matter what*."

I hung up.

"Fuck that," I said aloud. My job was to make Alexis Shane happy, not Samantha's sisters.

The woman from concierge led me back to the room next to Alexis's, where I met the Israeli security. I apologized but requested they switch rooms with Big Wayne. Like myself, they were uninterested in drama.

"We don't want any trouble. We were just doing what Vanessa instructed," one said.

The concierge led me into Alexis's presidential suite to double-check the rider. When we were in San Francisco, it had been so easy. But as I went through the list, I noticed half the things were missing. While I had time before Alexis arrived, I was still anxious. I was unable to speak the language, in the middle of nowhere, and without a car.

"Ma'am, I'm sorry, but where are the rest of the items from the rider?"

"This is the best we could do, sir. We don't usually have guests with requests like this."

Just at a quick glance I could see I needed the Diptyque candles, Fiji water, cauliflower chips, and Q-Tips. *What hotel doesn't have fucking Q-Tips?* There were also only four humidifiers in the room, but Alexis liked to have between eight and ten for her voice. And given that this was her first performance since my employment, I knew that was the most important item.

"Listen, I don't mind running around to get everything. But *please*, I need help getting more humidifiers."

The concierge told me she'd do her best, and kindly provided me with a driver to take me anywhere I needed. I climbed into the back of the town car to first head for groceries, when my phone rang.

"Hayden, it's Big Wayne."

"Hey, I—"

"I just wanted to say thank you for sorting everything out. I've always stayed in the room next to Alexis, for security purposes, you know? And I always have to check her suite to make sure there's no hidden cameras set up by hotel employees. I know that sounds crazy, but it's happened before. I just don't understand what all this drama is about. No management team has ever made my job so difficult."

"I, um, totally hear you," I stammered, after the mention of hidden cameras. "I just want to make your job as easy as possible. We're all here to make Alexis happy, and that's all that matters."

He agreed, and in that moment, I knew I couldn't just be quiet about Vanessa and Amber's attempts at sabotage anymore. The truth was *they* were the real sycophants, causing problems for no other reason besides wanting to be the closest to Alexis. Big Wayne wasn't going anywhere, nor did he need to. He was a good guy, just trying to do his job.

As I hung up, Vanessa called from thirty thousand feet in the sky.

"Did I hear you just switched Big Wayne's room?" she whispered.

"I did."

"And who gave you the authority to do that?"

"Vanessa, I'm sorry, but I'm not playing this game with you. I'm not a problem creator, I'm a problem solver. And right now, I'm running around a foreign country trying to make things amazing for my boss, okay? So, is there anything else you need?"

The line went silent.

"Yeah, actually," she said, ignoring my jab. "I'm gonna need you to pick up SIM cards to get Alexis's Apple TV up and running."

I wanted to say 'fuck you' after sending me to the wrong airport and terrorizing Big Wayne all day—but instead did as I was told. I redirected the driver from the market to the closest electronics store. I went in alone, but no one spoke English. The driver had to come in and translate. While checking out, I noticed a photo printer in the corner and logged in to print pictures of R&B to make Alexis feel more at home.

Luckily, when I returned from shopping, the concierge had been able to locate six more humidifiers. I spaced them evenly throughout the suite, with more around her bed—where I knew she'd spend most of her time. I placed white roses on the entry table, on the coffee table in the sitting room, and on her nightstand next to a Diptyque candle and pictures of the twins. On the notepad, I wrote, "*Welcome to Austria, Alexis! You're going to kill it!*"

Setting up for Alexis really did take all day. And when I finally finished, I decided to set the tone for the next few weeks in Europe by inviting both Big Wayne and the Israeli security to dinner.

The hotel restaurant was on a dock by the water, where locals could park their boats and come eat. It was such a different way of living here, and the view was beautiful, especially at sunset, with the water mirroring the pink and purple sky. After the drama and how hectic it had been running around, I finally settled in and felt gratitude, remembering that not long ago I was behind the desk at a salon in Beverly Hills.

We all got along so well at dinner that I was dreading the rest of the entourage's arrival. But an hour later, the Sprinters pulled up to the hotel. The back doors opened, and I couldn't help but feel bad for the bellmen when they saw how many bags they'd be carrying. I handed out everyone's room keys as they stepped out of the vans. As I went to hand Vanessa hers, she scowled and snatched it. The queen was, of course, the last to emerge—in a silk floral-print Versace tracksuit, and with a big smile on her face. I breathed a sigh of relief knowing she was in good spirits. Big Wayne led Alexis up the hotel steps, gracefully holding her hand, and when we reached the top, she turned to greet me with a hug.

"How was the flight?" I asked, making small talk as I led the group down the long hall. I'd never actually seen Alexis walk this far.

I opened the door to her suite, and the ten humidifiers let out a massive gust of fog into the hallway.

"Oh my God, Hayden! This is *perfect*!" she squealed. "This is exactly how I need it."

I finally relaxed as she toured the rose-scented suite and headed for the master bedroom.

"Hayden! This was so thoughtful of you." She held up one of the frames with a photo of herself with the twins. "Oh my God, you haven't met Marlo yet, have you?"

"I haven't," I said. I turned to Marlo, a fit black woman with fresh braids and flawless skin. I recalled Karen mentioning she was sixty, but she didn't look a day over forty-five. "It's nice to meet you, Marlo. Welcome to the team."

As Marlo went in for a handshake, Vanessa walked between us like a military woman on a mission to hook up Alexis's Apple TV. Alexis walked back out to the formal sitting area and sighed. "Marlo, do you mind ordering some salmon and capers to the room?"

When it arrived, Alexis sat down at the large dining table, and Samantha started going over the next day's schedule. She had barely started speaking when Marlo interrupted.

"Excuse me, Samantha," she spoke condescendingly, "but don't you think maybe you can go over this when she *isn't* eating?"

The room went silent. This new girl—well, *woman*—clearly hadn't been told about Samantha or her temper. I froze in anticipation, both scared and excited for her response.

"Excuse me, Miss *whatever your name is*," Samantha spat, "I will talk to my client as I please. We've been together for three years. JLT. Job long time. Now, if Alexis doesn't want me to speak, she will tell me. Got it? I'll give you the benefit of the doubt this time, but don't *ever* speak to me like that again."

WHILE I WAS EXHAUSTED FROM the shock of the breakup and the never-ending roster of errands executed the day before to prepare for Alexis's arrival, I couldn't rest. If I was idle too long, the flood of existentialism would crash upon me again, and I'd fret all over again about the purpose of my life—an especially difficult question now without Grayson in the picture.

Samantha texted me to bring an iced coffee to her room, exactly the kind of menial labor I was thankful for.

I knocked on her door, and Amber opened it.

"So, what happened with Big Wayne yesterday? You *idiot*," Amber said.

I handed Samantha her iced coffee. "What do you mean, what happened? I gave him the room Alexis wanted him in."

"Hayden," Amber said, "these people are trying to get us fired. You can't be friends with them."

"He seems like a nice guy. I don't know what you want me to say. I can't be mean to someone just because you and Vanessa don't like him."

"Would a nice guy, someone who claims to be her friend, continuously charge her two hundred and fifty thousand dollars a month, knowing she's broke?" Samantha interjected. "Other security teams will charge that fee for an entire year, Hayden. There's still a lot you don't know. When I started managing her, he handed over two million dollars in unpaid invoices, pressuring me to take care of them. These people who've been around her for a long time don't *love* her; they don't care about her at all. They're professional extortionists, and Alexis is their meal ticket."

It confused me how Samantha was so aware of someone like Big Wayne, yet her sisters were the same, if not worse. Was she really that blind to her own family? Or did she simply underestimate her sisters' backstabbing capabilities?

"Speaking of meal tickets, where's Brody?" I asked.

"He's not coming to Europe. That was part of the agreement. For business obligations, he stays home. As long as I stay out of her personal life."

Amber snickered. "Well that doesn't mean she didn't want him to! I went through her texts before we left, and she was asking if he'd come, at least for a couple days. But he responded he would rather drown than be on a thirteen-hour flight with Samantha."

I couldn't help but laugh.

Samantha choked while sipping her iced coffee.

"This isn't cold enough," she said. Her dark red lipstick stained the straw. "Alright, so Amber, now that I have you both here—I told Hayden a little about how it's going to work now, being that there's three of you. Marlo is the new day-to-day assistant, the bag carrier, the babysitter, the one who makes her tea and rubs her feet.

"Amber, you're now the head of wardrobe. And Hayden, you're the executive assistant. You do the scheduling, attend business meetings, work with the merchandise company, and you advance, just like yesterday."

"Oh, right. About that, I spent—"

"I have your credit card!" She pointed to her bubble gum pink Celine bag, at the foot of her bed.

It was like the gates of Heaven had just opened. Yesterday alone, I spent hundreds of dollars of my own money shopping around for missing items on Alexis's rider. At that rate, I'd be broke faster than I received my next paycheck.

"Why does *he* get a credit card?" Amber scowled.

"Because he's responsible!" Samantha said, rolling her eyes. "Now, like I was saying before I was so rudely interrupted: You're doing the schedule. So, every morning on the road, you'll send out a group chat to me, Alexis, Amber, and Marlo. For example, today," she said, dictating what I should type:

"2:30–4:30 p.m.: Sound check at venue
5:00 p.m.: Glam in Alexis's suite
7:00 p.m.: Depart for venue
7:20 p.m.: Arrive to venue
8:00 p.m.: Alexis on stage
9:00 p.m.: Alexis off stage."

"Won't she want to do glam *before* sound check?" I asked.

The two looked at one another and laughed.

"You realize she never goes to that, right?" Samantha said. "I mean, I've begged her to. Especially after the Super Bowl. But she refuses. Okay, now you two get out of here. I have some calls to make. Just please make sure glam is in her room before five p.m."

IT WAS GETTING CLOSER TO glam time, and I still had yet to see or speak to Alexis, so I went to her suite to check in. Marlo answered the door, her face puckered with disapproval.

"She already in glam. Whachu need?"

"I haven't heard from her yet today, so I just came to check in."

"Well she's not ready to see anyone." Marlo started to close the door.

"Marlo," I stopped the door with my palm, "I can sit right there at the table and wait. You don't have to lock me out like a dog."

She *was* acting like Alexis's security. But I wasn't going back to that place I had started in months ago, especially now that I had no life outside of work. Without Grayson, every mundane or irritable aspect of this job suddenly seemed crucial. Now more than ever I had to be vigilant, because if I lost the job or slipped a degree in worthiness in the eyes of Alexis, none of this would have been worth it. When Alexis finally emerged, she looked like a ghost of herself. She had dark circles under her eyes, and her face was swollen. I couldn't bring myself to act like one of the entourage clones and tell her she looked amazing when she didn't.

As we arrived to her dressing room at the venue, Amber and Marlo both clamored for her attention. Not willing to participate, I walked out to the front of the stage, or what's called the *front of house*, to check out the crowd.

There were servers on stilts, and women on stage climbing silk. Open bars framed the perimeter of the space, and knife imagery was *everywhere*—on the wallpaper and embossed into the carpet. There were knife-shaped candle holders, and six-foot-tall knife replicas. I looked up to see a second-story, enclosed glass box littered with celebrity guests like Leonardo DiCaprio and Jennifer Aniston. I glanced back down to find Samantha and Blair appear stage left. I waved them over to an empty table, just as an announcer took center stage.

"Ladies and gentlemen, we have a *very* special treat for you tonight," he said. The stage lights dimmed, and a spotlight came on. People shuffled in quiet anticipation. "Allow me to introduce you to the bestselling female artist of all time, *MISS ALEXIS SHANE!*"

An excited crowd surrounded the stage. The familiar song kicked in. I held up my phone, excited myself, and recorded a video for my Insta-story. But after the fifteen-second recording ended, I reviewed the video and was shocked at what I saw. I couldn't post this. I looked up from my phone to see if she looked as bad in person as she did in the video. *Fuck*. I knew she'd gained a few pounds, but I hadn't realized how heavy she'd become until seeing her on a spot-lit stage.

I moved from side to side of the venue, looking for a better angle, but it never appeared. The crowd became unenthusiastic—not only at what they saw, but what they heard. She sounded terrible. It was a cringey hour watching as Alexis wobbled around the stage, sounding out of breath, and unable to hit any of the high notes she was so famous for. People whispered to each other and exchanged dim looks. For all the pomp and fuss surrounding her, it was an anticlimactic moment.

I'd been so excited to brag to my friends, but I couldn't post anything. I felt too bad. This was right before her comeback tour, but it seemed more like a pitiful reminder that she was not what she used to be. I couldn't help but think this is what happens to something valuable when nobody takes care of it.

"WELL THAT WAS... SOMETHING," DYLAN said. He took a seat next to me at the hotel bar, shaking his head and scoffing.

"I don't even know what to say," I said.

"Sir, *sir*?" Dylan called after the bartender. "Could you bring the gentleman and I each a glass of champagne?"

"What happened to 'no drinking' on this trip?" I teased.

"Listen, if that was any indication of where this trip is headed, I'm gonna need it. I mean, did you see how she was acting at the after-party? She asked Leo to feed her—in front of *his girlfriend*!"

Dylan and I broke out into laughter.

One glass of champagne somehow transformed into four. I knew what I was doing, but I felt too good to stop. After all, a little flirtation after the stress of the past week was a welcome distraction. Otherwise, I would have been sitting alone in my bed ordering late night room service and thinking about what a sad, lonely old gay I'd grown up to be. When the inevitable question came, I didn't demur.

"So, where's your room?" he asked.

"I'm in 209."

"Oh. *Crazy.* I'm in 210."

As we walked back to our rooms, Dylan stopped short at mine. I fumbled with my obnoxiously large key, hyper-aware of his gaze upon me and the smell of his cigarette sweat.

"Should we have a nightcap?" he asked.

But before I could respond, he was opening the door himself. He pushed me into the room and onto my bed.

He straddled me, hesitated for a second, then went in for a kiss.

I WOKE UP ALONE, HOPING I hadn't made a mistake. Grayson and I were broken up, so I hadn't technically done anything wrong. But still, I felt guilty. I knew I wasn't thinking clearly. I'd been vulnerable and drunk and wanted temporary fulfillment now that there was a huge empty space in my life. Dylan was just there, making me feel good. *I shouldn't have crossed that professional line though*. But then again, did I? We're gay men. So, this wasn't abnormal, and I knew he wouldn't make it weird.

To distract myself, I scrolled through Instagram to look at what Alexis's fan accounts were saying about last night's performance. Some were defending her, and some were ripping her to shreds. The trending photo, however, was a side-by-side comparison of last night, and a performance she'd done in London the year before. I wasn't the only one who noticed the weight gain. Everyone was talking about it, mostly out of concern. One comment read, "*Is she okay?*" If only they knew.

I met Samantha for breakfast on the dock, where she gave me a run-through of the day's schedule. I wondered if I should tell her about what the fans were saying, when Amber called.

"Have you seen Dylan?" She sounded concerned.

Fuck. Was I busted? Had she seen us at the bar?

"No," I lied. "Not since you did at the venue last night."

"We can't find him *anywhere*, and he's not answering his door. Alexis needs him for glam."

Out of the corner of my eye, I saw Big Wayne descending the wooden steps of the dock with Alexis in hand and Marlo close behind. I became anxious. Alexis was never out in the daylight, and definitely not without glam. Today she wore dramatically oversized Christian Dior mirrored sunglasses instead.

As they joined our table, Big Wayne gave me a head nod to join him to the side.

"What's going on?" I asked. "Amber just told me Dylan went missing?"

"Well after he completely missed glam time, and didn't answer his door, the front desk gave me a key to his room. When I went in, he was unconscious, and every single bottle of alcohol from his mini-bar was empty and scattered around him. You don't know what happened to him last night, do you?"

"I have no idea," I said quickly, flushing.

I mean, I wasn't *lying*. He didn't even seem drunk when we had sex. And I didn't think anything of it when he said he preferred to sleep alone.

But did he drink all of that by himself? Even in the centerfold of glamour and wealth, the brokenness of people remained. I felt like the cracks of this lifestyle were beginning to spread. What were we, really, but a bunch of lost people—delusional, alcoholic, lonely, vengeful—desperately trying to believe in the false narrative that we precariously upholstered each day?

CHAPTER ELEVEN

I opened one eye, looked at my iPhone, and pressed ignore after seeing Samantha's name. She'd managed to book Alexis a last-minute job filming a commercial in Madrid, and I'd advanced the night before. Being driven through the dark city in the moonlight was serene and beautiful, with its religious overtones and architecture. Luckily, the Four Seasons was much more prepared for our arrival. Even my own room had a spread of fruit, cheese, crackers, and a bottle of red.

But it was now eight a.m., and I could hear the bustling city from bed. Samantha called again.

"Hello?" I groaned from underneath the covers.

"Hayden! Where are you?" Samantha said through a mouthful of food. I could tell she was becoming dependent on me. "Come over and eat with us!"

I threw on my "uniform"—an Adidas tracksuit—and headed for Samantha's suite down the hall from my own. Despite the excitement of traveling the world, so far it was looking like Alexis's life on the road wasn't much different than at home. The only place she wanted to be was in bed.

I knocked on the door, and Amber opened it. Samantha had failed to mention she'd invited her sisters too.

"Morning!" I said to the table of sycophants feasting on breakfast. "The commercial is tomorrow, right? Are we gonna do anything fun today?"

"Yeah. We're plotting to get rid of the poison," Vanessa said.

Wasn't there five minutes that could go by without her talking sabotage?

"It's *her*!" Amber interrupted, flashing the screen of her iPhone to the table, showing Alexis was calling.

"Put it on speaker! Let us listen!" Vanessa said, as she always did.

"Hello, *kitten*," Amber said upon answering.

"You forgot to pack something *very* important." I felt guilty listening to a conversation Alexis thought was private. "I'm gonna need you to fly back to Los Angeles for it. It's way too important to ship."

Fly back to Los Angeles for it. As if it were the same as running down the block for coffee.

Amber's mouth dropped.

"*Hello?* Amber?"

"Of course, kitten. I'll start looking at flights right now. But... what did I forget?"

"My Bible. You know I never travel *anywhere* without it."

Amber hung up, and the table burst into laughter at her having to jump on a twelve-hour flight. But not Samantha. She began pacing.

"This isn't fucking funny, you guys!" Samantha said. "She must not be taking her pills."

"Why do you say that?" I asked.

"Because when a manic episode is coming on, she always wants her Bible. So when she falls into it, she doesn't forget who she is."

Her serious tone quieted the table.

"Forget who she is? What does that have to do with her Bible?" I asked.

"Inside the front cover, she's written her name, birthdate, address, social security number, and Amex number," Samantha said, becoming solemn for a moment. "*But,* she also isn't wrong. She *never* travels anywhere without it. So, if Amber wasn't such a *fucking idiot,* she wouldn't have to spend the next twenty-four hours on a plane."

A FEW HOURS LATER, SAMANTHA and I stepped into an elevator together. As soon as the doors closed, she let out a sigh.

"Hey," I said. "Are you okay?"

"I'm just so tired. I want this contract done already. Then I can relax," she said, rubbing her temples dramatically.

"Contract? For the commercial?"

"Come on! Are you turning into Amber? Have you not been listening to me? *My* contract with Alexis."

"You never told me—"

"Hayden, *I did*!"

"You told me Brody was staying out of her professional life, as long as you stayed out of her personal. But you never said—"

"Hayden, c'mon. Remember? She and I are signing a contract for the next twelve months. It's really just to protect all of the deals I set up for the next year. But also, because I can't keep working in good faith when I have to constantly look over my shoulder for the next person trying to get me fired. It gives me a little security."

She'd never told me, but it wasn't worth arguing with her. Samantha explained their lawyers had been going back and forth, and after the European trip, before the tour kick-off in Las Vegas, Alexis was to sign. But now, Alexis wanted to use those few days off to charter a yacht in Capri.

"Here I am, busting my ass to make her all this money, and she's gonna spend another quarter-mil chartering a fucking boat. She doesn't even own a home! This is insanity!"

"Are you going on the boat?" I asked.

"No, and neither are you. She said she wants it to be *intimate*. So, I guess *intimate* means just Brody, Regina, Big Wayne, and Marlo."

While Samantha didn't say it, I knew she was worried that on this trip Alexis's *friends* would talk her out of signing. She wasn't going to let some fatuous, drunken afternoon destroy everything she had built and been through with Alexis.

ARRIVING IN PARIS WAS AS glamorous as I'd imagined, and the energy of the city was electric. I had advanced with Big Wayne and the stylist Charles, meaning we also were traveling with thirty of Alexis's suitcases—the cost of checking them was more than double my rent.

As we pulled up to the Plaza Athénée, I couldn't help but feel like Carrie Bradshaw in the series finale of *Sex and the City*. The hotel was just so *Paris*. From the exterior, every room had a balcony draped with ivy and red florals that matched its red awnings. The VIP hostess waited outside, impeccably dressed in a navy suit with a group of hotel employees in military formation. She greeted us formally, as one would expect for royalty, and assigned us each a bellman. Forget Carrie Bradshaw, I felt like Kate Middleton.

Alexis's suite was fit for a queen. I admired the detail in the crown molding, the lush rose-colored curtains, the chandeliers that sat over the formal sitting area, and her bed. The marble tables, the French furniture, and most importantly—*the view*. I let out an audible gasp when I looked out the window to find the Eiffel Tower.

I could have gotten away with not advancing to Paris at all, as the rider was not only completed as described, but they'd taken the initiative to do the personalized things I would, like buying white roses, and framing photos of Alexis and the twins. Our whole floor was even closed off to the public with security posted by each elevator, keeping anyone unknown from entering.

After double-checking her room, I went to the restaurant in the courtyard of the hotel, where suites with windows looked down at the tables full of smokers. Being in Paris felt like a dream, an oasis away from the rest of the world. I set my phone down on the pristine white tablecloth and admired the fashionably dressed guests. The waiter stopped by with an open box of cigarettes. "Sir?" he said, holding them out to me. I hesitated, as I had quit years ago, but *everyone* was smoking. It was glamorous here, so I lit up just as my phone rang.

"Hayden? We're boarding the jet now," Samantha said. "How is everything? How's the weather? The hotel is *fabulous*, right? Does she have the suite with the view of the Eiffel Tower?"

I never got used to Samantha asking a million questions before I could even respond to one. "Yes," was all I could muster.

"Listen, when we arrive, meet us out front. The hotel should already be setting up for the paparazzi."

"Setting up?"

"How do you think we're going to Paris last minute?" She laughed. "The hotel is *free* in exchange for photos of her checking in."

So, this was what people meant by once you're famous, you get everything for free.

BEING IN TOWN FOR ONLY Twenty-four hours, and knowing my alone time would soon end, I stepped out of our hotel onto Avenue Montaigne—the same street as all the designer shops. Paris in July was so uncomfortably hot, it encouraged me to stop into each of them. As soon as I did, I was swarmed by attractive salespeople with thick French accents.

"Things are much less expensive here than in America," they all said.

Exactly what *American* vibe was I giving off? I felt slightly disappointed, as everyone always told me I had European bone structure. I guess the real Europeans could tell from my profile that I was just another anonymous boy from Maryland.

When I arrived back at the hotel, I heard the shouting of Alexis's name, announcing the queen's arrival. Paparazzi were waiting behind the velvet barricades and had gathered the attention of a large crowd. The entourage hurried inside as Alexis stepped out of a Rolls-Royce in slow motion, wearing a body-hugging spaghetti-strapped white Dolce & Gabbana dress, oversized sunglasses, and diamonds dangling from every limb. She was merely checking in but looked as if she were arriving to a movie premiere. Fans continued shouting her name, begging for selfies.

As Alexis posed for the fans and photographers, Amber pulled up in a cab, rushing to Alexis's side—Bible in hand.

"Go inside," Alexis growled through her teeth. She could sense Amber's desperation to be seen and nudged her away. She shuffled quickly inside, her tangled bun bobbing on top of her head.

When Alexis finally entered the lobby, Amber wasn't even given a 'hello' after flying across the world.

"Why are you *here*?" Alexis rolled her eyes. "You aren't coming to Saudi Arabia, so why didn't you just meet us in Tel Aviv?"

Maybe Alexis didn't care as much about her Bible as she did about getting rid of Amber. But why, then, didn't she just fire her? I didn't understand the relationship between Alexis and the sisters. It's as if the three of them held a strange power over her somehow, like she felt responsible for them in some way.

After settling Alexis into her suite, I walked Samantha and Blair to theirs, Vanessa following close behind.

"We need to talk about Dylan," Vanessa said as we walked in. "What happened in Madrid was unacceptable."

"What happened in Madrid?" I said.

"At the end of the shoot, when Alexis sent you back to the hotel to check on the twins, he got into a screaming match with the director. I mean, he went completely *mental*. It was so unprofessional, and completely unacceptable for a *makeup artist* to be talking to a *director* like that."

I wanted to defend Dylan, but I wasn't there. I was gone for only an hour of the shoot, and *this* happened? I also considered who was telling the story.

"Hayden," Samantha said, "I know you're friendly with Dylan. So, I think it's best that you be the one to let him know we're sending him home."

"You're sending him home?" I looked to Vanessa, who wore a Grinch-like smile. "I'm talking to Sebastian's agent now, but I'm not sure he can make it until we get to Saudi Arabia. So, I just need you to keep Dylan calm and out of the loop until Sebastian gets here. Once Sebastian gets to whatever city we're in, you'll send Dylan home. I just hope he doesn't cause any more problems until then."

"Well, finally *someone* gets what they deserve around here," Vanessa said. "He left his makeup bag on the jet too. I, of course, left it behind—to teach him a lesson."

Who was this woman to think she needed to teach everyone a lesson? What did she not understand about working together as a team? Even if Dylan *was* in the wrong, Vanessa was too. I didn't want to hear it anymore and headed for the door, exhausted with their petty politicking.

"Let the boys know glam will be at eight p.m.!" Samantha shouted after me.

CHARLES HAD ARRANGED FOR RICCARDO Tisci of Givenchy to host an impromptu dinner at L'Avenue in honor of Alexis's last-minute trip to Paris. L'Avenue was comparable to Nobu or Mr. Chow in Los Angeles—places you go only to be seen.

I was excited following in Alexis's footsteps to the long table that awaited us, full of actors, athletes, and supermodels. After kissing Kate Moss and Naomi Campbell on each cheek, I expected her to be unhappy to see the beautiful women, but surprisingly, she was kind and elegant in her role-playing. Perhaps this is how she survived so long—having a chameleonic charm, being able to turn it on and off instantly.

Even though I was to take a submissive role at dinner, I had a seat by Alexis's side and was treated no differently than the Hollywood elite, being served champagne and complimented on my outfit. This was everything I'd fantasized this job would be. That is, until I received a text from Lion. He'd never texted me before, so I was surprised to see his name.

"I'm sorry to bother you, Hayden. But I'm going home."

Great. Any time I was really enjoying one of the highs that came with this job, someone was there to ruin it. But for Lion to be saying something must be serious. He was always so easy and unbothered by the drama that came with living in Alexis's world.

"WHAT'S GOING ON?" I ASKED when we returned from dinner.

I sometimes wondered how Alexis was comfortable around Lion, when Samantha had drilled into my head that she doesn't like to be around anyone younger, prettier, or thinner than her. He didn't identify as female but was gender-fluid. He was thin, six feet tall, and his perfect flowy brunette hair met his waistline. *I wonder if it's a wig?*

"It's just been really bad. You have no idea," he said, guiding me into his hotel room and taking a seat at the edge of the bed.

"What do you mean? With Alexis?"

"Hayden, I have *no money*. I didn't come to dinner tonight because I didn't want to just assume it's being paid for, and I can't pay myself."

"What do you mean, *no money*?" I asked.

I didn't understand because I now knew that hairstylists traveling with celebrities never made less than a thousand dollars a day. It was one of the most lucrative positions to be in.

"I've been working for Alexis since January, and I even stopped taking all my other clients to be on call for her. But I can't do it anymore. Not *one* of my invoices has been paid."

Really? I had to deal with this *again*? Alexis had to owe him a hundred thousand dollars by this point. How could she look these people in the face every day when she's booking jets to Paris and yachts in Capri? Did she really feel no sense of responsibility toward them?

"It's just gotten too hard at this point, being across the world with no money. I can't do it anymore. Not even for Alexis. I mean, my landlord is threatening eviction, Hayden. I'm owed *a lot*. I don't think it's too much to ask to be able to afford to eat and pay my rent."

"I totally hear you, and I understand. I'm sorry," I said, trying to remain calm despite the pile of bullshit that continually stacked itself against me. "I didn't know, or I would have helped you sooner. You've been sending all your invoices to Karen?"

"To Amber."

"Why have you been sending them to Amber?"

"That's what she told me to do. I keep following up with her like once a week, and she always says, 'I've got it covered, babe!'—but then nothing happens."

I wanted to strangle the bitch. She only saved face at the last minute, when there was no other option. There were many moving parts to preserving Alexis's image, but Amber's continuing neglect and laziness threatened to collapse it. Her team was the channel through which she interacted with the world, so when one of us was compromised, everyone felt it.

"Okay," I sighed, rubbing my hands over my face. "I'll take care of it."

"Thank you so much, Hayden. *Seriously*. I've had no one to turn to. I mean, I can handle being talked down to, but I can't handle not getting paid."

"Talked down to?" I asked in disbelief, knowing how much Alexis loved him. Her relationship with the glam gays was always much friendlier than with the assistants. Maybe because they were responsible for making her feel beautiful.

"Oh, not by Alexis!" he said. "By Vanessa. She's just so condescending, and constantly makes me feel like I'm in the way. Like I'm the help, and she's some important executive. But I'm not even really sure what she does. Technically someone with her job title is supposed to give us an itinerary before we even leave the country. It would say each place we're going to and the hotel information. We would be given an envelope with our per diems, and our bags would be numbered and delivered to our rooms. None of those things happen on this team. Everything's always done half-assed or last minute. It's such a mess."

I never understood exactly what Vanessa's job was either, but at least now I knew what she was *supposed* to be doing. So far, I only had evidence that she could plug an Apple TV into a wall, yet somehow that was important enough to fund her Range Rover.

"I can't disagree with you," I said. "I was actually thinking about talking to Samantha about it."

"*Please* don't bring me up when you talk to Samantha. I don't want any trouble."

"No, no. Of course not. It's coming from me, not you. Now what the hell is going on with Dylan? He missed glam in Vienna, and today Vanessa said he got into a fight with the director in Madrid?"

Lion sighed.

"Dylan… that's a whole 'nother issue. He was just trying to get the lighting how Alexis likes it. I mean, his delivery was wrong, for sure. But then Vanessa jumped at the opportunity to turn it into something bigger, to look like some kinda hero. She started yelling at him and calling him unprofessional in front of the entire crew and Alexis. So, he got embarrassed and fought back."

"*Jesus*," I said. "Yeah, it's been a little hard for me to defend him because I guess his room was full of empty liquor bottles in Austria."

Lion hesitated before responding.

"This has happened with him on other teams, if that's what you're asking. But he keeps getting jobs because he really *is* an incredible artist."

"Are you insinuating…"

"That he's an alcoholic? Yeah. He was drunk when he missed glam, and he was drunk when he fought with the director."

I thought life after mania would be smooth sailing, but the drama never stopped. Amber was incapable of doing her job, employees still hadn't been paid for months, and Alexis continued to spend frivolously. Not that I was helping matters, having fucked the alcoholic makeup artist, who I was now going to have to *fire*.

DYLAN CAME RUSHING AROUND THE corner with disheveled hair and sleep in his eyes.

"Well there you are," Charles said to him as Big Wayne permitted entry to Alexis's suite.

I always tried to keep my interactions with the stylist to a minimum, as he was a stereotypical gay man—always bitching.

"Dylan," Charles said, "I'm taking Alexis to see Thierry Mugler today. So, if you're coming with us, you may want to put a little bit of that concealer on *yourself*." He laughed unkindly. Being that Charles had been sober for years, you would think he wouldn't be so judgmental.

When leaving Thierry Mugler, photographers followed us through the streets of Paris and then pressed their camera lenses against the glass as we walked into Hermès.

It didn't take long for Alexis to find something that caught her eye—another one of the world-famous Birkin bags, of which she already had many. But this one was white crocodile with diamond hardware. Its price tag: €300,000.

"Amber, don't I have store credit here?" Alexis said.

"No, babe. Or what you do have, you can only use in the States."

"Where did Dylan go?" I asked the group, to no response.

"*Alexis*," Samantha whispered, grabbing her by the wrist as if she were her mother. "I can't let you buy this without calling your business manager. I love you, but you've spent a million dollars since we've been on the road. The whole point of this trip was to start saving and buy you a house in Los Angeles so you can stop leasing."

Alexis reluctantly called Karen, who sighed, but quickly gave permission. Her 'yes' disgusted me. Wasn't the whole point of a business manager to tell you when you're being reckless? The woman was living paycheck to paycheck, for fuck's sake.

I watched the salesman's eyes light up like Christmas, then noticed there was a second-story bar which Dylan had, of course, found. He threw back a mimosa. While his fate was sealed, I still didn't want him to embarrass himself. I spotted the elevator and tiptoed over. But as the doors opened, Dylan shouted, "Hello? Will somebody get me another *fucking drink*?"

CHAPTER TWELVE

ollowing the embarrassing scene in Hermès, Alexis insisted Dylan advance to Saudi Arabia with Big Wayne and me. He should have just been sent home immediately, but Samantha refused until Sebastian's flight landed. God forbid his plane get delayed, and Alexis be screwed out of glam just before show time. But even aside from Dylan, I was nervous traveling to Saudi Arabia. Amber opted out because of their treatment of women, so I couldn't imagine they cared much for gays either.

Once the flight took off, I googled *"LGBTQ rights in Saudi Arabia"* and felt even worse. I read that most members of the community would stay in the closet until death, and that "coming out" was rare. Last year it had been voted the worst place in the world to be gay, as there was no legal protection. No hate crime laws, no marriage laws, and when an LGBTQ rights group tried to form, the founder was soon after murdered—strangled to death by a rainbow flag.

The next morning when we had all settled into our hotel, Alexis unexpectedly wanted to hear the sound check and texted me to record it. Samantha called Vanessa for credentials to get into the venue, but Vanessa insisted I wouldn't need any until the performance that evening. So, imagine my surprise when I arrived to be met by security *checking credentials*. Luckily the driver who'd taken me from the hotel helped to translate and avoid a thirty-minute trip back.

Relieved to have simply gained access, I walked in, not knowing where I was going or how huge the grounds were. I stopped groups of people, hoping to find someone who spoke English, but no one even understood the word "stage." I'd never experienced being incapable of communicating with people before and became frustrated. I pulled out my iPhone to call someone from the band, but my phone didn't work without wi-fi.

I started hyperventilating, wandering aimlessly, unsure where to go or what to do—until I heard a familiar song in the distance. I ran in circles until I spotted a speck resembling a stage. I ran toward it, only to be able to record the last few seconds of the final song on the setlist.

A simple task that should have taken minutes took hours. Vanessa was sabotaging me, just like she had with Dylan and his makeup supplies, and with Wayne's accommodations. She wanted my failure to be in Alexis's face. I couldn't let her get away with this anymore. After returning to the hotel, I'd tell Samantha *everything* and give her the chance to fix it before involving Alexis.

But when I arrived at her suite, she had other things to discuss.

"Listen, Sebastian just checked in. So, you need to go have the conversation with Dylan. Vanessa already booked him on the next flight home."

"Samantha, I—"

"He's just gonna take it better coming from you, Hayden. But you need to tell him *now*. I don't want him showing up to Alexis's suite for glam and making her feel uncomfortable."

Hours earlier, I'd flown a drunk Dylan with me to Saudi Arabia, and now I was shipping him home. I felt sick.

"Hey," I said nervously as he opened the door to his hotel room, "is it alright if I come in?"

"Uh, yeah. Just give me a second." He quickly closed the door in my face. I could hear the clinks of empty bottles behind it. The door opened again. "What's going on?"

I walked in and leaned up against the wall. He took a seat at the edge of his bed.

"Sebastian's here," I said.

"*Sebastian?* I thought he was only flying in for the shoot in Israel?"

"I guess because of what's been going on, Samantha wanted to cover her bases. I don't want you to take this the wrong way, but—"

"But, *what?*"

"Well, you missed glam in Vienna, you got into a fight with the director in Madrid, you were shouting for a drink in Hermès. Not to mention

Wayne overheard you drunk and making comments about how upset you were to be missing Kylie Jenner's party."

"What are you getting at?"

"I get that your priority is *you*, Dylan. But ours is Alexis. So, I'm sorry to blindside you, but we're sending you home on the next flight."

His defensiveness abruptly stopped, and his eyes began to water.

"I'm saying this as a friend, *okay*? You really need to get home and take care of yourself."

He wouldn't make eye contact, and the crying intensified.

"It's just become pretty clear that you... have a drinking problem," I said, not wanting to overstep any boundaries but also feeling genuinely concerned for him.

He sobbed, I assumed, because he messed up an incredible opportunity. This was only the beginning of our travel schedule and he would now be missing out on an entire North American tour—costing him tens of thousands of dollars.

"Your flight information should be in your email any second," I said.

"I'm just, *I'm sorry*," he said between tears. "I know I'm not who you thought I was."

"No one in Hollywood is, babe," I laughed, trying to lighten the mood.

Seeing how Dylan was such a mess only reminded me how lucky I was to have been with Grayson. I zoned out as Dylan continued crying in front of me. I missed Grayson. Grayson would never put himself in situations like this. He worked too hard for what he had and was grateful for every opportunity. He was *home* to me—safe and reliable and loving—a feeling I was increasingly forgetting the more time I spent in this bestiary. I wanted to call him. But I couldn't. What would be the point? What was there to say? I fucked up. I couldn't salvage our relationship over the phone. Maybe Bethenny Frankel was right: You can't have both a successful career and love life.

As I approached Alexis's suite, Sebastian and Lion waited outside. Sebastian examined me from head to toe, as gays who haven't met yet often do—like a dog sniffing another dog's ass.

I held my hand out. "I'm Hayden."

"Hi there!" He waved my hand away and instead introduced himself with a tight embrace. "I'm Sebastian," he said into my ear.

His age was indeterminable, he wore all black, and towered over me—reminiscent of a vampire.

"How hot is Hayden?" Samantha yelled from down the hall after witnessing our interaction.

"*So hot.*" Sebastian played along, pushing me up against the wall dramatically before pretending to make out with my lifeless body.

I'd just gotten rid of one work boyfriend, and didn't want another.

COME PERFORMANCE TIME, A FLEET of black SUVs dropped our entourage close to the stage. I hadn't noticed earlier, but it was built on a waterfront. Alexis and Samantha hopped out and onto a waiting golf cart, leaving the rest of us to chase behind, tripping over cobblestones. We hurried backstage into a white-curtained dressing room. Through them, I saw red, green, and blue lights flash while an intro video of Alexis played.

Her longest-running number-one hit blared through the speakers, and the crowd went wild, shouting her name and waving homemade posters. She even looked like a different person from the night of her performance in Austria, now wearing a purple sequined bodysuit that flattered her curves, a high ponytail, and knee-high "fuck me" boots. She took the stage, hit her infamous high notes, and all my worries were swept away. This was the show I'd been waiting to see, and I was proud to Insta-story my boss confidently rocking the stage. All the headlong diving into madness was *worth* something, because it amounted to *this*. Still, I couldn't help but wonder if there was an easier way; if the chaos was a natural result of her international star power, or of the incompetence of those around her.

"Alexis wants you on the jet!" Samantha shouted into my ear over the screaming crowd.

"*She does?*" I shouted back, a little too excited, prompting an eye-roll from Samantha.

But I couldn't help it. We were to head straight from the stage to the jet, and I had never flown private before. Most of my knowledge of what it was like came from what I'd seen on *The Real Housewives*.

The show ended with fireworks being shot off into the sky and Alexis on a high, not wanting to leave the stage. I was about to leave for my luggage when she called my name over the microphone.

"Come take a photo of me!" she said.

I walked out center stage to take a photo of her posing in front of the cheering crowd. Goosebumps covered my body.

So, this is what it feels like.

The overwhelming energy of the adoring crowd suffused me with an ecstasy I had never felt before.

My car was the last to arrive to the jet. The driver hopped out to hand me my bags. I slowly walked up the steps, grateful I didn't have to advance—I assumed because Amber was already in Israel. At the top I was greeted by a stewardess who welcomed me aboard and took my bags. The jet sat eighteen passengers, and almost every seat was full. I marveled at the luxurious interior—creamy white leather seats with intricate stitching, and mahogany finishing so polished I could see my reflection. In the back was Alexis and a California king-sized bed with a charcoal suede headboard made custom to fit. I took one of the only two open seats.

"*Where were youuu?*" Alexis whined, now in silk Gucci pajamas. She made her way from the back of the jet to sit next to me.

"I'm sorry!" I said. "I just had to grab my bags, and I knew Marlo was with you so I thought it was okay. Did you need something?"

"No, no! I just *wanted* you here. You make things *festive*, Hayden." She took a sip of her favorite Pinot Grigio. "We could have just had Amber do that, you know."

I was grateful to finally feel needed by her and wanted to bask in the moment, but I couldn't help myself from saying, "Alexis... Amber's not even in this country."

She gripped my hand, and we burst into laughter.

THAT AFTERNOON, ALEXIS WAS HOSTING a press conference at the Dead Sea for the new haircare line, and fans were already waiting outside our Tel Aviv hotel when we arrived at five a.m. I walked out onto the oceanfront balcony of my room and squealed with excitement. Things had been moving so fast, I hadn't had a real moment to appreciate what was happening. I felt gratitude watching the sky change colors as the sun rose over the beach. When else would I have ever been able to travel like this? Of course, the vacuum of Grayson's absence pulled at me, knowing he would have loved it.

"Come on, let's go!" Samantha shouted later that afternoon, banging on the door of Alexis's suite. We were supposed to have left an hour earlier, but Alexis was still in the makeup chair. After being permitted access, Samantha joined the girl talk instead of putting on pressure.

"Oh my God, Charles. That ensemble is just *divine* on her," she said.

I too admired her now-curvier body in the nude pencil skirt with gold studs, a low-cut sweater that exposed the edge of her white lace bra, and a $300,000 diamond necklace, which had been a gift from Mark Kauffman.

I checked the time on my phone, knowing the Dead Sea was an hour drive from Tel Aviv. I was starting to get worried. The event was only supposed to be an hour long, meaning we'd now arrive at the time it was scheduled to end. I was embarrassed, and not sure how Samantha didn't feel the same.

When we finally made it to the lobby, there was a bus for the star and a second for the staff. As Alexis caught Amber starting to board, she called, "Amber! I'd really rather you stay behind. I'm going straight from Israel to Capri, and I need some new outfits for the boat."

We all knew the Dead Sea visit was the only thing on the itinerary Amber had been excited about. Her jaw clenched and she walked off the bus and back into the hotel without saying a word.

As we got closer to the Dead Sea, our buses twisted down dirt-covered roads. The textures of the deteriorating hills were mesmerizing, and the scene became even more stunning the closer we got to the bottom, seeing the clear blue sky meet with the world-famous teal water. I hadn't been aware, but the driver explained this was also the lowest point on earth, which made sense because my ears were popping.

We pulled up to the haircare headquarters to be greeted by a very upset owner, as even after being an hour late, Alexis refused to just walk in—she needed touch-ups. I felt bad for the owner, as he had obviously never dealt with a celebrity before, let alone the most notoriously difficult.

When Alexis finally stepped off the bus, the owner faked adoration. He led us through the double doors, where we heard Alexis's greatest hits blaring from the second story. Leading the entourage, I carried a sleepy Rhythm up the stairs to a table that had been reserved for us, right between fans and press. As Alexis hung behind, the entire room of guests turned to take photos of the sleeping twins, or worse, walked over in an attempt to *touch them*. I pulled Rhythm and Blue away from the aggressive fans, shocked at how comfortable they felt.

Front and center was a raised stage with two chairs placed before a giant step and repeat plastered with the company's logo and Alexis's name. While the intention of the press conference was to promote the haircare line, with Alexis's high-profile personal life, I knew where the questions would inevitably go.

Alexis entered the room to deafening cheers, which jolted the twins awake.

"What are you looking forward to doing while in Israel?" the first reporter asked.

"Honey, I don't know what I have time for!" Alexis said. She looked at me holding her son and smiled. "We're just so excited to be here. I've never been to the Dead Sea, and neither have R&B."

"You mentioned your twins. Beyoncé has twins, Mariah has twins, J.Lo has twins. Do you ever ask any of them for advice?"

"*Sweetie*, do I look like I need advice?"

Her response made the room laugh. She was quick-witted and great talking about herself, easily intuiting which side to reveal after a lifetime of publicity. But when the questions turned to the product line, she struggled.

"I mean, I'm just a very earthy girl," she lied. "And there's all these great vitamins and nutrients, you know?" She looked to the owner for assistance, but he was no help. "There's just so many great things when it comes to using the salt from the Dead Sea. I swear by it."

A presumably gay publicist stood up to ask the room if there were any more questions before we wrapped the press conference portion of the day.

"Alexis, will you sing for us?" one fan shouted.

"Sweetie, do you have a check?" she said, and winked.

The publicist then led us into an all-white room next door, where one-on-one camera interviews were to take place. The contract was for three reporters, yet fifty were lined up. Due to our tardiness, the haircare company figured they could take advantage.

"Um, *HELLO*!" Samantha shouted in the silent room. "Who's in charge of press here?"

"I am!" said the overweight, flamboyant publicist in rainbow-framed glasses as he formally introduced himself with a stereotypical snarky attitude.

"Well, I need you to get a little bit more *organized*, because we only agreed to three interviews. So, pick out who you want, and make it snappy."

"Excuse me! I am the best publicist in all of Israel, and you will *not* speak to me in that tone!"

The two were red-faced, arms flailing, and voices raised when an unknown woman from across the room ran up and started recording.

"What do you think you're doing?" I interjected. I grabbed the phone from her hand and deleted the video. After the Super Bowl performance and Alexis's documentary, Samantha's reputation had taken a big enough hit. "Who are you?"

"I'm his wife!" she spat, grabbing the phone back from me. I couldn't help but smile about the new guts I'd developed working this job, remembering how overwhelmed I felt on St. Patrick's Day.

Chuckles erupted from around the room, and the owner of the haircare line came to separate his publicist from Samantha. I felt bad for her, but the way she responded to conflict was always so erratic. I looked to Alexis to find her huffing at the attention being off her. She just rolled her eyes and sat in the white velvet chair, allowing Samantha's tantrum to run its course. Sure, she could defuse the situation herself. *She* was the star. But right now, she just seemed tired—tired of playing the part, of giving direction, of contriving her every appearance. Finally, the first reporter sat down, anxious to get his handful.

"Alexis, after your last visit to Israel, the Kauffman family got into a little bit of trouble."

"I don't pay attention to the news, sweetie," Alexis said.

"Well, they were at your show."

"What did I do? Someone wants to blame me for having an audience at my show?" she said, laughing dismissively.

I looked to Samantha, who was reading emails on her phone. Why wasn't she interfering? Why was *no one* interfering?

"The accusations against the Kauffman family are kind of a big deal here," he said.

"That sucks," Alexis said. "But all I can do is be responsible for myself."

"Okay, alright! *NEXT!*" I shouted to my own surprise, and Samantha's, who finally glanced up from her phone.

But the second journalist had even less tact, and Samantha, now aware, kicked him out within seconds. She warned the owner that this was his last chance, and to choose someone wisely.

The final interviewer was extremely handsome with jet-black hair, a square jaw, and dressed professionally in a suit—unlike the previous two. I felt optimistic.

"Would you say that you had a special connection with your ex?" he asked.

"Which one?" she joked.

"The billionaire."

"Like I said, *which one?*" Alexis laughed at her own joke. "I don't have much of a connection with anyone I date. I'm just there for the gifts and free food, you know? A girl's gotta eat."

"Why are the authorities so interested in the gifts your ex gave you during your engagement?" he asked, pointing to her necklace and the ten-million-dollar ring on her middle finger that she refused to take off.

"I was just around for laughs. Please sweetie, let it go."

"So, if they were to ask about your ex's current business dealings—"

"I don't know anything about that motherfucker!" Alexis said in her diva tone.

Her statement made the room erupt into laughter. The journalist was escorted out by Big Wayne, and next fans were to come in and take photos with Alexis holding the new products. They trampled in like animals. As they crowded her, I saw the color drain from her face and her eyes widen with fear. Sure, she could command a room, but she couldn't physically hold back a crowd. Why was no one stepping in? Security? Her manager? Alexis started to disappear behind them, until I rushed for her.

"Everybody, *FALL BACK!*" I shouted, again silencing the room. Vanessa's face turned red to see me insinuate myself—but I couldn't just watch the chaos ensue and not do anything. "Everyone get in a straight line, you get *one* photo, and then security will escort you out."

Was this chaos normal for A-list celebrities, or was Alexis just poorly managed? Maybe Samantha really was in over her head, or she didn't care enough at crucial moments to recognize when Alexis was suffering. Thirty minutes later, Alexis was ready to leave after a hellish day, but there was still one more obligation—the photoshoot in the Dead Sea. The Dead Sea is one of the seven wonders of the world, with a sodium level so high you float without even trying. They say it will dry up soon, so I was excited to go in—it felt like a once-in-a-lifetime opportunity.

Alexis changed into a sexy black Versace one-piece and a tiny matching sarong, before the owner led us out back to the company's private beach. As we approached the sea, the dried-up salt in the sand became painful, like needles pressing into the bottom of our feet. I came prepared with a bathing suit under my track pants and was ready to get in. But I stopped when I noticed no one else was. Everyone just stood around watching the professional photographer take photos of Alexis floating. It was awkward until Alexis herself invited me in to take photos on my own phone for her Instagram.

She posed as I snapped away. A few with her lips pursed, a few of her smiling with only her eyes, and a few of her grinning from ear to ear. We repeated the poses again after she tilted her head back to soak her hair. I smiled like an idiot, trying not to think about how insanely impossible this moment would have seemed to me as a boy—snapping photos of my hero in one of the holiest bodies of water in the world.

"Lemme see," she said, swimming toward me. But after looking, she became unenthused. "Sweetie, please do not post *any* of these before we Facetune."

"You look *gorgeous*!" I said, and she did. "But of course. I would *never* post a picture of you without your permission."

"I appreciate that," she said. "You know, some of these people…"

"They're bleak, sweetieeeee! They're bleak!" I responded in the same diva tone she used in her interview.

She laughed at me imitating her.

"The bleakness!" she said.

Alexis had me ride on her bus back to Tel Aviv so we could Facetune together. And after posting it to Instagram, the photo went viral. The headlines read, THE DEAD SEA—ALEXIS SHANE'S PERSONAL CHAISE LOUNGE.

"WHICH OF THESE ARE COMING with me?" I asked Marlo, overwhelmed at the sight of dozens of black suitcases in the entrance to Alexis's penthouse suite.

Not only was I being sent back to Los Angeles, but with *half* of Alexis's luggage. I was disappointed not to be included on the trip to Capri, but I didn't have a choice. When it came to personal life, there was a distinct line between Samantha's people and Alexis's people. And being that Samantha was how I got the job, *her people* is where I fell.

Marlo began pulling away which bags she could tell were meant for the yacht when Amber walked in.

"Why didn't you just wait for me, Hayden?" she asked. "You know *I'm* in charge of wardrobe."

"Sorry, I'm kind of in a rush. I have a flight to catch, and Marlo's been staying in the adjoining room, so I just figured she knew."

I rolled my eyes behind Amber's back, and Marlo laughed. Amber turned to catch me making a face with my tongue out.

"What the fuck?"

"Relax," I said, "I'm just joking."

"You want Marlo to think the two of you don't need me here, don't you?"

"Amber," Marlo said, "Hayden hasn't given me that impression once. You're too worked up over suitcases."

Her paranoia led her to believe that every move I made was to make her look bad. I didn't understand why, but it also wasn't helping matters that I'd quickly developed a friendly banter with Marlo, something Amber and I never shared.

Amber and I started to push the carts into the elevator when I heard a muffled Alexis talking with Marlo behind the suite doors. She must have just finished glam.

"I'm running late. I'm gonna go say 'bye' now so I don't have to come back up," I told Amber before walking away.

"I thought you left without saying anything!" Alexis said as Marlo opened the door to the suite.

"Never!" I smiled. "I'm on my way to the airport now though, so have fun in Capri and I'll see you in Las Vegas for the tour kick-off."

She half-smiled and looked to the side, as if she wanted to say something. Like maybe she really did want me in Capri.

"We're not even apart, and I'm already looking forward to seeing you again!" She gave me a tight embrace.

"Me too," I said. It made me glow to hear her vocalize that. She had a hardened exterior for a good reason, but once you got over it, there was real warmth. Her divahood was no match for her humanity, even if she was only vulnerable every now and then to show it.

Back in the hall, as the elevator doors began to close in front of me, a red-manicured paw stopped them.

"Hey!" Samantha said. She looked both ways before asking, "Do you want to come to Maui?"

"*What?*" I asked, my eyes bulging with excitement.

"*Shhh*," she whispered, "don't get me in trouble! I'm taking Blair for the week since Alexis is headed to Capri. We haven't had a vacation without her in years! Which, you know, is never a vacation anyway. So, what do you think? Want to come?"

"Of course! But why is it a secret?"

"You think Alexis Shane is going to be okay with me taking *her* assistant on *my* vacation?" It still seemed silly to me to feed into this underlying division in an entourage that was supposed to all be working for the same person. "Yeah, right. After you drop her bags off in Los Angeles, just hop on the next flight to Maui. It's on me."

It's on me. She said it as if she was buying me a drink.

CHAPTER THIRTEEN

After the sixteen-hour flight home from Tel Aviv, I considered staying in Los Angeles for a few days before heading to Hawaii. But when I got to my apartment, it was half empty. I knew Grayson had moved out, but seeing it felt different. It felt cold. His books were missing from the shelves, his toiletries from the medicine cabinet, his clothes from the closet. He'd left every photo of us, even his favorite from our first road trip to Palm Springs. And the Louis Vuitton backpack I had just gifted him for his birthday—I assumed because it had been purchased with the money I made from working this job. Seeing it made it all too real, and I couldn't stomach the idea of staying there alone. It was like standing in the brutal rubble of a place that used to be beautiful—devoid of the force that had made it a home.

So, after another six-hour flight, I landed in Maui. The deep blue ocean and sky full of lace was a world away from the entropy I was now accustomed to. For once, there was enough space and silence around me to just *be*, to let myself feel this heartbreak.

As I checked into the Andaz, Samantha called saying she'd get in sooner than expected. She didn't want to wait for a commercial flight, so she flew with Alexis to Capri and was chartering the same jet to Hawaii. "It's only seventy-five-thousand," she said, as if it were normal. It worried me that being in Alexis's world for three years had made her disconnected from reality, and I also felt guilty about her spending another five thousand to have me here. I changed into a tank top and bathing suit and made my way to one of the five restaurants on the property—the one closest to the beach, where I ordered a pineapple mojito. It felt good to have someone ask *me* what I wanted, and to know I could just be present in the moment, not having to worry about Alexis or her schedule. But at the same time, when I finally could relax, I constantly checked my phone. The chaos had become an addiction. How did I *relax* before? What did I *think* about?

Who was I, beneath all the noise, before all of this?

THE ANDAZ IN MAUI WAS the place to be for the Fourth of July, so I wasn't surprised when Lea Michele stopped me on my way back to the pool.

"Oh my God, *Hayden*! How are you? I heard you're working for *Alexis Shane*? Tell me *everything*!"

It excited me to see how ecstatic another celebrity was about my job being an *assistant*.

"Who was that?" Samantha asked, as I returned to the lounge chair next to her.

"Lea Michele."

"How do *you* know Lea Michele?"

"What, like I'm some kind of peasant?" I said. "The same way I know *you*. From the salon."

"Well, who's her manager?" She sat up on her elbows and lowered her bedazzled Gucci shades.

"We're not talking about *anything* work-related. You promised."

"Fine." She threw her body dramatically back into the lounge chair.

"You need to relax, lady."

"I can't," Samantha confessed. "She's supposed to sign the contract next week, and there's still so much to do before the tour."

"Samantha, we're in *Hawaii*. Please sweetieeeee, please," I said in Alexis's diva-tone.

She was silent for a total of thirty seconds but couldn't help herself. Her whole life was work, and she didn't know what to talk about outside of it.

"So, I was on the phone with Karen while you were over there," she said, then laughed, now aware of what she was doing. "We were trying to re-purpose some of Alexis's tour ensembles from last year to save money. But Charles just informed her it'd cost more to let them out from a size four to a size twelve than it would be to buy all new ones."

"*Size twelve?*" My mouth dropped. I knew Alexis had gained weight, but I didn't realize how much.

"I know. She was a size four as recently as March. But I think the combination of the medication, the drinking, the staying in bed—"

"*Okay*, enough! You're tricking me into talking about her again!" I climbed out of my chair. "Can't we just have a couple days? I'm gonna get us another round of mojitos. Maybe that'll shut you up."

But before I could make it to the pool bar, Samantha was shouting my name.

"HAYDEN!" she yelled from across the pool, oblivious to the fact that she was irritating relaxing vacationers. "Alexis is on the phone! She asked me to conference you in!"

"HAYDEN, SWEETIEEEEE, HOW'S SUNNY LOS Angeles?" Alexis cooed.

"Everything's great, Alexis! How are you?" I said, hating lying to her.

"Hayden," Samantha said, "Alexis is calling because the tour is about to start, and ever since Marlo came on board she and I have been in regular communication about everyone's position on the team."

"We have," Alexis agreed. "And when we were in Israel, things just became a lot clearer to me."

Where was this conversation headed?

"You know, Amber's in charge of wardrobe, Marlo is more of my day-to-day, and I don't want this to sound rude toward them at all but..." She lowered her voice to a whisper. "You're just *too smart* for those things."

"But Alexis, I love my job, and I—"

"Hayden," she giggled, "I'm not *firing* you."

Samantha joined in on the laughter.

"Like I was saying, the way you handled everything in Israel just really impressed me. So, I want you to work closer with Samantha. I want you to be a part of my *management team*."

My eyes welled up. I didn't know how to respond.

"Are you fucking *crying*?" Samantha cackled before remembering I was supposed to be in Los Angeles. "Is that why you're silent?" she said, covering her mouth, in shock at her own stupidity.

"Alexis, I don't know what to say." I cleared my throat. "Thank you."

"Alright, well, I'm glad that's settled. I just think with the tour coming up, Samantha doesn't need to be at *every* show, you know? She'll come to the major markets, and you'll be more of my day-to-day management, making sure everything is going smoothly. Samantha, will you call Karen after this and handle his raise?"

"Thank you so much again, Alexis. I don't even know *how* to say thank you."

"Of course, sweetieeeee. Now get back to enjoying your time off, a glass of bubbly is calling my name!"

"You're welcome," Samantha said smugly after hanging up. She reclined in her chair and took a sip of her fresh mojito. "You know this is just because she wants her boyfriend on the road, right? But hey, if that means I get to keep my job *and* not have to schlep around all summer on a tour bus to places like Kansas City, then it's fine by me. Either way, *you deserve it*. You work hard, you're smart, you're talented. You've proven what most people can't on this team—that you're irreplaceable."

I was already making $75,000 just to be one of three assistants. So, what would I make as part of the management team?

"Do you mind if I ask—"

"One-hundred-fifty is a good place to start, don't you think?" Samantha grinned, knowing it was more than generous.

I was in Maui, now making six figures, and about to travel North America with a living legend as part of her management team. What had my life become?

"I'm happy for you," she said, "but I think before you hit the road, you need to know about my history with Alexis. Because with this position comes a lot of responsibility."

I didn't think there was anything at this point that I didn't know, but Samantha took a serious tone.

"Sometimes you've questioned my decision-making, and I think that knowing everything that's happened will help you understand. You see, I signed Alexis three years ago by complete accident. I was never looking to do this."

I sat up in my chair, confused. Being that Samantha did come from the world of documentary production, fans wondered exactly how she became Alexis's manager.

"You know my friend, Quentin?" she asked.

"Of course." I'd only seen *Pulp Fiction* a dozen times.

"A few years ago, when Alexis and Rich were separating, the press was flooded with negative headlines about her. I only reached out to Quentin to connect me in hopes of making a documentary. I wanted to help her spin the narrative. And I guess Alexis had just confided in Quentin she was looking for a new manager to do the same thing. So, when I called, he saw the stars align."

Samantha felt bad for Alexis when they finally met, as she was basically alone, besides those on payroll.

"It was so sad, Hayden. She was even worse than she is now. Just so fucking overweight and lethargic—like a shell of herself. And she was needy to a point I hadn't experienced before. She'd call at all hours of the night pleading for me to come over and keep her company, then sleep the entire following day. 'I need vocal rest,' she'd say, even though there was nothing on the schedule."

After gaining Alexis's trust, Samantha got the job. During their late nights together, the two bonded over being women of a certain age in the entertainment industry and single mothers who had been cheated on.

"But the more time I spent with her, the more twisted I uncovered her life was. She didn't want to communicate with her business management and pleaded with me to handle her finances instead. You can imagine my shock when I found out the woman the tabloids claim is almost a billionaire is actually on the verge of bankruptcy. So, I made it my life's mission to turn hers around. I had to make her vibrant again. I had to make her money."

Her previous manager had been in talks for a South American tour, but Live Nation was ready to pull out.

"They told me, 'She's not well.' But I begged them to give me a chance to prove them wrong. So, I got her out of bed and into rehearsals. I did everything I could to add festivity to her life. I just wanted her to have *fun*, you know? I wanted her to remember that she's *Alexis Shane*."

Samantha proved herself and pulled together the tour, solidifying Alexis's dependency on her. So, when Samantha explained she needed to get home to relieve her parents and attend to her daughter, Alexis became upset.

"'*Nooo, Samantha,*'" she whined. "'Don't abandon me. Everyone always abandons me. I need a full-time manager. Someone who is with me *at all times.* Can you not do that?'"

"'How could anyone abandon you?' I asked her. 'You're Alexis Shane.'"

But it was true—Alexis had been through six managers the year prior. Not to mention Samantha had never made money like this before. So, she accepted the challenge, relocated Blair's life to the tour buses, and hired a teacher to come along to make sure she'd finish out the school year.

"I became not just her career manager, but her life manager. I didn't want that responsibility, but I wanted to make her happy. So, I did anything I could to help. Lawyers had been billing her hundreds of thousands of dollars per month, so I opened the line of communication between her and Rich, and personally settled their divorce. I hired a trainer to get her into great shape and would even stay up with her to do three a.m. workouts. By the first show, no one could believe how happy she was, how great she looked, and how amazing she sounded. Everyone had ruled her out."

Despite Samantha's earnestness and fervor, I couldn't help but think it was a little ironic Alexis had been in the same position only six months ago when I first was hired—lethargic, lambasted by the media, unmotivated, irrelevant. Perhaps these cycles were inevitable with her disorder, or perhaps Samantha didn't actually know what was best for her, as much as she claimed to.

Her appearance to the public was looking better. However, financially she was still a mess. Money wasn't coming in fast enough, and Alexis's business manager wanted to sell off her assets.

"The pressure was building as the IRS contacted Karen to inform her that if Alexis didn't pay her taxes, they'd come arrest her on stage to make an example out of her. So, I was taking meetings with everyone, trying to make money. But even after the tour, her reputation was so damaged that no one wanted to work with her. I went back to Live Nation again to sell them on a European leg. I thought it would be easy being that she had just killed it in South America. But they were concerned that it was too much, that she couldn't handle it. Still, I refused to leave without a yes, getting on my hands and knees to grovel. I've humiliated myself to save her from doing it herself."

While on the European tour, Quentin came to visit, and brought along Mark Kauffman—who quickly became Alexis's fiancé.

"I really thought I'd brought her back to life. She was skinny, touring the world, adored by fans, and now in this high-profile relationship. She was an A-list star again. But she couldn't help herself. She had to self-sabotage. It's the illness."

When the team had a day off in Sweden, Samantha walked into the bathroom of Alexis's suite to find her asleep in the tub.

"I was in tears, dragging her body from the bath." Samantha choked up. "I didn't know she had a pill problem. I just thought she was *eccentric*. After she woke up, I went through her bag and took all of them. There were benzos, Vicodin, Percocet, Ambien, Lunesta. I've never seen so many pills."

Now that Samantha wasn't just willing to let her do whatever she pleased, Alexis turned to Brody, a backup dancer who worked for her on and off over the past decade. He had a reputation in the industry for his obsession with fame, but Alexis didn't care. She just wanted someone to appease her addiction. And by the time the tour wrapped, they were in a full-blown affair.

The Alexis and Brody stories were so ridiculous that it was hard to believe. Like Brody breaking his arm while dancing on stage and *suing* Alexis in order to keep getting paid.

"She wanted to stay with someone who was *suing* her?" I asked.

"I just told you how dependent she was with *me*, so imagine how she is with someone providing her drugs and sex. When she's in control, she's in *full control*. But there are so many moments where she just goes away, Hayden, and that's when it's easiest for people like Brody to take advantage."

I didn't have the words to respond.

"Right. So now you can imagine why I don't really care for the schmuck."

"She didn't feel bad fucking Brody behind her fiancé's back?" I asked.

"Alexis told Kauffman she was saving herself for marriage," Samantha laughed. "She said she would just put on sexy lingerie and writhe around on top of him while he jerked off. Like she was in one of her music videos or something."

"So, why did she stay with him?"

"She said because of the kids. She wanted them to be taken care of for life. So, to keep Brody around, she paid what he asked, even firing her long-term choreographer to give him a position. But that wasn't enough. He wanted to sabotage the engagement."

Kauffman's team anonymously uncovered the news while en route to Fiji for the wedding and redirected the flight.

"I woke up to a voicemail from Kauffman crying hysterically, saying his team kidnapped him to keep him from marrying her."

I rolled my eyes.

"Seriously, ask Sebastian! He flew all the way to Fiji and got off the plane to find out there was no wedding. Then we flew home, and Alexis was so depressed—even though it'd been her own doing. She spoke about how she wanted to die like Marilyn. So, I knew I had to cut her ties with Brody. I'd built her up, and he was tearing her down. We bulked up security, changed her number, anything we could to keep him away. That was the first time I saw it."

"Saw it?"

"A manic episode. She'd sit in front of the mirror reapplying makeup for hours on end while talking nonsense. She'd lock me in the bathroom with her, and I'd wake up to find her wandering the house repeating, 'Please don't let me wind up like Britney Spears.' A week passed and I realized it wasn't just going away, so I called a shrink to the house who diagnosed her as bipolar. And now it's happened every other month since. I've had to sneak her in and out of UCLA or pay doctors to treat her at home. It's a constant up and down, and the only way to make it stop is to take medication."

When she came out of it, the IRS threats were intensifying. So, Samantha and Alexis, or I guess Bonnie and Clyde, plotted to sue her former fiancé. The infamous "annoyance fee" was to pay her taxes.

"Amber actually nearly ruined the whole thing. When she found out Mark was paying Alexis ten million dollars to go away, she hired her own lawyer and sued Mark as well. She made up this whole lie about him sexually harassing her."

"*What?*"

"Yeah, and he wound up paying her a million, too. I mean, I love my sister. But as if a billionaire would ever come onto her. She's a whale,"

Samantha laughed. "Anyway, that's the thing about this mental illness, Hayden. It's cyclical. Like in the beginning she was super depressed, in bed, heavy, lethargic. I brought her back to life, but she doesn't want to take her meds. She's her own worst enemy, and Brody feeds her drugs and alcohol to keep her reliant on him. I'm just tired of being the punching bag when all I've ever tried to do is help her."

"I don't even know what to say."

"I know this is a lot to take in. I just want you to *understand*. You question me, and you do give good advice. But you needed to know the full picture. Alexis and I were best friends, but once I uncovered her medical condition, I became enemy number one. This mental illness and addiction could take her life, but she doesn't care. That's the difference between her and me. I want her to be Cher, and she wants to be Whitney."

CHAPTER FOURTEEN

*I*n Vegas, I was woken not by my alarm, but by the thumping of the bass from the pool party outside my Planet Hollywood window. It was so loud I could make out every word to every song nineteen stories above the DJ. I called Amber to head over to Alexis's rental, a mansion twenty miles outside of the city, but was sent to voicemail.

When I stepped out of the elevator on the ground floor, I spotted her. At ten a.m. she already had a drink in one hand and was lying across the steps to enter the pool, having no consideration for the children struggling to get around her.

"Must be nice!" I said, approaching her.

The scent of the chlorine was so strong it made me gag. But it was probably necessary to kill whatever diseases these hotel guests were carrying.

"Get in!" she said, phone in hand, as if she hadn't just ignored my call.

"I've got way too much to get done over at the house. She'll be here before you know it," I said, expecting her to offer help.

"Oh, *please*. You have time," she scoffed. "Well, will you at least take some Insta-pics for me before you go?"

Amber handed me her phone, and comically lifted her large ass above the water, attempting to pose like a Kardashian. I tried not to laugh after noticing one false eyelash strip was half-attached.

I took what felt like a hundred photos—all hideous—before meandering my way through the casino in search of the VIP valet. Vanessa had sent a group email the night before, mentioning there'd be rental cars waiting for each of us to make traveling between the hotel and Alexis's home easy.

But when I found the valet, they had no clue what I was talking about. I let out a groan of frustration. Even the things she claimed were done never were. And I knew if I called to ask for clarification she'd be nasty. But I had no choice.

"Call the company," she said before quickly hanging up. But who was the company? There was no information in the email, so was I just supposed to call every car rental company in Las Vegas? It was like the only part of the job she cared about was what Alexis could see. The problem with that was a tour manager was responsible for taking care of *all of us*. But instead of causing myself unnecessary stress, I ordered an Uber to take me to the house.

The mansion was as large as her Beverly Hills home, but in this neighborhood, each place looked identical with matching beige stone and terracotta roofs. The key was hidden in an obviously fake rock, and I used it to unlock the heavy oak wood door. It opened to a long hallway, and to my immediate right was a large modern white kitchen with no walls, only floor-to-ceiling glass windows. Through it, I saw a deck overlooking a pool, hot tub, and basketball court.

I followed a handyman down the hall, passing a fully stocked restaurant-sized bar to our left, and next to it a large glass wine closet— stocked with only the best and under lock and key. The last door on our right was the primary suite. I walked in to find that every wall was also floor-to-ceiling glass—meaning it would need to be covered with black adhesive window film as Alexis had requested.

"Don't worry, sir," the handyman said. "I've done this for her before. It's easy! The hard part is taking it off after it's melted in the Las Vegas sun for weeks."

My phone vibrated in my pocket.

"When the U-Haul gets there, will you let me know?" Amber shouted over the blaring music at the pool.

"U-Haul?"

"This morning I had my friend John and his cousin load up Alexis's closet in Beverly Hills and start driving it to Las Vegas."

"Her entire closet?"

"Yeah. Alexis never seems to want me around anymore, so Samantha said I need to start going above and beyond. But if they get there before me, you can go ahead and start organizing."

Of course. Knowing Amber, she'd promised her friend thousands of dollars of Alexis's money without any instruction from Alexis herself. I'm not sure that's what's considered *going above and beyond*. It's more like theft. I started to strip the bed and replace the sheets when I heard yelling from the front door.

"Hello? *Hello?* I'm here to install the bounce houses!"

"The *what*?" I hurried down the hallway for the entrance, trying not to laugh-cry as everything piled up at once.

"The moon bounces."

"Uh, okay. One second," I said.

I called Samantha for confirmation, but there was no answer. And now everything began to arrive at once. Two dozen flower arrangements, Noah with a car full of groceries, and John with the U-Haul. All of this constant parading for one woman. It was incredible.

"I'll be with you in just a second, sir," I said, signing for the all-white rose arrangements.

With John and his cousin, I guided the forty rolling racks toward the primary suite's closet, which wasn't nearly large enough to contain them.

When I returned to the entrance to help the patiently waiting moon-bounce man, Vanessa pulled up to the house in a black Escalade.

"What's happening here?" she asked assertively.

"This guy is here for... the moon bounces?" I said, hoping she was familiar.

"Yes, it looks like I've got three in the truck for you," he said, reviewing his invoice. "The Barbie moon-bounce, the Spiderman moon-bounce, the water slide moon-bounce—oh, and a snow cone machine, too."

"Ahhh, yes," Vanessa said. "You've been here before, correct? You can go ahead out back and set up."

"Of course, I just need payment," he said.

"Well, *shit*. I don't have my company card on me," Vanessa said.

"Oh, I do!" I interrupted.

Vanessa turned to me with a furrowed brow.

"*You* have a company credit card?"

I pulled my wallet from my back pocket and handed my Platinum American Express card to the man.

"I mean, I kind of need one to be on the road." I laughed, trying to break the sudden tension. "If I spent my own money on all the things she needs, I'd go broke."

She wanted to make sure she was the only one able to charge super-fluous items.

"The handyman's installing the blackout adhesive now," I said. "The pool is working, the flowers are here. But I do still need to go buy the twins' beds. Maybe I could borrow your Escalade?"

"*Flowers?* Why did *you* buy flowers? I always buy the flowers."

"I didn't know, I'm sorry. I just did what Samantha asked."

Vanessa ignored my response and continued walking into the mansion.

"Hayden, come here," she said, waving me over toward the bar and pulling a key from her pocket. She used it to open the wine closet, then walked back to the bar, pulling specific bottles and passing them to me.

"What are you doing?"

"Pulling anything Brody likes. I need you to put them in the back of the wine closet so they are completely out of eyesight."

"But *why?*"

"Because when we stay here, Brody's bar tab is more than what it costs to lease the place."

Following Maui, I understood why Samantha did the things she did. But what about the rest of these people? Why were they trying to control Alexis's life? For entertainment? Did they really think they knew what was best for her? Is this what they called protecting her? But instead of saying anything, I did as I was told, not wanting to cause any more drama.

After hiding all the bottles, she locked the closet and dropped the key into her pocket.

"If anyone asks, we were never given a key," Vanessa said.

I HAD NEVER BEEN TO Candy Land before, but of course had heard of it. Founded right in the casino of Planet Hollywood, the chain was now a nationwide phenomenon. In Las Vegas, the way nightclubs gain notoriety is through their costly celebrity appearances. Candy Land copied the concept but with restaurants geared toward families. When attending, you knew you could rub shoulders with Kim Kardashian or

Rich Revolver, and then order their own creation from the menu. Kim came up with an oversized ice cream sundae, a scoop for every member of the Kar-Jenner family. Rich concocted twinning sugary drinks with Dry Ice and Swedish Fish, and Nicki Minaj had mannequin heads made of chocolate beneath cotton candy wigs.

I walked under the candy cane arch entry and passed signs proudly advertising it being the most Instagrammed restaurant in the world, finding Samantha in the far corner at a table full of older, professionally dressed white men. She looked right at home with her fiery hair and no-bullshit expression.

"*Alexis Shane's Candy Land*—it's a land within the Land," she explained. "So, when exiting Candy Land, you'll walk through a pop-up shop with diva-themed treats. Candy microphones, platinum albums, chocolate stilettos, champagne. We can even make Ring Pop replicas of every engagement ring she's been given! I mean, what an amazing opportunity for you guys to make even more money and provide your clientele with one-of-a-kind souvenirs to take home."

I didn't like it. It cheapened the Alexis Shane brand.

"And just so we're on the same page," Samantha grinned, "we don't want a *fee*. We want *equity*."

Following the meeting, venue security led the two of us through the bustling casino.

"They're willing to give our production company ten percent equity," Samantha explained, "and Candy Land is set to do three hundred million dollars this year, so that means Alexis and I will make thirty million dollars. Fifteen million each."

"*Fifteen million each?* I thought a manager gets ten percent."

"On incoming deals, of course, ten percent. But this is something I completely conceived on my own. So, it's considered one of our *productions*. And on productions, we split it. Fifty-fifty."

It sounded questionable, but what did I know?

"And all she has to do is make a few appearances and put her name on merchandise?"

"That's what she wants. I mean, fifteen million dollars is more than she's making for this entire tour. She said she doesn't want to schlep around the world anymore." Samantha shrugged. "But before we agree to anything, I need that fucking contract signed."

"Well she asked me to get comps for Karen and her lawyer tonight, so hopefully it'll be signed before they leave town."

"Yeah, and I have a lunch with them tomorrow to see what her notes are. So, it shouldn't be too much longer."

Security led us through the front of the venue, which opened to the stage.

"Oh my God!" I gasped. "This is enormous."

"No, it's not!" Samantha laughed. "She can still sell out sixty-thousand-seat venues overseas. Here there's only about five, and sometimes they even have to turn out the lights on the top balcony so no one can see they're empty. Yet another reason I'm trying to focus on opportunities like Candy Land."

We stopped talking as we reached the elevator and took it down to the dressing room where Big Wayne stood by to permit access. Samantha quickly passed him, walking through to see Alexis. But I stopped short and waved to Marlo from afar.

"Whachu doin' just standing there?" Marlo chuckled. "Come in!"

Marlo didn't tiptoe around Alexis like everyone else did. She just treated her like a normal person, which helped me relax.

"She ain't got nothin' you wanna see anyway!"

Alexis laughed at our interaction, then turned to whisper to Samantha. Something about a doctor.

"How's everything going, *supermodel*?" I asked Marlo, wanting to make it clear to Alexis that I wasn't eavesdropping.

"Boy, you crazy!" Marlo said. She lowered her voice to a whisper. "Are we not doin' rehearsal?"

"No," I muttered through my teeth. "I don't get it either."

"This a mess." She rolled her eyes. My phone pinged with a text message from Noah.

I typed, pretending to respond, but was instead listening in on Alexis and Samantha's conversation.

"Samantha, *I need one*," Alexis said. "I can't perform my best without it."

"Babe, you just had one. It's still in your system," Samantha said. "It's active for three days."

She was trying to talk Alexis out of something, but eventually caved. I sat quietly as Samantha dialed doctor after doctor, looking for anyone who would come last minute with something called Dexamethasone.

WHEN A DOCTOR DID AGREE, and quickly arrived, he, Samantha, and Alexis closed themselves into the bedroom of the dressing suite. I then jumped up, remembering I hadn't taken care of Alexis's ticket requests, and grabbed a lanyard from Big Wayne. I headed for the box office outside the venue, on my way googling "Dexamethasone"— a steroid shot, sometimes used by singers to reduce inflammation of the vocal cords. The most common side effect was weight gain.

"Hi! I work for Alexis Shane," I said to the man at the desk, holding up my backstage pass. "I just need to have a few tickets held for her business manager and lawyer."

"Sir, I can do it today. But Vanessa is the one who normally requests comps."

"That's fine. I'll let her know moving forward. I'm just in a time crunch."

But before I could even make it back to the dressing room, Vanessa was calling. She never missed an opportunity to bitch me out.

"Did you just go put in ticket requests at the box office?"

"Yeah, sorry. Alexis asked me to."

"Hayden, that's *my* job."

"I wasn't intentionally going around you, Vanessa. I didn't even know it was your thing. But it's close to show time and Samantha and Alexis are tied up, so I just ran over and figured it out myself."

Vanessa hung up. I sighed. It was getting exhausting trying to explain myself to everyone when my only intention was to do my job.

Back at the dressing room, I found Amber and Vanessa whispering in the lounge. The door closed behind me but was followed by a knock. Amber shook her head *no* aggressively, but I turned to open it.

"Hey man," Brody said.

I could feel the cold front moving in as Amber and Vanessa both glared in my direction.

"Hey!" I forced excitement, wanting to distract him from the glares. "So, when am I gonna meet all the hot dancers?"

"Whenever you're ready, man!" Brody chuckled. "Is she in there?" He pointed around the corner, to the glam room.

I nodded.

There was a level of excitement building up to the tour's kick-off show that I hadn't felt with her one-off performances in Europe. Maybe because this crowd was *paying* to see her. But in true Alexis fashion, she was due on stage at eight p.m., and it was nearing eight-thirty.

"THE HOUSE IS READY!" a production assistant shouted outside the dressing suite door.

Our entourage shuffled toward the door, when Brody stopped Alexis.

"Let's do it one more time, babe," he said. He picked her up awkwardly underneath one knee and twirled her in a circle.

We crammed into the small elevator and Alexis huddled in the corner, shielding her face with her hand from the overhead lighting. I held up my copy of the setlist to assist her, and she smiled. It was fun getting to know her quirks; it made me feel closer to her. The elevator doors opened, and we stepped out of Alexis's way as the production assistant guided her up the steps with a flashlight. It was dark with the curtain down, but I could still see the heads of the crew turning to get a glimpse of her. They didn't get to see her every day like I did. Samantha and I escorted her center stage, and the P.A. handed Alexis a bedazzled microphone. She checked her inner earpiece as Amber and Charles fluffed the train of her oversized red, orange, and yellow gown.

"You look gorgeous!" I shouted over the screaming fans.

Alexis blew me a kiss and fluttered her fingers delicately in my direction, her engagement ring glimmering in the spotlight.

The crowd was now chanting her name as the band began to play the first single she'd ever released. I made it to side stage just in time to watch the curtain go up and became emotional after seeing the fans lose it. *How was this now my life?*

I turned to Samantha. "Thank you," I said.

"Oh, come on, you queer." She rolled her eyes. "Let's go watch from the mix."

I didn't know what or where that was, but I followed her lead. Fans shouted Samantha's name as we walked through the venue, having recognized her from the documentary. And I felt important, powerful even, walking by her side with Alexis Shane credentials around my neck.

We squeezed into the mix in the center of the space, where all the equipment was. I watched excitedly as the screens behind Alexis displayed a beautiful visual of a phoenix rising from the ashes. The ashes contained images of iconic moments from her two-decade-long career and flew in every direction. The dancers moved dramatically across the stage and down the aisles with luxurious red, orange, and yellow fabric, making it appear as if her dress took up the entire venue. This was the show I had been waiting to see.

Samantha pointed to two open seats in front of the mix.

"What was that dexa-something about?" I whispered as we sat down.

"Sometimes singers get them for a little *boost*. But she wants one before every show. She's *addicted*." Samantha sighed. "I've even spoken to the doctors privately to try to have them give her a saline injection instead. But she can tell the difference."

I zoned out as Alexis began singing her most famous song, which contained a high note that I was unsure she could still hit. But to my surprise—she did.

"I TOLD YOU! I told *everyone*!" a wasted blonde shouted, pushing her friend teasingly. "SHE'S STILL GOT IT!"

"She really is incredible," I said proudly, turning to Samantha.

Samantha frowned. "Are you *serious*?"

"Yeah! The fact she's been doing this for so long and is still able to hit that note? I can't believe it."

"Well *don't*. That's not *her*, Hayden. Well, technically it is. But it's her... *in the year 2000*."

"What?" I asked in disbelief. The high notes were a backing track? It felt like I'd just found out Santa Claus wasn't real, and on Christmas Day. "Why'd you have to tell me that?"

"Didn't you watch the Super Bowl? That's why while she was singing nothing, the high notes continued to play in the background."

Once it was pointed out, I couldn't un-see it. Alexis would sing the lower register parts of the songs live, then lip the high notes while shielding her mouth and neck with the microphone so no one could tell. I slumped in my seat, disappointed.

"CAN YOU RUN DOWN TO the lobby and print off the invoices I forwarded you?" Samantha asked during our routine morning phone call.

"Then meet Karen and me at Carmine's for lunch. We're going over the contract with Alexis's lawyer. I also need you to have tickets at the box office for the studio heads from Universal. They're coming to the show tonight to hype Alexis up for award season."

I glanced over the invoices as I walked into Carmine's and felt sick to see Charles had charged Alexis $250,000 in styling fees over the past few weeks. I understood the magnitude of a couture gown, but how could anyone possibly justify such an egregious amount? After spotting the duo at a table in the corner, I handed them to Samantha. Without looking, she tossed the papers in front of Karen.

"Do you see this?" Samantha said. "Your job is to protect her, Karen. Why am I the only one who ever talks to her about budgets and over-spending? The money conversations are *your job*. I can't always be the bad guy."

Alexis was being paid seven million dollars for the tour. But after hair, makeup, wardrobe, backup singers, dancers, band, and crew, she was set to take home only about two—and Samantha wasn't okay with it.

"I just don't understand," Karen groaned. "How can she think this is okay?"

Overspending was a part of Alexis's mental health condition. Karen just didn't want to be the one to tell Alexis 'no' and potentially end her own payday. It was surprising to see that these people in such important positions had no backbone of their own. They were more barnacle than anchor.

"I'm calling Alexis now," Samantha said. "You have to tell her we need to cut Charles and the dancers. It'll save her a million dollars!"

"Samantha, wait!" Karen tried to stop her.

But Alexis quickly answered.

"Alexis? We're about to review the contract. But while Karen's here, we need to revisit this tour budget. Now listen," she lowered her voice to a whisper. "The whole point of this is to make you money. And that's not gonna happen when Charles is sending me quarter-mil invoices. Like, why? We already have the dresses, so let's let him go and have Amber dress you. I won't argue with you about the backup singers, but we should really cut the dancers. People are coming to hear *you*, not watch shirtless men. Are they really worth half a million?"

So much for making Karen do her job.

"Absolutely not!" Brody interrupted the call. "Alexis, you *need* the dancers!"

Because what fun would tour be for him without his friends?

"The deal was *you* stay out of business, and *I* stay out of personal," Samantha spat, her face now blood-red. "Alexis, let's revisit this when we can speak in private."

"Okay," she said.

"Before I forget, after Las Vegas, the team will predominantly be traveling by buses. I sent you the passenger list for each one last night. Did you see? Does everything look all right to you?"

"No, Samantha," Brody interrupted again. "The twins aren't coming on *our* bus. Alexis and I need alone time."

Samantha was biting her tongue so hard I thought it might fall off. How could he not want *her* kids on *her* bus? Some of those bus rides were long. Eighteen hours long. He was only concerned about his own comfort, which he clearly took for granted, seeing that none of this luxury would be available to him without her.

"Nosey! Can you get out of here?" Alexis shooed Brody like I had never heard before. "Just give me a few minutes!"

We heard the door to their bedroom slam behind him.

"Alexis, it's me," Karen finally spoke up after aggressive hand gestures from Samantha. "We need to get this spending under control, so that you can actually benefit from all your hard work. Now, I'm looking at Charles's invoices, and I can't let you pay this guy a quarter of a mil every few weeks."

"Karen... don't you think if I'm the one who has to schlep across the world, doing all of these performances, entertaining hundreds of thousands of people, that I should get to choose whichever stylist I want?"

Alexis was unwilling to change her twenty-year spending habits. Especially just after she had been living in the lap of luxury with Mark Kauffman.

Karen became silent.

"Alexis," I inserted myself to the surprise of the table. Samantha dug her red, freshly manicured talons into my hand to silence me. "I'm sorry if I'm overstepping. But I just want to say there are so many stylists in the world. Ones who would be so thrilled to dress you, they would do it for free. And I'm more than willing to spend the time to find you one you love."

"Hayden, I appreciate that, but—"

"*Listen*, I do better with material examples," I interrupted again, and Samantha's nails dug further into my skin. "So, to put it materialistically, you bought Charles a Bentley for a couple weeks of work."

The line went silent.

"Now would you rather buy Charles a Bentley, or *yourself*?"

"Hayden," she said now confidently, "get Charles *the fuck* out of here."

When Alexis hung up, I received an actual round of applause from the table.

CHAPTER FIFTEEN

W e only had two days off back home in Los Angeles, and it was spent doing damage control. Alexis's weight gain was now not just a viral meme, but national news. One headline read, THINKING ABOUT SEEING ALEXIS SHANE THIS SUMMER? THERE'S *A LOT* TO SEE.

I incessantly told Samantha we had to do something about it. To which she'd respond, "Alexis hates working out." But that wasn't my point. It honestly was okay if she didn't want to lose the weight. She just needed to address it and be in control of her own narrative. Maybe she could do a cover shoot with the caption reading, I'M PROUD OF MY CURVES, and we could turn this on the media for body shaming her and make her a hero to women everywhere.

But I knew Alexis Shane well enough by now to know she never wanted to be *that* girl. She wanted to keep up the appearances of old Hollywood glamour. Which meant if she gained a little weight, she'd take care of it quickly and quietly.

Samantha was nervous about the days off when Alexis had downtime with Brody, assuming he'd use it to talk her out of signing their contract. Even though it was only forty-eight hours, she was adamant about Alexis hitting the town. "We need to keep your face out there!" she said. And while Samantha was to meet with her lawyer in another attempt to finalize the contract, I was sent to Alexis's, who was due for a lavish celebrity dinner in honor of Demna, the creative director of Balenciaga.

"*Whyyyyy?*" Alexis whined, still under the covers, as I opened her bedroom door. "*Please*, Hayden. Just tell Demna I have too much to do before we leave again for the tour. He'll understand. And I really don't feel like being around all of those *whores* right now, anyway."

The whores she was referring to were Demna's muses, the Kardashian sisters.

Alexis sat up in bed and checked her reflection in a floor-length mirror. She didn't read the tabloids, but I knew she could tell how big she'd gotten. While I'd never talked to a woman about her weight before, I'd also never been a part of an artist's management team before. I knew I had to bring it up, but my stomach felt pitted out just thinking about it. I didn't like treating her like a commodity, but I knew she'd feel better once we addressed it, as another bout of barely breathable corsets was *not* preferential.

"So, I was thinking... Obviously, we have glam booked for the tour. But is there anyone else you would like to have with us? Should we bring Noah? Or what about... a personal trainer?"

"Hayden, I know," she said, avoiding eye contact.

"You know?"

"I've been doing this for a long time, okay? This isn't the first time this has happened to me. Obviously, I'm not very happy with the way I look right now." She sighed and fiddled with her finely manicured thumbs.

"Either way, you're beautiful!" I said quickly, caught off guard by her response. "But if you *do* want to work out, I just wanted to say I'm more than happy to do it with you. It's never really been my thing either." I laughed, trying to lighten the mood and hating every word coming out of my mouth. "But I'll do it *for you*."

"Let's just talk about this in six weeks, after the tour wraps. I don't want to have yet *another* person on the road with us if I'm not going to use them. And what I normally do... well, I'll need recovery time. And that's just not an option right now with the schedule."

I nodded, eager to make her feel better. "Whatever you want to do is your decision, and I support it. So, no on Balenciaga?"

"*No*. Please cancel it. I just want to rest, Hayden. *Please*." She slumped back into the bed, pulling the blankets up around her neck.

I didn't want to be like Amber and completely push Samantha's agenda. So, I obliged and took my boss's orders. I couldn't imagine the energy it took out of her to perform in front of thousands of people every night, and it wasn't fair to force her out of the house just because of Samantha's paranoia. It was her day off, and she wanted to relax and spend time with her boyfriend. But glam had already arrived, meaning that regardless, they were charging. So, after I sent my regrets to Balenciaga, I took it upon myself to make her a late dinner reservation at the Ivy.

"Alexis?" I called through the door, hoping she hadn't fallen back asleep. I peeked in to find her scrolling through Netflix. "I canceled Balenciaga, but glam did just arrive. I can either send them home, or if you want, I booked you and Brody a late dinner reservation at the Ivy on the shore. I figured maybe you'd want a little romantic dinner before the chaos continues."

Alexis sat up and smiled at me, genuinely, in a way she hadn't before. She was grateful I had done something for *her*. She climbed out of bed and whisked past me to the glam room to get ready for what *she* wanted to do.

UPON LANDING IN SAN FRANCISCO, we were driven by a fleet of black Escalades to the artist entrance of the venue, where we were greeted by the tour buses that we'd call home for the next six weeks. I remembered seeing them on the freeway when I was a child in Maryland, and I'd fantasize about which glamorous superstar could possibly be driving through my small town.

I hadn't yet seen the process of unloading the tour at a venue, as during the string of shows in Las Vegas, we stayed put at Planet Hollywood. I had no idea how many people Alexis really employed, and it was overwhelming to find a hundred employees running around in her tour tees. Some built the stage, some transported wardrobe and props, and others unloaded an entire eighteen-wheeler full of merchandise. There was even a catering team whose sole responsibility was to feed us. Now it made a little more sense where all those millions were going.

As the entourage reached the dressing suite door, we were met by Chad, the head of Live Nation touring, and an assistant with a handful of credentials.

Alexis scowled at him. "What are you doing in San Francisco?"

"I know Samantha's not here tonight, so I just came to make sure you're on stage by eight p.m. sharp!"

"I have Hayden, Chad. We'll be fine."

"Don't lose these!" the assistant interrupted, passing out the credentials, her hands shaking. She was trying to avoid eye contact with Alexis. "You need them to get around backstage. Venue security is different in each city. So, they won't know you like in Las Vegas. God forbid you get removed!" she said, laughing nervously.

I thanked her and followed the entourage into the suite, quickly noticing it was nothing like Las Vegas either. Because it wasn't one. It was simply a large dressing room with a mini-fridge, vanity, and sofa. Meaning no adjoining rooms for me to wait. I started to sit, thinking I was safe, until Amber shot daggers in my direction. She nodded her head toward the door. But as I made my way there, Alexis stopped me.

"Hayden? What have you thought about the setlist so far?" She tapped her nails against the song titles taped to her vanity.

I was welcome in the dressing room by the only person that mattered. *I made it*. I walked up and peeked over her shoulder, trying to act casual in what to me was a rather symbolic moment. "Well *personally*, I love it. And I know whatever you choose, your fans will love too. So don't stress! And if you decide one night you want to switch things up, we can. It's really no big deal."

She smiled.

After the simple booking of her reservation at the Ivy, I finally knew how to work with her. She'd become accustomed to being bulldozed by Samantha's opinions and wanted to know hers still mattered. It felt like I was dreaming as I followed her in a close pack down the long hallway toward the stage. As we got closer, the energy in the arena became palpable. Fans chattered in disbelief that *the* Alexis Shane was in their town and began chanting her name.

"*ALEXIS! ALEXIS! ALEXIS!*" This mantra was becoming familiar to me. I knew the sound of this devotion would mark my life forever, that this would amount to one of the most precious periods of my life. The drums kicked in, and Brody pulled me by the inside of the elbow through black curtains to stage left so we could catch Alexis emerge. As she sang the iconic first line to her debut single, a shiver ran up the curve of my spine. She was singing *completely live*. I couldn't just *hear* the difference.

I could *feel* the emotion pouring from her. I looked around in awe as the words she wrote touched every concertgoer's heart. The faux scandal of something as superficial as her weight mattered to no one in this moment. They were entranced with the way she made them feel, ten thousand pairs of eyes appealing to her with love.

AFTER FOUR SHOWS ON THE West Coast, we were headed back to Los Angeles for a performance at the Hollywood Bowl. Alexis's bus, of course, was glamorous and luxurious. But the rest of ours were *not*. In the front of ours was a small seating area and an unusable kitchen with a broken fridge, followed by a long hallway with sixteen coffin-like bunk beds, and in the far back, three couches and a television.

Sleeping on the bus was also pretty much impossible. If you were on the top bunk, you felt like you were going to roll out, and if you slept on the bottom, you felt every bump on the road. And forget it if Vanessa was above you. The creaking of her excessive weight left me wide awake with anxiety that the bed would collapse. So, I was thrilled to have one more night at home in my own bed, knowing there were another five weeks of touring ahead of us, though in the middle of the night I found myself reaching for Grayson. His absence was still hard to believe, especially because I was never home anymore.

I woke up refreshed after sleeping in, happy to know I'd be left alone until showtime. That is, until Marlo sent me a request from Alexis to push back the bus pick-up time. She reasoned that Alexis's home was only five miles from the Hollywood Bowl. But in Los Angeles, that doesn't matter. Five miles can take an hour.

"*I'll have the glam boys come to the house instead so she can have more time at home,*" I texted her. "*But we can't push it. She needs to be out the door not a second past 7 p.m.*"

I wanted to appease Alexis, but at the show in Sacramento, she was fifteen minutes late to stage. I received a furious phone call from Chad after Alexis insisted he go home, assuring him I was capable of holding her accountable. He warned that if she was late again, he'd incur a fine that was larger than my yearly salary.

The Hollywood Bowl is the most iconic venue in Los Angeles, the place

aspiring singers dream of performing. Pulling up to see "TONIGHT 9 P.M.
ALEXIS SHANE" across the famous marquee made me proud. I drove
in circles in search of the artist entry, and when I found it, I had to pass
through more security than I'd remembered seeing during a childhood
field trip to the White House. A quick flash of my backstage credentials
permitted access through most checkpoints, but as I reached the last one,
they weren't enough.

"What's your name?" the security guard asked me.

"Hayden."

"Hayden?"

"Hayden Baldwin," I said.

"Your name isn't on the list," he said.

Of course.

"Who provided you with the list?"

"The tour manager."

I called Vanessa twice. No answer.

"Sir, we're gonna need you to turn your car around," he said, seeing
that I was struggling to get ahold of her.

At the same time, I caught one of Big Wayne's backup security parking
his car after being let through.

"Sir! Sir!" I shouted, frantically waving him over. "I'm so sorry, I don't
remember your name. I work for Alexis."

"What's the problem?" he asked the venue security. "Hayden's part
of Alexis's management team. I can vouch for him."

With his acknowledgment, I was permitted access and led backstage
to Alexis's dressing room. I breathed deeply, trying to calm myself. I
was getting closer and closer to having a freak-out any day now over
Vanessa's unapologetic incompetence. Inside, Sebastian and Lion were
waiting patiently.

"What are you guys doing here?" I asked. "Did you not get my text?
Is Alexis here?"

"Nooooo," Sebastian said. "We went to the house and Marlo told us
to meet them here."

After twenty years with Alexis, he instinctively knew he was going to
be left with *minutes* to apply her makeup, which normally took *hours*.

"I hate when I'm set up to fail, you know? I need the time. Especially *now.* She's so fucking fat, and I need to shade her neck. Do you know how long it takes, trying to hide that massive double chin?"

Sebastian abruptly stopped talking as Samantha entered screaming into her phone.

"This is not a fucking joke, Amber! Alexis has to be on stage in *ten minutes*, or she'll be fined *thousands* of dollars!"

"Where are they?" I asked, instantly absorbing her anxiety.

"They're stuck down at the light! Where have you been, Hayden?" she hissed. "Did you not tell them when to leave?"

"Of course I—"

"Just stop!" she shouted, raising her hand in my face. "The power's out at the bottom of the hill, and their bus is stuck at the light. Traffic control isn't there, and she has to be on stage *like now*! So, we're gonna have to go get them."

I tried to keep my composure, but it seemed no matter what, inconvenience after inconvenience always stacked up against us. Everything was somehow inexplicably more complicated than it needed to be. "What do you mean, go get them?"

Samantha grabbed the sleeve of my tour hoodie and pulled me toward the artist entrance. After spotting a venue employee in a golf cart, she whistled for his attention.

"I need you to drive us down to the main road!" she said.

"Ma'am, I can't take this on the road."

"Just fucking go!" she shouted, and we both hopped in. "It's for *Alexis Shane*!"

The driver no longer hesitated. He stomped the gas, and we plummeted quickly down the frighteningly steep hill. When we reached the bottom, the bus was still at the light. Samantha hopped off with a worn-in black Birkin at her elbow and began to literally stop traffic. I followed her lead, and the two of us frantically waved our arms to stop cars to get the golf cart up to the bus door.

The door opened. Alexis, Samantha, Marlo, and Brody piled in and quickly took off back up the hill. Amber and I chased behind on foot, and fans waiting to enter the venue spotted Alexis and screamed in disbelief to find her chugging up the hill in a golf cart with her famous chocolate locks billowing behind her.

At the top, the team rushed inside. But being behind, Amber and I were again stopped by venue security.

"Ma'am! Ma'am!" security shouted at Amber as she ignored them and continued running through.

But another guard caught up and physically stood in her way.

"Get your fucking hands off me!" she shouted, although no one had touched her. "How dare you touch a woman! What the hell is wrong with you?" She raised her voice even louder, turning the heads of everyone in earshot. "ASSAULT! ASSAULT! *HELP!* THIS MAN IS ASSAULTING ME!"

"Amber, calm down!" I pleaded, wiping the sweat from my forehead. "He's just trying to do his job. Sir, I'm so sorry. She's with me. You and I met earlier."

"ASSAULT! What's your name, sir? I'm calling the police!" She pulled her phone from her pocket.

"Ma'am, we just need to make sure you're on the list. I can't have you running after Alexis Shane when I have no clue who you are."

"I'm her assistant!" she spat. "And you'll let me through, or you'll *never* work in this town again!"

While he laughed, I felt humiliated.

People thought Alexis Shane was a diva. But the truth was the people around her were so much worse.

I WAS NERVOUS FLYING AHEAD of the team to Houston. While I'd already been Samantha's stand-in between major markets, I now wouldn't see her for weeks, and she'd been my protection from Amber and Vanessa. With her gone, I wasn't sure exactly *what* they'd try to pull. Alexis had warmed to me, of course. But she wasn't exactly inviting me over to her suite for girls' nights either. Still, I couldn't pretend like being on the road wasn't fun. We always stayed at a Four Seasons, so I was never slumming it. And maybe it sounds silly, but it made me happy to set things up for Alexis and make her feel more at home.

The bus drive from LA to Houston was twenty-one hours, leaving me plenty of time to have dinner with family who'd relocated to the city after I graduated high school. But first, I wanted to call Vanessa and confirm their arrival time. No answer. I tried texting her, but still no response.

Luckily, I was able to get ahold of Big Wayne, who informed me the team was now due to arrive at six the following morning.

Knowing this, I should have felt more at ease. But I was nervous to see my father. My relationship with him had been strained for twelve years now, since he kicked me out of my childhood home during my senior year of high school after walking in on me with an older man.

"Well, look at you now!" my father exclaimed, walking through the lush hotel lobby. He greeted me with an awkward hug before giving me a head-to-toe examination of my matching Adidas tracksuit and new Gucci fur slides.

When I was young, he'd always been good at expressing his affection, but now when we saw one another there was an air of discomfort between us—no matter how much time had passed, or how many conversations were had. He also never asked if I was seeing anyone. I'd hoped when Grayson and I became serious, he might change. I hoped he'd see my relationship was "normal." But he never once asked about him, or how he was doing. It was as if he wanted to pretend my boyfriend didn't exist. So, I knew he was uninterested in hearing about my heartbreak.

My two youngest brothers, on the other hand, were always thrilled to see me. I was the cool older brother, now even cooler due to the fact I was traveling the world with a pop star.

"Can we see her room?" asked my youngest brother, Cameron, as we took a seat in the hotel's restaurant.

"Are you *crazy*?" my father corrected him for his brazen request before initiating his own line of interrogation.

"So, what exactly do you *do* for her?"

"You do *what* to her room?"

"How much does all of this cost?"

"When does she get in?"

What had now become normal to me mind-boggled my family, and I took glee in explaining my role. When the bill came, my father pulled out his wallet. But I stopped him.

"I got it," I said, to his surprise.

For the first time ever, at twenty-nine years old, I was able to pay for my family's meal. My father knew I'd always wanted to be successful, but we both had no idea if it would ever happen. I wasn't exactly ever interested in school, and one can't exactly bet on being a superstar's assistant as a future job. But somehow I had made it to the other side. I knew he was proud of me for my success, even if he wasn't forthcoming about it. He smiled as I signed the check.

"I'm gonna try to get you guys tickets for the show tomorrow night," I said.

"That would be awesome!" Cameron chuckled as my dad nodded his head in approval.

I said *try* because, with Samantha gone, I had to go through Vanessa. And being that she regularly ignored me, I couldn't count on it.

SAMANTHA INSISTED THAT PART OF my advancement responsibilities was to be up and waiting for the team upon their arrival—no matter what time of day. So, at six a.m. I hurried to the lobby and went out the front door to wait side by side with the bellmen, anticipating the buses to pull up at any second.

Five minutes passed. Fifteen minutes passed. Thirty minutes passed. The hotel employees continued watching my every move, also anxiously anticipating Alexis's arrival in hopes of getting a glimpse of the superstar. I took a seat inside the double doors and called Vanessa, but again no answer.

How was I going to do my job when the tour manager, the very person responsible for communicating with me—*wouldn't communicate with me*? An hour passed, two hours passed, and my frustration was growing. The staff looked at me with pity. Finally, after two-and-a-half hours of waiting, the buses pulled up. I shot off the bench and up to the door of Alexis's bus. In the one behind, I saw the entourage begin to unload. No one was exactly thrilled to see me. And I guess after being on a bus for almost twenty-four hours, how could they be?

"Welcome to Houston, ya'll!" I said as we entered the Four Seasons to blatant stares and gaping mouths from both guests and hotel employees alike.

On our way to the elevator doors, Vanessa wordlessly snatched from my hand the envelopes containing the entourage's room keys. She passed Marlo her envelope. "Hayden," Marlo said, examining the rooming list, "my room isn't next to Alexis's. It *has* to be next to Alexis's."

"I'm so sorry! I didn't actually choose the room assignments. That's Vanessa," I said. "Vanessa, can we swap her room with someone else?"

As the entourage loaded into the elevator, Vanessa stopped me from boarding by grabbing my wrist.

"We'll grab the next one!" she said through gritted teeth, a fake smile plastered across her face.

The elevator doors closed. I rolled my eyes in anticipation of whatever diatribe she was brewing.

She pushed me back with two fingers. "What's your problem, asshole? Don't you understand what I'm trying to do? We need to keep Marlo *away* from Alexis, not push them together."

"Vanessa, what are you talking about? Alexis Shane wants her assistant in the room next to her."

"Where *her* room is, is none of *your* business. That's *my* job, and I'm doing what is best for Alexis."

"What's *best* for her? That's not up to you! Marlo's room should be wherever Alexis wants, *period*. You're just trying to irritate Marlo to the point of her not wanting to be around. You want to make her life difficult, just as you do mine. Would it really have been that hard for you to tell me the arrival time, instead of having me wake up at six a.m. to sit outside for three hours? Did you really have to not include my name on the list at the Hollywood Bowl? And what about the ticket comps in Las Vegas?"

I gave her the opportunity to respond, but she didn't.

"When there are problems," I said, "I'm going to solve them. Okay? I'm not gonna have Marlo upset thinking that I'm not doing my job, to cover for your fucking game of chess."

I pressed the elevator button, ready to leave her behind. But as I went in, she followed silently. The doors opened to the penthouse, and I headed for Alexis's room.

"*Hayden!*" Alexis squealed, "Everything is *perfect!*"

"I'm so happy to hear that." I blushed, my heart still racing after laying into Vanessa.

"Seriously, Hayden. Thank you *so much*. You did all of this by yourself? You ran around and printed pictures from the twins' birthday and bought these gorgeous balloons?" She pointed to the metallic phoenix display in the corner. "Oh my God, and did you get us these cowboy hats too? I love them! *So* festive! How did you have time to do all of this, on top of the rider?"

I felt the heat radiating from Vanessa behind me. She walked around us to head for the television in the bedroom to begin hooking up the Apple TV—seemingly the only thing she could actually do.

"Will you take a photo of me in one of these?" Alexis held up two different cowboy hats. "I want to show the fans how excited I am to be here!"

Alexis tried on both the black and tan cowboy hats in a mirror above the dining table, before choosing the tan. She posed in front of me. But before taking the photos, I led her by the wrist to face better lighting. She beamed. After taking two dozen, I handed the phone back for her to review.

"I hope you don't mind, but—" I started to say, but my sentence was interrupted by screams from the twins. I lowered my voice to a whisper. "I bought some toys for the twins and put them in their room with a note from you. I just figured they deserved it after enduring that long bus ride."

"You are *so* sweet, Hayden." She hugged me. "Thank you so much for being so thoughtful."

I'd wanted to impress her, but had no idea it would be so well received. And after the scuffle with Vanessa, her joy was especially welcome. "Do you think you could get some Norwegian smoked salmon sent up from room service? I'm starving!" she said. "Also," she now whispered, "could you just have the Apple TV set up before I arrive? So when I come to the room, I can just relax. Instead of having this circus of people in here…"

"Of course!" I said nervously, knowing this request was *not* going to help me with Vanessa.

CHAPTER SIXTEEN

*S*amantha helped me get comps for my family in Houston, and I joined them in the audience to find them ecstatic about how close they were to the stage. I watched eagerly anticipating my legendary boss's emergence. I felt so proud to be working for her. But when Alexis finally did appear, their expressions told me maybe I shouldn't be. I turned my attention from their faces to the stage to find her looking heavy, stumbling in heels and struggling to hit the high notes. Once again, I was embarrassed. Her performances were completely unpredictable. Each night was either a hit or a disaster. There was no consistency in her life at all. But how could I expect every performance to be perfect when she was simply reflecting back to the world the chaos of her immediate surroundings?

The next week, I woke in New Orleans to the normal hurricane of missed calls and text messages from Samantha. But also, an *actual hurricane*. I made my way downstairs to greet the entourage at the double door entry, where water had begun rising up the handicap ramp into the lobby. Tiptoeing along the edge of the ramp, I climbed onto the guard rail to avoid soaking my sneakers and used the sleeve of my hoodie to clear the fogged-up glass door. I peered out to see panicked pedestrians holding on to anything that didn't move as the water level neared their knees.

When Alexis's bus arrived, it was unable to pull up to the hotel. It had to park on a corner a block away, unaffected by the flooding. And she had to be *carried in* by security. The rest of the team was not so lucky. To make it to the hotel, they had to sludge through the same street of rushing brown water that I'd just watched nearly carry people away.

Sebastian and Lion led the way, carrying hair and makeup bags over their heads.

My phone rang.

"Hayden? Where's security?" Amber asked.

"What do you mean? With Alexis," I said, eyeing her through the doors.

"Will you call Wayne? We're gonna need security to carry us in!" she shouted. "He isn't answering my calls. Or if he wants, I can try myself. But if I get hurt... somebody's getting sued!"

When I called Wayne, he laughed before responding.

"You think I'm gonna be able to carry those heifers across the block? Yeah, right. Three of us couldn't do that, my man. Just tell her I didn't pick up."

I couldn't begin to explain the glee it brought me to see Amber and Vanessa nearly swimming across the French Quarter. I basked in every moment as they winced and floundered their way across, their screams audible from half a block away.

"Hayden, you aren't hoping they float away, are you?" Sebastian chuckled.

I tried to contain my laughter.

"I mean, it did cross my mind."

BEING RAISED AS A YOUNG black girl in an all-white home was difficult for Alexis. She had talked about it in interviews over the years, but also with me during mania. She said she felt more comfortable around who she referred to as "my people." So, when Alexis took the stage in New Orleans, in front of a predominantly black audience, there was an electricity in the air. The crowd loved her, and she them, making it her strongest performance thus far.

But seeing her on stage wasn't enough. The super-fans wanted autographs and selfies. They trampled over one another out of the venue to gather by the artist entrance, laughing and shuffling in adoring anticipation.

Following touch-ups, Wayne opened the double doors to a mob scene. Fans of all ages were screaming and crying. Some holding up signs and phones, others trying to push their way through the barricades and venue security.

"It's not safe, Alexis. I'm sorry," Wayne said, "I can't have you go over."

"Wayne, *come on*!" she pleaded. "Just a few selfies!"

Until one fan actually did make it over the fence, falling to their knees, in a replica of one of the dresses Alexis had just debuted on tour. They got up, raced past venue security, and charged for her. Their hand reached to grab her, when Big Wayne intervened, picking up the fan by their neck and carrying them back to where they came from.

It terrified me. But not Alexis. She was used to it. She just raised her eyebrows and smiled.

"Hayden, was that a *woman*? Or a man in drag?" She laughed. "I really couldn't tell!"

"Uhhh…" I stammered, still in shock. "It was definitely a drag queen!"

"He looked incredible!" she said, interlocking her arm with mine. "Maybe we should hire him to be my body double?"

THERE WAS NO SUITE FOR me to prepare in Miami because, at the last minute, Alexis decided she wanted to charter another yacht. This took me off my flight and put me on the bus with Vanessa and Amber. *Great.* After everything I'd seen, I knew I couldn't trust them anymore. I became even more paranoid when, during the entire bus ride, Amber peered over Teddi's shoulder to read her text messages. As if the nanny was doing something worth spying on. She was absolutely crazed by this point.

When our buses pulled up to the dock, I threw my monogram poor-person Louis Vuitton duffle over my shoulder and walked to the front.

"Where you goin'?" Marlo asked me.

"Ummm… *the boat*?"

"*We're* going on it," she said, then pointed to my bus. "Not *y'all*. The rest of you will be at the hotel."

"Oh, okay," I said in defeat.

"Sebastian? Lion?" she shouted toward the bunks. "Boys, get up! You're comin' with me."

Every time I thought Alexis and I had gotten somewhere, I was knocked back to reality. I was still one of *Samantha's people*. Luckily, we were in a "major market" so I wouldn't be alone with Dumb and Dumber for long.

When Samantha landed, I was her first call.

"How's the weather? How's the hotel? Was Alexis happy with the boat? Where is everyone?"

I'd never been so happy to hear her thick New Jersey accent rattle off questions.

"As if I know," I laughed. "I'm hiding in my hotel room."

"We all need to sit down and hash things out," she said. "Let's meet in my room in an hour so we can get it over with and enjoy our time in Miami."

I walked out on my balcony to find Vanessa and Amber by the pool. The two looked like gluttonous whales surrounded by an excess of food they could never finish. But they didn't care, as Vanessa was undoubtedly putting it on Alexis's card.

"Fine," I said. "I'll see you soon."

An hour later, I was the last to arrive at Samantha's room. She was staying in the suite that was supposed to be Alexis's because the hotel refused to give a refund.

"All right," Samantha said, "we need to have a little group therapy. Because we're all on the same team, and we can't keep operating like this."

"Everything's fine, Samantha," Vanessa muttered, scrolling on her phone.

"Well, everything's not fine considering the phone call I got from you in Houston," Samantha said. "And then there was the one in New Orleans when you were upset about Alexis linking arms with Hayden. Should I continue listing cities?"

"Hayden and I just don't need to work together," Vanessa said.

"Vanessa, that's not really up to you. I'm the manager, and Hayden is an extension of management. He has been for months now, yet you refuse to accept it. So, let's get to the root here. What's your problem?"

"I just don't like him," Vanessa said brazenly, not caring that I was feet away.

"And why don't you like him?" She was a music manager but sounded like a kindergarten teacher.

"Because I don't trust him."

Samantha rolled her eyes. "And what exactly has Hayden done to make you not trust him?"

"This is *ridiculous*," I interrupted. "I don't like you either, Vanessa. But you've taken it to a place of making us look unprofessional. Not liking me shouldn't keep you from doing your job. You need to turn in ticket comps when Alexis requests them, and you need to put Marlo in the room next to hers if that's what Alexis wants."

"You are *not* the boss of me," Vanessa puffed her chest and crossed her arms. "I'll just speak to Alexis directly if she has a problem."

"You will absolutely *not* speak to Alexis Shane about any of this bullshit!" Samantha said in a raised voice. "Do you understand me? You never bother the artist! Are you fucking insane? Just do your job!"

"Oh, and I haven't even mentioned the plethora of things Sebastian and Lion have come to me about," I said. "They painted a pretty vivid picture of all the things a tour manager is supposed to be doing, that you're *not*. It's embarrassing, Vanessa. You're making your sister look bad."

"What?" Samantha panicked. "What did they say?"

"Why are you even listening to this bitch?" Vanessa asked.

"Vanessa, you need to get it together. I'm serious! Mania is long over, and I'm done with the games of sabotage. I want to *work*, not *babysit*. If you can't do your job, just tell me and I'll find someone who can."

Vanessa huffed her way to the door, slamming it behind her.

Sinking into her chair, Samantha let out an audible sigh.

"Did I fuck up by employing my sisters?" she asked Amber. "I wanted to give you both opportunities, but Vanessa's losing her damn mind! Why is she so paranoid?"

Amber didn't respond, probably afraid that she was next.

"I just... I need help, *okay*? I need you guys to make sure everything is running smoothly. I don't need you two making things more complicated."

"I understand," Amber said quietly.

"Then why have you been dodging Karen's calls? I know she's been trying to get ahold of you for weeks."

"I have nothing to speak to her about," Amber said.

"It's not about if *you* have something to speak to *her* about, Amber. She has something to speak to *you* about. Forget it. We're not talking about this in front of Hayden."

"I don't care if Hayden's here. I'll tell you right now. Under no circumstance will I give *permission* to cut my pay," Amber said. "It's not my fault Alexis hired Marlo, or that Hayden was promoted. Both of those things are not my problem."

"It's not permanent, Amber! Once the Candy Land money starts rolling in, you'll go right back to your normal salary," Samantha said. "You know her finances, so just have a little empathy. She can't afford to pay you four hundred grand a year right now!"

$400,000 dollars a year? My mouth dropped. I was over the moon with my $150,000. And she didn't do half of what I did. Actually, she didn't even do a quarter of what I did. It was hard for me to fathom Alexis being okay with pouring that much money into a useless output.

"I'm sorry, but this isn't my problem, Samantha. If you two can figure out how to pay Hayden and Marlo, then you can figure out how to pay me." She crossed her arms, scowling.

"Amber, I understand your frustration," Samantha said calmly. "You were given that salary because, at one point, you were a *slave*. But we have a large team now, so you get to share the responsibilities. And like I said, it's *temporary*. Karen only wants to take you down to three-fifty—and maybe I can find other ways to pay you the difference. Like when we book photoshoots and she has styling budgets."

"*NO!*" Amber shouted. "I will NOT agree to that, Samantha! What do you not understand? I don't want to make *less money*! I want to make MORE!"

"You're still making so much! Major television executives don't even make three-fifty a year! Don't you realize that?"

"I told you, NO!"

How had Amber's salary gotten that high anyway? I suspected because of Samantha. She'd already given me two significant raises in my seven months of employment, and with what seemed like little instruction from Alexis.

"You lucked out," Sebastian texted me once we were all back on the buses. "*The yacht was horrible. Lion and I were asked daily to give Alexis and Brody privacy, which meant we were banished to our room on the opposite side of the boat. Unless it was the middle of the night, of course. In which, Marlo would wake us for touch-ups.*"

I fell asleep mid-text and woke up hours later to shouting. I peeked out the maroon velvet curtain of my own coffin, and it was now pitch black. But I recognized Amber's voice coming from behind the closed door, where the sofas were. I closed my eyes again, trying to go back to sleep, but the shouting intensified.

We had an eighteen-hour drive from Miami to New York City and I couldn't listen to this the whole way. Samantha had flown ahead; she even said I could too. But to be fair and avoid jealousy I insisted on taking the bus, which of course I now regretted. Alexis owned an apartment in the city, so there was no reason for me to advance.

Annoyed groans started coming from the coffin in front of mine, until Sebastian peeked out his head, also curious about the commotion.

"I'll check," I said.

I climbed down from the top bunk and opened the door, assuming she'd been shouting at Vanessa. But Amber was alone, in tears on the phone. As I closed the door behind me, she fumbled to hang up.

"What's going on?" I whispered.

"I don't deserve this!" Amber growled at me through clenched teeth. "I've been here for two years longer than you, Hayden! TWO YEARS! You don't even know the half of what I've been through!"

"*Shhh!*" I whispered. "You're gonna wake everyone up."

I saw this as an opportunity to bond with Amber and get us on the same page. But as I sat down and placed my hand on her back to console her, I looked down at the screen of her iPhone to see the video she'd recorded of Alexis during her manic episode. Paused in the moment of her completely nude and sexually pursuing me. The color drained from my face. I didn't know how, but I'd forgotten about the video. Maybe because in every city we arrived, a new drama presented itself. Or maybe because I had chosen to forget because the idea of actually dealing with it was horrifying.

Amber, catching what I saw, quickly turned over her phone.

My voice shaking, I said slowly, "Amber. What is that doing up on your phone?"

She was silent.

"Amber, you need to delete that," I said. "You need to delete it *now*."

"Oh, *fuck off*!" she spat. "This is what's gonna keep me safe! She wants to lower my pay? She wants to fire me? I fucking *dare her*."

"Amber, you can't blackmail—"

"Hayden, you better keep your fucking mouth shut, or I'll make sure you're gone first!"

Remembering she'd extorted Alexis's billionaire ex-fiancé, I knew she was capable.

I was nauseous and had no one to talk to. I couldn't call Samantha. She was too erratic, and I'd be the one stuck on the bus with Amber for hours after she unleashed her fury. Even chugging Nyquil couldn't help me fall back asleep. I stared at the ceiling, caught between fear for myself and the guilt of responsibility. Sooner or later, this would come to a head. I just didn't know *when*.

CHAPTER SEVENTEEN

E ven though the dancers were cut from the tour, Brody still took every opportunity to join Alexis on stage—especially at Madison Square Garden. He walked her out, twirled her in a circle, kissed her hand, and even played peek-a-boo from behind her. Which was not funny, due to the weight gain. I didn't understand how she was so oblivious to the fact he was trying to turn her solo career into some sort of weird Sonny and Cher duo.

Alexis was confident on stage in her hometown of New York, yet social media was still buzzing about her figure. To keep things centered on the performance, Samantha granted *Page Six* an exclusive interview from the dressing room, knowing they had the most pick-up from other media outlets.

As a final question, the interviewer asked Alexis how she figured out who to trust with her level of fame.

"I don't know," she said. "People think I don't have feelings because of this *diva persona*. But that's manifested because of years of being hurt. So, yeah. It is hard for me to let my guard down. Every time someone says something to me, I think—Did they mean what they said? Or is that not true? And that's with *everyone*."

Hearing this made me even more nervous to come forward. Would she not believe me without proof? I knew I might destroy everything I'd worked for by telling the truth, but there was no other option. I wouldn't be able to live with myself if the video ever leaked, and I didn't do anything to warn her. Eventually, I was going to have to emerge from this neutrality I'd been trying to assume.

Being that I was no longer Alexis's personal assistant, days could go by without being invited to her home. I understood when she wasn't working, she wanted to relax. But we were in New York City, and the only thing I wanted to see was her apartment. She'd made it famous when I was a pre-teen on an episode of *Lifestyles of the Rich and Famous*. Even viewers who weren't fans were fascinated by her six-million-dollar renovation and over-the-top antics. The episode broke ratings records and led her to be the only celebrity to film a follow-up—this time, from her Beverly Hills abode.

"*Samanthaaaaa*," I whined during our morning call, "I can't leave New York without seeing her apartment."

"Well, you may be in luck," she said, "because Kelly just called to say *Vanity Fair* wants to see the inside of her closet."

"Are you serious?" I squealed with excitement.

"The catch is, they want to shoot it *tomorrow*," she said. "I guess Jessica Rodriguez pulled out last minute. I'll ask Alexis if she wants to do it, and if she does, you'll go over tonight to organize the clothes. I'm warning you though, it's a *disaster*."

After getting Alexis's approval, I hurried across the bustling New York block for her building, where she, of course, resided in the penthouse. The elevator opened, and I walked out into a long hallway of doors. But which was hers? I paced, wondering which to knock on, until I noticed the first was cracked and held a powder room. The *entire floor* was hers. Overhearing a guest arriving, Rhythm and Blue poked their heads from one of the doorways. Realizing it was me, they screamed and charged in my direction, both wrapping their arms around my waist.

"Hayden?" Alexis cooed from a staircase to my left.

"Hi, Lex!" I shouted.

"Wayne, are you down there?" Alexis called. "Will you show Hayden to the closet?"

"All right you two, I have to organize the *ensembles*," I told R&B, tickling their sides to release their grip. "Do you wanna show me where Mommy's closet is?"

I'd barely finished my sentence before each twin grabbed a hand and led me further down the gold-leaf-wrapped hallway to the closet. As it illuminated, I gasped.

The room resembled a high-end department store. It was lined with mirrors, well-lit, full of designer clothes, and one-of-a-kind couture pieces. In the far corners were walkways leading into even more closet space. One side brought you to handbags and shoes, and the other to lingerie. In the middle of the "closet" was a jewelry display that nearly blinded me. Inside were ruby teardrop earrings, a yellow diamond necklace, multiple versions of her iconic phoenix choker, and a collection of oversized engagement rings and wedding bands.

The twins began pulling on sparkly things and opening drawers—until Big Wayne caught up.

"Come on, you two!" he said, laughing. "Hayden has work to do!"

But how would I ever get anything done in here? Pieces from pop culture history kept distracting me. Stilettos she wore in a viral photo on the beach, knee-high boots from her film debut, a little black dress she wore to the Grammys, and paint-splattered jeans that had started a worldwide trend. The ten-year-old boy in me was shrieking with delight as I held in my hands all the greatest symbols of my childhood.

But after stepping back and seeing the mess, I snapped out of my daydream. Samantha was right. It was a disaster. Alexis had been predominantly living in Los Angeles, so the care of this closet had fallen by the wayside. Boxes of clothing were shoved in corners that looked to have been shipped back and forth between homes. And while there were many iconic pieces, there was no rhyme or reason to where anything was placed.

I spent the first few hours separating the items into categories—casual tops, dressy tops, jeans, athleisure, resort wear, evening wear. As the closet started looking cleaner, the video recording came back to mind. I needed to tell Alexis, but we were rarely alone anymore.

Just shy of midnight, I heard a high-pitched squeal over my shoulder that could only come from one woman.

"Hayden!" Alexis squealed again. "This looks *amazing*. You're gonna need to do this in Los Angeles, too! Management or not!" She giggled, clutching a glass of wine. "I don't know exactly *what* Amber has been doing."

"Of course I will," I said proudly, blushing. Her attention was as flattering to me as the first time I met her. I hadn't realized at first, but she'd come in only wearing a powder blue silk La Perla robe. I flashed back in my mind to her coming onto me in the midst of mania. I knew she didn't remember.

"Wait. You haven't been to this apartment yet, have you?" she asked.

"I haven't! But I've been dying to come over and see the place ever since we got to the city."

"You should have just asked! Let's go!"

She held out her hand, pulling me from the closet and onto the grand tour. We whisked through the halls, past glass cases full of hundreds of awards, and up the stairs to a second story. It opened to a palatial white room, pristine enough to be mistaken for a hotel. In the corner was a baby grand piano.

"It was Whitney's," she said proudly, pressing a button on the wall above it. "She gifted it to me just months before she passed."

On the wall across from us, lush ivory curtains opened in slow motion, exposing a breathtaking view of the Empire State Building.

"*Oh my God*," I whispered.

She took a step back, admiring the view as if seeing it for the first time. "I know," she said. "This was all I ever wanted when I was a little girl. A penthouse apartment in New York City with a view of the Empire State Building."

"Well, you did it!" I said, wondering if she felt the same at all, or if decades of fame eventually changes the essence of a person.

"This place was my first purchase, when I made it big," she said proudly.

In the reflection of the glass, I saw her eyes welling up. She smiled sadly, dabbing her lashes delicately.

"So much has happened since then," she continued. She stood silent for a moment, dreamy and nostalgic, before willing the tears away. She guided me around the corner to another hallway. Behind the first door on the right was her room, where Brody was sleeping. On the left was a spa with a giant chandelier above the jacuzzi, white candles everywhere, a flat-screen television, and his and hers massage tables. The rest of the hall held guest rooms, the twins' rooms, and even one dedicated to her fans, which was stacked to the ceiling with scrapbooks, posters, and letters.

"This is where I come just to remember I'm not alone. That people care about me. That I'm not, you know... completely worthless."

I pulled her back by the inside of her elbow, struck by the shock of her words. I suppose when people only value you when you match their fantasies, you start to wonder about the value of yourself outside of that. It was mind-boggling to imagine that when she left the limelight of audiences worldwide, she could feel anything even close to worthless. "How can you think that?" I asked. "*Worthless?* Forget about your unmatched vocal abilities. But the words you have written alone, Alexis. They have *saved lives.* I mean, who can say that?"

Alexis smiled but didn't believe me, her eyes still glistening. She closed the door behind us.

"We're not done yet!" Her tone changed, becoming excited again. She led me back down the staircase—two stories this time, where we were met by another long hallway of glass cases full of yet more awards. The first door on the left was a movie theatre, and on the right— "It's an aquarium," she said as it illuminated. Behind the glass were fish in every color of the rainbow.

Across the hall was a recording studio, the next door down was a full-service salon, and finally—a gym. I tried not to laugh.

"I almost forgot the best part!" she said. Clutching my hand, she led me back up the staircase, three flights to the very top.

The room was completely encapsulated with glass windows, lit only by New York's city lights. Luxurious leather couches, navy velvet chaise lounges, and expensive pillows in vibrant colors surrounded the perimeter.

"This is the Rhythm & Blues Room." Alexis drank the last gulp from her large glass of wine. "I come here to have a drop, think, write music."

"Wow," I said, marveling at it. "It's gorgeous up here."

Alexis headed to a bar in the corner to refill her glass.

"Do you want a *drop?*" she asked. She held up a fresh bottle of white.

"Oh, I can do that—"

"Hayden, don't be silly. I've got it!" She laughed, acknowledging her reputation.

She refilled her Baccarat wine glass, poured a second, then made her way to the center of the room, taking a seat next to me on a large custom sofa that looked like it belonged in a nightclub. We clinked our glasses.

Alexis turned her attention from the view, and toward me. She let out an audible sigh.

"Hayden..." she hesitated. "I can trust you, can't I?"

I shuddered as the memory of the video came back to mind.

She trusted me? She didn't trust *anyone.*

I didn't want to ruin the intimate moment we were finally sharing. I couldn't break this spell. I quickly convinced myself Amber wasn't actually going to do anything with the video, and I could tell Alexis another time.

"Of course you can," I said.

Alexis readjusted her robe and sat up on her knees to become comfortable.

"I can't talk to Samantha about this because she and Brody have had such a tumultuous relationship. And she'll say *anything*, if it means he's gone for good."

"I'm confused," I said. "What exactly are you asking?"

"Do you think…" She took a breath, then a large gulp from her fresh glass of Pinot Grigio. "Do you think Brody is… *gay*?"

I choked on my wine, not expecting the question, and spit it back into my glass.

Alexis laughed at the sight, making her choke on hers too.

"What do you mean?" I wiped the wine from the sides of my mouth. "Did something happen?"

"Samantha and Quentin have always told me he is. But like I said, who knows what their motive is for saying that. I get the whole 'he's a dancer' thing. But besides that, I want an unbiased opinion. Do *you* think he's gay? Or even if not, is he taking advantage of me?"

"Alexis, I don't know. I mean, the dancer thing is just a stereotype."

"We haven't had sex in months."

"Oh," I said with defeat, contemplating how to respond. "Well if he's bi, would that matter? I mean, you've had a relationship with a woman."

She laughed uncomfortably. "That was just a one-time thing."

Making eye contact with her, I sensed her sincere vulnerability. She was so comfortable with me, she hadn't even noticed the unflattering lighting in the room. In this moment she wasn't existing outside of herself. She was just *being.* I sighed and shrugged, unable to find a response.

"I don't know, Alexis. And the truth is, I can't answer that for you."

What could I say to make her feel better?

"Do me a favor and close your eyes," I said.

Alexis looked confused, but followed my lead.

"Just ask yourself that same question now. Whatever comes to you first is your answer. You need to trust your intuition. Only you know what your gut is telling you, Alexis. You've got to trust yourself."

Alexis's eyes stayed closed and a contagious smile came across her face. Not because she knew whether or not Brody was gay, but because there was someone in front of her who was not telling her what to do or what to think. There was someone in front of her who wasn't manipulating her. There was someone reminding her that the power to make decisions was hers.

ALEXIS INSISTED I NOT ADVANCE anymore, instead wanting me by her side at all times. As the weeks passed, our bond became obvious to the entire team. To the point Big Wayne knew to permit dressing room access any time I appeared. He was always kind to me and never threatened by my getting closer. So, when in Big Wayne's hometown of Chicago, he asked if he could bring his family backstage after the show. I was happy to oblige.

I strode into the dressing room. "Are you ready to kick ass tonight?"

"Hayden!" Alexis cooed. Her eyes were closed as Sebastian expertly applied a gold metallic shadow. "I've been asking for you! I want your advice."

"On what, Queen?" I teased.

"Stop calling me that!" she giggled. "I was wondering what your thoughts were on… getting back into the studio?"

Even being employees, both Sebastian and Lion's ears perked up. Alexis was a gay icon who TikTok was constantly pressuring for a new album. Sure, she had released singles here and there. But her last full body of work was five years old—*ancient* in the music industry.

"I think you should!" I encouraged her. "Honestly, that's what your fans want most. And wasn't that the whole point of renewing your contract?"

"I just…" Alexis paused, appealing to all of us. "Boys, *please*. Everything said in the dressing room stays between us girls."

The room of gays nodded in agreement.

"Don't get me wrong, Samantha's a great manager. I mean, she's a *hustler*. I just don't think she knows a lot about the *music* side of the entertainment industry."

"I get what you're saying," I said to the surprise of Sebastian and

Lion. They made eyes at one another but stayed quiet. "Like when you released your song from the documentary. There should've been an alert when subscribers opened their Spotify and Apple Music apps notifying them of a new Alexis Shane release. Or, at the minimum, a banner under "New Releases." I mean, it's all about streaming now. That's where our focus needs to be."

"See! Things have changed so much in the past few years, even *I* don't know what I'm supposed to be doing," she said. "Will you please loop Samantha in on this kind of stuff?"

"Of course," I said. "And I'll look into booking some studio time after the tour wraps."

Alexis gripped my hand to thank me, and I turned to exit through the back of the dressing room, closed off only by white curtains. But I stopped short when I heard Vanessa's voice on the other side. She was on speakerphone with Samantha. I craned my head up to the curtain to listen to the muffled conversation, which only drew Alexis's attention.

"What's going on?" she called.

"Samantha, he's gotten too comfortable," Vanessa whispered. "You have no clue how much time they've been spending together, and now he's talking about things he thinks that *you* are not doing. Are you really okay with that?"

"WHAT?" Samantha panicked. "What did he say?"

"I hate to remind you, but the kid also has access to your emails, and your phone. So, you need to change your passwords. Like, *now*."

"Vanessa, I don't know how to fucking do any of that!" Samantha said. "You know I'm technologically challenged!"

"Hayden?" Alexis called again, concerned.

I turned to head for the front door at the opposite side of the dressing room and passed her.

"Don't worry," I said. "It's nothing. Just thought I heard something."

The door closed behind me.

Had Vanessa finally turned Samantha against me?

"**WHAT THE FUCK IS** *SECURITY* doing bringing *his family* back here?" Vanessa said to Amber in the hallway following the show, as the dressing room door closed behind the last member of Big Wayne's group. "Who does he think he is?"

She of course had done this many times herself. But that was beside the point. Every bitch needs an object to direct their bitchiness at, logical or not.

"This is ridiculous!" Amber spat. "There's no respect for management!"

Teddi passed by with the twins, covering their ears with her hands as the cursing escalated.

"Oh fuck off, Teddi!" Vanessa said.

At the same time, Big Wayne and his family started exiting. They beamed to have had mere seconds with the legend and were already comparing photos.

"Wayne!" Vanessa shouted as he led his family toward the exit. "We need to talk."

"You guys go ahead," he said. "I'll catch up."

Wayne jogged toward Vanessa and Amber with a big grin on his face, still coming off the high of giving his family a once-in-a-lifetime experience. From now on his kids would think he was the coolest dad in the world. But that grin soon disappeared.

"Wayne, I know you know that I'm the one who's in charge of ticket comps and meet and greets. Well, I'm also in charge of the hiring and *firing*," Vanessa said. "So, do you think it was really smart of you to bring your family backstage without having a conversation with me?"

Wayne frowned. "I, uh... talked to Hayden. He said it was okay."

"I don't give a *fuck* what Hayden said. He doesn't have the authority, and you know better. So, I'm sorry, but we're gonna have to let you go."

Wayne laughed confidently in her face. "Samantha gave you the approval to make this decision? And Alexis knows?"

"Wayne, as far as you're concerned, *I'm* the manager."

"**WHAT IN THE HELL HAPPENED?**" Samantha stomped into the lobby of the Four Seasons Chicago to meet Amber and me—closely followed by Blair and a slew of Louis Vuitton roller bags.

After a phone call from Alexis, she'd hopped on the next flight. Wayne had frantically pushed his way into the dressing room to a bewildered Alexis, and after deciphering the situation, she announced to the room she was nothing but happy to have met Wayne's family after working with him for so many years. She then promptly called Samantha and insisted she fire Vanessa.

"I can't deal with it anymore," Alexis said. "I mean, technically she's your person, anyway. I'm using all my energy to entertain millions of people, so I can't be worried about what drama your sister is causing with my closest confidants. I don't want to see her anymore, Samantha. I'm serious."

Me reminding Alexis of her power had worked. But with the things Vanessa had witnessed over the years, and how unpredictable she'd become, Samantha still couldn't agree to the firing. There was only one show left, and she needed the split handled amicably.

"Hayden, will you start looking at jets?" Samantha said. "I'm not letting Alexis take the bus to Portland after this. I need to keep her as far away from that fucking lunatic as possible. She could be costing me my job. Doesn't she care that I'm a single mother? I have a daughter to take care of!"

I glanced at twelve-year-old Blair wearing a matching Prada tracksuit, metallic silver Balenciaga ankle boots, and a Louis Vuitton backpack. She seemed pretty well taken care of.

Samantha handed me her phone to call the travel agent, but when I typed in her password, it had been changed. I squinted at her. Did she really think I would comb through her emails and texts like her psychotic sisters? I got that Amber and I now dressed in the same tracksuit, but *come on*.

"I'll call from mine." I handed it back. "Just text me his after-hours number."

Behind us, Vanessa walked into the lobby.

"Just make sure he has the correct passenger list, and not one with Vanessa on it," Samantha said. "She can take the fucking bus."

Vanessa stopped in her tracks. "What did you just say?"

Samantha turned red and tried to explain she and Alexis needed some alone time to go over business deals.

But Vanessa wasn't buying it. She was stupid, but not *that* stupid.

FOLLOWING THE FINAL SHOW OF the tour was the launch of Alexis's partnership with Candy Land at the opening of their first location in Portland. It'd become clear after growing closer with Alexis that what she wanted to do with her career differed from Samantha's ideas. But I also knew this opportunity would pay her an easy fifteen million dollars, affording her the time to record an album.

We pulled up to the entrance to hear her music blaring and see a thousand fans waiting, already decked out in her new merchandise. It was bizarre seeing the over-the-top restaurant that had originated in Las Vegas, in Portland. The tour bus doors opened, and police escorts carefully carved out a path enabling Alexis and the rest of us to make it inside safely.

As she took the red carpet, I stood next to Amber.

"I know life on the road has been hard… and I know Samantha can say things that upset you," I said. "But I really want us to get along, Amber. I think you and I can turn things around, for *everyone*."

I was still hoping if I befriended her, I could get her to do the right thing. Or worst-case scenario, I could steal her phone and delete the video myself.

"Let's talk when we get back to LA," she said. "I'm just too exhausted for this conversation right now."

As Alexis reached the end of the red carpet, I heard whispers from the local media.

"That can't be Alexis Shane," one said, and laughed.

"It looks like Alexis Shane ATE Alexis Shane," another said.

In the same moment, mine and Amber's Google Alerts went off.

The headline read, THE TRUTH BEHIND ALEXIS SHANE'S MASSIVE WEIGHT GAIN.

CHAPTER EIGHTEEN

For a moment, I felt grateful during our flight back to Los Angeles, remembering how after my interview I'd fantasized for weeks about private planes and paparazzi. It had always been a dream of mine to be a part of this world. But when we stepped off the jet, we were instantly swarmed by a flurry of paparazzi, and I saw the other side. There were dozens of photographers outside the gates of the tarmac, all shouting horrifying questions.

"Don't you think you should watch your cholesterol, Alexis?"

"Brody, do you like your women *thick*?"

"Alexis, are you worried about being a bad example to your children?"

Black Cadillac Escalades were waiting for us, and as I climbed into the back of my own, I tried not to cry. Within the past twenty-four hours, the price tag on a shot of Alexis's cellulite and double chin had skyrocketed. I felt sick leaving her, but also didn't want to make her feel worse. Of course, I knew she'd become heavier. But I was also with her every day, so maybe I was blind to exactly *how much* heavier. Either way, the awful and invasive questions being flung at her were terrible to witness. I didn't know how she had a rock-hard exterior in a circus as cruel as this.

The next morning, her body was plastered across every single gossip site and news station. I turned off the television and prepared a portfolio of solutions. I remembered Alexis saying what she preferred to do would result in recovery time. But I wanted her to have options to make an educated decision. I started by calling the most famous celebrity personal trainers and nutritionists. Then, I anonymously made calls to all the top plastic surgeons in Beverly Hills. None were shy in their advertisement of the three most popular options among celebrities—the Obalon balloon, the gastric sleeve, and hi-definition body contouring.

While I'd briefly broached the topic months earlier, I still felt sick that afternoon, parking my car in Alexis's driveway. I was sent by Samantha to get contract signatures, but knew I had to use the opportunity to revisit the subject. Especially after hearing Kelly tell Samantha she had no intention of addressing it. I just hoped I could do it sensitively.

I waited for an hour until Alexis descended the grand staircase in a black silk robe with photoshoot-ready hair and makeup. It made me sad to know she was done-up, simply because *I* was over.

"Hi Hayden," she said, sounding lifeless.

She looked exhausted with bags under her eyes, and somehow even heavier than the night before.

"Hi beautiful." I stood to embrace her but could feel her discomfort at being touched. I pulled away. "How are you feeling?"

She shrugged, taking a seat next to me on one of the three oversized white "cloud" sofas in the formal sitting room.

"I can't even imagine how much energy it's taken out of you to do thirty shows," I said. "But the good news is, besides the tour wrap party and the New York charity show, you're off for the next two months."

"Hayden," she said, biting her lip, "I'm not done yet. I still have so many things I want to accomplish."

"What do you mean? Of course you're not done. Why would you think you're done?"

The weight aside, Samantha's management style had relied heavily on Alexis's lengthy list of accomplishments from the decades prior, making her appear as a nostalgia act. Yes, Alexis was forty years old, and some could even say her prime had passed. But it didn't have to be over. There were plenty of artists, like Madonna and Cher, who'd released hit records well into their *fifties*.

"I just want to bring the focus back to the music, like I said to you on tour. All these money-making opportunities have been great to pay the bills. But I'm starting to see things have been run like I'm a Kardashian, and... I'm not."

"I agree with you one hundred percent. Music needs to be the focus," I said. "So, let's take these two months off to strategize on your next moves. That's actually why I'm here anyway, and I want to preface this with... this is not an easy conversation to have. But your image for the past year, especially over the past few months..." I began sweating. "What I'm trying to say is, all people are talking about right now is—"

"My weight." Her eyes teared up.

Suddenly I felt like by even mentioning it, I was the problem. I couldn't make eye contact with her, as my eyes too began to well.

"Listen, this has nothing to do with how *beautiful* you are," I said. "But I wouldn't be doing my job if I didn't tell you what people are saying. And yes, all everyone is talking about is your weight."

A single tear fell from her eye, mascara staining her cheek. I tried to force out words, but I had a lump in my throat. I had to change directions. Maybe she *would* be comfortable turning this around on the media. Maybe she could be an advocate like I'd hoped.

I grabbed her hand.

"Fuck all of these people, Alexis. Seriously, fuck them! This is about *you*. Are you happy with the way you look? Because if you love your curves—which plenty of women do, then you should embrace them. We can turn this around and say body shaming is not okay and encourage women everywhere to love themselves."

"But, Hayden. I'm *not* happy with how I look," she said, wiping her eyes gently.

"Then we'll fix it." I reached behind the couch for my new Gucci backpack and pulled out my binder of weight-loss options.

"You can't help yourself, can you? Even your weight-loss presentation is immaculate," she laughed, her tears now drying.

"So, the first section here. These are the top celebrity trainers. I've spoken to all of them, and they're each willing to come to the house so you don't have to go anywhere. I also have nutritionists here that will check your blood, see what's going on, and be in regular contact with Noah—so he's only preparing meals that'll help you see the quickest results."

"I appreciate that, Hayden," she said, "but I want something that's gonna work faster than diet and exercise. I wanna feel good about myself when I take the stage again in New York."

"Alright, then." I grabbed the second tab in the binder and flipped the page. "These next few options are the most popular weight loss surgeries for celebrities right now. There's the Obalon, which is interesting. You swallow three pills, and they expand to full-size balloons in your stomach. I guess it suppresses your appetite, being that there's little room for food."

"I did that one before. It worked great. But removing the balloons after is painful. Not to mention, the weight came right back," she said. "Is there anything a little more... *permanent?*"

"Well, I would say one of these then." I flipped back and forth between two pages. "There's the hi-definition body contouring, where they suck all of the fat from your body, then use only what's necessary to reshape you. Like for example, if you still wanted to have an ass. However, that one is pretty invasive. So, recovery would be substantial. It may be pushing it too close, being that New York is only six weeks away."

"Yeah, I'm not sure about that."

"And this one is called the gastric sleeve. They remove a large portion of your stomach, leaving it the size of a banana. And within weeks, the weight just falls off."

"That's the one," she said.

"Are you sure?"

"I'm sure."

DURING THE NEXT MORNING'S CHECK-IN with Samantha, I relayed the message about redirecting our attention to the music.

"Do you have any idea how many times over the past three years I've been in the studio with Alexis? She always says that's what she wants, Hayden. But then we get there, and all she does is drink and get high. She never *actually* records anything." Samantha sighed. "But if that's what she wants... I'll connect you with her favorite producers and you can start scheduling studio time."

"All right, I'll get studio time on the books—for January though, after the *Hope* holiday promo tour wraps. And before you get into scheduling changes, that's another thing she mentioned. For right now, she's just wanting to lay low for the next two months besides the wrap party, the surgery, and the charity performance. I think she feels we've been saying 'yes' to too many things."

But Samantha ignored what I said and informed me of all the schedule additions.

"Now that tour is over, our number one priority is getting the Academy Award nomination for *Hope*. But that's more work for you and me than her. Aside from that, let's see... I've gotten an offer to honor her at the MTV Music Video Awards. I'm gonna say yes to that. We're gonna shoot a *People* magazine cover next week to promote the *Hope* tour. Kim's emoji company wants to meet with us in two weeks. Netflix finally confirmed that they do, in fact, want another doc. Oprah wants her at her birthday party. Heidi Klum wants her at her Halloween party. I said yes to filming an episode of *Bridgerton*. I said yes to her performing at the iHeart Radio Music Festival. And I know it's September, but I think if we hurry, we could rush out a line of makeup in time for the holidays."

Our schedule went from blank to overbooked, and with no real thought or direction.

"Samantha, you're not listening to me. I know she's thrilled about the Academy Award campaign. And I mean, that's *amazing* for her career. But besides that, she's just expecting to relax until the *Hope* tour. It's been a rough year, and she needs time to decompress."

"Hayden," she said sternly. I waited for her to remind me of the chain of command. "The surgery alone is a hundred-thousand-dollar expense. Where do you think that money is gonna come from?"

"She just made seven million dollars touring this summer."

"Have you not been paying any fucking attention? After paying everyone out, she took away two million, and half of that goes to taxes. She then chartered two yachts this summer—one in Capri and one in Miami. That's half a million right there. Oh, and don't forget, you also watched her buy a three-hundred-thousand dollar bag at Hermès."

"Well, what about the Candy Land deal?"

"It was just announced, and she's paid quarterly. So, she won't get her first check from them until January."

"I understand what you're saying. But then let's have a conversation with her, figure out a way to pull back on her expenses and only schedule what's necessary. I don't want to blindside her with this overbooked schedule."

"I've been trying to get her to pull back for three years! She doesn't care! She wants what she wants!" Samantha shouted. "What do you not understand? If she wants this surgery, she has to *work*!"

REGARDLESS OF ALEXIS'S CURRENT FINANCIAL state, she had to protect her mental health, and that meant learning to take control herself. I gave her a heads up about the drastically changed schedule, but explained that ultimately, *she* would have to tell Samantha 'no'. And impressively, for the first time, she did. She canceled both the *Bridgerton* cameo and the performance at the iHeart Radio Music Festival. Samantha had always been able to push Alexis before, but now Alexis was clear on only wanting to do what she was passionate about, which was having Samantha follow through on her promise of the Academy Award nomination.

Samantha and I spent the few days we had leading up to Alexis's surgery with the team at Universal Studios, completely focused on what we could do to secure the nomination. But with an aggressive award campaign, the schedule again began to fill. At least now the reasoning was career-changing, musically driven, and something Alexis really wanted.

Award season was to be kicked off in November right before the *Hope* tour, with Alexis getting a star on the world-famous Hollywood Boulevard. What I didn't know was that even when awarded, the celebrity actually pays for the star and installation themselves—which of course cost another $100,000. The ceremony would be followed by a press conference, then a performance of *Hope* for the Hollywood Foreign Press Association.

Everything was falling into place, and the only thing Alexis would need to do herself was deliver a memorable performance. Something I was confident she could do with the touching lyrics she'd written.

On the way back from our meeting with the Universal executives, I said, "How did Alexis agree to host a wrap party tonight anyway? The tour wasn't exactly something worth celebrating."

"Vanessa organized it before the tour even started. I guess she'd been in touch with Alexis's agent or something, who invited a bunch of celebrities. Anyway, it'll be good for her to get out of the house. Because after the surgery tomorrow, she's gonna be on bed rest."

"I thought Vanessa was gone for good..."

"She is. I mean, this is her swan song. You won't be seeing her again after tonight. I've been interviewing new tour managers with Karen. But Vanessa was already in town as a witness for a mediation between Alexis and Kauffman, so I didn't want to cause any more waves by telling her not to come. But after this, *she's gone*. So, don't worry. Just go home and get ready."

On my way home to change, Sebastian called.

"I'm just headed to Alexis's now for glam and wanted to see if you were going tonight?" he asked.

"I am. I mean… of course, there are places I'd much rather be than where Vanessa is. But I've gotta be there for Alexis. You'll be there too, right?"

"No, I'm not gonna make it. I have a job in New York in the morning, so I have to go straight to the airport."

"*Nooo!*" I whined.

"But speaking of Vanessa, I thought maybe I should tell you…"

"Tell me."

"Well, I've actually been to the building where the dinner is being held. It's the only high-rise of condominiums in Beverly Hills, nicknamed the "Twenty Thousand." They invite well-connected people in the industry to host parties on their rooftop, and for every A-list celebrity the host brings through the door, they get paid twenty grand. It gets the building's name in the press, and they're also hoping it'll prompt the guests' interest in a unit." Sebastian sighed. "They've asked me to host parties there before, but it just feels so icky."

The celebrities on the guest list were more fans of Alexis than friends. So, Vanessa wouldn't just be making $20,000 off Alexis, but $20,000 off of every other celebrity that walked through the door to see her. She'd be making more money in one night off this scam than I would all year.

I arrived at the *Twenty Thousand* at eight p.m., and security escorted me to the top floor, where I was greeted by a rooftop overlooking all of Los Angeles—from Downtown to Santa Monica. Each guest was elegantly dressed in either a designer gown or suit and had a recognizable face. An hour passed, and I began hearing whispers about whether Alexis was actually going to show, and jokes about her notorious tardiness.

Two hours after the time the invitation stated, she appeared through the glass elevator doors, and the crowded rooftop fell silent in awe. Even with the weight gain, she looked stunning with her hair slicked back in a high-pony and wearing an elegant navy Ralph Lauren evening gown that'd been altered yet again to expose an excess of cleavage.

After the guest of honor did a round of air-kissing with everyone from Britney to Beyoncé, we were able to take our seats at the three long tables that had been delicately garnished with rose petals. All the names on the place settings were famous, aside from those that belonged to our team. I started looking for my name, and quickly spotted Alexis and Brody's. I saw Amber's name, Marlo's, Samantha's, Blair's. I circled all three tables twice before realizing there wasn't a seat for me.

I found Samantha in her chair and squatted down next to her. Alexis sat across, eyeing me.

"There's no seat for me," I whispered.

"What do you mean, no seat for you?"

Samantha turned in her chair to eye the room, finding that every seat had been taken. She looked to her left to find one empty with a place card for Emma Stone. She picked it up and tossed it aside.

"Sit here," she said, and pulled the chair out with her patent-leather Saint Laurent stiletto.

"Samantha, *I can't*," I said.

"Excuse me!" Emma approached from behind, annoyed after seeing her place card had been thrown.

"Samantha, you girls don't need me here anyway," I said. The non-stop sabotage from Vanessa had finally taken its toll. "I'm sorry, but I can't do this with her anymore. I'm leaving."

"You're not leaving!" Samantha grabbed my wrist as I stood up. "I'll make her fix it!"

"What's going on?" Alexis called from across the table, drawing attention from Britney.

"I'll talk to you guys tomorrow." I pulled away and hurried for the elevator, embarrassed and at my limit with this petty bullshit. It would have been great to wine and dine with the world's most famous celebrities, but I was losing my composure by the second. Vanessa couldn't leave soon enough, and now neither could I.

When the valet retrieved my car, I climbed into the driver's seat and let out a scream of frustration. Like Alexis, I was tired. Too tired to be fighting with anyone anymore.

I turned right onto Santa Monica Boulevard and pulled over at Dan Tana's. I felt pathetic walking alone into a fancy Italian restaurant in Beverly Hills on a Saturday night. But I was starving and desperately wanted a drink.

The waiter had just delivered my first filthy martini with blue cheese olives when my phone rang. I cringed getting it from my pocket, waiting for Samantha's incessant squawking.

But the caller ID read *Queen*. Why was Alexis calling me? She never called me when I wasn't expecting it, and definitely not when she was in a room full of people—let alone *famous people*.

"Hayden, where are you?" she whispered. "I want you to come back."

"I'm just down the street having a drink. I'm sorry, Alexis. I hope I didn't cause a scene. I just can't deal with Vanessa anymore. But please just enjoy your night. We can talk about it tomorrow."

"I'm not staying here without you, Hayden. This is *my* wrap party," she whispered. "These people don't care about me or my tour. You were there for me, *every single day*. Now tell me. Where are you?"

"Dan Tana's," I said.

The line went dead.

"Alexis?"

I set my phone down, hoping she understood, then took a gulp of my martini before sinking into the red leather booth. Watching all the dining couples toasting and laughing made me miss Grayson terribly. Maybe this was all not in fact worth it. The wholesomeness and safety of that relationship felt so far away from me. I finished the rest of the martini, anxiously awaiting another.

Ten minutes later, I heard a commotion coming from the front of the restaurant. The front door flung open, and I was blinded by the flashing lights of the paparazzi. It was Alexis. Followed by Brody, Marlo, Samantha, Blair, and security. No Vanessa or Amber in sight.

"Hayden!" Alexis squealed with excitement.

"Alexis?" I managed to say after picking up my jaw. "What're you doing here? What about your party?"

"There is no party for me if there's no seat for you." She smiled, taking a seat next to me in the booth and gripping my arm. "So... what are we having?"

I couldn't believe that *Alexis Shane* had just walked out of a room full of celebrities for *me*. So maybe it *was* all worth it, if only to be able to say this happened. Vanessa had tried so hard to get rid of me, but what she didn't realize was the more she pushed, the closer Alexis and I became. I looked around the red and white checkered tablecloth, and it was like I could see the storm visibly passing. The people who were supposed to be here were here.

"You're the boss, you pick! I'm just gonna run to the restroom real fast," I said. I felt a little tipsy and wanted a moment to sober up.

The bathroom door closed behind me, but quickly reopened as I stepped in front of a urinal and unzipped my fly.

"Hey man," a familiar voice said.

It was Brody, coming to use the urinal beside me.

"Oh, hey!" I said, surprised to see him.

"Thank God we came over here, man. That party was a bust," he sighed, shaking his head dramatically.

"I really appreciate you guys coming to meet up with me," I said.

"She really likes you, Hayden."

"It makes me happy to hear that. I really like her too." I zipped up my fly.

Brody began to sway sloppily, examining me from head to toe.

"Do you always wear your shirts undone that low?" he asked, slurring.

"My shirt?" I asked. I looked down to find my top three buttons were undone, leaving my chest hair exposed. "I guess I do, actually," I laughed.

"You do, I've noticed," he grinned.

He's not... There was no way. I backed away and headed for the sink.

"I've actually been looking all night," he said.

He is. I didn't respond. I kept quiet, scrubbing my hands anxiously.

"Come here," he said.

I hesitantly walked toward him, but kept an arm's length between us.

Brody turned his body toward me, exposing his hard cock. He started to stroke it, then reached for me, digging his hand into my chest hair.

"Brody, no." I pulled away. "Don't."

But he grabbed me by the neck, pulled me in, and pressed a tequila-tasting kiss against my lips. I couldn't even look back at him as I rushed out of the bathroom.

I WOKE UP WITH A pounding headache, not knowing how I got home. But my confidence was soaring, recollecting how Alexis had left the party for me. Vanessa, on the other hand, knew she fucked up and was obsessively calling Samantha and Alexis. But neither would respond.

As a last resort, she called me.

"Hey, Hayden. I'm *so* sorry about last night. Not sure what happened," she said. "I had them bring in another chair for you, but you left."

She wasn't sorry. She hadn't apologized for *anything* over the past year. She just knew she was officially cut from the entourage and was willing to say whatever it took to make her way back. But with my newfound confidence, I didn't care.

"Lose my number," I said, and hung up.

It was the morning of Alexis's gastric sleeve surgery, and Samantha and I were taking her. I quickly showered and hurried down the stairs. But when I walked into my apartment's garage, my car was missing.

I called Samantha.

"Hey, I'm sorry, but I'm gonna be a few minutes behind. I think my car was *stolen*!"

"Are you *serious*?" She laughed. "Do you not remember? I drove you home. You left your car with the valet."

"Oh my God."

"Yeah, you came back from the bathroom and were guzzling martinis. So, I couldn't let you drive."

Fuck! My memory flashed with Brody coming on to me.

I'd quickly pulled away and returned to the table, pretending as if nothing happened. But instead of continuing to sober up, I got wasted to shake my guilt. Brody too, did the same, and we avoided eye contact for the rest of the evening.

What was I supposed to do? Go back to the table and tell her the night before she goes into major surgery? Right after she'd abandoned her celebrity peers for me?

I Uber'd to pick up my car from Dan Tana's, then became panic-stricken when I parked outside of Alexis's. Having this on my conscience now on top of the video recording made it feel like there was a hand squeezing my heart, ready to pull it out at any moment. Sweat dripped down my back as I opened the front door, and inside stood Brody—with Amber's contractor friend, John.

"Hayden! How's it going, my friend?" John said, approaching me with a handshake. "Come check out the ball pit."

"The ball pit?" I said, ignoring Brody's presence.

"Amber said Alexis wanted it installed in the den."

Initially seeing Brody had shocked me, but then relieved me, knowing that if he was here, she didn't know, and I could relax. Still, Alexis trusted me. How long could I let these things build up before I told her? The longer I waited, the more it only made *me* look bad.

I followed Amber's friend to the den at the opposite side of the mansion, just off the kitchen. All the furniture had been moved to the garage, and a wood frame had been built around the perimeter of the room. The inside was padded, and two dozen giant boxes filled with rainbow-colored Chuck E. Cheese balls were about to be unloaded.

"Where should I send the invoice?" he asked.

"You can just give it to me," I said.

He crossed the room for his clipboard and returned to hand it to me.

I looked down to see the total at the bottom: $100,000.

"What the fuck is this?" I spat. I pointed to the bottom and then waved it in his face. "Are you *insane*?"

I sounded like Samantha.

"These balls are very expensive, Hayden." He shrugged.

"I'm gonna need a breakdown," I said. "I'm also gonna need numbers for the vendors you're using, so I can verify these prices."

Either he himself was a thief, or Amber had instructed him to do so, ensuring herself a profit.

"Hayden? Is that you?" Alexis cooed from the kitchen.

I exited the den to find her perched against the white marble island, sipping on tea. She wore an ivory silk robe and looked beautiful with her hair still slicked back in the high pony she'd worn the night before.

"How are you feeling?" I asked, ignoring my own anxiety.

"I'm nervous," she said. Her hand was trembling as she raised the teacup to her mouth.

I grabbed it from her and set it down on the island.

"Alexis, if you don't want to do this, you don't have to."

"I have to, Hayden. I don't want to be a joke anymore." She peered over my shoulder to see if John was listening. "Let's go to the formal sitting room."

I followed her to the front of the house, where she and I had last spoken about her weight.

"After the surgery, like I said, things need to change around here." She took a seat. "Last night just really opened my eyes. That drama was so unnecessary, and you didn't deserve it. Vanessa has been calling me all morning trying to apologize. But I'm *done*. I was done after what she did to Wayne in Chicago. I'm just sorry that you didn't feel comfortable enough to come to me sooner."

The list of things I didn't feel comfortable coming to her about was growing. And here she was, giving me permission to tell more. But still, it wasn't the time.

"I won't bore you with the details of everything she's done. But every move I make is always to make your life easier. Vanessa has told me verbatim that *she* knows what is best for you, regardless of what *you* want. I just didn't want you to think I was whining or couldn't handle the pressure."

Alexis sighed. She stared blankly out the window across from us.

"This job is not about Vanessa," she said, "and it's not about Amber, or even Samantha. This job is about *me*. It's about making *me* happy. And *you* make me happy."

"That's all I want to do," I said.

"I had no idea when I came into this business more than twenty years ago... I know, I know, I don't do numbers." She grinned. "But I had no idea about all of the sycophants that came with fame and success. I wanted to be famous to validate my own existence, and I had no idea people would wind up using me to validate their own."

I couldn't help but feel sorry for her. I was seeing all this for the first time this year. But who knew how many times the same situation had presented itself over the past two decades?

I called the surgeon on our drive down the hill for instruction on how to enter his office without being seen. He'd closed his practice for the day to ensure maximum privacy. But it didn't make Alexis feel any more at ease. She was terrified in the waiting room, her hands trembling. If you have the money, it may seem like an easy decision to make. But once you're in the doctor's office with the gown on and he's explaining how he's about to cut you open, it's no less scary. She, or *we*, were choosing elective surgery due to the pressure of society, and I felt an enormous amount of guilt. I mean, she had children. Children that I loved. What if something went wrong?

Alexis took off the ten-million-dollar engagement ring she still wore on her middle finger and slid it onto mine. I choked up as she was wheeled away.

The doctor came out after a few hours to inform Samantha and me that it was taking longer than expected, as Alexis hadn't mentioned having a tummy tuck after giving birth to the twins.

I sat in the lush but sterile Beverly Hills waiting room, praying for the first time since I was a child.

Please God, don't let anything happen to her. Alexis is a good person. She's a mother. I'm begging you, please just keep her safe.

CHAPTER NINETEEN

After the surgery, Alexis was on bed rest, an all-liquid diet, and required to stay off her bipolar medication for six weeks. It made me nervous, as the longer she was off it, the more likely a manic episode became. But there was no way around it. Amber and Marlo took turns checking on her, but both ignored the aftercare paperwork, granting Alexis wine when she requested it. The acidity made her violently ill and forced the doctor to rush to the mansion.

Even major surgery couldn't keep Alexis's addictions at bay. Alcohol was now off the table, so she instead pleaded with the surgeon for more substantial pain medication. The doctor called Samantha confidentially to explain that Alexis had already been given much more than required and refused to give any more.

As the weeks went by, things began to pile up, and we now needed Alexis's participation to secure the Academy Award nomination. She needed the time to recover, of course. But her elective surgery didn't mean the rest of the industry paused. Both the record label and movie studio were requesting her input on everything from press to photo shoots to social media posts. But she became unreachable to *everyone*, including Samantha and me. No matter what time of the day or night.

"She's sleeping," both Amber and Marlo would say upon answering—whether we called their phones or Alexis's.

Initially, Samantha and I had wanted to give Alexis her space, and we had plenty of work to keep us busy. But following the home visits, the doctor started reporting back to Samantha that Alexis was doing better.

So, after nearly a month of being ignored, Samantha snapped, insisting that it was time for us to get Alexis back to work. Even if that meant showing up to the house unannounced.

I arrived at the mansion first and walked into the sound of the twins playing in the ball pit. Hearing their voices again made me feel like I was back home. I made my way toward the den, passing Noah in the kitchen, and dived into the ball pit headfirst. The twins screamed with glee and threw balls in my direction.

"What the hell are you doing?" a familiar siren admonished me.

"Hey lady, you said a bad word!" Rhythm shouted at Samantha, before throwing a plastic ball in her direction. "And you're not the boss of him!"

"I actually am!" Samantha laughed.

"Mommy is!" Blue countered.

Hearing Alexis's voice coming from the kitchen, I quickly climbed out of the ball pit. She headed our way, calling for the twins in full hair, makeup, and a fitted Roberto Cavalli maroon dress. She looked gorgeous, and while still heavy, was easily thirty pounds lighter. After spotting Samantha and me, her mouth dropped. Still, I approached her with a hug and teased her, as I too was in all maroon—an Adidas velour tracksuit.

"You look *incredible*! And I'm so glad you're feeling better!" Samantha said. She wrapped her arm around Alexis's waist and led us through the dark house for the office.

"I'm so sorry to just show up," Samantha continued, "but I can't seem to get ahold of you. We need to get you into your studio downstairs to finish the vocals for your soon-to-be-nominated song. I told the record label and Universal we want to keep the press schedule to a minimum. But to win, you'll need to do a little. Okay?" She glanced through her iPhone calendar, and continued without giving Alexis an opportunity to respond. "Let's see, I also need the set list for the charity performance in New York. Oh, and I need to confirm a musical director for the *Hope* promo tour."

Samantha continued to ramble as I examined Alexis from head to toe. She seemed fine, so why had she been ignoring us? It seemed so out of character, especially considering how close we'd become. I assumed she'd be excited to see me again.

When out of the corner of my eye, I spotted Amber hovering in the doorway glaring at her sister. Could *she* have something to do with this?

THE DAY BEFORE WE WERE due to leave for New York, I met Samantha in the glam room of her Calabasas home. Following our seemingly successful visit, Alexis had returned to ignoring both Samantha and me. Samantha now had no desire to go.

"Samantha, you have to," I said. "I'm sorry, but I know this has something to do with Amber. You didn't see the way she was looking at you. I mean, come on. She's been in that house with Alexis for six weeks, and now *neither* are speaking to us?"

I felt like Samantha not going was a huge mistake, like she was forfeiting her job. But after three years of unpredictability, she was too exhausted to fight back.

"Amber isn't speaking to me because of the pay decrease. And she blames you because of your promotion. I'm not going, okay? End of conversation. I'm not just some abused animal who's going to chase Alexis Shane around the world when she isn't even taking my calls. Just book her jet. Maybe I'll take Blair to London for a few days instead."

I gave up and reached out to Amber to ask what time Alexis wanted the jet to take off. And to our surprise, the inquiry prompted a phone call from Alexis to Samantha. The first in six weeks.

"Hi, my beautiful girl!" Samantha answered enthusiastically, resuming their relationship as if the past ten minutes had never happened.

"So, is Hayden the new Vanessa?" Alexis asked.

"Is Hayden the new Vanessa?" Samantha repeated, looking at me confused. "Alexis... what are you talking about?"

"Well, Amber just told me that Hayden is booking the jet."

"Yeah, Hayden is booking the jet to New York because we don't have Vanessa anymore. But he's only helping out until we find you a new tour manager," she said. "I have some candidates for you to meet. But I can never seem to get you on the phone."

"I'm sorry, Samantha. I just haven't felt well. You know? This recovery has been *abusive*."

Samantha rolled her eyes, knowing she was lying. There'd been photographs of Alexis, Amber, and Marlo over the past week jogging around her neighborhood in Beverly Hills.

"Okay, well no. Hayden is not your new tour manager, and I'm not sure why Amber would allude to that."

"I mean, she's made it pretty clear that Hayden was trying to take Vanessa's job, like all summer. And now he's booking the jet. So, I just figured—"

"Is she *insane?*" Samantha raised her voice an octave. "Hayden never wanted Vanessa's position, Alexis. He was just picking up the slack when other employees would complain about the fact that she wasn't doing her job."

What the fuck? I mouthed silently to Samantha. I was shocked at the accusation, especially being that the last time we spoke she was telling me how happy I made her.

"Everything he does is to help you, Alexis. I mean, the rates he's pulling for jets alone are *thousands* less than Vanessa. The new travel agent he's found is saying that it looks like Vanessa was working with someone who would overcharge and then give her a kickback."

"*Big surprise*, someone else taking advantage of me," Alexis said.

"Well she's gone now, so it's one less asshole to worry about."

The line went silent.

"*Alexis?*"

"Samantha, just have Hayden book the jet for ten tomorrow night."

"Okay. And you want me to come with you to New York, *right?*"

The line again went silent, and I knew Samantha giving her the option was a mistake.

"No, no. You don't need to come," Alexis said. "It's just one quick show, and then I'm back to LA."

"WHAT DO YOU MEAN SHE *re-hired* Vanessa?" Samantha shouted over speakerphone to Karen. "We were just talking about what a piece of shit she is!"

"I don't know, Samantha. But she made it clear she doesn't want Hayden booking her travel."

Karen's words were a punch to the gut.

"I don't understand. *Why?*" Samantha said. "Just weeks ago she left a celebrity-filled party that was thrown in her honor because Hayden left! She *loves* Hayden!"

How did the relationship I spent all summer building with Alexis just get thrown out the window? What could have happened? Did Brody say something? Or did—

"Amber," I said as she hung up. "I'm telling you, Samantha. I know she's behind all of this. I mean, *think about it*. Alexis hasn't been taking her medication, and Amber knows she gets paranoid when she's off of it. Why else would Alexis suddenly want Vanessa back after insisting you fire her? They're using Alexis's mental illness to turn her against us."

"You're giving those morons too much fucking credit," Samantha said. "Just go home and pack. Because even if I'm not going, *you are*. I need you to be my eyes and ears."

Oh, I was going. I had made too many excuses, thinking it wasn't a good time to approach Alexis about the video and hoping Amber wouldn't really sell it. But now Amber was manipulating her mental illness. There was nothing she wouldn't do. So, after the show, I was telling Alexis… *everything*.

AFTER TWO HOURS OF WAITING backstage in New York, Alexis emerged in a custom gold-beaded gown. The weight had fallen off faster than I'd ever seen happen to anyone. She had to be fifty pounds lighter.

"Alexis! You look *gorgeous*!" I said, chasing behind as she confidently led the way to the stage, followed by Wayne, Marlo, Amber, Brody, Sebastian, and Lion.

"Thanks, Hayden," she said.

She was pleasant, but short. There was a wall between us I hadn't felt since I started the job almost a year ago.

As she took center stage, I made my way to the back of the crowd. Lion followed.

"As you all know, I've gone through some really *tough times* this year," Alexis explained to the audience. "And I just want to thank you all for standing by me, and let you know that the best… is yet to come."

"That was weird," I muttered to Lion.

"*What?* That she's made a charity performance about herself?" He laughed. "No, that's not weird at all."

"No… It just felt like some kind of… subliminal message."

Lion shifted on his feet. "I don't know if I should say anything."

"What? What do I not know?"

"I'm not sure," he said. "But Amber did just ask me in the dressing room if I've been talking to you lately."

"Okay?"

Lion sighed. "She was basically telling me not to. She said you have no idea what's going on, and to only come to her moving forward."

Fuck.

As the performance ended, the entourage followed Alexis toward the dressing room. But for some reason, Amber jogged around the group. And when we reached the door, I saw why. Vanessa was there waiting with her arms crossed.

The two headed inside and the rest of the entourage followed. But I was stopped by Big Wayne.

"Wayne, *what the fuck*?" I said as he closed the door behind everyone. "What the fuck is going on?"

"I don't know, Hayden."

"What the hell is Vanessa doing here?" I reached for the handle. "I need to go in."

"I can't let you do that." He crossed his arms.

"Wayne, *you know* that Vanessa and Amber are bad people. I can't just let them go in there and start telling Alexis a bunch of lies. Especially when I've kept all of the horrible things they have done to myself," I said. I backed away and began pacing in front of him. "And I can't lose my job! I need to tell her what's really been going on, before it's too late."

Wayne sighed, then glanced down each end of the hallway.

"Listen, I've been instructed to guard the door... per Alexis. So, there's nothing I can do. But I'm being honest, Hayden. I have no idea what's going on." He hesitated before continuing. "But what I do know, is that if you walk down that hall and take a left, and then another left, you'll be on the other side of the dressing room. It's only a curtain, the same way it was when we were on tour."

I thanked Wayne with a bear hug, then ran to the other side of the dressing room, bumping into backup dancers, singers, and venue security. I stopped when I saw the white curtain and crouched down to the floor.

"She's a fucking *liar*!" Vanessa yelled. "You can't trust her, Alexis. And you never should have! She's been stealing from you for years! We've just been too afraid to tell you. She charges whatever she wants to her company credit cards, *and* she's been overpaying herself with the help of Karen. Like do you even have any idea how the Candy Land deal is set up?"

"And she abuses me!" Amber chimed in, forcing out crocodile tears. "She emotionally and physically abuses me, Alexis. And I haven't told you this, because I've just been *so scared* of her! But that's not even the worst of it. She's also... *a racist*!"

Amber hadn't been trusted with a card of her own, so when shopping for Alexis, she always used Samantha's. *What had Amber been charging?* They must have been planning this for months. And with how sensitive Alexis is about race, Amber knew what to throw in for good measure. "Vanessa's up to date on all your upcoming work, and she's also gained access to Samantha's emails," Amber said. "This is your chance, Alexis. I know you haven't been happy with her. So, get rid of Samantha and have Vanessa take over management. And we don't need Hayden, either. I mean, he's not *your assistant*. So, what is he doing here? Spying for her?"

A panic attack was coming on. I started hyperventilating and struggled to stand up, holding the wall to keep my balance. At the end of the hall, I called Samantha. But it went straight to voicemail.

I snuck out of the venue once I overheard Brody start validating their arguments. Samantha's own sisters had turned against her and were giving Brody everything he'd wanted all along. So, what could I have done? Barge in like a crazy person? It would be three against one, and after Alexis had specifically asked Wayne to keep me away from the dressing room, I didn't want to get him in trouble either.

I continued to incessantly call Samantha, but she never answered. I refused to leave the news on a voicemail because she was unpredictable. There was no telling what she might do. I had a way of reasoning with her, and we needed to talk through all of our options before any moves were made.

After being filled in on the details of the contract, Alexis skipped her scheduled appearance at Candy Land. I couldn't blame her. I myself felt that something was off about the deal. But how would we pay for her star on the Hollywood Walk of Fame now? Vanessa and Amber weren't just sabotaging Alexis's relationship with Samantha and me, but the Academy Award nomination.

I tossed and turned all night, convinced I'd lost my job. Had I just poured my entire soul down a black hole the past year for nothing? Around two a.m., my phone started buzzing.

"Samantha? Where the fuck have you been?"

"I'm in London, *hello*! Did you forget? It's five hours ahead here. What's going on? Why so many calls?"

"I told you that you should have come! You need to get to New York, *now*. The two of us are about to be unemployed."

"I can't just fly back to New York! Whatever it is, I'm sure—"

"You're sure, what? Your sisters cornered Alexis in the dressing room after the show. Vanessa's trying to take your job! She's accusing you of being a thief and saying all of Amber's charges on your company card are from you!"

"Hayden, I've been asking Amber for receipts and to code my credit card statements for months now. You know this!"

"Well, that's not even the worst of it. Because Amber went on to accuse you of physical abuse, *and* of being racist."

"Hayden, come on. *My sister?* My sister could never call me a—"

"Well she did, and then Vanessa explained the Candy Land contract and convinced Alexis not to show up to her appearance. So, we lost the hundred grand to pay for her star on the Walk of Fame."

The line went silent.

"Jesus Christ," Samantha said. "Okay, okay. I'm on my way. But don't tell *anyone*."

I was tortured for the rest of the day with images flashing into my memory of the racks and racks of designer clothing in Amber's room, scenes of Samantha yelling at her for receipts, and of course, the video recording.

Why hadn't I gone to Alexis sooner? Yes, I wanted to build trust between us. But the truth was, I was scared. Scared that I would be the one kicked out of her world. I should have been braver. It was my fault these criminals were still in her life. I had simply gotten used to tip-toeing around the issues just like everyone else in her world, which was hurting her more than helping.

I tried texting Alexis. I pleaded, saying it was important, saying I had to see her.

But the messages never said "Delivered".

THAT EVENING, WHEN SAMANTHA ARRIVED in the city, she came straight to my hotel room at the Four Seasons Tribeca with Blair in tow. Alexis was due on TikTok Live to announce the drop of the *Hope* song, and we were sure she'd skip it. But I got a notification on my phone that her account had just gone live. Samantha and I anxiously tuned in to find the camera on Vanessa's dirty socks, which then panned up to Alexis.

"Today's the day! My new song from the Universal movie, *Hope*, is now on Spotify!" Alexis paced around her New York apartment's kitchen. "So, I'm just here celebrating." She started walking in dizzying circles around her island.

"Alexis, sit down!" Amber mumbled in the background.

"I don't want to!" Alexis continued to pace. "Do the fans love the outfit? What are they saying? What do we think, fans? Yay? Nay? Amber, Vanessa, follow me upstairs!"

Alexis left the shot, headed for the hallway, and when the camera caught up to her, she was frantically walking up the same staircase she'd taken me up months before. She then began to pace back down the steps, and then back up the steps, and then up another flight of steps for the Rhythm & Blues Room. Alexis opened the door and took a seat on the same chaise where she and I had shared a moment. I thought things would have turned out a lot differently then.

"Don't film me from my bad side!" Alexis corrected Vanessa, then repeated her initial intro. "So, today's the day! My new song is now available on Spotify!" She stood up, left the shot again, and headed down the staircase. Halfway down, Alexis stopped in her tracks and waved the camera away in an attempt to end the live feed.

"But we need to answer some fan questions, Alexis!" Vanessa said.

The camera panned to Vanessa's feet, then back up to catch Alexis again walking quickly up and down the staircase. Her speech was mumbled, fast, and nonsensical.

"Fuck, fuck, fuck!" I shouted. "She's fucking manic."

"It's not full-blown mania yet. But it's on its way. I kept telling Marlo that Alexis needed to get back on Lithium after the surgery, but she told me not to worry about it. She's said she's got it, and to *trust and believe*! Fucking *bitch*. She doesn't even know what it's like when Alexis is unmedicated."

"You can't blame *her*, Samantha. Amber's the one who knows better and intentionally didn't give it to her."

Suddenly, our Google Alerts went off with the headline, IS ALEXIS SHANE OKAY?, immediately followed by a call from Kelly.

"What in the hell is going on? Why is Vanessa handling this announcement?" Kelly asked. "Why are you guys not there? Do you realize how bad this looks?"

"They've cut our access to her!" Samantha shouted. "None of Hayden's messages have gone through. I don't know what to fucking do."

"This is bad, Samantha. I mean, it's obvious she's not of sound mind. I've already gotten calls from *Entertainment Tonight* and *TMZ*. Not to mention the record label and studio. I mean, we're talking about the *Academy Awards* here. They've already shelled out hundreds of thousands of dollars in support of her. So, I'm sorry to say this. But with her current state and her reputation... they're contemplating *pulling out*."

Samantha's email pinged, this time with a message from the head of Universal.

"To: Vanessa
From: Universal Studios C.E.O.
CC: Samantha

Vanessa, any answers you need can be provided by Samantha."

"What the fuck is this?" Samantha spat. "Kelly, I'll call you right back."

Samantha scrolled further to find Vanessa had been trying to take control of the Academy Award campaign and was now asking Universal if they would cover the $100,000 cost for Alexis's star on the Hollywood Walk of Fame.

"What the fuck is she doing?" Samantha said, furiously auto-dictating,

"Vanessa, you are *not* on the management team! CEASE AND DESIST IMMEDIATELY."

As difficult as this job had been for Samantha, she didn't want to lose it. She began frantically calling Alexis's cell phone and apartment. No answer. She sent maniacal text messages and emails about Amber, Vanessa, the credit cards, and the Candy Land deal. She pleaded for an explanation as to how Alexis could ignore her after she'd taken care of her health, her twins, her taxes, her divorce from Rich, her split from Mark Kauffman, and her Super Bowl snafu.

But the messages all went undelivered.

"All right... Hayden, Blair, let's go!" Samantha rushed for the door. "We're going to her apartment!"

Blair and I hurried to keep up with Samantha, making our way to the elevator, then marching across the street to Alexis's building. But when we stomped into her lobby, we were quickly denied access.

"I'm sorry, Samantha. Alexis doesn't want to see you," the woman at the front desk said.

"FINE!" Samantha yelled, stomping in a red-haired fury.

We regrouped out front by the doorman. "I didn't fly all the way from London to New York City just to sit in a fucking hotel room!" Samantha said.

"Well, what can we do? Who will Alexis listen to?" I asked. Samantha continued calling Alexis's apartment. "Is she even coherent? I think you should reach out to Sebastian or Big Wayne. They've known her the longest and both know Vanessa and Amber's motives."

Samantha's phone rang. It was Alexis's lawyer.

"Samantha? Hi," he said, "I want you to understand that this wasn't an easy decision for Alexis to come to. But she asked for me to relay the message that it's time for the two of you to part ways."

Samantha's face flushed of all color. Her eyes were completely vacant of emotion. It was as if she couldn't process that this was real life. She had given her heart and soul piece by piece to reviving Alexis's career, and now her *sisters* had ruthlessly stolen that from her.

"With affection, of course," he added.

With affection wasn't how anything was ever done in Alexis's world. And more importantly, what did this mean *for me*?

CHAPTER TWENTY

The flight home to Los Angeles was silent. Samantha was devastated to have lost her job, but knowing she no longer had to look over her shoulder, she was able to sleep. I stared out my window for the next five hours, brainstorming how to keep my own. But being a part of the management team, I knew I was next.

When the plane landed, my fears manifested. I received an automated email from business management cutting off my company credit card. Samantha and I separated outside LAX, both climbing into our own cars. I immediately called Karen.

"What's going on?" I asked. "Why was my credit card cut off?"

"I don't know, Hayden," Karen lied. "I really don't know."

"Am I being fired?"

"I don't know. But I mean—"

"Okay, Karen, *whatever*," I said. "I just need you to tell me what time Alexis's jet lands in Los Angeles."

"I don't think I'm supposed—"

"*KAREN!*"

"They should be landing any minute."

I hung up.

"There's gonna be a change of address," I told my driver. "I need you to bring me to Beverly Hills."

"How long are we gonna be waiting here?" the driver groaned.

"Until my boss gets here!" I snapped. "You're getting paid by the hour anyway."

Almost two hours later, a black Mercedes Sprinter van pulled up to the gate. As it began to open, I hopped out of the Escalade and chased the Sprinter into the driveway. Big Wayne was the first to exit.

"Yo! Who's there?" he yelled after spotting my shadow.

"It's Hayden!" I shouted back, hurrying toward him.

"*Hayden?*" he said. "What're you doing here? It's really not a good time."

"I don't want to hear it! I need to talk to Alexis, and NOW!"

The entire entourage—Brody, R&B, Teddi, Sebastian, Lion, Marlo, and Amber—all peered through the Sprinter van's windows to see what the commotion was about.

"I don't need to be with her alone. You can be there. But I need to talk to her, and I'm *not* leaving until I do!"

"Hayden," Alexis cooed, appearing at the van's door, "let's go inside."

I was relieved to find her in control. The manic episode appeared to have subsided. But from experience, I also knew things appeared better before they got worse. And it was still strange to me how aloof she was acting, as if she barely knew me.

Big Wayne delicately grabbed her by the hand and I followed them toward the mansion's entrance. Once inside, Alexis headed for the formal sitting room.

"Let's go downstairs to the movie theatre," I said. Alexis stopped in her tracks. "What I need to tell you, I don't want anyone else to hear."

The two looked to one another, concerned, but still followed my lead.

"And Wayne, do you mind keeping a lookout in case anyone tries to eavesdrop?" I asked as we descended the staircase. "Amber always hides around corners to listen in on conversations."

Alexis frowned at my request as we took our seats next to one another in the front row of the movie theatre. She was wondering how long I'd known that.

"I know that you fired Samantha, and honestly whatever is going to make you happy is what I want for you, *truly*." I spoke quickly, nervously, anticipating being thrown out at any moment. "But when my flight landed today, I received a notification my credit card was shut off. I need you to know that I took this job to work for *you*. Okay? I didn't take this job to work for Samantha."

Why are you fucking talking about your job security? It was just another attempt to put off mentioning the video, even for a second longer. But I had to do it. It was the reason I came. The pressure in my chest mounted.

Big Wayne peered out of the movie theatre entrance and up the stairs, where Amber was now squatting on the floor, trying to listen.

"Yo, Amber!" he shouted. "Go unpack Alexis's bags or somethin'. I don't need you here lurking!"

Alexis shook her head. "Vanessa and Amber came to me after the show in New York explaining you were antagonizing them all summer and doing whatever you could to make them look bad, so you could take their jobs. You know, Vanessa used to set up my rooms and book my travel. Amber used to schedule my glam. But for some reason, all their responsibilities have become yours, and I just have to wonder—do you really have my best interests at heart? Or *your own*?"

My mouth dropped. Not because of the accusation, but because she *believed* them. Vanessa and Amber had taken what was true about themselves and said it about me. I looked to Big Wayne, whose eyes widened.

"Wayne, she doesn't know about anything that really happened on the road. So, you have to back me up here. Remember Vienna? Vanessa was trying to keep your room away from Alexis's. *I'm* the one who fixed it. Remember? And then in Houston, she did the same thing to Marlo. And *hello*, what about what she did to you in Chicago?"

Wayne looked at me stone-faced, knowing I was right, but unsure if he should interfere.

"Alexis, just weeks ago you were telling me that I made you happy and that these people have made you miserable. I don't understand how that could have changed so quickly. Don't you know me at all?"

Alexis looked taken aback, as she was suddenly recollecting our conversation and now questioning herself. Was her paranoia and caprice because of the bipolar disorder? On the one hand, she was a commanding superstar whose talent and expertise ascended her to the highest levels of fame—but on the other, she was as helpless as a child, believing whatever was the last thing told to her.

"But what about the credit card? They said you've been using your credit card for personal use." She spoke without conviction, trying to tape together a straw man she didn't even want. I felt bad watching her, as I could tell she was truly confused.

"I've kept every single receipt and can explain every single charge. That's just a flat-out lie, Alexis. I haven't even charged a bottle of water for myself to your card. Why wouldn't you just ask me? Why would you just believe that?"

"I don't know, Hayden," she said sincerely, with a sense of disappointment. "They were both just so passionate about it, and seemed so convincing, and—"

"They have been torturing *me*, Alexis, for the entire year, and things got worse over the summer as they saw us grow closer. I set up your rooms because Samantha asked me to. I didn't even know it used to be Vanessa's responsibility. I started working on travel when Vanessa had been let go. I started booking glam because Lion was gonna fly home when we were in Paris. He hadn't been paid in months because Amber never turned in his invoices to Karen."

Alexis seemed overwhelmed at the excess of information that I'd been keeping from her.

"All I've been trying to do is clean up their messes without you knowing. You already have so much to worry about, and I want your life to be easy. I just thought that was my job."

Wayne came up from behind and rested his hands on my shoulders.

"Alexis, you know who this kid is," he said. "You know his heart."

"I'm sorry, Hayden," Alexis said. "So much has happened this year, and I just don't know who to trust. I *never* know who to trust."

I looked to the side, knowing I couldn't make eye contact, but that I had to tell her. It was why I came. My eyes filled with tears and my heart began to pound. Somehow I had to tear through the moment I'd been fretting over for months now.

"My priority is and always has been to protect you, Alexis."

"And I appreciate that," she said.

"But things are a lot worse than you know."

"What do you mean?"

Losing any sense of confidence I had mustered, I burst into tears.

"I don't know how to tell you this," I said, "but I have to. I can't fix this alone."

I looked up at her through my tear-soaked lashes and saw terror on her face.

"Hayden, what is going on? You're scaring me," she said, her eyes wide and lost.

"I'm sorry," I said, trying to hold back the tears. "I'm sorry I didn't say anything sooner. I didn't know how, and I didn't want to embarrass you."

Alexis now had tears in her eyes as well, anticipating the worst.

"This past spring, when you went to Puerto Vallarta for your birthday. Sorry, *holiday*. Well, when you came home, you weren't in a right frame of mind, and I—um—have never been around someone with bipolar disorder during, you know, an *episode*..."

"Spit it out, Hayden!" she said.

"Samantha had me stay here at the house with you and Amber a lot. I'm not sure if you remember."

Her blank stare told me she didn't.

"Amber was mocking you, making fun of you, telling me you wouldn't remember anything. So, I tried to make sure after that day, I never left you alone with her. And when you came out of it, you and I still barely knew each other. I was scared to say anything. I just... I didn't want to lose my job."

"What do you mean, making fun of her?" Big Wayne interrupted.

"Like, when you're—manic," I said without looking her in the eye, "you don't really speak clear sentences. You ramble and jump from topic to topic. Amber was imitating you, mocking your speech, laughing at you. At one point, she even pushed you."

"So, you've felt *this* guilty about her being mean to me?" Alexis asked. She lifted my chin with two fingers and looked relieved as we made eye contact.

"It's not that." Again I looked away. "This is where her pay comes in. This summer, on tour—"

But I couldn't finish my sentence. I couldn't look at Alexis, and I couldn't look at Wayne. My face went red, I buried it into my hands, and began sobbing uncontrollably. I kept trying to muster out that I was sorry. But words wouldn't come out—only gasps for air.

Big Wayne came from behind and kneeled in front of me, grabbing me by my shoulders and trying to look into my eyes.

"Hayden, what the hell is going on?" he asked sternly. "What happened?"

"I'm sorry—I—" Tears continued to fall. "When she found out that her pay was going to be decreased, she showed me a... *video*."

Alexis's hands were now trembling.

"It's from when you were manic. I'm sorry. I thought not leaving you alone with her would be enough," I sobbed. "But it happened when I was here, and I'm so, so sorry."

"What the *hell* is on the video?" she shouted.

"Amber was hiding when she filmed it. I didn't even know she was there. It's you and me. We're in your bedroom. I was cleaning up because you kept changing. At first, you're wearing a robe, and then you—"

"I, *what*?"

"You get undressed. You're naked, and you're trying to get me to have sex with you."

Alexis's chocolate skin went gray. She immediately looked away.

"I'm so sorry, Alexis. It's just that I've seen and heard everything these people have done to Brody, and to your ex-fiancé... and I didn't know what to do. I've been so scared of losing my job and I just thought if I spent the time building a relationship with you, that when I finally did tell you everything, you would know you could trust me. But they came to you first, and with lies."

Alexis had tuned out. She didn't remember the incident, but knew it was true.

"Amber showed Samantha and me the video and told us that if you let her go, she was gonna sell the footage and buy herself a house with the money. But it's not just her. It's Vanessa. Vanessa said she was gonna hide it in a Dropbox. I don't know why Samantha hasn't told you herself. I can only assume because, having brought these people into your life, she feels guilty by association."

"Why didn't you come to *me*, Hayden?" Wayne shook me angrily. "Where is the video now? Did Vanessa hide it?"

Alexis's shock had subsided, and the panic set in. She too began sobbing.

"I am so, so sorry," I cried alongside her. "I don't know, Wayne. I don't know if she actually hid it. I'm sorry that I didn't come to you sooner."

"We've gotta get that phone from Amber," Wayne said.

"But it has to be done in the right way. If you ask her about it, she'll get rid of it and call me a liar," I said. "Wayne, you need to just take her phone. You need to take it and delete it."

I moved closer to Alexis to wrap my arm around her. But she pushed me away.

"Hayden," she said, "I think you should just... go home."

I CLEARLY WASN'T THINKING ABOUT timing when I rushed over to Alexis's, because when I got home, I remembered it was the night before her Walk of Fame ceremony and performance in front of the Hollywood Foreign Press Association. What if she was so upset it led to another embarrassing performance? Or what if she didn't show at all? Did I just set her up to lose the Academy Award nomination? So much for delicate timing.

Samantha, too, was worried. Being that Alexis had skipped her Candy Land obligation, she knew the ceremony was not paid for.

"How the fuck is she gonna pay for it?" Samantha said to me over the phone. "People are still expecting a solution from *me*, because no one knows we've separated. Karen just told me if the Hollywood Chamber of Commerce doesn't receive payment within the hour, they're going to cancel the whole thing. I mean, press is already lining up! She's going to be humiliated!"

I debated whether I should tell Samantha about what happened the night before, but decided against it. "Samantha, I'm sorry, I don't want to be rude. But... why are *you* worried about this? This isn't your problem anymore. Maybe things like this will need to happen for her to realize she's making a mistake. You still have had no communication?"

"She won't fucking talk to me! And Vanessa had me served a letter from some bogus lawyer telling me to stop slandering her name. *How dare her!* Fucking cost me my job and then threatens me!"

"I know—"

"No, you don't know, Hayden! These are *my sisters*! This is my livelihood! I have a child! Fuck, hold on. That's Adam, the CEO of Candy Land, beeping in."

Samantha merged our calls.

"I'm not sure what's going on, Samantha," he said. "Because you know Alexis didn't show up for her appearance in New York. But her business management office is calling and asking for payment anyway. They want it as an advance and are promising she'll do an appearance at a later date."

"Jesus," Samantha scoffed. "I don't know what to say, Adam. Alexis and I are separating," she said aloud for the first time. "I could be nasty and malicious and tell you not to. But I really don't wanna see her fail. So, if you could do this… as a favor to me. I promise, she'll make up for it."

Samantha wasn't the evil bitch everyone thought she was. Freshly fired, she had the opportunity to humiliate Alexis, and she didn't.

ROADS WERE CLOSED, TRAFFIC WAS crazy, and all I kept thinking about was the last thing Alexis said to me. *Go home.* So, I went home and climbed into bed. I knew she didn't want me at her Walk of Fame ceremony. But did not going make me look like I was somehow in the wrong? I obsessed over it for hours, until I saw on Instagram she was happy and smiling, posing in front of her star. I couldn't just give up now. I couldn't miss her performance in front of the Hollywood Foreign Press Association. We had worked too hard.

I pulled up to the valet at the Hilton in Beverly Hills when my phone rang with a call from Samantha. She too was headed my way.

"Are you sure that's a good idea?" I asked.

"I just realized, Hayden… I *have* to be there. Everyone in the industry is coming, and I worked hard for this. *I* made this happen."

Alexis did say she wanted to separate with affection. So, Samantha should be able to finish out a duty as big as an Academy Award campaign. But then again, who knew what headspace she was in after the bomb I'd dropped on her? "But—"

"Hayden, *don't.* Do you have any idea how much money I'm owed? I made sure that every single one of you were paid before me this quarter. I'm owed three-hundred-fifty grand in commissions, and for the rest of this year, I was due to make another six hundred. If I don't come, *everyone* will be asking why, and having just lost my job, it's important I maintain these relationships. She can take my money. But I'm not gonna let her ruin my reputation."

As strong as Samantha was, she was nervous and insisted I meet her out front. Walking in with her side-by-side, I was worried it would appear I was being disloyal to Alexis. But I felt partly responsible for her demise. After all, me calling out her sisters for not doing their jobs was the cause of them turning on her.

We spotted Big Wayne by the entrance of the ballroom, looking dapper in a well-tailored black suit. My anxiety spiked, not wanting him to mention my visit from the night before.

"I'm sorry, Samantha," he said, "but you can't see her before the performance. I'll tell her you're here, though."

"Of course. I don't want to distract her," she said. "This is a really important day."

Once enemies, Samantha and Wayne now embraced. I don't think anybody anticipated those bitches betraying their own blood. At least their lack of integrity gave us something to rally around.

Wayne scowled. "They did you dirty, Samantha."

Through the entrance of the ballroom, we saw the backup singers and band taking the stage, meaning Alexis would be out any second. Wayne led us inside, and I spotted Amber peeking out from what I assumed to be the dressing room door.

"I just don't want things to end badly, Wayne. I really don't," Samantha said as we took our seats in the second row. "We can do this amicably."

How could Alexis and Wayne let Amber still be here? Had nothing been said? Did they not believe me?

The door opened again, and my mouth dropped as I watched Vanessa walk Alexis toward center stage. I could feel the heat radiating from Samantha beside me. Alexis greeted the crowded room, made eye contact with Samantha, and smiled kindly. She looked more beautiful than ever in a sequined rose-gold floor-length gown, her hair styled like her idol, Marilyn Monroe.

The band kicked in, and I listened intently as Alexis performed her song live for the very first time. My body was covered in chills as she sang about being in the darkest of times, and then coming out if it in a better place. A place of gratitude even. I remembered the first time she sang it to me alone in her recording studio, and how that was the first time I truly made her laugh. Tears fell down my face for all the joy and heartbreak this job inflicted. Wherever and whenever this journey was due to end, I was grateful to have experienced it at all.

She did better than I ever could have imagined. She was everything anybody could have wanted her to be, and she looked *happy*.

I looked to Samantha; she had tears in her eyes. She knew it was over. She'd hoped coming today would change Alexis's mind. But Alexis didn't want to see her after.

WHEN I WOKE UP, THE news had broken. The headline read, ALEXIS SHANE SPLITS WITH MANAGER.

I opened my laptop to find it plastered across every entertainment and gossip website. It surprised me at first to see it was such a big deal. But their relationship had been highly publicized due to the documentary and Super Bowl fiasco.

Fuck. I buried my face in my hands.

My phone started buzzing incessantly. Not just from Samantha, but from coworkers, friends, family, acquaintances. All asking the same things I wanted to know. *What happened? Are you okay? Do you still have a job?*

Fans were speculating on social media as to why Samantha hadn't been seen at the Walk of Fame ceremony. Upon confirmation of her firing, they flooded her Instagram with snake emojis and insults. Not knowing Alexis's struggles with addiction and mental illness, they always blamed Samantha for Alexis's career missteps and were now celebrating her demise.

I wanted to wrap my head around this before I spoke to her. But she wouldn't stop calling.

"Hello?" I finally answered.

"Where the fuck have you been?" she shouted. "Have you seen the news?"

"I have. I'm sorry, Samantha."

"Hayden," Samantha's voice cracked, and she began to whimper for the first time since her firing. Reality had finally sunken in. "How did this happen?"

"I don't know," I said. But I did.

"These people, they're my family," she sobbed. "How could they do this to me? How long had they been planning this for?"

"I don't know what to say. Money, fame, power... it can bring out the worst in people. They didn't want to lose their access to that. Even if it meant betraying their blood."

The social media harassment only got worse as the day went on. I felt sick reading Alexis's fans tell Samantha to get HIV, cancer, or for her and Blair to kill themselves. Then the narrative took a turn when a private account started making accusations of Samantha threatening to expose Alexis's bipolar disorder. In my heart, I knew Vanessa and Amber were behind it. They were satisfied with nothing less than total destruction of the only person who had helped them reach their privileged lifestyles in the first place.

I was left confused in the days that followed—I was still getting my direct deposit, but no one was speaking to me. So, when Big Wayne called I was elated, hoping it meant I'd get some answers.

"Alexis wants to know if you'll come with me to her lawyer's office in Century City?"

"Of course I will. Is this—"

"It's about what you told us the other night. We need to make sure we're taking the right precautions. I'll text you the address. Could you meet me there in like... an hour?"

"I'll be there," I said. "But Wayne, I need to know. *Am I fired?* I still haven't heard anything."

"Let's just handle one thing at a time. Okay? I'll see you soon."

My twenty-minute drive from West Hollywood to Century City felt like an hour, and I had a knot in my stomach, reminiscent of when I'd been called to the principal's office in high school.

The doors to Alexis's lawyer's office opened on the twenty-seventh floor, and Wayne was already waiting for me. He led me into a conference room where Alexis's lawyer was sitting.

"Hayden, thanks for coming," he said, shaking my hand. "As you know, you had a conversation with Alexis and Wayne a few nights ago, and you made some *very* serious allegations. Which is why we're here today."

"I understand." I took a seat across from him.

"Let's start by having you repeat to me exactly what you told them. So we're all on the same page."

When I got to the point in the story where I had to describe what Alexis was doing to me on the video Amber had recorded, I couldn't speak. Instead, a loud whimper came out.

"I'm sorry," I cried. "I'm sorry."

"Why are *you* apologizing, Hayden?" Wayne interrupted.

"Because I feel horrible. I feel guilty even repeating this incident to you guys. It's private, it's personal. It's embarrassing, it's fucking *humiliating*," I said. "I don't see her as Alexis Shane. I see her as Alexis. I see her as Rhythm and Blue's mom. I see her as a woman struggling with mental health. I just... I don't know how Amber could do this to her."

The two men looked at me, and then at one another. There had been doubts about whether or not I was telling the truth. But now they were confident I was.

Wayne slammed his fists on the conference room table, the vibration knocking over an open bottle of water.

"How the *fuck* are we gonna get this video out of her hands?" he said.

Suddenly my phone rang, interrupting us. It was an unknown number, so I pressed ignore. But they called again.

"Go ahead and answer it," the lawyer said.

"Hello?" I said, trying to sound like I hadn't just been crying.

"Hayden? Hi! This is Spencer from *Entertainment Tonight*."

"What? Who? How did you get my number?"

The two men looked at me bewildered.

"We've just gotten confirmation that Alexis Shane had what is called *gastric sleeve surgery*. I wanted to see if you were interested in being a source, or if you had any more information on this?"

My shock loosened the grip on my phone, and in slow motion, I watched it fall to the white marble floor. The screen shattered.

"SIRI, CALL SAMANTHA," I COMMANDED my iPhone after closing the door to my car and making sure I was out of Big Wayne's sight.

"Hello?" she answered on the first ring.

"Why did you do this?" I said. "Why?"

"I don't know what you're talking about," she said. But I knew she was lying.

"You know exactly what I'm *fucking* talking about! *Entertainment Tonight* just called and asked for my comment! How did they get my phone number, Samantha? How do they even know who I am?"

"I don't—"

"Don't fucking lie to me!" I shouted. "I have been nothing but good to you!"

"Well... Hayden," she sighed, "this is her karma. This is what she gets."

"Her *karma*? Because she fired you? This is even worse than if her Walk of Fame ceremony had been canceled. I thought you didn't want to see her fail? What the fuck is wrong with you?"

Our call dropped as I pulled out of the parking garage, and by the time service hit my phone again, the news broke.

The headline read, CONFIRMED: ALEXIS SHANE UNDERGOES GASTRIC SLEEVE SURGERY.

CHAPTER TWENTY-ONE

*I*t was the day of my thirtieth birthday, the day I'd dreaded for years. All year I had been fantasizing about spending it with the legendary diva. I mean, who could say they spent their thirtieth birthday with *Alexis Shane*? But now we weren't speaking, my friendships were non-existent, and even Grayson didn't send his best wishes.

I got in my car and drove to Alexis's mansion. I wanted an answer about our future together, and now... I mean, it was my *birthday*. That had to bring me some kind of luck. Right? I would just apologize again for not coming to her sooner and she'd understand. Because she knew me, and like Wayne said, she knew my heart.

I pulled up to the gate off Beverly Drive and typed in the code. The grounds security on duty must have been clueless because he simply waved as I parked my car. Normally, I'd have just walked inside. But considering the circumstances, I rang the doorbell.

No answer. I rang the doorbell again, and this time, Alexis opened the door. My memory flashed back to my first day on the job.

"Hayden!" she shouted enthusiastically, holding out her hand for mine. "Come!"

Alexis yanked me up the grand staircase. *Where is everyone?*

When we reached her closet, I felt a familiar pit in my stomach. She quickly undressed in front of me, then put on a Swarovski-encrusted bra, tied a plaid button-up around her waist, and pulled on a pair of Ugg boots. She grabbed my hand and led me back toward the stairs. As we descended, she nearly tripped over a pair of Rhythm's swimming goggles, but stopped to pick them up and put them on. The whole time, she mumbled nonsensically, leaving no room for me to respond.

"Have you ever seen *Bambi*?" she asked. "I've been *Keeping Up with the Kardashians*. Have you seen my phone? Where's my phone, Hayden? Donald Trump is our president, and Caitlyn Jenner is our VP. I'm tired of people telling me that I'm not black enough. You know?"

At the bottom of the staircase, Alexis let out a familiar bone-chilling howl.

"What are *you* doing here?" Marlo said, running in from the kitchen.

"I..." I stammered, "I just came to talk to Alexis, because I still haven't heard anything about my job."

"Well now isn't a good time!"

"Clearly, I can see that," I said. "But Marlo, do you need help? Because you haven't been around her during an episode. Have you called her doctor? Do you even have her doctor's number?"

"We got it, Hayden!" Marlo said.

"This isn't just something you can handle on your own. It can last for up to a month," I tried to explain, "and it's going to get worse before it gets better. Here, I'll call the doctor."

"*No!* You need to *leave*!" She placed her hand on my lower back to guide me toward the mansion's entrance.

"Just promise me, Marlo. Promise me Amber isn't here."

"AMBER! AMBER!" Alexis began to shout. "AMBER!"

I could hear the pitter-patter of tiny footsteps headed our way, until Rhythm and Blue appeared in matching SpongeBob pajamas. They greeted me by hugging my waist, and I picked Rhythm up to hold him.

"Mommy's being crazy again," he whispered into my ear.

"It's gonna be okay, buddy," I said, before setting him down. "Hey, how 'bout you guys go play some video games in the movie theatre? I'll be down in a few." The thought of leaving the twins now made me sick, like I was abandoning them in this circus.

The twins followed my instruction, and I returned to questioning Marlo.

"I'm serious, Marlo. Where's Amber?"

"She's in the guest house."

"She's in the guest house?" I said. "You need to be a little less worried about me, and a little more worried about her! Amber's been secretly recording Alexis. That's why I came here the other night, to tell her. She's been threatening to blackmail her!"

"What's going on in here?" Big Wayne said, walking in from the mansion's entrance.

"I'm sorry. It's just, it's my birthday, and I wanted to see Alexis. I wanted to find out about my job. It's all I've been able to think about," I said. "I had no idea she was manic, Wayne. How the fuck is Amber still here? You know I wasn't lying. How could you put Alexis in harm's way?"

"Hayden, you gotta go," Wayne said. "I talked to Amber and she explained this is just another one of Samantha's elaborate schemes to save herself. Need I remind you of what she did to Brody?"

"Are you fucking kidding me? This isn't about saving Samantha—or me, for that matter! This is about protecting Alexis! You were there when I told her. You were defending me! How could you think I'd make something like this up?"

He just shook his head, continuing to push me out the door. "You need to let it go, Hayden. It's *over*. Alexis doesn't wanna be around anyone who is associated with Samantha," he said, followed by a heavy sigh. "I would just take a little time to yourself, enjoy the holidays with your family, and I'll see what I can do about getting you a letter of recommendation before the New Year."

"She's a liar!" I spat. "Did you even check her phone?"

Alexis was incoherent, now pretending to swim across the foyer. She breast-stroked her way to the accent table where her car keys were, pulled them from the drawer, and headed for the home's entrance. Alexis opened the door and the ground security guard's mouth dropped at the sight of her in the peculiar outfit.

"FUCK!" I shouted. "FUCK! FUCK! FUCK! I'm only trying to protect her! And you're just going to throw me out like I'm garbage?"

"You need to leave, Hayden," Wayne said, though I could tell he wasn't happy about it. Clearly nobody here knew what to believe anymore.

"I have to at least say goodbye to the twins," I choked on my words, holding back tears, knowing they were waiting for me in the other room. How could a house full of capable humans completely fail to protect those two kids?

"I don't think that's a good idea," Wayne said. He placed his hand on my back and guided me toward the door.

When the gates closed behind my car, I sobbed. I was thirty, friendless, fiancé-less, and family-less—besides Oma. I'd given up everything for this job, and now it was over. It had all been for nothing.

IT WAS A STRANGE FEELING, going from chaos to silence. I didn't know what to do with myself, as I'd been isolated from everyone for so long. I also didn't *want* to tell anyone. I'd gloated about my dream job, and in an instant, it was taken away. I'd confused work with a life. I didn't leave bed, instead surviving only off DoorDash over the following weeks. Not just because of being lied about and losing my job. But because I was worried about Alexis and the twins.

I considered reaching out to Rich, but I didn't even have his phone number. He'd been almost invisible for the past year. So, what was the point? He only seemed to care about Rhythm and Blue for an Instagram post.

Not helping my depression was my social media stalking. On the day of the *Hope* movie premiere, I laid in bed anxiously refreshing my feeds to see if somehow they'd gotten her to show up. But she didn't. However, her absence didn't keep Brody from making an appearance. He even posted a photo in front of a blank Hollywood star on the Walk of Fame. The caption read, *"Someday my name will be here, too."*

Fucking loser.

Wanting to be the first to deliver the news, Samantha called.

"Did you see she isn't at the premiere? She's *fucking manic.* Karen just told me," Samantha scoffed. "We worked so hard on this, and it was all for nothing. I hope when she comes out of it, she realizes what she's done."

"I saw," I said. "And the *Hope* tour kicks off the day after tomorrow. So, if she's manic, there's no way that she—"

At the same time, both of our Google Alerts went off. The headline read, ALEXIS SHANE CANCELS TWELVE SHOWS CITING LARYNGITIS.

"Fucking liars!" Samantha spat.

"Well what the fuck do you expect them to say, Samantha? That she's bipolar, manic, and not taking her medication?"

"Do you even know how much money she's losing canceling twelve shows? Three million dollars! All because of Amber!" Samantha said. "She should be held responsible. She's ruining her entire life and career!"

The news of the cancellations didn't sit well with her fans either, especially coming off the heels of her highly publicized elective weight-loss surgery. Their comments read:

"Diva? More like unreliable has-been!"

"Hope the gastric sleeve was worth it, you fat bitch!"

"We're done with you! Retire already!"

I WANTED TO LET IT go, but I couldn't. I spent day after day in bed obsessing over the lies Amber told. I knew she had a ridiculous salary with few expenses, but something still felt off.

I thought about the racks of designer clothing in her room. I remembered the time Alexis's publicist Kelly saw them and joked they had to be stolen. I recollected the four-thousand-dollar shoes she signed for, which mysteriously went missing. Then there was the time when she and I went to Gucci, and I suspected she charged her clothes to Alexis's account. And also the time she had me double-check Alexis's credit card statements, although she knew I was incapable.

Vanessa wasn't without blame either. I knew she'd been receiving thousands of dollars in kickbacks from our travel agent.

If I could just get proof of these things, it would discredit Amber and Vanessa. Suddenly I had a new purpose, and I wasn't going down without a fight.

So, I threw on my Adidas tracksuit and headed for Rodeo Drive.

The employees in the stores Alexis frequented all knew me and didn't question my requests for her receipts. I made my way from Louis Vuitton, to Gucci, to Saint Laurent, and when I walked into Hermès, I remembered the day Anna and I had come to return a stack of scarves.

"Thank you so much for all these receipts. You're a lifesaver!" I told the saleswoman. "I do have one more question, though. Is there any store credit left under Alexis's name?"

"Hmmm... let's see," she said. She clicked the mouse a few times on her computer. "No, Hayden. There's no credit here!"

"Are you sure? Because I swear..." I pushed further. "Maybe they were somehow returned under Amber's name? Could you check? Her last name is—"

And there it was. Not $10,000—but nearly $100,000 of credit that had been accrued over the past three years.

"I don't mean to be a pest. But when Amber comes in to buy something for Alexis, it comes from the store credit, even though it's under her name, *right*? Like, she's not making a new charge to Alexis's credit card."

"Well, that's strange," she said, inspecting the account. "It looks like Amber is returning items under her own name, but never using it. All purchases for Ms. Shane are always made to her credit card."

IT TOOK DAYS TO PREPARE binders before having them sent to Karen and Wayne. Inside was a letter, which kicked off with my first day at work explaining how strange I felt after seeing Amber's closet. I said it seemed like an expensive wardrobe for an assistant. But I ignored it after finding out her salary. I recalled that weeks later, a pair of four-thousand-dollar shoes made custom for Alexis had gone missing. I looked up the tracking information online to find Amber had accepted the package. Yet when I asked her, she denied it. Behind the first tab in the binder, I attached a copy of the tracking information, along with her signature.

I went on to explain that being new at the time, I wanted Amber to like me. So, when she asked me to help out by cross-checking her credit card statements with her receipts, I obliged. I explained that I did tell her there was no way for me to check that the receipts were accurate, being that she was the one who had made the purchases. But Amber told me not to worry about that. I also explained my first trip with her to Gucci, how I suspected that she charged things for herself to Alexis's account. Behind the second tab in the binder were copies of Alexis's receipts from the past year. *Just check and see*, I wrote. *See if any of these items are in Amber's closet.*

The saleswoman who'd helped me at Hermès spoke with a coworker who regularly assisted Amber. She confirmed that Amber would return things claiming they were gifts to her from Alexis, and then have the credit placed under her own name. Behind the third tab in the binder was a letter from the manager explaining that a hold had been put on both of their accounts until confirmation was received from Alexis that the $100,000 was in the right place.

I even paid a travel agent to make a spreadsheet comparing their prices to the ones Vanessa's travel agent had been charging. After making it, he shared it with the president of his company who was so horrified that he himself insisted on writing a letter explaining that no one—no matter how rich or famous, should be taken advantage of in the way Alexis had been.

But weeks went by, and no response.

Her mania passed, and Alexis kicked off the *Hope* tour in Los Angeles. I continued following her on Instagram, and she looked happy, living what appeared to be a chaos-free life. The cancellations only helped the other shows to sell out, and the press started turning around for her. She was receiving rave reviews, not only for her performance, but for her appearance. And her new song reached the top ten on the Billboard charts, something she hadn't accomplished in half a decade.

I wanted to be happy for her, but I was too upset. The positive press rolling in right after she fired Samantha made it appear as if Samantha was the problem. Yet the tour, the weight loss, the song, and the Academy Award campaign were *because* of her. Because of *us*.

I jealously watched the entourage travel from London, to Paris, to Tokyo, and finally New York. I'd been looking forward to returning to New York for the holiday season as Home Alone 2 was my favorite Christmas movie. Grayson had surprised me with a stay at the Plaza Hotel the year before, where the film took place. In a few weeks I was traveling to Oma's in Maryland, where Christmas had regularly been spent since the year I was born. So, after missing the last one, I knew I couldn't show up depressed. It was her favorite holiday, and who knew how many more we'd have together. Already East Coast bound, I convinced myself that maybe a New York pitstop first would lift my spirits. I deserved it after the year I'd endured.

But when I got there alone, it wasn't the same. I watched families in the Rockefeller Plaza taking photos by the tree before making my way toward Saks Fifth Avenue to see the holiday light show and window display. Overhead, I spotted a full moon. I remembered how the full moon was supposed to represent the end of a chapter. Maybe I had learned all I could. Maybe it *was* time to move on, though I didn't feel ready.

I stumbled through the cold, gazing up at the moon, wondering where I'd be at the same time next year. I hoped not alone.

My phone buzzed in my pocket.

"Did you see?" Samantha said through whimpers. "Did you fucking see? She got the nomination, Hayden!" Samantha gasped for air. "I worked so hard to get her that! *We* worked so hard!"

I opened my Instagram to find a video of Alexis in her dressing room with Brody, Marlo, Amber, and Vanessa. They clinked champagne flutes, celebrating the nomination none of them had worked for.

"I'm sorry, Samantha," I said, "I really am."

I, too, was heartbroken, in a busy street full of cheerful people ready for the holidays.

"What are *you* apologizing for? You're the *only* person who stood by me. When I was wrong, you *corrected* me. You didn't *sabotage* me," she said. "I'm so sorry I even entertained the idea when they said I couldn't trust you. I know this job wasn't easy on you."

"Thank you, Samantha," I said, "For bringing me in and giving me this opportunity."

As difficult as the year had been, Samantha saved me from being another thirty-year-old in Los Angeles working a dead-end job. She was the first person to really take a chance on me, and I couldn't help but feel grateful. After all, she was the one who made the nearly impossible dream of working with my favorite superstar a reality.

I SPLURGED ON AN UPGRADE to first class for my flight to Maryland. It would give me the opportunity to lie down and sleep, a luxury I'd become accustomed to flying in advance of Alexis. It would be my last splurge, I told myself, just happy to be headed home.

But when the plane landed and my phone service hit, an excess of voicemails and text messages rolled in. Even more than I'd received on the day Samantha's firing went public. The difference was, these were all from family. My mom, brothers, cousins, uncles, and aunts. There was only one person who I didn't have a message from.

"Mom? What's going on?" I said frantically. "I just landed."

But all I heard was sobbing.

"*Mom?*"

"It's Oma. She's in an ambulance on her way to the hospital. She had a heart attack."

The wind was knocked out of me.

My Oma was a short, frail woman in her mid-eighties. But she was much healthier and more active than anyone I knew. I had just spoken to her last week and she seemed so cheery.

"I'm on my way to the hospital," my mother said. "What airport are you at?"

"I'm at BWI. I'm on my way now."

I knew there was no way my grandmother could die. She was invincible.

But as I climbed into the backseat of my Uber, I got the call. She didn't make it.

I LAUGHED IN THE UBER, remembering how when I was a young boy who wanted to play with dolls, my Oma would buy them for me, despite knowing it upset my parents. "Who cares?" she'd tell them. "They're no different than action figures!"

But I also cried on the drive, remembering my dad dropping me off on a street corner with my bags, saying it was because he loved me. She didn't hesitate to pick me up and take me in—showing me what unconditional love really looked like.

I hadn't packed for a funeral. So, when I needed an all-black outfit, I drove to the nearby Kohl's. She always purchased our Christmas presents from there off the sale rack, as she was naturally thrifty, having been raised during the Great Depression. I remembered bickering with her once at the register when she left a coupon at home and insisted we leave and come back. To avoid another trip, I tried buying the items for her myself. But she refused. Never wanting to waste money, I figured she'd passed this time of the year on purpose. Traveling was expensive, and we'd already be home for Christmas.

My brothers and I carried her casket down the same aisle of the church she had married my grandfather in. It didn't feel real. We set the casket down at the front of the church before taking our seats in the front pew with the rest of our family.

At the end of the service, "Wind Beneath My Wings" began playing through the church's speakers. I started hyperventilating, remembering watching *Beaches* with her as a child, and Facetiming her as I stood in front of the stage at the Hollywood Bowl. I let out a noise that I'd never made before, a groan of desperation, and hands came at me from every direction in an attempt to soothe me.

I needed air.

I hurried for the back of the church with my head down, not wanting looks of sympathy, and pushed through the double doors. I could smell the snow coming down before I even looked up. And when I did, there stood Grayson.

"What are you doing here?" I sobbed, falling into his arms. My tears soaked his coat. It felt like an eternity since I'd last seen him, and the scent of his cologne overwhelmed me with a loving nostalgia. In his arms, I realized just how much I'd missed him.

"Your mom called me. I couldn't not come," he said. He was trying not to cry himself. "I'm so sorry, Hayden. I know how much you loved her."

"I'm so sorry," I cried. "For everything."

"I know," he said.

"Life just became warped with the money, and the travel, and the fame. I lost my grandmother, I lost you. I lost *myself*."

"You didn't lose me," Grayson said.

"Okay, well good then," I said. I broke my tears with laughter. "Then I'm hoping you didn't come all the way here just because you're my friend."

"Hayden…" He laughed, and lifted my head. "You and I will *never* just be *friends*."

GRAYSON WAS ONLY ABLE TO stay for a few days before returning to Arizona to finish out the holiday season with his own family. We said we were going to take things slow, but we seemed to pick right back up, almost as if my time in Alexis's world had never happened.

My mom, my brothers, and I stayed at Oma's house for weeks following her funeral. It felt like we were just waiting for her to come home, not wanting to admit it wasn't going to happen.

I did my best to avoid anything Alexis-related, not wanting to rub salt in my wounds. I just told myself that this bizarre chapter of my life had closed—like the full moon predicted.

But eventually I caved and looked at her Instagram. She was spending Christmas in Aspen with the twins and posting photos with Santa. I wasn't missing anything. So, I closed out of the app to start looking for plane tickets home—when my Google Alerts went off.

The headline read, ALEXIS SHANE RETURNS TO THE SUPER BOWL FOR COMEBACK PERFORMANCE.

Wow. This was a big deal. If done successfully, this performance would get her back in the public's good graces, and just in time for the Academy Awards. I felt a pang of jealousy to not be part of it. And within seconds, my phone was buzzing with a call from a number I didn't recognize.

"Hello?" I said.

"Hayden," a familiar voice responded. "How are you?"

"*Marlo?*" I said in disbelief, convinced she'd called by mistake.

"Alexis wants to know if you'll come meet with her. In New York, in a couple weeks."

The dates she gave me coincided with the Super Bowl.

I went silent as I wondered what I'd say to Samantha, what I'd say to Grayson.

"Hello? Are you there?"

"Um... yes! Of course I can come," I stammered. "But, do you know why—"

"Okay, perfect! I'll let Alexis know, and Karen will take care of your flight. We'll see you soon!"

She hung up.

IT WAS THE COLDEST DAY on record in New York City, and I patiently waited in my hotel room at the Four Seasons for instruction to head over to Alexis's apartment. But the time kept changing, reminding me of my interview process a year earlier. I'd been traveling with the same few items of clothing for over a month. So, that morning I stopped into a Zara to find an appropriate outfit to meet her in. I paired a beige slim-fitted suit with a heather-grey turtleneck. Considering everything I'd been through over the past month, I looked and felt great.

The hours went by, and I now expected our meeting to be postponed until the next day. Which made sense. I mean, it was one thing to meet. But on the day of her Super Bowl performance? Why would she want to have any kind of potentially stressful conversation before that?

But at the last minute, Marlo sent me instructions to meet them at the Giants stadium.

On a golf cart, venue security drove me through the bustling stadium toward Alexis's dressing room. Outside, Big Wayne greeted me with a huge grin.

"I'm so glad to see you here," he said. He shook my hand professionally, as he never had before. "She's been waiting for you."

Waiting for *me*? Was I dreaming? He knocked on the door, then placed credentials around my neck. I looked down to read "Management."

"Hayden!" Alexis said, beaming with excitement as Wayne opened the door.

"Alexis!" I matched her tone, and we smiled at one another through her well-lit glam mirror.

She hurried out of her chair, nudging aside Lion and Sebastian to hug me.

"Boys, will you give us a minute?" Alexis batted her lashes. "I need to talk to Hayden before taking the stage."

The boys each gave me a hug as they passed before joining Big Wayne in the hallway.

I held Alexis by her hands and stepped back to admire her from head to toe. She looked like a movie star, wearing a nude illusion gown that amply displayed her bosom, and over her shoulders was draped an ivory faux fur.

"You look beautiful, Alexis. Like a real *diva*," I said, still in disbelief that I was there. "They don't make them like this anymore."

"You're right, they don't. I'm the last!" she said, laughing. "The last living diva!"

I flashed back to a vision of myself, squatted on the living room floor of Oma's home. It was my senior year of high school, and I was watching her latest music video on MTV. She seemed a world away then, and now she was right inside of my hands.

"I know we won't get a chance to talk after because you're gonna be swamped with press. So, you need to know. This wasn't all Samantha's fault. She really does love—"

"Hayden, *enough*." She released her hands from mine and took a step back.

"Everything you said was true. That's why you're here," she said. "We double-checked everything you sent over. Last night, both Amber and Vanessa were arrested."

"*Arrested?*" I said in disbelief, trying not to smile.

"For stealing from me, for filming me, for blackmailing me," she said. "Everything only got worse after you left. After you sent those binders, Wayne bugged their hotel rooms in each city and busted them talking about the video."

"I'm so sorry, Alexis, I—"

"And, Brody, well…"

"*Brody?*"

"When we were in Tokyo, he was caught with another one of our *male* backup dancers, getting a little too handsy in the restroom." She laughed. "I mean, I'm a smart person. What the hell was I thinking? A backup dancer? Of *course* he's gay!"

I laughed with her, relieved to know I didn't need to share my own experience with him.

"But you," she said, "you always had my best interest at heart. You proved that time and time again. You were the only person I could really trust over the past year."

"Well, Samantha," I said, still not wanting to take all the credit.

"Samantha, *nothing*! Do you think I don't know *everything*?" she said. "Regardless of his sexuality, do you think it was right how she handled Brody? Do you think she should have been controlling my life to the degree she was? Do you think it was right how she tried to use *me* to leverage fame for *her daughter*?"

"I don't," I said truthfully.

"I don't want Samantha to be my manager. *Okay?*"

"Okay," I said.

"I want *you*."

"You want *me*?" My eyes welled with tears.

Memories from the entire year began flashing before my eyes. Meeting Alexis at the music video shoot. Driving the glittery-green Ferrari on St.

Patrick's Day. Being locked in the house with her during mania. Traveling the world. The blackmail video. The end of my relationship with Grayson. My grandmother's funeral.

"Alexis, we're about to go live!" a producer shouted through the cracked door.

"So, what do you say? And before you say anything, I want you to know that I'm back on my medication. I've figured out a routine that works for me. I don't want you to suffer through what you did before. You mean a lot to me, Hayden, for sticking with me through it all. This go-around will be different."

I couldn't. There was no way. Grayson would never be okay with it. Would he? And how could I do that to Samantha?

"Um, *hello*?" She waved her hand in front of my face to break my trance.

"I'll do it," I said confidently.

Alexis squealed and embraced me tightly.

"Do you know how much *fun* we're gonna have?"

"We are," I said, returning the smile. "Let's do this! But Alexis–" I stammered, knowing it had to be different this time, that I couldn't just blindly repeat the same entropy that ruined my relationship. After all, I didn't want to spend my *fortieth* alone, too. "Do you promise it will be different? I don't think either you or I can survive another year like the one we just had. *You* come first, before anything else. As long as you can agree to that—"

"Hayden," she interrupted, her eyes glistening with surprised emotion. "Of course I promise." She nodded, squeezing my hands tightly. A smile radiated from her face. She looked clearer than I had seen her maybe *ever*.

"I also need you to promise me that I won't go a week without spending time with Grayson. Even if that means he joins us on the road."

"I promise," she said. "But wait... who's Grayson?"

I couldn't help but laugh. "My fiancé."

"Hayden, you have a *fiancé*?"

"I do."

"Well *hello*, why haven't I met him? Please bring him by the house for dinner once we're back in LA."

Outside the dressing room door, golf carts waited to drive our entourage to the center of the football field for the stage. As we reached the steps,

I walked Alexis up them, as I'd seen Samantha do many times before—forgetting the one hundred million eyes on us. Cameras followed our every move, and I caught myself on the big screen behind Alexis as I escorted her center stage.

"I believe in you." I kissed her hand and left her to do what only she could.

The stage went dark before a spotlight appeared, and the silhouette of the bestselling artist of all time came into focus. The inevitable ripple of wonder coursed through my body.

"As you know, this year for me was really difficult. But what you don't know, is it was a lot more difficult than what you've seen. People have lied to me, stolen from me, taken advantage of me." She spoke with strength in her voice, as opposed to the stereotypical diva tone she often used. "But one guy, one guy was honest. The one person who truly cared about me. My manager, *Hayden*. He's why I'm still here today. So, even in the darkest of times, all you need is that one person. That one person who believes in you."

The crowd cheered as Alexis began to sing what in two weeks would both win her an Academy Award and become her latest number-one single.

Back in Calabasas, I imagined Samantha's jaw drop, seeing the interaction on live television. No doubt she was hurling expletives at her television screen in her thick New Jersey accent.

I wanted to be sorry. But I couldn't say no. After all, this was Hollywood—and it was my turn now.

ACKNOWLEDGMENTS

Rose, I know you were guiding me through this entire process. I felt you with me every step of the way.

To my mother, Angela, and my best friend, Ali—thank you for answering every phone call over the past seven years, listening as I obsessively talked about this book. It was all I could think about, and you were the only two people who witnessed every stage of its creation—from the moment I came up with the title to the cover design. Your unwavering love and support carried me through, and I am forever grateful.

Mariah Carey, without you, this novel wouldn't exist. The time I spent in your orbit changed the direction of my life, giving it meaning and purpose. You taught me what it means to be an artist, how to lead with empathy, and how to recognize the right and wrong people to have by my side. For that, and for so much more, I will always be thankful.

Sam Lansky, thank you for teaching me how to write my first chapter. The guidance you gave me in those early days provided the tools and knowledge I needed to write the rest of this book.

To my editors—Patrick Price, Alex Foster, and Dominic Wakeford—thank you for helping shape this novel into what it was meant to be. Your insight and expertise gave me the confidence to put this story out into the world.

Vanessa Mendozzi, thank you for bringing *The Last Living Diva* to life with your stunning cover and interior design.

And finally, to you—the reader. Thank you for taking this journey with me. I hope you loved reading this story as much as I loved writing it.

MATTHEW STEVENS resides in Los Angeles, California.
A former celebrity assistant, he's now the CEO of Illusion
Bronze, a custom self-tanner tailored to clients' eye color, hair
color, and skin tone. With nearly 500,000 TikTok followers, he
reviews skincare products and shares stories about life, dating,
and celebrity gossip.